Still Waters

Still Waters

Sara Warner

Still Waters

Black Bay Books
1939 Sand Basin Road
Grand Ridge, FL 32442

Printed in the USA
First Printing in 2012

ISBN-13: 978-0-9624878-7-3

Book Design by Sara Warner

First Print Edition

Still Waters is sheer fiction. Any resemblance of names, places, characters, and incidents to actual persons, places, and events results from the relationship which the world must always bear to works of this kind.

For my person, Pete.

And with gratitude to public servants who make this a better world.

April 10, 2001

In the beginning of anything words can fail you. Like in that first moment when you realize someone's been in your house, tracked over your rug, rifled through your underwear, opened your closets, sat down at your computer and taken all the work you've done, the very thing that's kept you alive for the last miserable year. Then the adrenaline prickles through your blood like nettles and you know it all very fast—in an instant. But your mind is a complete blank, as if every word you ever cared to say had been taken away on that hard drive.

I picked up the phone and speed-dialed 1.

"Mel?"

"Teena. What's up? Why aren't you on? Max is in the chat doing his doomsday thing. Littoral's going berserk—"

"My hard drive," I stammered. "My drive's gone."

"Somebody stole your computer? Have you called the cops? Teena, you should get out of the—"

"No, no, the drive. Somebody *removed* it."

"Are you sure it isn't just, like, you know, mega-crashed? There's a virus—"

"Mel, I'm looking at the hull. I've got it open. The frigging drive is *gone*."

"I'm coming over."

"It gets weirder."

"What?"

"He left a printout of that window that says *this program has performed an illegal operation and will be shut down*."

"Get out of the house. Get in your car and lock the doors. Call the cops. I'm leaving now."

She hung up. I grabbed my cell phone and started for the door. Even with every light in the house on it somehow still seemed that I was walking through a long, dark tunnel, reaching for a brass doorknob that glowed at the other end like the eye of a Cheshire cat. A strange odor hung in the air that made me think dimly of my Aunt Jane.

The cell phone bleated. I stuck it to my ear expecting Mel's play-by-play: I'm at Copeland and First, I'm turning onto Wandaland, I'm three minutes away. . . .

"If you want your files back keep the police out of this." The voice was confidential, almost friendly, male.

"Who is this?" Then silence, not even breathing.

"You've got a lot of work to do if you want to get this right."

"Look," I said, "I need my files. I'll pay."

"Don't be cheap," he said. He sounded angry. "Money isn't going to buy what you want."

"What do—"

"We both understand that money isn't where this is going. *You know* money is the enemy of art. And that's what we're talking about, isn't it? Your fulfillment? I'm going to help you with that."

"What do you want?"

"I want you to get it right." Silence. "I know you're special." Silence. "Are you ready?"

Through the window I could see Mel's Kia at the corner, turning as if in slow motion. Everything was losing its rhythm; the words were breaking into waves, particles of sound spaced too widely apart to carry meaning. "I, uh, what do I—"

"Get back on line and wait. I'll be in touch. Lovely expression, don't you think? Don't you? Think?"

"Look, I just—"

"Here's the thought for the day: *Écriture.* Have you got that? Oop, time to go. So nice talking to you." He was gone.

Then Mel was pulling up to the curb and getting out of her car, coming up the stoop, across the porch, flinging open the door, standing in the middle of the floor. "For christsake Teena! If you were going to stay in the house anyway then just use the phone. I was trying to get you on your cell the whole way over here having gruesome visions of someone beating you to death with the latest in wireless technology."

"That was him."

"What was?"

"The guy, the creep—he called my cell."

"What did he say?"

"That I have to get it right."

"Get what right?"

"I don't know. He said to get back on line."

"How are you supposed to do that without your hard drive?"

We stared at each other until we realized no answer was going to drop in from the blue. Then Mel went to the kitchen and got my bottle of cheap scotch, two glasses, ice. We sat on chairs and stared at the empty computer hull—still wired to the monitor, keyboard, mouse—and the printout of the error window tucked into the crib of the missing board. We drank.

"Mel, do you smell something?"

She stuck out her nose like an Irish Setter and tested the air. "What *is* that?" she asked, scrunching up her face and taking another whiff.

"I think it's *him*."

"You mean his *body odor?*" She got up as if to follow the scent to its source, sniffing her way around the den.

"Yeah, or his cologne or shampoo or something. It smells like oranges."

"You don't think he's still here, right? I mean, you went through the house when you—"

"Right, right," I said, trying to decide if I had done anything remotely like checking through the house. All I could remember was thinking something was amiss—maybe that odor more than anything else—the bedroom door slightly more open, then glancing into the den, seeing my computer tower pulled askew, the panel off.

"Where's Willow?" Mel asked.

"I haven't seen her since I got home. She probably freaked out and split through her cat door."

Mel took a turn around the den, looking closely at the drapes, the windows, the rug, the things on my desk.

"Where are the frigging cops?" she finally said.

"No cops. He said no police."

"Teena, you didn't call the cops? This guy's a lunatic."

"But Mel, my novel, everything—"

"Yeah, but you've got back-up files you can work from." She looked at me. "You do have back-ups, right? Don't you have it on your computer at work?"

"No. I took it off everything at work when they started with all that special access crap. I might have an old disk." I got up and went to my desk, pulled open the disk tray. "Son of a bitch," I said, staring at the empty drawer. "He took 'em all."

"We're calling the police."

"Wait Mel, I just need a minute to put this together. Something he said."

But Mel was leaning over the printout, studying it with unwavering concentration. "Teena, this doesn't say 'program,' it says 'person.'"

"What now?"

Her body didn't straighten, not a muscle twitched. Her voice seemed to come from deep behind the curtain of her wavy, red hair falling across her face. "It says, 'This *person* has performed an illegal operation and will be shut down.'"

I let her call the cops. A paunchy officer came to the door, took down my story on a tiny notepad, then went over the house trying to lift prints of the thief. Little piles of his black powder collected beneath each doorknob, under the handles of closets and cabinets. Black smudges appeared behind the drawer pulls on my desk and all over my computer.

"There aren't any prints here," he said finally. "Not even yours. Everything's been wiped clean."

"Is that *normal*?" I couldn't help noticing that the word sounded strangely hollow, as if there were no such concept in the English language and I was just making it up, knowing even deep in my confusion that no one would have the slightest inkling what I was talking about.

But Officer Tom Kirkland seemed to know the word. "I've never seen it before," he said evenly, "and I've been working burglaries for 23 years. Still, you get a lot of things these days you never used to would."

"What do you make of this message he left?" Mel asked.

"Well, he's somebody who knows computers."

Mel and I exchanged a glance.

"We've got a guy at the precinct who'll be able to tell us more about that," Officer Kirkland said, ignoring our innuendo. "Do you know any computer geeks?" he asked.

"Sure, people at work who take care of the computers." I said, reaching for my bag.

"And you work where?" He stood with pencil poised over his tiny notepad.

"Environmental protection, State Lands. I do historical research." I handed him my bureau card.

He looked at me, squinting his eyes like he thought this might all be an elaborate hoax. He made a note. "Anybody else?"

"People online I dialog with probably know computers. But I don't know how they would find me here."

"That might not be as hard as you think," he said. "Was there anything about your recent interactions that was unusual? Anybody mad at you?"

I couldn't think of anything. Mel told him about the chat room we frequented that hosted discussion on politics, philosophy, literature. "There are always some whacky types on there," she said, "but nothing personal, really."

"Was there anything about your hard drive that would make someone want to steal it?" It seemed to be dawning on Officer Kirkland that everything about this case was weird.

"No-o," I said, trying to think what would be of any interest at all. "All that was on there besides my email and bookmarks was a novel I was writing. Some photos, software." I was fading into black. I knew they wouldn't be able to catch the thief, wouldn't recover my book, couldn't protect me in the unlikely event that this weirdo had more fun and games planned. And now I would never get my hard drive back because I had called the police.

I realized with a start that I was assuming the thief already knew I had called the cops. Even recognizing how improbable that was, I couldn't shake the feeling that he was omniscient, that he somehow knew my every move.

Officer Kirkland assigned me a case number, said a detective would be in touch within 24 hours, and drove away. Mel packed my nighties and led me out, locking the front door behind us. I remember wondering vaguely why this was happening, why this creepy guy was screwing with me. But I was too troubled to think clearly. As we turned onto Wandaland the sun spiked over the eastern horizon, casting a red pall over the gray city. *Shut down.*

Chapter One

Jessie Weston had watched the surveyor wading the lakeshore all morning. She sat on the edge of the steps where the porch rail would keep her from seeing her father, sitting still as a stone while the sweat ran down his neck and darkened his shirt back. She could hear him grunt softly each time the surveyor straightened up from his transit to make notes, sighting from the water's edge to the willows along the dike. She could hear her father wheezing the air through his nose while the surveyor pulled up his tripod and settled it in a new location. Snippets of red tape dotted the lakeshore behind him.

The newspaper lay under the porch rail where her father had flung it down. She could see part of the advertisement Bud had circled in red. Next to the obituaries, in bold type: Notice of Public Hearing, Lake Ponder, Ordinary High Water Line Boundary. Down by the dike the surveyor took off his hat, mopped his face with a red kerchief, ducked his head back under his hat. He waved an arm at one of his crew, motioning with a pointed finger due east, then angled his transit for a shot across the dike toward the big oaks upland. "Son of a *bitch*," Carl Weston drawled softly.

Out at the highway a car slowed to turn, then came on fast, spewing dust into the sky in a steady stream along the line of the drive. "That'll be Bud," she said, leaning back to glance at her father's face.

Her father nodded once, then sat watching the younger man climb out of his car and come up the steps. "Is this what you call taking care of things, Bud?"

"All right, C.W., all right," Bud said. "Did he say anything?" he asked, poking his chin toward the surveyor.

"He's the State," Carl Weston stated matter-of-factly. "He doesn't have to *say* anything. I thought Sandy was going to keep them out of this. Isn't that what he told you? To leave it to him–that the district could keep them out? We might as well just pull the plug, Bud, once the State gets in it. You can go to your grave fighting the goddamn State over this ground . . .".

Jessie got up and strolled to the end of the porch, but the surveyor had moved down the lakeshore, out of sight. He had driven in so early she almost hadn't seen his jeep in the green half-light. But from the barn, down close to the groves, she'd heard it. He was coming in slow, as if he were working out something he didn't want interrupted, but she had waved him down anyway thinking he might be lost. His name was Reese Kessler, State surveying and mapping. He said his office had sent a letter to Mr. Weston about fixing the ordinary high water line. She'd asked him if it was broken, and he looked puzzled, then laughed and said it was a long story.

She said, "I know," and he sat back a little and looked at her.

They had surprised each other, laughing there in the black edge of morning, and for a moment they waited to see what would happen next. Reese had been thinking of his wife as he drove through the groves, had, in fact, thought of nothing else for weeks. Then suddenly he wasn't thinking of his wife anymore, and just before he realized that he was becoming uncomfortable, sitting there saying nothing to this woman, he felt sharply that he wanted to go on looking at her, laugh with her and keep looking at her. He glanced up the drive. "Mr. Weston at home?" he asked.

Jessie turned from him and looked toward the house. She seemed to consider the question as if it were a matter of considerable weight. The truth was her father might be at the house. But she knew he could be any number of other places too, even feeding calves at the other end of the ranch. "I can show you the lake," she said.

He sat for a moment watching the light play over the cordgrass down at the water's edge, the pale shades of green sliding into dark under the slight breeze. "I need to talk to Mr. Weston first."

"Well, I've got to feed these horses before I do anything else," she said. "You can try at the house or you can wait."

He had turned back to her, nodded. "Thanks," he said, and put the jeep in gear. In the barn the horses were shifting, knocking their hooves against the stall doors.

"Jessie have you gone to the moon?" Her father was half out of his chair and twisting to look at her. "Would you get that roll of plats off my desk for Bud to take back. And bring me some ice water. If I don't have a heart attack today it'll just be so the State can screw me into kingdom come."

Jessie patted his arm as she passed and heard him sigh. She didn't like to see him get worked up, but she knew it was better for him to rant and get it out. Then, he would make his peace with it and move on. She entered the cool dark of the house and went down the long hall to his study. This room had always seemed to Jessie the heart of the ranch. From this space flowed the life blood of every plan, beginning as a spark in her father's mind, then a drawing, phone calls, lists of figures, notes about new equipment, until one day it pulsed out onto the ground and took shape as a new barn, a grove, a road or holding pond. A dike system.

The public hearing was to be on Thursday morning in the town hall annex. For a week her father had been on the phone constantly, meeting with Bud and Sandy Stockard from the water management district. To hear Carl Weston tell it, their problems had all begun three years before when his step-son, Bud, had come to him with a plan to build a golf course and condo community along the lakefront. For fifteen years ranchers had been selling off lakefront for development, retiring on the windfall. Then, just when he had decided to follow suit, the environmentalists had raised a stink—some hogwash about water quality—and, when the water management district issued his permit anyway, a group of them filed a petition. He had gotten a notice that there would be a hearing on the matter, but he and Bud had not been concerned. Dempsey Partin, the hearing officer, was a first cousin of one of the district board members, and they were ranching folks—people who had settled this part of the State; fought mosquitoes, malaria; run off the Indians and bought the first swamp and overflowed lands deeds the State issued. Dempsey wasn't about to take up with a bunch of tree-huggers. He had limited the hearing to the issue of whether Carl Weston's pump system was adequate to protect the proposed development in a 100-year-flood event. He had required hours of expert technical testimony. Then he had upheld the permit.

But the greenies weren't finished. They appealed the decision and the matter went up to Tallahassee, where tree-huggers had gained a foothold. The matter would be heard the following fall. In the meantime, the governor and cabinet—who were charged with the protection of the State's sovereignty lands—asked their staff at State Lands to determine what interest the State had in Carl Weston's permit. The State Lands Director sent a memo to Sam Donnovan, chief of the Bureau of Surveying and Mapping, asking him to look into it. Donnovan sent Weston a letter explaining that the boundary between the sovereign lands of Lake Ponder and Weston's own uplands was the ordinary high water line. A survey team would be working in the area over the next several months to locate the line.

As soon as he opened the letter, Carl Weston knew it was a fatal blow. He also knew he could not accept it. Occupying his place in the world just meant having to fight—for the principle of the thing, for the other ranchers, and for Bud—even if he recognized that the particulars in this case put him in the wrong. He had always been a logical man and a man of will. Usually these aspects of his character harmonized, energizing him to accomplish whatever he put his mind to. Now he knew he must work divided against himself.

Jessie thought the trouble had begun long before the brouhaha over the permit. The way she saw it, it had all started with the dike. She remembered the year they built it as a war. Her father, Bud, the ranch hands, and the mud, the endless mud that transfigured the shape and color of everything in those oppressive months fifteen years ago. The smell of the muck permeated the house, the pumps droned night and day, and the men came and went like zombies before dawn and after dusk, leaving black footprints across the porch and piles of clothes stiff with the dried muck. Each night Bud would fall asleep over his plate and her father would have to shake him awake to send him to bed. For a month they made steady progress.

Then the rains began, and the lake rose to take back the land they had claimed. They brought in more pumps, more men. But the rains came harder, and the dike began to melt and slide beneath the rising waters. For Carl Weston it became a battle of wills, and he allowed no doubt that in the end he would prevail. But the waters of the lake persisted, as only the blind force of nature can in the face of such a man. Carl Weston gave ground, fell back a hundred yards and built a dike twenty feet high and fifty feet wide, impounding some three hundred and sixty acres of river marsh. Jessie was seventeen that year and for the first time in her life she was glad her mother wasn't alive to see her father's hardening anger. Only years later did it occur to her that her father wasn't raging against the rain or the mud or the rising waters of the lake, but against her mother's absence.

Jessie glanced at the photograph on his desk of the woman who still seemed so present. She was standing on the old pontoon boat in a red sun hat, her black hair waving gaily in the breeze, her yellow blouse billowing in stark contrast against the bright blue sky. So full of life. The famous smile. Picking up the bundle of plats, Jessie nodded to the woman in the photo and left the room.

"I'm going to the barn." She handed her father a perspiring glass of ice water and went down the steps.

"Watch out for that yellow cow," he called after her. "She should'a had that calf by now, but I didn't see her today or yesterday."

April 11, 2001

It seemed like I might as well go to work, even on an hour of sleep, just to keep up appearances. I couldn't shake the eerie feeling that everything I did was in full view of this creep, like he was god or a cameraman for one of those stupid tv shows where you live with cameras trained on you day and night until you lose your mind and then they give you a bunch of money. As if it would do you any good then.

Getting off the elevator, though, I right away began to have second thoughts. Bonnie, my trusty assistant, waved me down in the hall, tapping her watch and saying, "Steve's looking for you. Better hit his office first thing."

"Thanks," I said dubiously. "What's up?"

"Something about the judge is all I heard. Maybe we're finally going to get our date with destiny." She waggled her eyebrows at me and ducked into the women's room.

I went down the hall past my office, stopping only long enough to stick my bag and briefcase inside the door before going on to Steve's office. Steve Donneroe is the Bureau Chief of Surveying and Mapping, in the State Lands Division of the Department of Environmental Protection. He hired me straight out of graduate school for a job no one had ever had in his bureau and one he didn't want a whole lot of people to know about. "Your official title will be Research Associate or Government Analyst or whatever the hell you want to pick for your resume. But your true identity will be War Dog," he said, relishing the words in his mouth. "When I have to go to court, I like to go in a pink Cadillac." He squinted his right eye almost shut and looked hard at me out of the left. "It's your job to make sure I do." He spent most of an hour telling me about the "cloud on the horizon," a powerful group of people who seemed bent on transferring sovereignty lands—the lands under navigable waters—from the public trust that was supposed to protect them, to private ownership. *Their* private ownership. "Then, if we deny them permits to build condos and golf courses all over the lakebeds they can sue us for 'takings.' We end up paying them not to use land they stole from the State to begin with." At the time, I didn't know whether to think he was psycho or a brilliant strategist. Today—eight years later—it's perfectly clear.

"Yo," I said, sticking my head through his doorway. "You lookin' for me?"

He motioned me in, nodding his head meditatively. I went in and took a chair, settled in and waited. He sighed deeply. Steve comes up to things in his own good time. Prodding doesn't help. He has an innate sense of the drama inherent in words uttered ripe. He reminds me of a wine commercial: "We will pour no wine before its time." I've sat in his office more than once with enough time to wonder whether the *its* in *before its time* has an apostrophe or not. On this day, though, he seemed agitated, out of rhythm, like he knew all he had to pour was a sour bottle. "The AG's talking about a settlement," he said with as little intonation as he could manage.

"On what?"

"Your baby."

"Lake Ponder?" I asked, incredulous.

He nodded, pushed back his chair, settled in.

"How do they think they're going to do that?" I began. "If we don't give Wesson the dike, he won't settle. He's got to have the dike for his development. If we do give him the dike, it makes a complete joke of all the case law that protects sovereignty lands."

He bit his lower lip and stared at his phone.

I geared up. "How will we ever stop *any* encroachment on the lake beds if we give this away?"

He folded his hands, bobbing his head quickly and ever so slightly. It could either mean he agreed with me—which I knew already he did—or that his head was about to explode—which I knew already it was.

"If we can't bust Bob Wesson, we can't bust anybody." I was exasperated. I had seen the plug pulled on cases before, but there had always been a good reason.

"Every word you're saying is true," he said. "And you know as well as I do that that's exactly the position they want us in."

"Not the AG's office," I said, unwilling to face the possibility that our one staunch ally had at last been bent by the political winds.

"No, but apparently they're having trouble holding out against the Gov on this one." He looked at me and I could see him struggling not to get really mad. He prided himself on being the longest surviving bureau chief in State Lands, but in moments like this one you could glimpse the toll it took.

I had learned a lot from him over the years, about hanging tough through a grueling deposition, keeping a low profile with our more volatile supervisors, maintaining a clean record with the accounting office. I'd seen him keep his cool during a marathon grilling—a two-day cross-examination by a junkyard dog corporate attorney in a high-stakes trial. I'd watched him play the guy into a corner, all the while maintaining a cordial geniality and an earnest attention to his questions. A lot of people might not realize what it took to do that, but I'd sat on that hot seat enough to know. To get it going your way when a nasty, split-tongued lawyer is doing his best to discredit you hour after punishing hour, riling the jury with lies which he keeps phrasing as questions by prefacing them with "and isn't it true that . . ."—even though the judge keeps sustaining your lawyer's objections—I knew to keep control like that took imagination and real nerve. Lately, though, I had begun to realize that Steve's amazing ability to contain his anger might have its limits. Facing an administration that continually worked to tie our hands, to keep us from doing the job we were hired to do, he was frustrated in a way that might prove unbearable.

We had discovered not long after the new governor and his appointees began operating that our efforts to protect public lands were persistently undermined. Of course, it was a secret war. If that bunch on the hill had their way, they'd give away all the lakes and rivers to their big landowner cronies as political tender. But they couldn't quite afford to be that obvious. They had to at least *look* like they were protecting the public trust. During much of my nine-year stint at State Lands, we'd had fairly consistent support from the Trustees (the governor and his cabinet)—and unwavering support from the attorney general's office. But the winds had shifted in the last election when the son of a former bigwig—who had managed to lose a mere $55 million of Savings & Loan money in the only business he'd ever tried to run—moved into the governor's mansion. Dud!—you had to wonder if the exclamation point was the work of some public relations genius faced with trying to sell Dudley as *anything* but especially governor of Florida, or the work of his mother who was faced with, well, *him,* or maybe just the work of the nurse who was eating a chocolate donut over the clipboard where his birth certificate was filled out—anyway, Dud!, like his father before him, was rabidly big business.

He had spent the first ninety days of his administration slashing budgets for any kind of regulation, but especially environmental regulation, and issuing edicts designed to privatize as many of the functions of state government as he could get away with. Fat contracts were handed out to his buddies, while long-time staffers in food and janitorial services, state parks, and personnel—just to name a few—were "let go." For those of us still left after the carnage, he pushed through changes in the State's employment contracts, making it the rule rather than the exception that state employees could be fired without just cause. This policy meant your job was on the line with every decision you made, and it was having its intended effect: eliminating the professional independence of the State's civil service and making us mere rubber stamps of the governor's will. Now really doing our job required the creation of a surface layer in which we always seemed to be doing nothing much. It was like learning to live in an occupied city.

"Get used to it," Steve said as if reading my mind. "No one's going to be able to stand up to this kind of gall. We're just in for it."

If this had been *The Big Sleep,* he would have been Humphrey Bogart slapping the dopey sister. I knew he was doing it for my own good. Knew he was doing it because he expected me to take it standing up—like he was going to. Knew also he was doing it to shut me up and get me the hell out of his office.

"Put together some kind of draft," he said. "You know," he smiled, "bring in the usual suspects. Figure out what we could live with."

"Can we stall?" I asked.

"By end of day."

We gave each other our twisted mouth grimaces and I left.

I went back to my office and sat in my chair, stunned. Were they really going to be able to get away with this? I booted up my computer, thinking vaguely about my stolen hard drive, my novel. I had thought I would come in this morning and clean up my C-drive, spend a few minutes looking for any old files I could use to re-create the pages I'd lost. Maybe even go down to the basement and see if the computer techs could scrounge up some archived back-up files. We constantly joked about our paranoia that every report or memo we'd ever written was "down there" somewhere, waiting to ambush us in the crucial moment of a brutal cross examination:

Opposing attorney:
"So you are testifying here today, Dr. Shossie, in front of these good people, that you never considered Jumpin' Jimminnee Creek to be non-navigable?"

Me:
"Jumpin' Jimminnee Creek is clearly navigable. You see in State's Exhibit 402 a photograph of the creek in the pre-drainage era with a steamship pulling up to the dock."

Voice from the peanut gallery:
"Hey isn't that the Exxon Valdez rounding the bend in the background?"

Opposing attorney [smirking]:
"I have here in my hand a copy of a memo to your assistant I obtained from the DEP computer archives. Would you please read it to the court."

Me:
"Going to look at JJ creek mañana. If it looks non-navigable we can get the early flight. Book me for the 5:55 and I'll call the airline if I need the 8:07. TS."

Opposing attorney [triumphantly]:
"I ask you again, Miz Shlostick, is it true you *never considered Jumpin' Jimminnee Creek to be non-navigable?"*

Of course, if you actually *needed* a back-up file to restore something you'd lost—or had stolen—you could just dream on. In the first place, the only people who hadn't bailed out of the computer squad under the governor's "new deal" were either jackheads who couldn't stay out of cyberspace long enough to perform mundane tasks like backing up our files, or hopeless geek wannabees who couldn't make the jump to the big-time corporate stuff but felt mundane tasks should be beneath them by now. In the second place, everyone was too paranoid of the computer people to ask for any favors. One of the "improvements" the new administration had implemented was the capability of the computer techs to "step in" to our computers as we worked. This new "special access" would save the techs from actually having to come to your office when you had trouble with your computer. Instead, they could simply commandeer your controls from where they sat, big-brother-like down below, viewing whatever you had up on your screen.

When this special access was first announced with all the fanfare of a wonderful new time-saving breakthrough—as if we were really too dense to understand the implications—I'd gone to Steve, who sighed, then sent me to talk to the deputy director. I worked on confidential files, I told him, that were shared only with the Attorney General's office. If the techs had "special access" to my files, I needed to know they weren't security risks. With a perfectly straight face he assured me the techs would only use special access after calling me to make sure it was a convenient time. A million things went through my head standing there trying not to guffaw in his face. Fortunately, Steve was one of them. I smiled. Tilted my head back slightly and closed my eyes. When I lowered my chin and opened my eyes I was able to say in a wonderfully even voice, "I'm so relieved. Thanks for your time."

Of course, it wasn't the techs we worried about so much as who might be paying them for a peek. We had learned the hard way not to take lightly the value of our files to our opponents. Once, in the middle of a tough court battle down by Lake Okeechobee, the corporation that owned the county pulled some strings and had us evicted from our temporary war office. The fire marshal came around while we were in court, intimidated our office assistant, and posted a notice of eviction giving us 8 hours to move. During the confusion of moving everything into the Glades Hotel—a rickety, rundown building with signs pasted on the mirrors saying No Cleaning Fish or Game in Rooms—an entire file cabinet went missing. Of course, we could never prove anything, but I had been impressed by the lengths people will go to to undermine their enemies. And it wasn't lost on me that their target had been the files I had spent years building—files we all relied on to protect sovereignty lands.

I realized I was putting off the inevitable. I had to put together something to give Steve by the end of day. I opened a blank document and typed "Lake Ponder Proposed Settlement, DRAFT." I tried listing the issues, tried summarizing the situation, putting the conflicting viewpoints in two columns. I tried every trick I knew to get myself started writing a settlement proposal. At 2:30 when Bonnie stuck her head in and said, "Well?" I was still nowhere.

"We're folding."

She stepped in, closed the door behind her. "What happened?

"Nothing."

"Don't the bosses think we can win?"

"I think it's because we can win that they're settling. The Gov wants to give it away." Saying it made my eyes sting.

"Shit, Teena." She perched on the edge of my worktable, studying my face. "You wanna' get out of here? Get some beers?"

"Steve's making me draft a proposal."

"Well that sucks. You'd think if the AG wants to give it away so bad he could get one of his boys to write the damn settlement."

"It's not their office. They're getting the order from on high. They just want to keep their jobs—same as us. We're all assuming the position."

"What are you going to do?"

"Yet to be determined."

"Need anything?"

"A different world?"

She left me to my misery.

I had worked on this case for the better part of nine years. In fact, it was the case Steve had hired me to do. He had sensed the groundswell coming ten years ago when, in an unusual spate of court cases dealing with sovereignty lands, the same players seemed to be showing up at the lawyers' table and in the back of the courtroom. When the same bunch showed up at the cabinet's hearing of the Wesson Ranch permit, he'd started putting out feelers for a streetwise researcher with impeccable credentials. He'd settled for me. Within a week of coming to work at the Bureau, the Wesson Ranch case landed in my lap.

I had been wondering what Steve meant by driving him to court in a pink Cadillac, but after a few months on this case, I knew what he was looking for: the clincher, the goods that no judge or jury would be able to ignore in spite of whatever political winds might be blowing. It was a complicated case, but I followed the paper trail and I learned. The history of Florida, the huge water control projects, agricultural diking and draining, government surveys, navigable waters, sovereignty lands, the natural boundary, the law—when I found out our sister agency had actually busted Charlie Wesson, Bobby's stepfather, for the dike way back in 1980, I began to understand how it felt to drive a Cadillac. I searched for and found the old permit applications, correspondence, and enforcement files on microfiche in the dusty basement of a DEP warehouse across town.

It was then that I began to understand something about the untold heroism of civil servants. It turned out the Department of Environmental Regulation had made Wesson breach the dike, returning the waters of the lake to their former lakebed. But it had not been an easy task. Permitting was a brand new ball game, and few people even knew what you were talking about if you uttered the word "environmental," much less in the same sentence with "regulation." Ranchers and farmers were accustomed to governmental support, if not always monetarily, then at least through a hands-off policy that allowed them free rein in the conduct of their operations. A handful of pencil-pushers in Tallahassee telling Charlie Wesson to take down his dike must have seemed no different to him than his children urging him to give up smoking. And he probably handled the two requests in pretty much the same manner. He appeared conciliatory, he blitzed you with information, he stalled. Again and again, correspondence showed the staff at DER meeting with Wesson, making patient explanations of the law, the boundary, the impact of the dike on the lake, on water quality. Charlie responded with obfuscation, excuses, promises. The water was too high, he needed a permit from the Corps of Engineers, he was going to make arrangements for a bulldozer.

After a year and a half of this song and dance, DER sent a simple two-sentence letter, registered mail, return receipt requested. Charlie Wesson's file would no longer be considered a restoration in progress.

It was being forwarded to the enforcement division. Charlie spent a few moments revisiting his options. Then, deciding that retreat might prove a useful strategy in a war against bureaucracy, he shut down the pumps, hauled out the bulldozers and cut 12 breaches in the dike wide enough to drive a yacht through. There's no telling what went through his mind that day, when, standing atop the ruptured dike, he watched the waters of Lake Ponder pour slowly over the green shoots of his best pasture. Field inspections were performed, reports filed, the DER went home. As far as the Trustees of sovereignty lands were concerned, all was well at Lake Ponder.

But Charlie Wesson wasn't about to leave well enough alone. He bided his time and talked to every dirt lawyer he ran into, until he met Andy Ratzlaff at a Farm Bureau fundraiser for their legislative hopeful. Ratzlaff must have listened to the older man's grievance with studied attention, sensing a case that could put him on the map, and knowing that he had an edge on problems of this kind. He probably gave him a card, told him to call Myrna on Monday and make an appointment. "I can help you with this," he might have said, nodding his head like a dashboard doll. However it had come about, Ratzlaff had taken up Charlie's cause and paid a visit to his old law school chum, Darren Sloan, who just happened to be the executive director of the water management district.

Ratzlaff's visit was not part of the official record. He filled out no application that would have been reviewed by the professional staff at the district. He didn't even sign the guest register. Only because of two people did I ever realize what had happened. The first was an unknown staff person, who left a handwritten note in the district file. The staffer had written: "DS [Darren Sloan] requested the permit file on the Wesson Ranch for a meeting with Mr. Ratzlaff. I told him that all we have is an enforcement file of DER correspondence." The note was initialed JC, but I'd never been able to track down who JC was, or where the enforcement file had ended up. I found out the rest of what happened only because the district enforcement officer, Eddie Barfield, had put a memo in his files outlining Sloan's directive. Apparently Eddie was uneasy enough with the director's hands-off order—given to him by telephone—to want to document his understanding of the deal. His memo described a closed-door meeting with Sloan in which Ratzlaff had secured a "verbal okay" to "maintain an existing dike" that was supposedly "functional throughout its length." Of course, Eddie had been on the job when that dike had been breached; he'd seen the water pouring in, returning the lake to its former lakebed. If that piece of swiss cheese could be called "functional throughout its length," then Eddie would be damned if he knew what words were good for at all. In spite of that, or maybe because of it, Eddie wrote.

Finding Eddie's memo taught me to hope for such things, to rely on the intrepid nature of the public servant. It made the world look pretty different than I'd conceived it until then—and infinitely better—that regular people with nothing to gain and a lot to lose so often did what they could to protect Florida's lakes and rivers, the fragile marshes and floodplains, all in the face of an entrenched power that could chew them up and spit them out in a Tallahassee minute behind closed doors.

But by 1989, Charlie Wesson had refilled the breaches in his dike and was pumping water off the marsh every time it rained. In the early 90s he dusted off the plans he'd drawn for a lakefront development and hired an engineering firm to design a pumping system for three-hundred-plus condos, a golf course, and marina.

If it hadn't been for an airboat cowboy named Chris Farlow and his boating club, The Far Out, the Trustees might never have known about the development—or at least not until it was too late to actually stop it. But sportspeople are frequently the whistleblowers when anything fishy is going down. They don't like people tampering with the water, closing off the marshes, keeping boaters off public lands. When Farlow saw the bulldozers filling in the dike one cool morning in the fall of '89, he called the president of his airboat club, who called an emergency meeting. They formed an organization called DIKES B GONE, set up a telephone operation, and rallied local environmentalists and sportsmen. With a little freebie advice from a girlfriend's brother who was in law school, DIKES B GONE filed a petition at the water management district asking the governing board to deny Wesson a permit for the pumping system. When the board reviewed the matter and found no reason to deny the permit, DIKES B GONE appealed, and the matter went before Administrative Hearing Officer Dempsey Partin. Mr. Partin likewise found no reason not to issue the permit. DIKES B GONE appealed again. Now their case would finally get out of the neighborhood, so to speak. It went up to

Tallahassee to be heard by the governor and cabinet sitting as the Florida Land and Water Adjudicatory Commission—FLAWAC. It was the fall of 1993.

And that's where I came in.

My phone rattled. I hit the speaker button and Mel's voice came over the airwaves. "You want to go by ComputerYou on the way home? I need some zips."

I glanced at my screen margin, saw the time was 4:54. "Oh wow. I'm supposed to have a settlement draft to Steve in six minutes. I've got nada."

"E-mail him something unreadable. Mark it draft. Leave the building. I'll pick you up out front."

Normally I would have told her I had to stay, get it done. But I couldn't help thinking of JC, that unidentified file clerk, and Eddie, the enforcement officer, who had in their own small ways registered their resistance. Maybe none of us alone could make any headway against the powers. But I wanted to believe that together—even spread out over decades and separated by hundreds of miles, never having laid eyes on one another or shaken each other's hands—that we could make a difference. "Parking lot, five minutes," I said and rang off.

Chapter Two

Stepping from the bright sunlight into the cool dark of the barn aisle, Jessie paused. The sound and smell of horses had always affected her in contradictory ways, calming her and quickening her pulse at the same time, and she stood for a moment letting her eyes adjust to the dim light and taking in the familiar sensations. She had come back to the ranch two years ago, formally ending a marriage that had been over long before. At college she had thought she wanted a career in agricultural engineering, but she had ended up in environmental sciences, married to a young professor whose passion was avant-garde literature. She had thought she was building a life for herself. But after six years she realized her life was waiting for her in the cool shade of the groves, among the bawling cattle, the heat and dust, and in the lightning-fast motion of a good horse. Nothing else seemed remotely real.

She saddled her horse, a dark Quarter Horse stallion she had taken to the reining championships the first year she came home. They had finished third. Her father had pushed her to compete him again the following year, but she knew that, even if she tried, it would come to nothing, and she hated to frustrate the horse's competitive spirit. He liked to win. But winning took a kind of unyielding focus she knew she couldn't muster, and she had spent the year riding him through the groves, working cattle, and swimming him behind the dike when the pumps were shut down for maintenance. She was back in her own skin, but not unscathed, and she waded into each hour knowing that the full extent of the damage was still untallied.

She let herself through the gate into the south range and rode toward the bluffs above the lake. This time of day the herd would most likely be sheltering under the big oaks, and, if she could catch a glimpse of the yellow cow, she could at least set her father's mind at ease about that. Rocket swung along in his big, eager walk, pushing his nose out ahead of him as if parting the waves of orange-scented air. Crossing the open ground, she set him in an easy lope and within minutes they reached the trees. She could hear the cattle stamping their hooves on the oak roots as she eased the horse into the hammock.

She didn't know whether to think of it as the superior instinct of his breed, perfected over generations by savvy horsemen, or the unusual intelligence that marked his unique personality, but stepping into the dense woods she felt again the masterful current that was the very being of the horse. He moved among the cattle with easy command, calming a flighty cow with an almost imperceptible, but deferent, shift of his glance, warning a rowdy youngster with a hardened jowl and flattened ears. Each gesture was precisely sufficient to accomplish its task, and Jessie marveled at the efficiency and concentration with which Rocket worked. Within twenty minutes they had canvassed the herd, but the yellow cow was not there. A breeze had come up as the sun settled toward the lake. The cows were beginning to move out onto the grass.

It occurred to her that she was thinking of a borrow ditch at the western toe of the dike, and she reined Rocket in that direction with a new sense of urgency. A cow in trouble calving could suffer an agonizing death, and Jessie felt there was no room in her now for such grief. She pushed Rocket in a steady trot as long as she dared, but the ground was harder here, uneven, and peppered with dense blackberry thickets. The last two hundred yards they were forced to a slow walk, as Rocket picked his way through the shrubs, lifting each hoof clear of the clinging briars. It took most of an hour to reach the west end, but as she rode up onto the dike she thought she heard the cow moaning. A few minutes later she saw her, down in the borrow ditch in a thick patch of buttonbush. She looked dehydrated and spent, but she was still on her feet. Beside her lay the calf, but from this distance Jessie couldn't tell if it was alive or not. She rode along the edge of the dike, looking for a way down to the cow, but she could find no likely place. She knew Rocket would go down the sheer bank if she asked him, but between the twenty-foot drop and the thick brush it would mean certain injury, and she didn't know how they would get out. Yet she hesitated to ride all the way back to the house for help. By the time they returned it would be dark and the danger of injury or of losing the cow would be greater.

Eventually, about a quarter of a mile west, she found a gully in the bank, a washout from the heavy spring rains. It might just be possible to get down it and haul the cow out. She cursed herself for not bringing a rope, but she considered her roping skills more a source of embarrassment than aid, and it did not usually occur to her to carry a rope. Suddenly Jessie realized that for some minutes she had been hearing an engine approaching from the west. She stopped still and waited. It was coming closer. After another moment she spotted it. It was a jeep, coming along the dike. She could see two men, one with a red bandana and broad-brimmed hat, and she rode toward them waving her own red visor.

It was Reese Kessler and one of his crew. As they drew closer, he slowed the jeep and stopped, letting her bring the horse alongside. Not just anybody would know that, she thought, not to run a vehicle right up on a horse, and she wondered briefly if he knew about horses or just about danger. He seemed already to realize this wasn't a social call.

"You having trouble?" he asked.

"I've got a cow trapped in the ditch back there. It's going to take some doing to get her out."

"What do you need? We've got some straps down at the boat."

"I'm not sure. I'm going to need to get a trailer. She's not going to be able to walk far even if we can get her out. And she's got a calf. I don't know if it's alive."

"Do you want to call back to the ranch?" Stepping from the jeep, he pulled a cell phone off his belt and came quietly toward Rocket. When he was close by the horse's shoulder, he reached up and handed it to her. She dialed the house. In a moment Juanita answered.

"Juanita, is dad there?"

"He and Bud are gone to Mr. Sandy's meeting," she said. "You are in town?"

"No, I'm here. I found the yellow cow, but she's stuck. I need one of the boys. Is Carlos around?"

"I didn't see them since this morning. They are spraying trees."

"Ok," Jessie said, hesitating. "Uh, ok. I'll be in in a little while. If you see Carlos, tell him to hitch up the cattle trailer and stay by the phone, ok?"

"Everybody's out right now," she said, handing Reese the phone.

Reese nodded. He seemed to wait for something, then turned back toward the jeep. "Richard," he called, "run back down to the trailer and get the straps and any other rope you've got on the boat. And bring Bo back with you."

A dark-haired man in his mid-thirties jumped out and came around to the driver's side. "Be right back," he said, nodding at Jessie. He backed the jeep around and was gone.

"Let's go have a look," Reese said. "We'll get her out and then we can run get your trailer." Jessie dismounted and they walked back along the dike to the gully.

"I think this little gully is the only chance we've got—such as it is," she said. "I can slide down and try to get something around her."

They walked on along the dike, looking for the cow below. In a moment they saw her, her head hung low, her front legs wide apart. Jessie thought they didn't have long before the cow went down.

"We've got a cooler about half full of water," Reese told her. She nodded. "I can't see the calf," he said.

"It was behind her awhile ago when I first found her. I can't see it from here either."

They heard the jeep coming. Jessie felt everything in slow time now. It all seemed to unfold like a fast piece of music being played at half-speed. They walked back to meet the jeep at the gully. Reese introduced her hurriedly to Richard and Bo. They nodded and Richard came forward and shook her hand.

"Nice to meet you," he said, looking directly into her face. "What's the plan?"

"I'll go down," Jessie said, "take the straps and wrap her up. Is there any rope?"

"About twenty-five feet is all we got," Bo said.

Jessie and Reese exchanged glances. It wouldn't be enough to bring her out through the gully.

"We'll just have to hoist her straight up the bank," Reese said, watching Jessie. He could see in her face she knew it wouldn't be ideal. It might not even be possible. She looked grim, but she said nothing.

"How you want to haul her out?" Bo asked.

"If we can get the rope secured, Rocket can help pull her up," Jessie said.

"Why don't we use the jeep," Reese said. "It's got a winch on the front bumper. No sense chancing gettin' your horse hurt."

Jessie nodded. She led Rocket a safe distance away and ground tied him. Then she picked up the three long straps and headed for the ditch.

"Ms. Weston, put one of those around your belt and let us hang on to you while you get down," Reese said. She secured a strap around her waist, feeling the awkwardness of his formality, of her reliance on his help, and the nature of his business at the ranch. He seemed to feel it too, and when she handed him the end of the strap, they glanced at one another, and he grinned and shrugged.

"It's been nice knowing you," he said, as she went over the edge into the brambles.

The descent was so nearly straight down that she gave up getting any footing from the bank, trying instead to brace against the buttonbush stalks. Finding the gully this treacherous made her wonder how they would manage the steeper bank above the cow. Only halfway down, already her arms ached from trying to hold her weight and once she slipped, banging her cheek against something sharp. She could feel the blood well up and trickle down her jaw, but she also felt the strap holding her steadily from above, and leaning against it, she found she could make better time and keep her face clear of the brush.

"How we doing?" Reese called.

"Almost there."

At the bottom of the ditch she discovered her hands were exhausted from gripping the strap. Trying to untie it from her waist seemed to take forever.

"I'm at the bottom," she called up. "Let the straps down."

"Hold up a minute," Richard called. "Reese is coming down."

After a moment she heard the jeep start, then the brush cracking above her. She scrambled out of the way and watched him come down the precipice. He was obviously fit and remarkably agile, yet he maintained the slow, rhythmical motion of a careful man. Jessie thought of her own lay-up with a shattered ankle the summer she was twenty-eight and wondered what had made him feel his mortality. Then he tumbled out of the bushes at her feet and stood up, his eyes fixing on her cut cheek.

"Clear," he called up, and the straps slackened. "Ready?" he stepped out of the straps and wrapped them over his arm.

"Ready," she answered.

They made their way west toward the cow, the jeep tracking their progress on the dike above. Walking along the uneven ground with Reese following behind her, Jessie tried to focus her energies on the task ahead. She was not at all sure they could get the cow out of the ditch even using the jeep to winch her up. In all likelihood she had suffered major injuries getting herself into this spot. It was surprising she had been able to deliver the calf. Jessie wished she had brought a rifle. She worried about someone getting hurt trying to help her. She wondered if Reese thought this a lost cause as much as she was beginning to.

"There she is," he said quietly. When they approached, the cow groaned weakly. Her right leg had been cut badly and had bled and swollen shut, but none of her legs seemed to be broken, and Jessie allowed herself a small measure of hope. Reese was bent over the calf, listening. "He's alive," he said, looking up at her. "Only barely though."

He took a strap to the other side of the cow and passed it under her belly to Jessie. They fashioned a harness around her haunches, trying to secure her bulk. "Should we try to water her before she goes up?"

"Let's just take her on up," Jessie answered. "I doubt she'd drink anything the way she is now."

Reese called up for the rope to be lowered as nearby as possible, and in a moment they saw it come down through the brush with a water jug tied to its end. It looked too thin to hoist an 800-pound cow. They tied it to the straps beneath the cow's neck.

"We got lucky there," Jessie said. "If she'd been further away, we would've gotten to see if we could carry her to where the rope reaches."

Reese grinned. "Yeah, I'm a little disappointed not to have that challenge today—we're on such a roll. You ready to do this?"

"I wish we could do something to protect that leg. It's going to start bleeding again at the first bump." She thought longingly of the first-aid kit hanging in the barn.

"Use this shirt," Reese said. Before she could protest, he had it off. "I never liked it—so you'll be doing me a favor," he said, handing it to Jessie.

"I won't start saying 'I owe you' now," she said. "Remind me later to buy you a drink." She wrapped the leg, watching the dirt and blood seep into the blue cloth, hoping the shirt wouldn't be ruined in vain.

"Ready now?"

"Ready."

"Haul away," Reese yelled, and they heard the jeep engine rev, then Richard and Bo calling instructions to each other.

When the rope tightened, the cow began to struggle. Jessie feared the rope would break and the cow would come tumbling back into the ditch. If they could get her lifted clear off her feet, she would have no leverage to fight. But the brush and the bank angle made it impossible to keep her clear while they reeled her in. About half way up the bank, though, she gave up, slumping against the rope and allowing herself to be dragged over the rough ground. Jessie wasn't sure if it was a good thing or not.

"This may all be for naught," she said as evenly as she could to Reese.

They watched the cow disappear over the bank top, waited for some word. The jeep engine cut off. In a moment they heard Richard's voice. "Straps coming down."

"Come ahead," Reese called. "He's a good man," he said to Jessie. "He can do anything with a boat, a gun, a rope—he can survey anything, talk to anybody—a really good guy. I don't know how we keep him, much as he could be making in the private sector." She nodded, realizing he was trying to divert her from the cow's misery, and she wondered what kept Reese in public service. The strap end came down. Reese handed it to her and went to gather up the calf.

"Let me get the strap around me," he said tying it on, "then help me get this little guy over my shoulders. He'll have an easier trip up if I kind of buffer him."

"I'm not sure he's going to appreciate it," Jessie said.

"Yeah, probably not. But the lady who owns him is threatening to buy me a drink, so he's going to have to put up with it."

They made the calf and Reese as secure as they could manage. Pulling and pushing the calf onto Reese's bare shoulders gave her a strange sensation, and Jessie fought the familiar urge to hurry that came with fatigue and wanting to be out of a sticky situation. This was the danger zone, she thought, when you're thinking the worst is over. And then something happens, and you're not sharp enough to catch it fast enough. Lives change at such moments, or end.

"If something happens," she said, "let him go, okay?"

"Yep," Reese said. "We'll be fine. See you at the top." He tilted his head back and called, "Haul away."

As they lurched and swung up the bank, Jessie saw his muscles tense, gripping the strap in one hand and the calf's legs with the other. She thought about the final round she'd lost the year before that cost her the reining championship with Rocket. She'd been unfocused in the last go; she'd kept him from winning and nearly gotten him hurt when a big rangy steer tried to come past him at the fence. She'd told her father it was fatigue, that she just wasn't fit enough yet. But she knew she had simply choked, let her mind get cluttered with doubt. At the time, she had cursed the events of her life that cost her the easy confidence she'd once known. Now she wondered if such doubts were not the price of survival.

With a tremendous sense of relief, she saw Reese top the bank, and listened to the men laughing about the calf around his neck. They seemed unperturbed by the unexpected turn in their day, as if they regularly met damsels needing their livestock hauled out of treacherous ditches–which their fathers had dug illegally.

The strap appeared and she fastened it around her waist. "Ready anytime," she yelled.

April 11, p.m.

My message light was blinking when I got home, but I went on to the den with my ComputerYou bag and began right away to install my new hard drive. Loading software would take time, and I could answer calls while I waited for the rows of empty little cubes to fill with blue time. Smudges of the black powder Officer Kirkland had used to look for prints dotted my desk front and rug. It didn't seem to blow away or wipe up. It stuck to everything and smeared when I brushed it. I needed to sleep. I could feel a dense aridness behind my eyeballs. My reaction time was stretching out like hot taffy.

But I got the drive in without any trouble, inserted the operating system disc, flipped through the start-up dialogue til I got to "install," then went to listen to the messages. The first was from my mother. Evidently Mel had called her and told her about the break-in. I knew I'd have to call her back, but I could have written the script of our conversation before I ever dialed. She would insist I move into a gated community, get a Rottweiler or a boyfriend, and buy a gun—just something little, you know there's nothing wrong with protecting yourself Teena. The next message was from a Detective Deo. He needed to interview me as soon as possible. He left a number. I dialed while loading my internet software.

"Logan Deo." He pronounced it Day-oh.

"This is Teena Shostekovich. I had a message to call you."

"Dr. Shostekovich. I'd like to go over your case with you as soon as possible. Fill in some gaps. When would be convenient?" His voice had a slightly exotic quality I couldn't identify.

"Uh. Any evening after 6."

"How about now."

"I'm in the middle of loading my new hard drive."

"I could come to you. I'd like to see the situation for myself."

"That'll work. I guess you know where."

"I'll be there within the hour."

I hung up and loaded more software. The last message was from Mel. "Well I'm sure you've heard from your mother. I didn't mean to tell her, but she called me to find out what she should get you while she's in London. Don't get your hopes up. You know no matter what I told her, you're going to get another funny tourist hat. Anyway it's better for me to tell her." Right on both counts. "Email me when you get on."

I went to the fridge and got out leftover Chinese, grabbed a fork and went back to the den. Time to log on.

Everything came up just fine, which totally amazed me, since it had never happened before in my life with a new system. My text program checked out, internet was nice and zippy. I took a deep breath and clicked on my email inbox.

I scanned the list. Nothing unusual. Somehow this simple fact completely undid me. On one hand, the normalcy of the list made it seem that nothing had happened. No break-in, no aromatic emanation, no stupid note, no creepy call. Nothing was any different than it had been two nights ago, except that my story, all my work on the novel I was trying to write, was gone gone gone. Like a stone dropped in the ocean. And the waters were threatening to close seamlessly over, leaving not a trace of what had been lost. On the other hand, the fact that creepboy hadn't sent me an email meant he *did* know everything. He'd said no police, and I had ignored his warning. I felt tears welling in my eyes. My nose was stinging. I just knew he was watching me every second, listening to all my calls and conversations and thoughts and knew the police were in on it, knew they were on their way over here this very second, and I would never get my novel back, never get my—the doorbell sounded. Time for losing it was up. I grabbed a paper towel from the kitchen and blew my nose. I hated crying. It made me mad. And, the thing is, when I get mad I can't think, I can't talk, I can't breathe, and I repeat myself. The buzzer again. I was right in the middle of a thought like if I ever get my hands on creepboy I'll feed his gizzard to the cat, I'll feed his gizzard to the c. . . still sniffling, red-eyed, when I opened the door.

I'd been prepared for another version of paunchy Officer Kirkland. But Logan Deo was never going to be that. I was immediately embarrassed in that way you can only be when you've been caught in a manic moment by someone who has no way of knowing this really isn't you, but who is, himself, plainly one of those rare people who's alive, awake in a way most people never have been. He held forward his badge as if he really wanted me to look at it.

"Dr. Shostekovitch," he murmured, "you really should check to see who's ringing before you open your door." There it was again. Something strange in his speech. In the pattern itself. He put his badge away and handed me a card. "I'm Detec— Logan Deo." He was having trouble figuring out how much eye contact would indicate professional courtesy without seeming to notice that I'd been crying.

"Do you drink tea Detective?" I stammered.

He stood in the kitchen with me while I boiled water.

"Ok…". His voice trailed off. He paused. "You live here alone?"

"Yes. I have a cat."

He took his time digesting this information.

"And last night you came home to find your house had been broken into?"

"Yes. And then he called me. He took my hard drive." I realized I sounded like a total boob.

"What time did you get home?"

"Around one-thirty. There was a retirement party for one of my co-workers."

"Show me exactly what you did."

"I came in the front door. Something wasn't right. I smelled something . . . weird. My bedroom door was a bit more open than I leave it." I gestured down the hall.

"May I see?"

"Of course." I led him down the hall unable to escape the unfamiliar feeling of being alone with a man, headed for the bedroom. He stepped into the room and stopped, looking carefully in each direction, scanning the dresser, the bookcases, the pictures on the walls. I wondered what he read in those objects.

"So you came in here first? Did he take anything in here, or move anything?"

"Not that I could tell. But the officer said he had wiped everything down. All my drawer pulls, closet handles." Logan Deo nodded, seeming to understand the implications.

The teakettle was beginning to whistle. We went back down the hall.

"What did you do next?"

"I was going to the kitchen to call my friend. I was a little nervous someone might still be around."

"And your friend, I'm sorry, who was it you were calling? I don't mean to pry, but you understand I have to ask you some personal questions."

"Right. No. Mel is my best friend since college—we were roommates. Melody Costner."

"Do you have a boyfriend, ex-boyfriends, ex-husband? Anybody who might want to scare you?"

"No. My ex-husband works in the Middle East. He designs water systems for a company out of Orlando. They do a lot of contract work with the UN through US AID—that's a water resources program." I poured steaming water into the teapot, got mugs from the cabinet. Black powder gathered on my fingertips.

"You own this house?"

"Yes. The bank, actually. I'm buying it."

"I realize this seems peculiar, but I have to rule things out. Is there anyone now, a boyfriend—or girlfriend, who might want to shake you up a little so you would be inclined to have him or her move in with you—as protection?"

That this scenario was so common as to need ruling out struck me as an ironic comment on my own disengagement. "No. I haven't really seen anyone seriously since my divorce," I said. I could feel my face reddening and I wasn't sure if it was because of the half-lie or the awful truth. "There isn't anyone," I said again. As I said it I realized it sounded like someone trying to convince herself it was true, or finally realizing it was true. It must have sounded like that to him too. I couldn't have told you what changed in Logan Deo's face, but something happened. Like a cloud passing over in the blink of an eye.

"And that was . . ?"

"I'm sorry, what?"

"Your divorce took place when?"

"Three years ago."

He nodded. "What did you do next?"

"After the divorce?"

"After you started to call your friend—Ms. Costner. Did you call her?"

"Well, as I was going past the den, I glanced in and saw my computer tower pulled askew. When I went in I found the panel open. My hard drive had been removed. There was a piece of paper stuck in where the drive should have been."

"Do you have it?"

"Yes."

"Show me."

We took cups and teapot into the den and I showed him the printout of the error window. He sat in the armchair by my desk looking at the image, then spent several minutes examining my computer set-up. I sat in front of my computer screen staring at the list of unopened mail.

"Ok, now go back. You said you smelled something when you first came in."

"Yeah. It reminded me of my aunt. I don't know why."

"Is it possible she might have stopped by?"

"Oh, no, she lives in Orlando. She would call if she were coming up."

"Can you still smell the scent?"

"I did when I first came in the house tonight. I don't think I can really smell it now."

"Where was it the strongest?"

"In here. He must have been in here several minutes getting the board out."

"Ok. I'm going to take some air samples if that's all right with you."

"Sure." I had it now. It was where the spaces fell between his words that was unusual. He spoke like someone who was listening at the same time, so that there were very slight pauses in odd places, and it went through my mind that he was listening to someone speaking to him through a wire and repeating their words as he heard them. I watched him walking slowly around the room filling vials and sealing them with a tape that seemed to melt like wax. "What will you do with those?" I asked him.

"I'll have them analyzed to find out if there's anything unusual in the air. I'll have to get more samples later, when the air is closer to its usual state. That way we can compare. And, we'll create a chemical print of the air. Just because he didn't leave fingerprints doesn't mean he didn't leave any traces."

"Wow, that's cool," I said, thinking how badly I needed sleep and how moronic I sounded.

"I'll also keep a sample in case we want to use it later with a canine unit." He turned and looked at me. "You must be tired. I would imagine you were up most of the night. We can do the rest of this another time," he said.

"Oh that's ok. What else do we need to do?"

"I want to talk to you more about what was on your drive. I'll need some information about your co-workers. And I would like you to show me your regular stops on the internet."

"The officer mentioned a guy who does computer forensics. Do I need to talk to him?"

"Oh." Logan Deo looked startled and then slightly embarrassed. "He was talking about me," he said. "He exaggerates my credentials. I'm not trained in information systems, it's just something I find useful to pursue."

"Ummn." I nodded.

"There is one other thing you should tell me now if you feel up to it. While it's still fresh in your mind."

"Ok."

"You said he called you. Had you ever heard his voice before? Was it familiar?"

"No. But . . .". I was trying to think of something that had stuck in the back of my mind during the call. Detective Deo waited while I squeezed the bridge of my nose, trying to think. "It seems to me that something about the call sounded different." He waited some more, his body motionless, his eyes on my face. "The dead spaces when he wasn't saying anything sounded completely quiet. I know that doesn't make sense, but I noticed it."

"Like the call was filtered?" he asked.

"Something like that. So his voice might have been altered too."

"Can you tell me what he said? What was the first thing he said?"

"He told me not to call the police or I wouldn't get my files back."

"So he knew there was something valuable on your disk?"

"I don't know. Probably everyone's files are valuable to them."

"That's a good point. He may have just been testing the waters to see how badly you wanted your data back."

"Except he knew already. I offered him money and he chided me. 'Don't be cheap,' he said. He said something about money being the enemy of art."

"What do you think he meant by that?"

"It just struck me as some Marxist hooey he'd heard somewhere. I thought he was showing off, like a lot of people do when they first read something or hear about it. Some of the people in my chat group spout Marxist stuff without really knowing much about it."

"What significance does Marxism have to you?"

"None in particular. It's sort of a knee-jerk reaction cult-critters have when they first figure out there's something dark about the free market."

He paused for a moment and I wondered if I'd stepped on any nationalistic pride or other pet beliefs with my little spiel. "Cult-critters?" he asked with raised brows.

"Sorry—cultural critics. I dialog online with people who do cultural criticism—politics, philosophy, literature. Some of them are really smart—probably grad students somewhere. A lot of them are just starting to read stuff and you can tell they're not really used to talking about ideas yet."

"Have you ever identified yourself to any of these people? Said where you live or met any of them in person?"

"No."

"Did he say anything that made you think he knows you personally?"

"He said he knew I was special, that he wanted me to get it right. That he was going to help me."

"With what?"

"My fulfillment."

For the second time that evening I saw something flash over his face. It was as if the myriad tiny facial muscles tightened for the briefest instant before he willed them to relax, to give nothing away. "Officer Kirkland's report says you had photos on the disk and a novel you were writing."

"Yes."

"What was the nature of the photos?"

"Mostly pictures I took in the field—waterbodies I was working on, the people I work with, water marks."

"Was there anything of an erotic or sexually explicit nature about any of the photos?"

I shook my head. "Just my friends, airboats, birds, shorelines, trees, some of the scientists I work with from time to time."

"Is there anything in your novel that would prompt this guy to think you need 'fulfillment'?" he asked.

I opened my mouth to say no. Clearly the novel was not suggestive in the way Logan Deo was thinking. But the word *fulfillment* hung in the air, and I realized I was denying it its due. I wanted to ask him if he'd ever read a novel. I wanted to tell him that all any novel was ever really about was the longings we want fulfilled. I had begun my novel right after my divorce. I hadn't had sex with my husband in more than two years. I'd lost faith in my own abilities, in my very person-ness. To make matters worse I had waked up one day to realize that I was in love with someone who was way off limits. I imagine my need for fulfillment was the first thing any stranger passing me on the street would notice. It would have been impossible for the novel not to signal a person all too familiar with lonely. But I also knew a novel has its own longings.

"I took him to mean it artistically," I said. "That he wanted to see me fulfill my artistic potential."

Watching his face I was unsure whether he understood me at all. I wondered if he thought me the most naïve woman alive, or whether I had just suggested something so strange to him that he was now reeling backwards from a possibility he had never considered. It was almost as if he'd suddenly realized there was another voice in the wire, one he should have been hearing all along, and he was trying to figure out how he was going to listen to it too, all while carrying on with his apparent conversation. At that moment my mail chime sounded softly and a new envelope appeared in the inbox on my screen. "It's from Mel," I said.

"Do you need to answer?"

"Pretty soon, or she'll worry."

"There's a lot more we need to talk about," he said. He looked at me as if gauging whether to press for more. I must have looked like hell. "But we'll continue another time." He made it almost a question with the tilt of his head.

"Sure," I said. I felt vaguely disappointed to end our conversation so abruptly. His questions stimulated me. His eyes on my face, his simple presence in the room brought relief from an ache I'd forgotten I was living with. We stood and made our way through the hall. At the door, he turned to face me. He was tall and easy in his body like people are who've always counted on an innate athleticism. "Tomorrow would work for me," I said. "Around seven?"

He nodded once and smiled slightly. "Dr. Shostekovich, until we get to the bottom of this, you should take precautions for your safety. This guy might be pretending to be an artist in order to attract you. Or he might be genuinely engaged in artistic pursuits, but that doesn't mean he's harmless. He expresses several behaviors characteristic of a stalker. I don't want to frighten you unduly, I want to caution you. Ok?"

Fatigue was washing over me in waves, but I remember feeling his energy like coiled electricity inside his shirt. I looked at his face and wondered what it was like when he wasn't working. "I'll be more careful," I said.

He stepped out onto the porch and Willow shot past him into the house. "Your cat, I presume." He laughed. It was a good sound. "Well, good night. Bolt your door."

"Yes sir," I said with mock seriousness. But I stayed for a moment on the porch watching him walk to his car. It had been awhile since a man had made me so aware of his presence, and, even tired as I was, I didn't want to miss any of it. As he drove away I saw a curtain in the house across the street wave slightly, like a silk scarf in a soft breeze.

Chapter Three

Reese Kessler lay on the bed in his hotel room thinking about the events of the day. His body ached from the strain of loading the cow onto the trailer, and he had gotten a nasty gash in his forearm carrying the calf up the bank through the buttonbush thickets. It had been years since he felt so alive. He let himself savor the sensations that had overtaken him from the first moment he saw Jessie Weston that morning, standing by the drive in the thick green light. From a distance, her strong, slender build made her seem almost boyish. But when he saw her face and heard her voice, realized she was teasing him for patronizing her, he found himself staring at her mouth and wondering why he was trying so hard to stay married to a woman who didn't want him. He knew it was foolish to lie there, thinking of Jessie that way, but that only added to his delight. He couldn't remember the last time he'd felt bare-bottomed goosey over a woman.

He'd thought about her all morning while laying out transects along the lakeshore. From one station he could see her sitting on the porch with her father and he'd felt peculiarly self-conscious knowing she was watching him. He wondered what she thought about him being there, knowing he was with the State, knowing that more than likely he was going to report that her old man's dike was standing on sovereign lakebed. He hoped she could see it was nothing personal. Every time he thought about the way she'd laughed at him his heart beat so hard he could feel it pulse in his fingertips. You're an idiot, Kessler, he said to himself. She's probably just playing you for a sap so you'll go easy on her old man. But it wasn't like that, he knew. Getting that cow out of the borrow ditch she had been amazing. He'd never been around a woman like that, working shoulder to shoulder. He felt like they had read each other's minds, so easily had they fallen into a rhythm together.

He remembered the last time he'd had to work with Vivian. He was helping her move into an apartment in town. She had decided she needed space. Carrying her bed together down the steps of the farmhouse had felt like trying to push a cart with a square wheel. Going up the stairs to her apartment she had almost managed to knock him down with the table they were toting. Then she had yelled that he was so hopeless he couldn't even see her slowing down. They were so out of sync in every way. For a long time Vivian had seemed irrational to him. He had tried to be understanding, but the truth was he didn't understand her. She seemed to take everything personally, like a tired child, and they had never formed the habit of talking over their problems. He found it difficult to speak to her as an adult, a friend. Over the years, their exchanges became formulaic, and no matter how he tried to steer them along a different course, they ended up in the same place. When he had first met her he'd been attracted to how much she seemed to need. He knew there was no toughness in her, but he was twenty-six, and he took for granted his own steadiness, thinking it sufficient for them both. Now, approaching forty, he could see she didn't want his steadying influence. Her ways were home to her, no matter how unreasonable they might seem to him.

What had surprised him today was how easily the realization had come to him that it was over between them. Seeing Jessie Weston's strength and quiet self-possession had made him feel how much he longed for a partner and friend. And, though he knew it was unlikely he would ever get to know her, she had made him think of being with a woman in a different way than he'd ever imagined.

He would always want to remember Jessie's face when she came over the top of that bank. She had cut her cheek on the way down and the wound looked painful. He knew she must be about done in. But her eyes were already surveying the damage. She saw that the cow had gone down, and she'd looked quickly around for the calf. Then she'd seen his arm, freshly cut and still bleeding. Now, he thought, she'll lose it. He saw her pull her bottom lip between her teeth, and then she'd looked at him and said, "I'll go get a trailer. Would you guys stick around and help me get her on?" They sure would, he'd told her. She caught her horse and mounted him. "I've got a first aid kit at the barn. We can clean up your arm," she said. And then she reined her horse around and was gone. He'd left Richard and Bo and followed her in the jeep. He could still see her ahead of him, loping her horse slowly along the top of the dike, her red visor like a flag on the skyline. Then, as she rode down off the dike and onto the broad sand road, he'd seen the horse stretch out into a wide-open gallop. The last half-mile to the barn she had let him fly.

The sharp jangle of the telephone startled Reese from his musing. He expected it would be Richard, calling to see if Reese wanted to go with him and Bo to get dinner. Instead, it was his boss, bureau chief Sam Donnovan.

"How's it look out there?" he asked.

"About what you'd expect from the aerials. That dike is well below the average water level. There's maybe a good hundred yards in most places before you get to anything like a break in elevation."

"Oh boy."

"Yeah."

"Did Mr. Weston play nice?"

"Well, he didn't shoot at us. But he wasn't real happy. They're planning to show up at the hearing."

"That's Thursday?"

"Yeah, morning."

"I expect you better plan to head on over there first thing. Be on hand to answer technical questions. Keep the director out of trouble."

"That might be easier said than done. I think most these people would just as soon see us run out of town on a rail."

"Nothing new there. Those airboat cowboys'll be friendly though. You probably ought to look up that Chris Farlow guy beforehand. Just touch base so you'll have somebody to cover you if you have to make a run for it."

They chuckled half-heartedly. "I made a little good will today though," Reese told him. "Weston's daughter had to ask us to help her get a cow out of that old borrow ditch. Son of a gun was really stuck down in there—with a calf."

"That's a hell of a thing. Did you get it out okay?"

"We got her out, but I don't know if she'll make it or not. Jessie took her on to the vet."

"Jessie, huh?"

"Yeah."

"You watch out down there, boy. Old Mr. Weston won't take kind-lee to you barkin' up that tree." Sam laughed.

"I s'pect that's right," Reese laughed too. He felt unaccountably pleased at the thought of trouble over him seeing Jessie Weston. "Anything in particular you want out of this hearing?"

"Just try to get the old-timers to talk about where the water was before the dike went in. If we end up in court on this, we'll have an easier time if we don't have to go with just the gauge data. A lot of people still mighty suspicious of all that scientific voodoo we do."

"Me included," Reese laughed.

"A'ighty," Sam said. "Be careful down there."

"Yep. Talk to you later."

He hung up and went into the bathroom to shave. He suddenly felt like getting out, maybe just walking through the streets of the town and looking at the people going in and out of shops, sitting at outdoor tables eating dinner. He didn't want to hear Richard and Bo talk about what had happened today. He was already wondering if Richard hadn't thought about getting to know Jessie himself over the next few weeks, and Reese didn't want to hear him say so. Richard had a lot going for him. He was younger. And single. He liked women, and had an easy way with them they seemed to respond to. Reese had worked with him, traveled and been out on jobs like this with him enough to know Richard usually got what he wanted.

Reese studied himself in the mirror, wondering what a woman like Jessie saw when she looked at a man like him. He finished shaving and was buttoning his shirt when the phone rang. He thought about not answering it, but it would be better to let his crew check in with him. He could beg off easily enough and give Richard the plan for tomorrow. "This is Reese," he said, picking up the phone.

"Mr. Kessler. It's Jessie Weston."

"Hey there," Reese blurted out. Suddenly his pulse was racing again, and, half panicked with surprise, he struggled to sound normal.

"I'm sorry to disturb you," Jessie said, "but I'm just leaving the vet's and I wanted to let you know that both your rescuees are still among the living. And I wanted to make sure that you were too."

"I'm glad to hear it," Reese said. He tried to focus on the news of the cow. "What did the vet say about her?"

"Well, the leg's a concern, but no other serious injuries. She was severely dehydrated. Apparently the calf did nurse, so that was good for him, but hard on her. I think they must have been down there a couple of days. Anyway, they're both on IV's and I'm hopeful they'll make it."

"That's good news." Reese wished she would go on talking about the cow or the vet or the cost of green cheese. He didn't want her to hang up.

"I wanted to thank you for all you did, and Richard and Bo. You guys were great," she said. In a second she would be saying good-bye and that would be it.

"Look, I was just about to go out and get some supper," he stammered. "Would you join me?"

The line seemed to go dead. For at least a half-second there was no response. Reese imagined his heart suspended mid-beat, waiting for the world to breathe again. Then she said, "I'd need to go home first. I look like a train wreck. Could you give me an hour?"

"Any hour you want," he said, and they laughed.

"How about Posie's at eight?" she said. "I'll buy you that drink."

Reese could not have said how he spent the next hour. He had certainly called Richard and made some excuse for not going out with them, had probably told him about the call from Sam and gone over the plan for tomorrow's work. He must have asked directions to the restaurant. At 7:45 he found himself walking along the riverfront behind Posie's, vaguely aware of the fading light, the pelicans perched on the dock pilings, the sound of an old record playing from a window above. The stars were beginning to glimmer in a clear turquoise sky, and the words of the old song carried intermittently on the breeze.

He couldn't remember ever wanting so much to be a part of something larger. It seemed to him that he could feel the gears of the universe turning endlessly on their sprockets, and he imagined them carrying him toward something undeniably his. He made his way into the restaurant and told the hostess he would like a table for two, somewhere quiet where they could see the boats come and go. He hoped Jessie would like that.

When he turned he saw her crossing the street, and he went out front to meet her. He had wondered how it would be now, if they would be shy and formal with each other, or relaxed and easy. He was like a man who had escaped history, standing with the world before him ready to remake. But when he saw her coming toward him, her dark hair blowing free in the wind and her white blouse billowing against her breasts, he was uncertain whether he had language.

"Hi," she said, smiling into his face. "Doesn't the air feel wonderful, after such a hot day too."

"You look great," Reese said. "How's the cheek?"

"Ugly," she laughed. "At least your battle wounds are easily concealed." She stretched her forefinger toward his arm and touched his sleeve just below the outline of the bandage. "How's it feel?"

"Wonderful," he laughed. "Would you like to go in?"

"Or we could sit outside. They have riverside tables out back."

"Perfect. Of course you run a greater risk of being seen out there," he warned her, "consorting with the enemy."

"Oh, let them talk," Jessie said. "They're so grateful for new grist they'll probably cast you in bronze."

"As long as they don't leave me inside the cast."

They went leisurely through the timeworn rituals. Deciding where to sit for the best view, choosing a bottle of wine, ordering food. Each action felt to Reese as if it were being performed for the first time, as if it were the definition of time. When the wine came he told the waiter, "You better let Ms. Weston do the honors—I've got a tin tongue."

"Now you're not going to keep calling me Ms. Weston, are you?" she protested, lifting the glass to her mouth. "Ummmn," she nodded at the waiter, "that'll do just fine."

Reese waited for the waiter to pour the wine and leave. He folded his hands and studied her face. "What shall I call you then?"

She gazed across the river, squinting her eyes. "How about Woman-with-Cow-Stuck-in-Ditch," she giggled.

"And what will you call me?" he asked, smiling.

"Heap Big Help."

"Ok, but I'll have to call you WWCSid for short."

"Sounds like a world war," she laughed.

"And you better call me Heap," he said, enjoying her laughter. "If you call me Help, somebody might get the wrong idea and throw me out of here." Reese thought he would always like to see her this way, and he wondered if she was like this with other men, joking and happy, really beautiful.

"So, Heap," she grinned, "what were you doing down at the lake today?"

"Ah, Sid, so you are a spy. I have to warn you I've spent years in training to resist beautiful women trying to pry state secrets out of me."

"So you're un-crackable, huh?"

"No, I've never been able to resist yet—that's why I'm still in training."

"I see," she said. Reese thought her expression sobered. She was quiet, and they watched a sloop, sails folded, motoring slowly into its mooring, its crimson light splashing the foaming wake.

Their food came. He watched her peel shrimp and spear florets of broccoli while he cut his steak and buttered his potato.

"What we're doing," he said, "is locating the ordinary high water line of the lake." She poured more wine. "We lay out transects from the lakebed to the uplands. The lake is down right now, so we can see a lot of change as we go up. We flag changes in the vegetation, the soil, places where the ground breaks up sharply. We shoot elevations to determine where those changes are occurring."

"But the dike has changed everything," she said softly.

"Yeah. But we'll compare it to other places on the lake that haven't been diked. Try to get some idea of where the water would be. And there are still indications behind the dike from when the water was in there."

"Will you be at the hearing?"

"Yeah. Just to listen to what people say. Make sure what we're finding correlates with what they know."

"How long have you been with the State?"

"I got on with them while I was still in college, cutting line in the summers between semesters. That was 1980. So, fifteen years. After I graduated I went with them full time. I like the pace and the people."

"You were at Gainesville or Tallahassee?"

"U of F–G'ville."

"I guess I just missed you. I went up in '81."

"What did you study?"

"I thought I wanted to do something in ag engineering. But I took an ecology class, and then I took a wrong turn–to hear my father tell it anyway. Got into natural resources–microbiology, though, not management. Cell biology was just starting to be taught. When I first looked at pond scum under an electron microscope, I fell in love." She laughed softly and Reese nodded, hoping she would go on talking. "I loved looking at those little invisible worlds. They seemed like conversations going on that I couldn't quite hear. And I thought if I got really still and quiet–inside myself–I would be able to make them out." She folded her napkin.

"Did you finish a degree?"

"Yeah, but I got side-tracked. Married an English professor. Took a dead-end job so I could stay in Gainesville."

"And it didn't work out." Reese said.

"And it didn't work out." She seemed to hesitate, and Reese wondered what fatal flaw the marriage had foundered on. "He thinks he owns out to the section line," she said. "He says it's in his deed."

It took Reese a moment to realize she was talking about her father. "That's a mistake a lot of people make."

"He showed me the deed once. I couldn't tell anything one way or another," Jessie said.

"It probably is described in his deed that way. It's just that that kind of deed can't convey navigable waters below the ordinary high water line. The land was parceled out in huge tracts, but people were supposed to know that they didn't get any navigable waters within those tracts."

"That's what he won't hear. He acts like a deed is a writ from God."

"I'm sorry there's so much at stake here," Reese said. He felt helpless to express to her how little he wanted to fight her or her family.

"He's a good man," Jessie said. "It's just that we've had a way of life here that works. Now, everything's changing. He knows that the world has arrived on his doorstep. He wants to cash in on all the development–for me, really, and my stepbrother, Bud. Not for himself. But along with all those people who want to buy his land comes more government, more oversight. He's used to calling the shots." She shrugged and smiled. Reese thought she looked tired.

"How bad is this going to hit him?" Reese asked.

"I'm not sure," Jessie said. "I need to talk to him when this all settles down. See what he thinks we should do. I think financially he can probably weather it just fine. But he's not one to give up in a fight. He'd probably rather it kill him."

They finished the wine and Reese paid the check. He felt unsure of what should come next. He wanted to go on talking to her, but she was probably ready to be away from him.

"Would you like to walk a little?" she asked suddenly. "It's nice along the river."

"Sure, if you're up to it," he said.

A gibbous moon had come up in the east. They walked along, listening to the sail riggings clanking against their masts in the steady river breeze. Reese found himself imagining they had been married for a long time–as long as he and Vivian had, or longer. He felt her beside him, felt her concern for her father, felt her thoughtfully mulling over the problems they faced in the weeks and months ahead. He knew he couldn't already love her, but he liked imagining he had loved her all his life. How different life would be with a woman like that. He wanted to take her out on the water, go flying across Lake Ponder, pitch a tent on Moccasin Island, lie on the shore and eat wild oranges. At one point in their walk, they had to pause and yield the boardwalk to an older couple, and he took the opportunity to place his hand gently against her back as if in support against the uneven footing. He thought he felt her lean into him very slightly.

"We should go back," she said. "We've both got early chores." Still they lingered, watching the lights of the town glittering like stars in the waves. When at last they started back, the boardwalk was deserted. As he walked her to her truck, he thought of kissing her, wondered if she expected it, wondered if he could still kiss a woman. It had been so long. She turned to face him.

"I'm glad I met you today," she said. "And I haven't forgotten. I still owe you that drink." She stretched up and kissed his neck just below his jaw, climbed in her truck, and drove away.

April 12, 2001

I was dreaming we were on the airboat at Lake Ponder flying over the rough blue water just ahead of a storm that was closing fast around us. I could feel Steve's arm against the back of my life jacket, and his thigh pressed against mine as Richard swung the boat across the waves and punched the throttle full open. Lightning ran through the gray air to the ground, arcing like the finger of god pointing at some hapless sinner. I felt Steve turn back toward Richard, his hand reaching across my body to hold me in. I heard his muffled shouting. We can't make the landing. We can't make the landing.

But the roaring engine turned into Willow purring against my shoulder. I looked at the clock. Time to go. I rolled out, showered, made tea, fed Willow, and was out the door before I let myself think of anything. I was going to have to talk to Steve about this break-in thing. Detective Deo had said he would need information about my co-workers, and I needed to clear that with Steve and just let him know that . . . what? That I was all right? That there was nothing he needed to do? That I would be careful about what I said? He already knew these things. Didn't he?

I didn't want to break my pact with myself about confiding in him. It was still the thing I missed the most, the long conversations we used to have. They would start with our wisecracking about some political outrage that was in the news. We would be sitting in his office, finishing up the day discussing some case we were working on and one of us would make some comment about the sorry state of the world. Then we'd be off and running on that, cracking jokes and ranting about politicians until long after other employees had gone home to their TVs and families. By the time the cleaning crew came in we would be well along to sorting out our philosophical differences with the world. We would walk out to the parking lot together, happy, stimulated. Then came a long, drawn-out case we worked on together in Vero Beach. What had been our habit of afternoon discussions in his office turned into long talks after the day's work in the courthouse or on the water. We would eat dinner at a little Italian place and then drive over the bridge, sit on the banks of the Indian River, and talk. Of course the topic shifted from politics and philosophy to our childhood memories, our teen-age adventures, our divorces, our current domestic dilemmas, music, how wonderful the air felt. I knew he had a girlfriend. He knew I had a cat. Sometimes we would go out to the oceanfront, to a little dive we found called the Blue Parrot, where a trio of scruffy guys played primo raw rock and roll. Sometimes we would just sit in the car down by the pier, listening to Stevie Ray Vaughn levitate off the face of the earth with his guitar. We kept telling ourselves we were just great friends—really great friends.

One night we were sitting on the pier watching the phosphorescent whitecaps in the churning surf. We would be going home the next day. We sat for a long time not saying anything. Finally he said, "I guess we've said it all, huh?" He got up, took my hand and pulled me to my feet. He said, "Are we going to do this?" And then we were kissing.

The following months were a roller coaster ride. I vacillated wildly between deciding to quit my job so we could be together and trying to stay away from him totally. He denied being in love with me, said he was leaving his girlfriend, said he couldn't leave his girlfriend, said he was taking a job in Missouri, would I stay in touch—would I come with him, he was crazy in love with me, he couldn't sleep couldn't eat couldn't breathe the air, the wonderful air. He couldn't leave right now, we had to be careful, he could get fired if people knew how we felt. Maybe someday things wouldn't be like this. We spun into mania together, tried to land softly, to shield one another. Finally, sitting on the porch drinking alone on my birthday I decided. Enough.

I stuck my head in his office. "Got a minute?" I tried to sound upbeat.

"Got a settlement draft?" he responded.

"I'm working on it. I'll probably have to coordinate with Jack though. There's just a lot of stuff I don't know how to approach—legally."

"I hear you stalling," he sang, paraphrasing an old blues song.

"On another subject altogether—"

"You know I could just let the AG do this. I want you on it for damage control. You know—"

"Somebody broke into my house and took my hard drive. Left a weird note. Called me up. The police think he might be stalking me."

He sat back and looked at me. I could see his confusion. I could feel the air between us like a current, an undertow pulling us out to sea. I went on.

"There's a possibility the police will want to interview some of the people I work with—especially people who know about computers."

"Are you all right?"

I could feel the hot pressure behind my eyes. I knew if he was nice I would start to cry and everything would get worse.

"Don't make me cry," I said, trying to laugh. "You know. I'll get mad, and when I get mad I can't breathe, I can't talk, I can't think, and I repeat myself—"

"You do what?"

"I repeat my—repeat myself," I said, taking the tissue he held out to me.

It was an old joke between old friends who had once tried and failed to find their way to something more, who would go on working together and caring about each other while mostly living their lives apart, with other people. But not without regrets.

"I don't think anything's going to come of it," I said. "I just wanted to give you a heads-up in case the police call you. And because they seem to think there may be a security issue."

"Ok. Do you need—" he winced and looked away. Sighed. "Why can't things work out?" he said softly.

"Maybe they do," I said. And I got up and left.

I thought about going to the cafeteria for some breakfast, but my stomach was queasy. I thought about the Chinese leftovers I'd downed last night. Maybe not so good. I went to my office and called Mel. Mel is an attorney with EARTH JUST IS, an environmental legal defense group. We share information, update one another on the legislative scuttlebutt, provide each other moral support, and talk over cases, mothers, and love affairs.

"What would happen," I asked her, "if we went to court and Wesson won on the estoppel issue?"

"Not much," she said. "The estoppel issue is particular to this case. Wesson's arguing that representatives of the State authorized the dike, so therefore it must be on his private property. If he won the estoppel argument, you would lose that piece of Lake Ponder, but it wouldn't affect your ability to bust other encroachments."

"And the location of the ordinary high water boundary wouldn't come into it, right?"

"Right. He would get everything in his deed—sovereign or not."

"What would happen if the Trustees won the estoppel issue?"

"Then you'd have to set the boundary. You'd end up going back to trial over the ordinary high water line. That would get pretty ugly. They want to challenge everything about that line."

"Hey, let 'em bring it on. We've done our homework. Our methodology is sound, fair—Chris Farlow would say conservative."

"That's the AG's least favorite option. They don't want to risk all the progress they've made over the last five years that helps protect sovereignty lands."

"What's it worth if we can't get this dike off the lakebed?"

"A lot, even if it's just a starting point. This case could wipe it all out in a heartbeat. And you know with a local judge in a big landowner county—Teena you're just not going to win on what matters."

"There are a lot of things here that matter."

"I know what you're saying. But you know what I'm saying."

"Yeah." My stomach was rumbling, my mouth had a metal taste.

"What don't you like about just losing it on estoppel?" she asked.

"Because Mel, we didn't fuck this up. Saying the State is estopped is like saying the people who worked so hard to get that dike breached didn't do their job—and they did. Wesson can't rely on that sniveling consent Sloan gave him to refill the breaches—not as proof of ownership. He knew he was on public land. I have the correspondence, the memos, the notes. I have his signature on a piece of paper saying he agreed to restore the marsh. He *did* the restoration. He knew he wasn't supposed to be on that lakebed. We just shouldn't lose this case. It's like letting him steal this really important thing and not doing anything about it."

"It's not like that," Mel said. "It *is* that. It's just that losing on estoppel is the best way out—from a legal standpoint. Just from a legal standpoint. That's why the AG wants to settle it out of court. Just make it go away."

"How do we do that? On what basis can we just give him the dike?"

"You're going to have to use his version of events—even though you have evidence out the yahzoo that his version is just a pack of sleazeball lies. Then you just admit that you're estopped and give him the damn thing."

"I don't think I can make myself do that. Even though everybody agrees that's what needs to happen."

"What are you going to do?"

"Yet to be determined."

"Have you talked to Steve about this?"

"No."

"Are you going to?"

"He thinks I'm stalling."

"He knows better than that. He just doesn't know how to help you get through this. He wants it over fast so you can put it behind you."

"Don't make him sound nice. I need to hate him. And I *am* stalling."

"Ok. How'd it go with the detective last night? Your email sounded a little whacky."

"Hmmmn, could be interesting."

"Cut to the chase."

"Ok, he's a hunk. We did it three times—once on the rug, once on the table, and once in the front yard as he was trying to make it to his car," I joked. "Anything else you want to know?"

"I'll want full details later."

"Ok. Thanks pal."

I hung up and buzzed Richard's office. No answer. I sent him an email asking him to get together with me on the Lake Ponder thing. Then I pulled my file containing Bob Wesson's "Chronology of Events" and "Fact Sheet"—tall tales Wesson, or more likely Ratzlaff, had cooked up in 1997 to schmooze the Cabinet into giving him the lakebed. At the time, I'd gone point by point through his assertions and shown they weren't accurate accounts and didn't take into consideration little things like the law. It had the desired effect: the

Cabinet declined to consider the matter. Now I was supposed to just go with Wesson's hogwash? I spent the rest of the morning and all afternoon trying to walk a mile in his Cole-Haans. I didn't get very far.

At lunchtime I tried to choke down a sandwich. It wasn't like me to be reluctant to eat, but somehow food was not working for me. I chucked it in the garbage can.

At four o'clock Bonnie stuck her head in. "You got the email about the staff meeting tomorrow?"

"I haven't checked."

"Mandatory. 8:30."

"Thanks."

"How's it going?"

I made a face.

"Need anything."

"A double shot of Johnny Walker Red."

"I'll check the supply cabinet." She ducked out.

In the interest of keeping my procrastination list under some kind of control, I dialed my mother's number. Her neighbor, Mrs. Myers, answered and told me she'd left this morning on her trip. "I'm just here to bring in the mail," she said. "I'm sure she'll call you when she gets checked in to her hotel. You doing all right, dear?"

I lied and told her I was great, chatted her up enough to find out that she was fine except that her feet hurt when she shopped too long. I told her she should shop the internet, and she laughed and said she was afraid she'd get mugged.

I spent the last half hour searching my C-drive for old versions of my novel files. I found an ancient file called "Novel Notes" that outlined some ideas, but nothing substantial. Nothing like the hundred and ninety pages that had kept me alive for the last six months.

As soon as I got home I pulled up my email and scanned the list nervously. I really didn't know if I wanted to see anything from creepboy or not. There was only one it could be. A message entitled Do you read me? from one Ed Itori at an unknown address. I glanced at the time. Logan Deo would be here in half an hour. Maybe I should wait 'til . . . . My hand moved the mouse almost involuntarily. My forefinger clicked. There wasn't going to be any waiting. The message came up, filling the screen all the way to the edges.

My, aren't we gay, and such a nice looking young suitor too. Just the cat's meow. MeeooOWwwuh! **HAHAHAHAHAHA.** Oh but enough of this frivolity. Matters press.

Let's see. Where to begin. Perhaps a cautionary tale: Oh but you **MUST** have heard the story of the young Gustave Flaubert, who began his writing career — surprise surprise — as a Romantic. What, our Gustave? Author of the grim grim grim *Madame Bovary?* The very same. He himself admitted to being addicted to the "disease" of Romanticism. The story goes that he once presented an early draft of some of his "diseased" work to his friends, and, what do you think? These trusted allies made cruel sport of his efforts! -—Guffawing, my dear, IN HIS ***VERY*** **FACE.** So scathing, so trenchant, were their remarks on his sentiments that he quite vowed *never* to be vulnerable to such criticism again. He remade his very sensibility, my pet. "I refuse to consider Art a drain pipe for passion," he wrote. Instead he resolved "to render ignoble reality artistically." Having ascended to this critical vantage point he could then see the hollow and sordid society of his time for what it was — sick with romantic self-indulgence, bloated on bourgeois rapacity. To this awakening we owe the creation of his masterpiece, which ended the classical solidarity of art with the bourgeois consciousness.

Oh but a thousand pardons — how droll of me to go **ON** so. My point — yes yes — to the point: What meek drivel you have been writing! To put such talent as yours, such sensitivity to the beat of language as you possess, to so menial a task as this little romance. One might almost imagine that you grew up chanting All you need is love, deetah deetah dum. Really, my dear, a heroine falling in love with her father's enemy! Galloping around on horses. For shame, forsooth, from this day forward promise me more MORE **MorE.** You have greatness in you, and mistake me not:

I WILL GET IT OUT OF YOU.

So, now, we shall make this beginning concrete. **HAHAHAHA.** All good editors give concrete assignments. I shall expect you to post a paragraph of your new and evolving style — oh tsk tsk, let us use the proper term---your new *écriture* — to your favorite little chat site by Sunday evening.

Or you will *pay* ***the price!***

AHAHAHAHAHAHA;)!

Your Ed

I probably read the message through four times before I realized I was starting to read it again. I felt sick, I was outraged, I was scared. The most horrible part, though, was that I was intrigued. I realized, even then, sitting there shocked and shaking, that my mind was already engaged in the story of Flaubert, was already thinking of the writing in *Madame Bovary* with a certain concreteness. I had taught the book in a World Literature course as part of my graduate teaching. There was something else too about the message that seemed familiar. Classical art, its solidarity with the bourgeois consciousness—that was something creepboy had said on the phone. And the word *écriture*—what had he called that—the thought for the day. That should be a dead giveaway, I knew. If this was going to be an intellectual game, I was going to need to think. I should already have been able to place those ideas, to name that theorist. Instead, I could feel the sluggishness in my gaping synapses.

I forced myself to analyze the document a sentence at a time. It was then that I realized the implication of the first paragraph. Willow! I felt the blood drain from my face and a wave of nausea wracked through my esophagus. At that moment the doorbell sounded. As I tried to stand, the room lurched crazily in my vision. Walking towards the hall I felt the floor tilt crazily. The air hummed with agitated black bees. The bell rang again. I crumpled to my knees and felt my way into the hall bathroom. I remember retching in the toilet, hearing Logan Deo calling Dr. Shostekovich, Dr. Shostekovich, are you there? in an increasingly louder voice, until finally I heard him saying Teena, Teena—are you all right? I'm coming in. And the door opened and he came down the hall just as I was sitting up and trying to wipe the spittle from my nose.

"Teena" he cried, "are you ill?"

I shook my head, but stayed on the floor, seeing ghosts of the phrase "ignoble reality" swirling through my jittery vision.

"Let me help you. Keep your head down."

"Call Willow," I blubbered.

"What's that?"

"Would you help me to the door, I have to call Willow."

"Of course, your cat."

I nodded. He walked away. I could hear him open the door and step out onto the porch. I couldn't have imagined what would come next. Everyone knows that you call a cat kittykittykittykiiiitttttty!? Instead, I heard Detective Deo, in a perfectly cordial voice, say, Willow, would you step in please. Dr. Shostekovich would like to see you. I was mustering all my strength to yell **Do you see her?** when cat and man appeared in the bathroom doorway, both in seemingly excellent health.

When Logan had settled me with Willow in the armchair by my desk and propped my feet on the ottoman, he went to make tea. I tried hard not to think about how embarrassed I was going to feel as soon as I revived enough to care. I tried even harder not to think about Willow shooting into the house last night, the soft wave of the curtain in the window across the street.

"Better?" he asked. I nodded, drinking. "You still look pale," he said. "Did something happen?"

"Something I ate," I mumbled, pointing to the message on my screen. He sat in my desk chair, rolled closer to the screen, and read. I watched his eyes. He read it twice through before sitting back. "Do you feel like talking about this?" he asked.

"I . . . yes."

"What do you make of it? Tell me what you thought when you first looked at it, if you can."

"I kept reading it over again. I got caught up in the allusion to Flaubert—I taught that book when I was a grad student so it got me thinking about what he was saying. I kept thinking I should be able to identify the critic or school he was hooked into. He talks about the bourgeois relationship to art. He sees Flaubert as occupying a sort of watershed position in literary history. He refers to *écriture* as a 'term.' He said similar things on the phone."

"And these are things you are familiar with?"

"Yes. I studied them intensely at one time. But I haven't thought about them seriously for years."

Logan got up and refilled my teacup, dropped in two lumps of sugar, stirred. "Do you have any soda crackers?"

"I think so. In the cabinet above the fridge."

He went to the kitchen and I could hear him rustling around. It was very weird having him take care of me. It felt like we had known each other in a different way.

"Did something in particular upset you?—not that the whole thing wouldn't," he said handing me a plate of crackers and five bite-sized pieces of cheese.

"I guess the first few times I read it I sort of breezed over the first part. I got hung up on the mention of Flaubert. But when I went back to look at it line by line, to see—you know—what was going on in the document as a whole—that's kind of what I'm trained to do actually—I realized from the first paragraph that he's watching me all the time. He was here last night."

Logan was very still. I could see the effort it was taking, but I don't know how. "What about the first part indicates that to you?"

"He makes an allusion to a suitor. You were here last night. When you left I thought I saw someone across the street in the house upstairs—actually just a curtain—"

"Why didn't you call me—or just dial 911 and tell them you're in trouble—you don't seem to realize, tonight your front door was unlocked, I just walked right in when you didn't—" He stopped. "You have to be more careful," he said. His shoulders relaxed. He took a long breath. "You were saying something and I interrupted you."

I kept looking at his face, wondering what I was seeing there. "The part about the cat's meow upset me. I think he might have been outside the house. I was afraid he had done something to Willow—remember how she ran into the house when we opened the door—that's not usual for her."

He nodded.

"Of course I probably imagined the whole thing last night. The curtain could easily have been a nosy neighbor." I didn't add what we were probably both thinking: How did creepboy know about Logan being there if he wasn't nearby watching? "Is there another way to interpret that first bit?" I asked. "Maybe I'm just being paranoid."

"Perhaps there are other ways to interpret it," Logan answered. I thought I detected a note of tension in his voice. "But you are not just being paranoid. This guy wants to scare you, and normal, harmless people don't go around doing that."

I found myself listening to the little pauses in his speech dropped like notes in a jazz improvisation. "So what's next?"

"It seems from his message that it's your writing he's focusing on."

"It's Roland Barthes," I said suddenly.

"Who?"

"The critic, writer, the theorist creepboy is glossing—it's Roland Barthes. I just realized. It makes sense—Barthes is a name that crops up in the cyberchats. He described a mass culture controlled by the bourgeoisie in order to encourage conformity to its own values."

"Controlled how."

"I don't have a fast answer to that. But Barthes saw language and objects as a system of signs already being used when we come into the world. With language, we begin speaking and writing these signs, thinking of them as a given, as natural—neutral. But really they are already appropriated by the existing power group—they are spelling out the world as the powers would have it be."

"Are you talking about political powers?" Logan asked.

"Yeah, but broader. Think of the picture of life that corporations and politicians create to try to get the rest of us to act in their interests. The 'powers' are the people who control that. Did you know, for example, that most of the books published, the records recorded, the films made, the newspapers, television—it's all produced by half-a-dozen mega-corporations. That's a lot of influence over what we see as our world. That's power that for the most part stays hidden, but it can be used very effectively to maintain a particular story of reality."

"So the 'powers' tell the story that helps keep them in power?"

"Right. Think of how powerful stories are. A lonely woman reads a romance, which reinforces a notion that relationships between men and women follow a certain formula. She buys make-up, shampoo, perfume, clothes, a car even—all based, at least in part, on that idea. That's not lost on people who market products. They use the signs she's already familiar with to sell her their products."

"Meanwhile, the guy in the cubicle next to her is thinking he would like to talk to her but her perfume is too strong and her make-up scares him," Logan grinned.

"Maybe. More likely he's thinking he'd like to talk to her but he's afraid his deodorant isn't working and he has a stain on his shirt. So, he needs to go buy something."

He tipped his head back and laughed softly.

"We're all using language that has baggage, and we're constantly tempted by the familiar version of reality that it conveys. So really it's like language is using you."

"What relevance does that have to your novel?"

"Barthes saw writers were faced with a particular difficulty because of their reliance on language. Even though a writer might want to present a different view of the world, of the possibilities for our lives, language has a history that tends to lead us back to the familiar stories of the powers, and the way they present the world. The special danger to a writer is that these dominant stories are like favorite bedtime stories. They lull us to sleep in a comforting way. They reinforce what we already think the world is, and make it more difficult for the writer to see and express a different vision of the world."

His face registered absolutely nothing. Then he said, "Tell me again what it is you do in your work."

"I work to protect sovereignty lands. They're lands under navigable waters that belong to the public."

"And how do you do that?"

"When we get a complaint of someone encroaching on sovereignty lands, I do the research to find out what's happened to the waterbody and the land, what deeds are relevant, what permits have been issued, what drainage projects have affected the waterbody, whether boats have used the water for trade. If we get into court, I work with the legal team to help them figure out the case and build their legal strategy, and I testify about the research I've done."

He sat for a moment letting his eyes scan back and forth across my keyboard as if he were reading the letters for signs.

"And you think—'creepboy'," he paused and smiled at me, shook his head—apparently there was something he enjoyed about my dubbing "creepboy" so irreverently—"you think he knows this theory of Roland Barthes?"

"I really can't tell from what we have to go on. He knows something. A lot of paranoid cyberpunk types really get into Barthes. I mean he's a cool guy in his own right. But my guess is this nut is on thin ice when it comes to the implications of any theory to literature. So far the stuff he's spouting he could've gotten in one afternoon cruising the web. Parts of it sound like they're from a lecture or an article."

"Couldn't he be an academic? Someone who saw you at university?"

In that split second, my ear caught the idiom, and I almost asked him about it. I suspected he wouldn't answer though. He didn't seem like the kind of professional who wanted to chat about his personal life, and I imagined him trying to spin it as just mumbling. So I answered as if I had only been pausing to consider his question. "His characterizations of romance and realism are general. He's probably had a few classes in literature that got him thinking about these issues, but I'd be surprised if it was more than that."

"Still—and correct me if I'm wrong here—he seems to be pointing to a connection of this theorist to a writer. And, if I understand you, Flaubert is not a contemporary writer?

"He wrote in the 19th century."

"So our pal has some inkling of literary history."

"You're right. Barthes' interest in Flaubert was specifically literary—within his critique of bourgeois society. Roughly speaking, romanticism would represent only the privileged views of the world—the 'powers,' while the creation of the new literature—realism—focused on the horrors of life for the underclasses. But Barthes' interest in Flaubert went far beyond that simple division. He was interested in Flaubert's various inventions in literature for unmasking what's really going on."

"This writing assignment he's given you. Do you know what he wants you to do?"

"My guess is he thinks I'm naively writing a romantic story and thus inadvertently doing the bidding of the oil companies that own the publishing houses and bookstores and all the rest of the media. He seems to think that if I exposed the love affair as sordid and made it all 'grim' like Flaubert did, that that would address the problem."

"And it wouldn't?"

"There's a lot more to it than that. Barthes would want to see the writer unmask the power structure—not confirm that if only you were white, American, and middle class everything would come out all right. But it's never clear from the outset how that might happen. Flaubert, for instance, in trying to avoid indulging in gratuitous sentiment, actually invented one of the most intimate forms of discourse a writer can place in the mind of a character. And a few critics have argued that his novel was *condemning* a world that would deny Emma Bovary the legitimacy of her passions. Of course, most have seen the book as a brutally realistic account of a silly bourgeois woman. So exactly which power structure—or structures—are being unmasked becomes a layered question as well."

He sat for a moment, his hand covering his mouth. It gave me the odd impression he was trying not to say something he wanted to say. "What is your novel—about? like? I don't know the right question."

"Those are the right questions. It has to do with finding what matters. I don't know what it is yet. I was writing it to find out."

"But not naively." He smiled.

"Well, you never know," I shrugged. "You're not usually naïve about the thing you've got your eye on." I realized my eyes were on his face. "It's all that other stuff you're not even thinking about that gets you." He sat in my desk chair looking at me and waiting. It reminded me of the days in Vero with Steve, the luxurious sense of time stretching out and words floating in the air between people who were listening for something not said. "But I'll tell you something weird," I went on. "Ever since I first started to write the two main characters, I've had to fight against their love affair taking over the novel. I've felt it as this pull I had to constantly guard against, and yet it's also the reason that I'm writing—in some way I don't know how to say yet. It's possible that may be what creepboy's feeling too. He could be picking up on that, and he would be right that it's one of the problems I'm trying to write my way through."

Logan Deo's mood seemed to shift suddenly. "Don't make any mistakes about this, Dr. Shosteko—"

"Please call me Teena," I broke in. "Otherwise I feel like I'm being cross examined."

He seemed not to have heard. His eyes didn't waver from my face. His voice had an urgency I hadn't heard before. "Don't underestimate this situation. He wants you to let your guard down because you feel that he understands you, your work. Teena." He said my name so quietly I almost couldn't tell if I'd heard it.

"Why are you spending time on this case?" The thought had come to me suddenly and I'd asked it without thinking. But this time I was looking straight at his face and I saw the shadow pass over it, as if the blood had drained suddenly from his skin and then rushed back, like a violent tide. "I mean, nothing of value to anyone but me has been stolen. No harm's been done." I was torn between wanting to give him time to compose himself and wanting to find out what I was seeing, what he was reacting to so involuntarily.

"Well," he forced a small laugh, "my curiosity has been piqued. I want to see you get your novel back so you can finish it. Besides, I want to read it."

I didn't laugh. Listening to the hollow sound of his words I'd felt a small prickle of anxiety on the back of my neck. "Look," I said, "you don't need to patronize me. Is there something about this thing I'm missing?"

"I'm not patronizing you, believe me," he said earnestly. "There are things about this I don't know yet. But this may be something we've seen before—part of a pattern. I'm trying to find out what this guy's after, but I need your help. And I need you to be careful."

"A pattern of what? People's novels being stolen? Their writing criticized? What the hell is going on here?"

"I'm not sure yet. I'll tell you as much as I can, but to figure this out I need you to tell me things without any preconceptions. We need to rule things out."

I sat there feeling utterly frozen with my mind chanting desperately: I have to think, I have to think. Something about this wasn't right. I was vaguely aware that Logan Deo was telling me nothing, but I felt as if he'd told me creepboy was a known axe-murderer. At that moment Willow jumped out of my lap and went to Logan. She settled into his lap like they were old pals. I breathed. "All right," I said. "Let's keep going."

"I'm assuming that your work is fairly political—that you make enemies with the kind of testimony you give."

"Not that many, but a few. And they're powerful—used to getting what they want. A handful of people in Florida want the boundary on lakes and rivers changed to give them the benefit of more land. They keep bringing cases they think will overturn the public trust doctrine."

"How are your computers set up at work?"

"We have a network, desktop computers, internet access, email."

"How much security?"

"I really don't know. You'll probably need to talk to the guy who does all that."

"Do you know any of those guys personally?"

"No. If I have a problem, they come fix it. Actually, they don't even do that anymore. They have a thing called 'special access' where they can 'step in' to your screen while you're working—remotely—so they don't even have to come up the stairs."

"So it wouldn't be that hard for one of them to look at what you were working on?"

"Well, actually, I take precautions. I don't know how much they help. Probably any two-bit hacker could get into my files."

"What precautions do you take?"

"I keep sensitive documents on my C-drive only. I don't store them on the network. I keep my office locked. I lock my computer and keep the key in my bag."

He took his time thinking about that. "You've thought about this a lot, haven't you?"

"I don't like what these guys do. They take land that doesn't belong to them. These are environmentally sensitive lands. They want to make a lot of money screwing everybody else, and sometimes they play really dirty pool when you call them on it."

"Have you ever thought someone was 'stepping in' when you were working on sensitive documents? You know, to get a look at the document while you were working on it?"

"I worried about it. Right after the department started the special access thing, I fixed my cursor so it would show any small movement—any little jump shows up as red glitter. And I made a macro on my keyboard so I could exit into a dummy document even if they took control of my mouse."

"Wow," Logan was leaning toward me, eyebrows raised, absorbed. "Did it work?"

"Yeah," I said, pleased that my scheme impressed him. "But the two times I actually caught someone in my files they didn't take over the mouse, so I wasn't sure what was going on until it was too late. It was strange because both times it was after hours, and the first time it wasn't documents at all—it was my novel. I was in the habit for a while of working on my novel after everyone had gone home. It was kind of a hard time for me and I liked doing that—sitting there in that empty building, writing. I suddenly had the feeling something changed—like everything slowed down just a fraction. Maybe the response time to my keys. Not quite anything I could be sure of. So I stopped for a few minutes like I'd gone out to the bathroom or something, and just sat there watching the screen. In a minute I saw all the text boxed blue, like it had been selected to be copied or cut, and then it went back to normal. I was sure someone copied that file."

"Did you tell anybody?"

"No. At first I expected to get fired."

"For using the computer for your own work?"

"Ostensibly, yeah, but really because I help win cases."

He nodded. "There must be a break-over point. Where the professional staff gets buffered from the political will. Who protects you?"

"It's hard to know where it is at any given time. It shifts. My bureau chief protects me. Sometimes the division office protects him, but only if it's in their interests. It hasn't always been that way. But he walks a thin line these days."

"But the excuse for firing you—that you were misusing state resources—he wouldn't be able to protect you from?"

"That's what I was afraid of. They want to clean house of anyone who isn't on the bandwagon of the new administration. Believe me, nobody really cares about me taking up a few sectors of the State's hard drive with some stupid novel I was writing to keep from killing myself." I hadn't meant to reveal how thin my emotional edge was, but this time Logan Deo didn't look away.

"You've been through a lot." He wasn't asking. It was strange to hear it said out loud in such a nice way.

"I've seen good people lose everything as a result of Dud!'s little party. It's been a really rough time."

"But nothing happened—about the file you think was copied."

"No, I did finally mention it to Steve, my bureau chief, just so he wouldn't get blind-sided. And I took everything to do with my novel off the C-drive and took it home."

"And that was when?"

"Over a month ago."

"What happened the other time you caught them?"

"I was working late on a case that's turned into a real hot potato. The opposition is trying to parlay it into an all-out challenge of the way the State interprets the boundary on waterbodies. We're trying to contain it. There's so much to lose if we lose that fight in court—all the fragile lands around the edge of the lakes and rivers. Anyway, I was writing a description of the dikes on the property, how they had once been breached by order of the State. Then the landowner filled the breaches back in. I was sitting right there writing and all the sudden my text was all selected—the same as before—like to copy it. I hit my macro to try to exit from the file, but I'm not sure I got out before the copy was made."

"Did you tell anyone about that?"

"I called Steve at home right then and told him what had happened. He said he would talk to the division office."

"Do you trust him?"

I have no idea how long it took me to answer. So many things crowded into my mind when confronted with that simple question, I might have sat there for a full minute before I took a breath. "Yes."

"But?"

"No, I trust him not to be involved in undermining that case. I also trust him to protect me, and in his judgment that might mean not talking to division. I'm not sure he wouldn't call someone entirely different."

"Like?"

"Like an old friend of his who used to head up enforcement investigations."

Logan sat for a while, thinking. "And how long ago did the last event happen?"

"Not long after the first one—maybe a month ago."

"Could you be precise if it mattered?"

"I can look at the date the file was created."

"Which file of your novel did he copy?"

"Chapter six."

"Ok," he said softly. "Feel like eating?"

"I'm starving."

"Let's go—my treat for abusing you so."

"Do you think it's okay, you know, for us—?"

"If you mean officially, I got off work a half hour ago, and I assure you I will not run the least bit afoul of police tradition if I keep an eye on you unofficially. If you're thinking of creepboy, he already thinks I'm your 'suitor', so it'll just look normal."

"Give me a minute to change."

I put on a skirt I knew I looked great in and a white cotton blouse. I brushed my hair out and put on lipstick. It made me feel funny looking in the mirror trying to decide if I was interested in Logan Deo in the middle of all this mess. But he certainly seemed to bring out the girl in me.

As we stepped out onto the porch I realized I should've told him before which curtain had fluttered, and I looked over at his face to see if he was watching the windows across the street. I didn't think about til later how uncanny it was that he seemed to glance straight up to the third floor window at the far right end of the building. Where I'd seen the curtain wave the night before. At the time, I must have wanted very much to miss that sign.

Chapter Four

Jessie brought two horses into the saddling paddock the next morning before the light was good enough to see color. She liked feeling her way into the dark intimacy of the band, finding the horses she wanted by their shapes and movements. They all knew her well, knew her as comfort and order. She slipped ropes around Knuckle, her father's chestnut gelding, and Rounder, the dark bay youngster she'd just started under saddle that spring. She'd spent the last few weeks working him in the round pen, teaching him the alphabet of a riding horse. Now it was time for him to go out on the open range, and that was better done with a steady, older horse along to show him how to be.

She'd timed his training just so. Just as her mother had taught her years before. To go safely over open range, a young horse needed to understand go, stop, and turn. He needed enough strength to carry a rider over uneven ground for at least an hour. And he needed to keep a level head with a rider on his back who he had only recently decided wasn't a predator. A colt's range debut was the first real test of what you had after all the time and money you'd put into breeding that colt, getting him safely on the ground, raising him and teaching him to think straight in a human world. And the first time he saw cattle out in the open was a telling moment. It didn't do to rush a colt to this point. But the very last thing you wanted was to ruin his spirit in the round pen, drilling him on the endless circle, with his fragile joints aching and his young mind bored and turning sour. Her father not only understood the importance of this timing, he enshrined it as he had every practice of her mother's. This, Jessie was counting on.

She hoped the colt was ready. Beyond that, she hoped he was awesome. For some time she'd felt the need to shake her father out of his mania, to bring him home to what he loved. Over the weeks she'd brought this colt along, a longing had developed in her, then a plan. As the public hearing on the lake boundary approached, and she had seen her father falling into a seemingly bottomless vortex, she'd worked each day to meet her target. Today was the day. The hearing would be tomorrow, and he would have to see the writing on the wall. He was not going to get to build the golf course for Bud, or the condo development. He was going to lose on every point he was fighting for. She wanted to give him something to take into that building that he would come away with. She wanted him to remember what he loved about this life. Not the development of a condo community, a golf course on the lake, but ranching. If he could see the colt, out there on the hills for the first time, figuring it all out, maybe something would happen.

She saddled the horses, making sure to go slowly with Rounder. It wouldn't do for him to pick up on her nervousness. Everything needed to be like old hat. Her mother had always said that. She double checked her father's gear and led both horses out of the paddock up the drive to the house. She worked to slow her pulse as she made her way around to the back of the house. He would just now be in the kitchen, with a cup of coffee and a ham sandwich. She was thankful he still dressed in jeans and boots every morning, in the long habit of a rancher, even though it had been years since he had ridden regularly. Any delay—a phone call at the wrong moment, if he had to go upstairs for anything—would likely kill her plan. She could see the top of his head through the screen door, bent over as if he were reading.

"Papa," she called. "Papa, come out here."

"Jessie?" he rose and came through the screen door onto the porch. "I didn't know you were up. Looks like you've gone to riding tandem. Who've you got here?"

"Knuckle and Rounder. Come ride out with me. I need to take Rounder for a spin around the block."

"Is he ready for that?"

"I believe so." She could see him hesitating, starting to run his list of things that needed him to do before lunch.

"I got that hearing tomorrow, Jessie. Lots to do. Can't you get George or one of the boys to go?"

She fought back a wave of panic. If ever Carl Weston dug in his heels, you'd get nowhere trying to reason with him. She had to be careful here. A logical answer would only remind him more of his obligations. She took a slow breath. "Come on, Papa. We haven't ridden out together for a hundred years. Besides, you gotta see this little guy go. Tell me if you think he's worth messing with. We'll be back in an hour."

For a long second he stared at her, standing in the drive with the two horses snuffling the soft morning air. Suddenly he grinned and ducked his head like a truant schoolboy. "Ok," he said conspiratorially, "but we better go before Bud gets here. If he catches me playing hooky, I'll never be able to hold his feet to the fire." He set down his coffee cup on the rail and took Knuckle's reins from her.

He led the horse to the bottom step and mounted, settling softly into the well-worn saddle. "Howdy old thing," he said to Knuckle. Jessie mounted and brought the young horse alongside and they rode down into the side yard and away from the drive, enjoying their thickening conspiracy to avoid detection. Rounder felt keen in the early cool, and emboldened by the presence of the older horse. Jessie hoped he wouldn't act up. She dropped in behind Knuckle and worked to keep the young horse's attention, shortening and lengthening his stride, making him keep three lengths back. She wanted to remind him of his lessons and put him in a working attitude before he got out in the open. A quarter-mile from the house they came to a gate leading into the ranch's largest tract of range. Here would be the first test.

"Want me to get it?" her father asked.

"Let's let him have a go at it first," she said. "He likes a challenge." She brought Rounder alongside the gate and asked him to halt. He stopped squarely and she felt his weight settle evenly into all four legs. "Good boy," she said softly. "Steady now." Leaning down she released the bolt on the gate latch and caught the guide rope in her left hand. As the gate swung away she closed her legs and asked Rounder to follow the gate. For a moment he seemed unsure of what to do. He understood the simple direction of her aids, but the gate swinging away confused him, especially since he seemed now to be connected to it by the rope in her hand. He hesitated. Jessie waited for him, relaxing very slightly. And then, as casually as if she were asking him to eat an apple, she reapplied the aids telling him to go forward, to follow the gate. He stepped toward the gate and found the connection acceptable. "Good boy," Jessie murmured. Her father rode through quietly, knowing she was concentrating on the young horse's performance. Now she dropped the rope and turned Rounder, bringing him back alongside the gate again. Leaning down, she took up the rope once more. But this time he would have to allow her to push the gate, not merely follow it as it opened. She stepped him toward the opening, trying to angle him so that the gate would come with them. In the first few steps, though, he got ahead of the gate and she had to stop him and ease the gate against his rump, edging him more to the side. Then he jumped a little and she had to rein him in. But at that point the gate was in front of him and he happened to push it slightly. "That'a boy," she said, releasing the reins. They sat for a moment before she asked him to step forward again. This time he kept the gate in front of his shoulder and edged towards the gatepost. In short order they had the gate closed and latched.

"First rate!" her father called out. "You been working him on that?"

"That's his first try," she said proudly.

"Smart boy," Carl Weston said to the young horse, patting Knuckle as he spoke. "Let's head over to the bluffs," he said. "The ground's good that way and maybe we'll run into some of the herd." They let the horses trot on, then picked up a lope. Rounder felt steady, not overly eager, and Jessie breathed a little deeper. When they reined in for a break, she brought her horse up beside her father's.

"I guess George told you we got that yellow cow out of the ditch yesterday," she began.

"He told me you had to have her to Doc Helm."

"Yeah, she'd gotten down in there good. Had the calf probably two days ago and couldn't get to water. That survey crew helped me get her out. They were working over that way and came up and hauled her out."

"Hmmph. Calf make it?"

"Yeah, he seemed like he'd be okay. Mr. Kessler hauled him out wrapped around his neck so he wouldn't get all banged up."

"He a cow man?"

"I wouldn't be surprised if he'd been around 'em. He seemed to know what needed doing."

They rode on in silence. Then as they topped a small ridge they saw the herd, spread out over thirty acres of dewy grass. "Now, there's a good sight," Carl Weston said softly. They reined in and sat their horses. At the far edge of the herd several does and two yearling deer grazed with the herd. A thin mist was dissipating in the rising heat. In the cloudless blue sky a flock of ibis floated lazily towards the lake. "You want to take him down there and see how he acts?"

"Yeah," Jessie replied. "If you get a chance, show him something." They eased the horses down the incline and into the meadow, giving the herd plenty of warning of their approach. Jessie hung back, letting her father lead, and as he skirted the herd, she sensed the constellation of small events swirling around them and she knew something would happen. It always began this way. The cattle shifted and began to move toward the trees some three hundred yards off. Knuckle was circling the far end of the herd when she saw her father rein him between two cows and ride directly into the herd. Within seconds he had separated three cows from the rest. She eased Rounder into the gap behind the older horse just as the biggest of the cows jumped straight for Knuckle, trying to spook him off. Then the cow bolted to the side and tried to slide around him. Knuckle sat down and swung hard to his left, flattening his ears and baring his teeth. Carl Weston had slacked the reins to let the horse work, and with one hand on his saddle horn to steady himself, he was sitting tall. A thrill ran through Jessie. She eased Rounder to the right, anticipating a break by one of the other cows. He danced a little and shoved his nose out against the bit.

Now Knuckle sprinted left, staying in front of the big roan cow. The cow pulled up and turned her back, then broke back to the right. Knuckle spun hard and, in three strides, bore down on her. Now the cow cantered back to her cohorts and turned to reconnoiter. Before she even settled, though, a little black cow broke from the threesome, stampeding hard to the right. Without thinking, Jessie sent Rounder jumping forward to cut off the cow's escape. He leaped into a dead run, closing the distance to the black heifer in ten huge strides. The cow hesitated. Jessie reined in and, for a split second, felt the horse struggle for balance. Then, it happened. He lifted his neck, raised his forehand, and sat back on his haunches, and, bouncing twice, he swung to face the cow. She darted left. He lunged at her, snaking his head viciously and snorting. The cow started back to the right. This was Rounder's weaker side, and the cow almost slid by him. But Rounder's blood was up. He bore down on the little heifer like a tornado, full of fury. The cow yielded, turned and trotted back to the other exiles. Jessie reined Rounder away and patted him. "That'a boy," she said, breathing hard. His neck was damp and his sides heaved, but she could feel his satisfaction.

Then she saw her father's face. He was skirting around the three cows to send them back to the herd, and for fifty yards or so he let Knuckle open up, chasing them as they high-tailed it. His face was beaming like a little boy's, and he raised his arm and let out a whoop as he reined Knuckle in and rode back to join her. "That beats a second cup of coffee any day," he called out happily. "And that young fella catches on quick. Nobody has to show him how to tell a cow off. Did you see the way he shook his head at that old bossy? That's a nice horse."

"Boy, Knuckle sure fell to, didn't he? How long do you reckon it's been since he sat on his butt like that?"

"Too long," Carl Weston replied. "I should get him out more. This old boy's got some giddy-up left in him."

"I'll say. He'll probably be stove up tomorrow, but he flat sure wasn't letting that big mama by." They grinned at each other, clapping the horses on their shoulders for work well done.

"He won't be the only one stove up. We better take it slow going home. Let both these old boys get their air back. You looked like your momma out there Jessie. She'd be real proud of how you've brought him along."

They hung their reins on their saddle horns and let the horses walk, their heads stretched low to the ground, their backs swinging. Her mother had always insisted on long, slow cool-outs for hard-working horses, and Jessie knew it was part of her secret for keeping horses sound. When other competitors were folding because their horses were stove up, her mother had gone on, winning national reining championships, her horses as keen as on the first day of the campaign. Her father knew it too. It was one more part of the canon that he kept sacrosanct, and, like most rituals, its performance provided a deep satisfaction.

"Let's ride back on the dike," Carl Weston said. "There'll be a breeze off the lake."

They stopped at the stock tank and let the horses drink. Then riding along a connecting arm, they came out onto the perimeter dike just west of the old borrow ditch. Jessie waved her arm to the west. "That's where she was, down in the far end there."

"I wonder how in the world she got in there." Carl Weston said.

"I wondered that yesterday. Where we hauled her out was so steep I don't believe any cow in her right mind would've gone down there."

"She might have been having trouble with the calf. I've seen 'em try to get between two boulders to support their labor. Maybe she thought the buttonwood trees would help her."

"She almost sheered her leg off. Cut it close to the bone. Luckily it was on the forearm where there's a lot of meat and it swelled and stopped bleeding."

"That must've been a hell of a job getting her out of there," he said, looking at the steep incline.

Jessie didn't reply. She remembered Reese's bare shoulders, the red and brown pigment of his deeply tanned skin, the scar along his shoulder, the fresh gash on his arm. She wondered if she would see him again.

"Looks like they're hard at it again."

She followed her father's gaze and saw the survey crew launching the airboat down at the shore about a quarter-mile off. Even from that distance she could pick out Reese by the angle of his shoulders and the way he carried himself when he moved. She saw him look up to the dike, saw him wave his arm in greeting. She raised her hand and waved it once through the air in reply.

"I wish Bud had taken more to ranching," her father said. "You'd think he would've, being around all this, but I guess it isn't in his blood."

"Some people never learn to like the out-of-doors," Jessie replied. It had always been a sore point between her and her step-brother. Jessie had loved horses from the day her mother took her down the front steps—as just an infant—to visit with Ditto, her mother's favorite horse who was grazing on the front lawn. Her mother taught her to ride almost before she could walk, and very early Jessie expressed a keen interest in every aspect of the ranch. This made her a natural favorite of both her parents.

Bud had been only seven when Carl Weston married Lacey. Lucinda Blake was a striking young woman, widowed when the plane her husband was piloting crashed into Tampa Bay during a routine training flight. At the time of the crash, they had been married only two years, and his death had left her the sole parent of Bud, his young son from his first marriage. For Lacey, a lifelong horsewoman, the move to Carl Weston's ranch was one which harmonized perfectly with her deep, natural love of the land and horses. But for Bud, the ranch was overwhelming with its vast spaces, lightning storms, heat, bugs, and Mexicans. He missed the familiar sidewalks of his neighborhood, with its well laid-out streets, tidy school and park. To make matters worse, it seemed to him that he was now losing Lacey to her new husband and to the horses that seemed to occupy more and more of her time as she settled into her new life. When Jessie was born, Bud's sense of alienation grew. He frankly blamed Jessie for what he perceived as a lack of attention from Lacey and Carl, and he stubbornly clung to his childish desire to undermine her, even when this tactic earned him repeated scoldings. To Carl Weston's credit, he'd taken particular pains to be a father to Bud, but it had not been easy with a boy who pointedly did not want to take part in the daily life of the ranch. In his teen-age years, when Bud began showing an interest in business, Carl taught him to read blueprints and decipher ledger sheets. And, although Carl was temperamentally not disposed to Bud's talent for politics, Bud's penchant for development found an easy resonance with Carl's own love of building, and over the years the two had become enthusiastic partners in planning the lakefront development. But Jessie had sometimes wondered if they would be in this whole mess if Bud had liked to ride horses.

"It kinda seems a shame to think about this all being changed into a golf course," her father said. "We've got plenty of ground for you to go on ranching. But sometimes it seems like we're selling the best part of the ranch to a lot of strangers. You know what I mean?"

Her father's frank sentiment startled Jessie. She knew all too well the feeling he was describing, but she was surprised to hear him voice it. She had wanted to make him realize the development wasn't everything, but she hadn't suspected how close to the surface those feelings already were. She hadn't imagined she would ever hear him speak in such a wistful manner. Still, she knew her father wasn't about to skip out on all he and Bud had planned—even if privately he'd had second thoughts, and the lakefront was the natural place for the development. "We'll make it work if that's what ya'll want to do," she said.

"Ah, Jessie," her father said. "I wish you had more of your mother's fight. She wouldn't stand for all this dicking around with her ranch. She'd have thrown us out for even talking about a golf course on good grazing ground. As it is though, I've got to get into this fight with the State. I hope we don't all live to regret it."

Jessie heard these words with a heavy heart. The last thing she would have wanted was to make her father feel the pain of what he was doing to the ranch. She knew he would fight for his and Bud's plans as if he were single-minded. But the fact that he wasn't, she now realized, was a worse burden, not a lighter one. She remembered just last night telling Reese he might rather die than lose the fight. But clearly, seeing again the beauty of the land and feeling close once more to her love for the ranch had made his job harder. Her plan had worked disastrously well, and she longed for a way to undo the damage.

She wondered what her mother would do. Whatever it was would be brave, bold, brilliant. Her special gift had been for seeing clearly what to do when everyone around her was confused. And she never flinched from any action she perceived as necessary—even when that action had cost her her life. Jessie knew all too well what it was to live in the shadow of that legacy, and she felt deeply for her father.

As they neared the barn she tried to rally her spirits. It wouldn't do to let her father see her depressed. She watched him unsaddle his horse and feed him treats from the sugar jar. Sometimes, she thought, things worked out for the best even when you did everything wrong. She hoped this one would. They led the horses out to the paddock and turned them loose. "Don't worry about things Papa," she said. "We've got a good life and we work together. We'll be all right."

He smiled a tired smile at her. "I wish we didn't have to deal with the State on this thing," he said. "I'm just afraid that's going to be a black hole that'll keep us tied up for years and eat up all our money in lawyers."

"Yeah, but maybe, you know, time can work to save you from something you'd regret."

He nodded, pulling her to him, and kissed her on her forehead. "That's a good youngster you've got there. Let's think about getting back to the Nationals next year with him and Rocket, huh?"

"You'll have to help me."

"You know I will, Baby. If I'm still walking and breathing, nothing could keep me away. Thanks for the ride." She watched him walking back up the drive toward the house, his back straight and his head slightly bowed, and she wondered if time really did offer any refuge at all from regrets.

At 4:30, Jessie pulled into the vet clinic parking lot and let herself through the back gate into the barn area. Over the years as a client she had become part of the clinic family, and when Beth Helm had taken over the practice four years ago they had become fast friends. Leroy, one of the helpers in the barn area, called out to see if she needed help. "Just checking on my cows," she called back.

"They should be about ready to go home," he called. "I turned them out this morning and that little one's ready to roll."

Jessie leaned over the rail looking at the yellow cow and her calf. Now they would be pets. Live in the small herd of crippled and maimed creatures who had grown tame through some misfortune, who had gained a place in her affections, who lived by the barn where she could tend them each day and spoil them. She had often wondered how long she would go on running cattle after her father retired. She had never had the heart for raising an animal for slaughter, and it had earned her much derision in her family over the years when she refused to eat beef, or any other meat from animals she might care for. She thought about shifting the ranch more to horses, maybe even host a riding school. But she would need to solidify her own reputation in order to make a go of that. The oranges were good income, but with citrus one needed a hedge against the weather and other misfortunes. Diversity was good in the precarious world of ranching.

The lakefront was the sticking point. Her father was right that in many ways it was the heart of the ranch, but she valued different aspects of it than Bud and her father did. She had learned to appreciate the value of the lake to the entire operation when they built the dike. There had always been good grazing on the floodplains—even in drought years. When other ranchers were scrambling for forage and buying hay, the Weston Ranch had had plenty. But once the dike was in place everything had changed. Run-off collected behind the embankment and had to be pumped back into the lake during rainy seasons. In dry seasons the land behind the dike—once rich marshland—dried out, compacted, subsided. When the State had made Carl Weston breach the dike in the early 80s, she had watched the lake waters flow back into their old home, and gradually the marsh returned. When Bud and her father rebuilt the barrier several years later, the same pattern of damage emerged. The land became a liability to the ranch instead of the boon it was in its natural condition. She knew what she would do if she had no one to consider but herself. She would take the dike down for good, return the floodplain to its natural condition.

"Hey there!" It was Beth. "I'm almost through in the clinic. Want to get a drink or some supper?"

"Yeah. I was hoping you'd have time to get away. How's our patient?"

"Let her stay here til the end of the week—just so we can keep that leg really juiced up. I think she's going to be fine."

"Great."

"Is she going to join the petting zoo?"

"You know it." They laughed.

"You're going to have to apply for non-profit status. Send out those pitiful fund-raising appeals for support."

"I like it. In the meantime you better hope my oranges don't ever freeze. I won't be able to pay my bill."

"I need to leave some instructions and then I'll meet you at Nick's, ok?"

"I'll get us a table."

Jessie drove the three blocks to the restaurant and parked. She thought she recognized the DEP truck and trailer in the parking lot and she was startled to realize how much she wanted to see Reese. More actually, to be alone with him and talk about their lives. She had been surprised by how easy he was to talk to. He seemed equally comfortable being serious or silly, and he had made her feel free in an unfamiliar way she seemed to long for.

She stepped into the dark interior and waited for her eyes to adjust. As she was scanning the room she saw Richard coming out of the men's room. He was walking right toward her.

"Hey there," he said. "It's Richard from the survey crew."

"I remember," she said. "I owe you a huge debt–and a drink."

"No, no debt. I'm glad we could help. Would you come join us? Me and Bo were just having a beer."

"Thanks, but you have to let me buy."

"You're a nice lady. Here we go." He steered her into the booth opposite Bo and slid in after her. "You remember Bo. Bo, Ms. Weston."

"Hey," Bo said.

"Jessie. You can't call me Ms. Weston or I won't drink with you."

"Jessie it is," Richard said, smiling. He motioned for the barmaid. "How's your cow?"

"Doing good. Doc says she can come home in a day or two. In fact, the doc will be here in a minute–she's a friend of mine. We're meeting for a drink."

"Well, maybe she'd join us. The more the merrier." Richard held up his Killian bottle. "One more of these. What will you have Jessie?"

"That'll be fine for me too."

Bo tapped his Bud and held up a finger. Jessie wondered if he was always so quiet or if he had clammed up because of her.

"My uncle was a vet," Richard said. "He just retired and sold his business last year because his wife made a lot of money in her investments. I think he misses it though. He always seemed to enjoy it."

"Yeah, that's the way Beth would be. She loves her work."

"I'd go broke as a vet," Bo stammered. "I'd fix all the dogs even if people didn't have the money to pay. I hate to see them all mangy and needing their shots and stuff."

"You'd just have to marry a good business woman," Richard said, "so she could lay down the law to people and get them to pay."

"Yeah, or if they were too poor to pay she could get them to clean the kennel for us," Bo said.

"Beth was just kidding me today about being such a softie," Jessie told them. "She said I should start one of those foundations like the Salvation Army for dogs. We could stand outside the grocery stores at Christmas, Bo, and ring the bell for collections." They laughed.

"I'd probably like that," Bo said.

Beth came in and found them, ordered a gin and tonic, and slid in beside Bo. "So you're the dreaded survey crew, huh? Come to rape and pillage the poor villagers." She grinned.

"We just goes where we's sent, m'am, and calls 'em like we sees 'em." Richard said. They laughed. "Actually we're just hoping to make it out with our hides intact," he said.

"Noble and loyal servants of the people," Beth joked. "Seriously though, what's going to happen tomorrow?"

"Well, our boss is going over to the hearing," Richard explained. "There'll be some other bosses down from town–Tallahassee–to get feedback from the public on the lake boundary. But if this hearing is like others I've seen, it's pretty chaotic. Most people use it as a forum for any gripe they've got against the State. The State just wants information from the public–what they know about the lake levels and whatnot. But they never get that across, and people get mad because the State's not telling them where it thinks the line is."

"So everybody gets frustrated," Beth said.

"This hearing is to gather information then," Jessie asked, "not tell people where the line is?"

"That's what I understand," Richard said. "You can check that with Reese. He'll probably be along in a little bit. He had some phone calls to make and whatnot."

Reese Kessler held the phone in his hand and hesitated. He wanted to call Jessie, but when he tried to think about doing it he got flustered. He wasn't sure what was appropriate. On the one hand, he wanted to see her, and he didn't want to fail to call her in case that's what she expected after their date last night. On the other hand, he didn't want to come on too strong, give her the wrong idea about what he was after. There was also the problem of Vivian. He hadn't told Jessie he was married. It wasn't that he'd meant to keep it from her. It simply hadn't dawned on him until he saw her this morning, riding along the dike, that he was still a married man. He needed to think straight about this. He didn't want to screw it up.

He also needed to call Chris Farlow and talk to him about the hearing tomorrow. Anything that might lessen the tension would likely help the situation in Jessie's family, and it was Reese's opinion that people made better decisions when they weren't under the gun. He'd spent a large part of his day deciding how he would present information about Carl Weston's property if he were asked, and he'd thought a lot about how he would talk to Mr. Weston if he got the chance. He wanted to establish good relations with Farlow. If Farlow trusted him to be fair, it would help keep the talk from getting hotheaded. He decided to call Farlow. That way he'd have something to tell Jessie when he talked to her.

But first things first. He dialed Vivian's number.

"Viv—it's Reese."

"Hey Reese."

"How's it going? You doing all right?"

"Yeah."

"I wanted to check with you and see if we could get together and talk, maybe this week-end."

"I'm going out of town this week-end."

"Well, how about next week sometime?"

"Look Reese, I don't think it's a good idea. Just tell me what you want on the phone."

Reese felt the familiar pressure in his chest. It made him sad that his marriage had come to this. He wondered if he had done things to alienate her that he would never know about, things that he would go on doing. He wondered what would happen if he tried again with someone else. Was it possible that in ten years someone like Jessie would talk to him this way?

"I want to know if you're coming home," he said softly.

"Oh God. Look. That's not going to happen, ok. In fact you should really just try to get your mind around this Reese because that's not going to happen."

"Well what do you want to do?" Reese asked.

"I'm thinking about it Reese but I just don't know right now. The beautician school starts a course next month. I might go to that."

"That would be great Viv. But, I mean, what do you want to do about us?"

"What do you mean?"

"Do you just want to go on living apart?"

"I told you Reese. See I tell you and you just keep asking me the same thing over and over. You just cannot possibly conceive . . .". She sounded on the verge of tears.

"Okay, Viv. Tell me again. I'm listening."

"Look Reese. I've got a life and you have to accept that. I'm through just sitting around waiting for you to come home. I'm not going back to that."

"Well I think that's good Viv. You shouldn't just sit around waiting for me. But, I mean, it's not like we're even married anymore with you living in town. I just want to know if you want to keep going or what?"

"I'm not going back to that Reese. I've told you and told you."

"But it wouldn't have to be like–" he began.

She slammed the receiver down.

Reese sat back on the bed and breathed a long sigh, his legs jumping nervously. He felt a peculiar mixture of relief and sadness, and was surprised that those feelings didn't cancel one another. Whatever was in Vivian's mind could easily change tomorrow, he knew. Nothing about this exchange was any indication of how she would feel next week. He made a mental note to ask Sam Donnovan to recommend a lawyer. The idea of talking all this over with Jessie struck him as an immense relief. Yet he was afraid. His attraction to her probably far outreached any interest she might have in him, and very likely she would wonder why a complete stranger wanted to discuss his failed marriage with her.

He called Chris Farlow and was glad to find the man articulate and pleasant. He offered to meet Reese for a drink around nine.

"Sorry to make it so late," Farlow told him, "but I've got two more parties to take out before I'm through for the day."

"A man's gotta work," Reese replied. "You got a favorite watering hole?"

"How about the bar in the Granville Hotel. There's a barmaid there—I keep hoping I'll get lucky with her."

"Sounds like a plan. Nine o'clock then."

He dialed the ranch and was told that Jessie wasn't home. He was about to hang up when the woman said, "I think she goes to Dr. Beth for the cow." Perfect, Reese thought. Maybe he could catch her at the vet's and get to talk to her for a while before his meeting with Farlow. For the first time in a long time he wanted to hurry. Suddenly every second seemed too long. He fought the impulse to speed through the city streets and tried to slow his racing thoughts.

He'd managed to stay calm most of the day. At one point Richard and Bo had teased him for not having on his wedding band, and Reese realized with surprise that he hadn't replaced it after his shower last night. It must be lying by the sink in his hotel room. He wondered if Jessie had noticed the white band of skin where the ring usually sat. He'd told them that Jessie had called to thank them all and that the cow and calf were expected to recover. Richard had been strangely quiet when he mentioned her, and Reese tried not to speculate on the reasons why. He was tempted to tell them about having dinner with her. He knew that would be taken as a sign that he was staking a claim on her. It would likely keep Richard from moving in. For some reason, though, he'd kept quiet. He hadn't wanted to discuss the evening with them. But it wasn't just that. It seemed to Reese that Jessie was pure destiny. She had entered his mind full-blown as someone who would change his life forever, and it seemed demeaning to think of her as something to fight over, to manipulate and jealously guard. Not that he didn't feel jealous of her. He'd been wondering all day if she was dating anyone seriously. But he thought of her as a woman who knew her own mind. If she wanted Richard or anyone else there was nothing for him to say.

As he turned into the vet parking lot he could see they were closed. Disappointment welled in him. He got out of the jeep and stood staring over the paddock fences at the barn. When he saw a lone figure pushing a wheelbarrow full of muck along the isle, he called out without thinking, "I'm looking for Ms. Weston. Have you seen her?"

Leroy set down the wheelbarrow and pushed his cap back. "She was here earlier. I think they were going to Nick's."

"Where?"

"Nick's. You know—bar down on Granville Ave."

"Thanks," Reese called, waving his arm. Suddenly he felt lucky. At any moment the whole world might conspire to help him find Jessie, maybe even to have her fall in love with him. His divorce would go through quickly and painlessly and he would have his whole life ahead of him. He hummed an old tune as he turned onto Granville Ave. Nick's must be near the Granville Hotel. He'd be close to his rendezvous point with Farlow.

He spotted the bar simultaneously with the hotel and steered into the parking lot. Immediately he saw the Bureau truck with the airboat trailer parked along the side of the building. Damn it all! Why hadn't he told Richard to stay away from her? He bolted from the jeep into the bar.

He could hear Richard telling one of his tall tales as soon as he came through the door. And he could hear laughter. He made his way toward the voices. Then he saw Bo and a red-haired woman sitting beside him listening intently to Richard's story. Jessie sat beside Richard on the inside of the booth. Her back was to Reese but he was certain he could hear her laughing. Confusion overwhelmed him. He stood there trying to decide if he should go in, pull up a chair and casually join the party, or bolt out before anyone saw him. What was the matter with him? He didn't want to seem to be chasing after Jessie but he didn't need to run away. It occurred to him that it was normal for him to track down Richard and Bo after he'd finished his calls and paperwork. Settle down, he told himself. Still his mind raced with fragments of fearful thoughts as he edged into the room. Damn it to hell. How had Jessie come to be here with Richard? He took a shallow breath and tried to walk forward. Bo had spotted him, was waving him over.

As soon as he saw her face he felt himself grow calm. He knew she was glad to see him. It was just like last night walking on the riverfront. He felt he had known her for a long time, that they read each other's minds and acted in concert even when the people around them detected nothing. He shook Beth's hand, pulled up a chair to the end of the booth, and waved for the barmaid to bring a round.

"I know ya'll have already discussed that cow up one side and down the other, but give me the update," Reese said, smiling at Beth.

"She's going home Friday, barring any unforeseen turns," Beth said. "Ya'll did good getting her out. It sounded like she was in a real tight spot."

"Why would a cow go down in a place like that?" Bo asked.

"I've been wondering that too. How she'd even get down there is hard to imagine," Richard said.

"If she was in a lot of pain she might have wandered too close to the edge and tumbled in," Beth said. "But it is unusual. Is it all as steep as where you found her? I mean, could she have wandered in from another area and couldn't find her way out again?"

"That could happen," Jessie said. "I saw one area that was eroded from heavy rain at some point. It didn't look much like anything a cow would go down, but there might be other places like it further along the ditch that are less steep. I should ride out there tomorrow and look. I sure don't want to have to get down in there again to get a cow out."

"Oh come on," Richard nudged her with his elbow. "You know it was fun."

"Hmmmn. Like a stomachache on a tilt-a-whirl," Jessie laughed. She turned to Reese. "I hate to bring up business after hours," she said, "but I'd like to talk to you about the hearing tomorrow. Are you free for dinner tonight?"

Reese was dazzled. He had been wondering how to get her alone and she had simply asked him to have dinner, right in front of all these people. "I'd be delighted," he said.

Beth moved to go. "I better get back," she said. "I've got rounds to go before I sleep."

"I'll walk out with you," Jessie said, poking Richard in the ribs. "S'cuse me," she said brightly. "I'll catch up with you in a few minutes?" she told Reese as she slid out of the booth.

"How are the steaks at the Granville?" Reese asked.

"I hear they're edible."

"Meet me over there in a few minutes?"

"I'll be there," she said, smiling.

In the parking lot Beth waggled her eyebrows at Jessie. "Does the sleeping beauty stir?" she asked.

Jessie squinted at her. "I don't know what you could be talking about."

"Ok, but when it does dawn on you that it's race day—you know, sometime during your stroll to the starting gate—you should realize he's already at the quarter pole. When you asked him to dinner just now he got completely starry-eyed."

"Oh he did not. You're just a hopeless romantic."

"Mmmmhmmmn. And you are glad to hear every word I'm saying." She squeezed Jessie's shoulders. "Call me later—even if that means tomorrow," she giggled. "Oh, wait. I know what I meant to talk to you about. Is this thing tomorrow a big deal or what?"

"From what I can tell I think it's just going to add to the confusion and make people mad—you know, a good ole public meeting. But the one thing it probably won't do is make it clear to Bud that this development isn't likely to happen. I keep hoping he'll move on to something more promising. I think Daddy's kind of torn about the whole thing, but of course he'll fight like a pitbull over it."

"He'd probably just as soon drop the whole thing and get on with ranching," Beth said.

"I get that feeling."

"Well, let me know what goes on. Maybe I can take Bud out and get him drunk. Talk some sense to him."

"That might be helpful," Jessie grinned at her friend. "But you'd have a lot more fun asking that surveyor out."

"Who says I didn't," Beth grinned back and climbed into her truck.

"You go girl." Jessie laughed. "Talk to ya."

"Mañana." Beth said.

Reese watched Jessie fold her napkin into a tiny square and place it on the table. During dinner they had briefly discussed the hearing, but then she had begun to tell him about the young horse she was training, about her hopes for competition and her fear of winning, or not winning—she wasn't sure which it was. He liked the ease with which she could laugh at herself. Yet there was never any doubt about her seriousness. He understood that the horses were connected to something ultimate. He knew whatever it was might always elude him, but it didn't matter. He had the sensation of touching a deep current between them, and he wanted to wade in until it was a raging torrent all around him.

With a start he realized it was almost nine o'clock. He had told her nothing that he'd meant to—nothing about his marriage, about his marriage ending—and he didn't want to just blurt it out in a rush and then have to leave. She had that expression on her face he was coming to recognize as characteristic of her, a striking mixture of sadness and joy that made him want to soothe her and stand in her glow.

"I hate to say it, but I have to meet a guy on business in a few minutes," he said, watching her face.

An unmistakable flash of disappointment passed over her features. "Oh. That's a shame," she said evenly. "You really put in long days."

"I'm hoping this meeting will make things smoother tomorrow. This fellow, Chris Farlow will be at the hearing on behalf of the airboaters. He's head of the outfit that's challenging your permit."

"Chris Farlow," she said, lowering her head. "I went to high school with him. We were in the same class."

"Really?" Reese didn't know why that should surprise him in such a small town. He wondered what expression her lowered face concealed. He tried to imagine what she had been like in high school. Tomboy? Homecoming queen?

"And it's not my permit," she said with a grin. "I run the ranch. The golf course is not my thing."

"Duly noted," Reese replied. He marveled again at how often situations he came to with a simple assumption turned out to be so complicated. He wouldn't have guessed the first day he met the Westons that they weren't all of one mind about the development project. But the more he knew about Jessie's feelings the more he had to wonder how she maintained a sympathy with her father and stepbrother. At that moment a blonde, sunburned man came through the arched door of the Granville dining room and headed straight toward Jessie.

"There he is now," Jessie said. She stood up.

"Hey girl," Chris called out. "What are you doing downtown besides breakin' hearts? You get prettier every year." He grabbed Jessie's shoulders and kissed her on the cheek. "Can't you get that ornery old man of yours to take down that damned dike so I can get back to fishing? I don't like all this lawyering."

"You know better," she said, shaking her head. "How are you Chris?" She smiled at him and his gaze stayed on her face. "Do you know Reese Kessler? State surveyor."

Farlow swung towards Reese and shook his hand heartily. "I didn't know you were going to enlist the most irresistible woman in five counties to do your bidding," Farlow laughed. "I've heard the State doesn't play fair. Now I know it's true."

"Actually, I was just leaving," Jessie said. "Mr. Kessler and I have had our meeting."

"You don't have to go on my account," Farlow said. "Anything I have to say is public record, and you already know it all anyway Jess." They laughed.

"Thanks Chris, but I've got early chores. It's good to see you." She smiled and stood up. Reese stood up too.

"I'll just see Ms. Weston to her car," he told Farlow. "I'll be right back."

"Take your time Reese. I've got a little business I can attend to while you're gone." He winked at Reese. "Night Jess."

They walked out into the warm spring night and crossed the street to Nick's parking lot. "He seems like a decent guy," Reese said.

"He cares a lot about the lake, the whole river system. He probably knows it better than anyone. His father used to keep Chris out of school and have him drive them up and down the river fishing. He had an old ratty tugboat he got from somewhere."

"Why couldn't his old man drive it?"

"Too busy drinking I imagine. But he was a mean old bastard. He might've just done it to keep Chris from having any friends."

"Hmmn. That's hard luck."

"Well, Chris never seemed to hold it against him. I think because he loved the river so much he didn't care about all the trouble his old man caused him."

They had reached her truck, and she turned and leaned against it, looking at Reese. "I'm sorry to have to cut our evening short," he said. "There were some things I wanted to talk to you about, but I let the time slip up on us."

"I'm afraid I blabbered on about horses and never gave you a chance to get a word in edgewise."

"Not at all," Reese said. "I can't tell you how much I enjoy hearing about your horses and your plans."

She smiled. "Are you heading home Friday?" Jessie asked.

Reese hesitated. He hadn't even thought about what he would do about the weekend. The survey crew usually headed home on Thursday night. Fridays were his paperwork day. He felt an urgency to let her know about his situation. The last thing he wanted was for her to find out he was married without him having a chance to tell her the whole story.

"Actually I don't have any reason to make the drive," he said. "I'm thinking I'll just hang around over the week-end, relax, take care of some paperwork. Crew'll be back Sunday night late and we'll work our way on up the lakeshore next week."

She nodded. "Well, I guess I'll see you then." She started to push herself away from the truck door.

"Jessie—" Reese said. His hand went out to touch her shoulder and she stepped toward him and into his arms. Her kiss was soft and hot on his mouth, and when his tongue reached out to taste her lips, they opened to a deeper kiss. Reese had the sensation that flashbulbs were going off behind his eyes. A strange pressure built in the back of his head. He felt his body arch toward her and gather her to him. Then she released her hold on his arms and stepped back.

"Good luck tomorrow," she said. She stroked his forearm once, letting her finger trace over the bandage under his sleeve. Then she got in her truck and drove away.

April 12, p.m.

The Blue Moon was crowded with couples intoxicated by the mild, spring night. Under the draping strands of patio lights, the murmur of conversation wafted over soft jazz, and the fragrance of African dishes floated in the air. We headed for a table between the garden and the bar, and I felt Logan's hand on the small of my back like a warm shadow. During the drive to the restaurant he had regaled me with stories of his mother's cats, a Siamese named Hituch and a Persian named Onslo who engaged in endless skirmishes for toys, turf, affection—anything the other one had. Logan painted a picture of them as two charismatic warriors, making lightening fast forays into each other's territories, raiding, pillaging, giving no quarter.

"The bloodied fang and claw of politics," I suggested, and he nodded, smiling.

"I call them the fur-in-powers," he said.

He ordered wine and food, and I found myself wondering if it wasn't unusual for a detective in Tallahassee, Florida to cultivate such exotic tastes. But nothing about him fit my stereotype of a detective. I was trying to form a question that would get him talking about himself without seeming inappropriately nosy, but when I glanced up, he was studying me intensely, and I forgot what I was going to say. His mouth formed a crooked smile as if half of him wanted to be happy and carefree but was weighed down at the other end by concerns he couldn't shake off. He seemed embarrassed that I had caught him looking at me.

"You're not what I expected," he said.

"And what was that?"

"I guess I'm trying to figure that out," he said. "Being surprised makes me realize I had some expectation about you, but I wasn't conscious of it until I began to realize you don't fit it."

"Actually I was thinking something similar about you," I said. "I must have a fairly outdated notion of the Tallahassee Police Department, because you don't fit whatever it was I thought."

"I've always run a bit askew of expectations," he said. "Even my own." He looked at me evenly and directly now. "I think that might be true of you as well."

I could hear that thing in his speech that seemed part of something altogether else. He was too well spoken for a cop. But I told myself I was being awfully narrow-minded. I realized dimly that he had a mesmerizing effect on me. His eyes were so dark I couldn't tell if they were blue or brown or black. For a moment he seemed to me like a wild animal hypnotizing its quarry. I had a sudden vision of wrestling with him in tall grass, rolling through patches of snow, wanting to be overcome and still survive.

"Now why would you think that?" I tried to shake myself into a more vigorous consciousness. It felt like I was being enveloped in a cloud.

"You don't fit the mold," he said. "All your training would suggest an academic career. But you ride around in airboats, stomp through marshes up to your waist, swinging a machete. You put yourself on a line and tell some pretty tough guys not to cross it."

"Obviously you've never faced a classroom of forty-some-odd students," I laughed. "Stomping around with alligators is a walk in the park compared to that."

"I see," he said, smiling.

"How do you know about my field work?" I asked.

"The pictures in your den," he answered. "Where were they taken?"

"That's a big marsh down by Lake Okeechobee. We had a court case down there several years ago. It had to do with whether a creek feeding into the Lake was public or private property. We had to prove it was navigable at the time of statehood if we were going to claim it as public. But the marsh was a problem."

"How'd it come out?"

"We traced all the changes in the area. There had been lots of flood control over the years. It had damaged the navigability of the entire creek system. We were able to show that the creek naturally flowed through that marsh area and connected to the Lake. So the jury found it navigable, public."

"I bet that made you some friends."

I nodded. "I learned a lot. I'd never really seen a power struggle of that magnitude from so close up before. There were a few times I wondered if we would get out of that little town without someone getting killed."

Our food came. It was all on one big tray underlined with a flat bread that served as spoon and sponge. Logan demonstrated by pinching off a piece of bread and wrapping a bit of fish and what looked like a brussel sprout into a bite-sized sandwich. I followed suit. The textures and tastes startled my tongue, warming and expanding into a delicious and stimulating flavor.

"Mmmmnn. I wish the first bite of everything could be so wonderful," I said.

Logan nodded. "Good food is a daily miracle. It's funny, you know, I once had a theory that cultures that eat delicious food are more peaceful nations than those that subsist on mean rations."

"Sounds possible. Is it true?"

"More likely the contrary—that the more aggressive nations end up with the best food. But the idea was to eat my way around the world investigating the hypothesis. I haven't made it yet." He poured more wine. "The curry in this is just right though. It's got that subtle little nip that comes in at the end—do you taste it?"

There it was again. A mannerism, a way he had that I found totally unexpected. What anyone else would treat as a polite but purely rhetorical question, Logan seemed earnestly to ask, and then to wait for a reply. He was smiling at me, holding a bite of bread and vegetable up as an example, watching me for my response. Was I mad? Was this the way people normally talked to each other over dinner? Not people exactly. Men and women. It had been so long since I'd had dinner with an attractive man who was paying close attention to me. Maybe I was over-reacting to what was just normal courtesy. Keeping my eyes on his face, I nodded slowly, and he went on describing the composition and properties of curry. Coriander, cayenne, cardamom seeds, tumeric, ginger, mace, saffron.

"The merchants of Sheba traded with you," Logan quoted, cocking his wine glass at me. "They exchanged for your wares the best of all spices, precious stones and gold."

"What is that?" I asked.

"Probably Ezekiel, don't you guess? One of those Old Testament stories. The Arabs were the masters of the spice trade a thousand years before the time of Christ. They kept Europe completely in the dark about where the spices were coming from—which of course was the Orient. Whenever they were questioned about the sources, they told horror stories about the dangers they had undergone to get the spices from mysterious foreign lands."

"Too bad the Europeans didn't have Barthes to clue them in about signs."

"Yes," Logan nodded. "There it is again, isn't it. Stories being used to obscure the source of power."

"You're a quick learner," I said, smiling.

"We've forgotten what a source of power spices were. There were no potatoes or corn then. No lemons, no sugar. No tea or coffee or chocolate."

"Horrors."

"Exactly. Cattle had to be slaughtered and salted in the fall because there was no fodder for them that could be stored. Spices made food that was barely edible, delicious—or at least palatable."

"You know a lot about this," I said, biting into something unrecognizable but luscious.

"My theory, remember. While waiting for the money to materialize that would fund the travel, I did a lot of reading," he said. "I'm still reading." He smiled ruefully. "The appeal of spices went even beyond what we think of as civilization—that is, Europe. The barbarians soon realized that spices kept their meat fresher. That improved their food supply during their constant forays. When Alaric the Visigoth laid siege to Rome he demanded 3,000 pounds of pepper and an annual tribute of 300 pounds."

"That must have been something to see," I said. "Horses and camels carrying sacks of pepper. The storehouses under guard. The whole city sneezing."

"In London in the Middle Ages it was counted peppercorn by peppercorn. The guards on London docks had their pockets sewn shut to make sure they didn't steal any. People paid their taxes and rents with spices; a sack of pepper was worth a man's life."

He spun the story of spice and power, mysterious lands, trade routes, the young Marco Polo, the downfall of the Arabian Empire, sultans, horses, murder and love. I watched his hands gesturing in the air under the yellow and blue lights and thought it completely unfair that the overall effect was to give him an aura, a golden aura.

How do you know when to give yourself over to the sensuous world? Descendents of the Puritans, we shut out the world's beckoning hand. We never lift the veil for fear of being taken over by beauty. Taken in, or shut out, we fear them equally. We live in no man's land so as not to be fools. Make me a fool, I thought, looking at the triangle of tan skin above Logan's open collar.

"Whether spices came by sea or by land, they had to come through Cairo," Logan was saying. "'Whoever is lord of Cairo may call himself lord of Christendom,'" Logan quoted with a flourish, "'since all spicery from whatever direction can come and be sold only in the land of the Sultan.'" Logan suddenly looked sheepish.

I laughed. I knew the feeling well, of getting swept away on that tide of something you'd studied and loved and rarely been able to share with anyone. "You should teach," I said. "You have the gift."

We drank more wine, enjoying the sensation of the soft, dense air and the sussing of the palm fronds swaying in the light breeze.

"You said before that you were having trouble with your characters' love affair taking over your novel," Logan said, watching my face. "What does that mean?"

"Well," I paused, not sure how to embark on such uncertain ground—ground so close to home. "Love scenes can set—or upset—the whole tone of a book. They easily fall into rather pat, canned language. They can feel too predictable. If you get them wrong, they can erode the complexity of your characters. Practically speaking, it's hard to get the sex right. Too much explicit detail and the book veers into seediness. Also it's hard to recover from really hot scenes and get on with the book. But if your love scenes have too little heat in them the whole endeavor is unsatisfying. It feels patted down, safe, and that reflects on the characters. I tend to write rather steamy love scenes because I create complicated characters who want to break out of their isolation—to connect with life more intensely. That tends to be cathartic, not deliberate or even playful." I looked at Logan's face. For the first time since I'd met him he seemed wholly absorbed, as if the wire in his head had gone silent and left him to listen to one thing. I shrugged. "But I usually end up cutting them—playing safe."

"But you keep reaching for something more," Logan said. It was almost a question. "Looking for a way to give the characters that intensity without having it take over everything."

I tried to laugh. "It does seem to me that it should be possible. And sometimes in the middle of trying it feels pretty grand. But later it just seems pathetic or wrong-headed."

Logan nodded. "Like in life," he said evenly.

It began to rain softly and steadily, and couples came crowding in from the garden under the tiny canopy over the bar.

"Shall we?" he asked, half standing.

I nodded. Logan pressed a wad of cash into our waitress' hand and we made our way out, walking through the rain as if it were sunlight bouncing off our shoulders. In the car, I leaned back against the seat, feeling that struggle still going on inside myself. To let down my guard or remain vigilant? There are so many ways to end up a fool.

"Feel better?" Logan asked.

"That was great," I said.

"Want to get dessert somewhere? Coffee?" He had his hand on the gearshift, waiting to pull out of the parking lot. I wondered if he was the first man I'd ever gone out with who asked me these questions. They seemed so strange. Had Mack never asked me if I wanted coffee? Surely Steve had. I'd been alone too long. I was a sitting duck for anyone coming along who was nice to me.

"I better pass this time," I said. "It's getting late."

We drove through the drizzle watching the tree limbs sway. There was some lightning north of the city.

"Looks like we might get more weather," Logan said.

I wondered if he ever thought about lying in a dark room with the windows open, listening to the rain and watching the lightning, touching the lovely tan triangle of a warm throat. When we pulled in the drive, he got out and came to the door with me. He stood, waiting, while I unlocked the door and switched on the hall lights.

"I'll just stand here for a minute," he said. "Walk through the house and make sure everything seems normal to you."

I went through the hall glancing into the kitchen and the den. In the bedroom I opened the closets and looked behind the bathroom door. I wondered what boogeyman I was looking for. The whole idea of danger had begun to take on the quality of a hallucination. I checked the second bedroom, flicked on the back porch lights, and went back through the kitchen to the front door. Willow was there, rubbing her sides against Logan's pants legs.

"All clear," I said.

"Ok then. I'll be in touch. Good night." He stood looking down at me with the wind buffeting against his shirt.

"Thanks for dinner."

He nodded, still looking at me.

"Go inside," he said. "Lock your door. I want to hear it lock."

"Yes sir," I said.

I took one last look at his face. It was such an intense mixture of concern and comfort. I wondered if it bore any relation to what was in his mind. I couldn't have said at that moment whether I was happy or miserable. I just went through the door and closed it, threw the dead bolt and went to bed.

Chapter Five

Reese chose a seat along the wall towards the back of the meeting room. It was early—a good twenty minutes before people would start coming in, but he wanted to watch everything unfold and be on hand when the bosses arrived. The building was a concrete block annex that had been built behind the courthouse during the late 1960s, and Reese supposed its garish yellow, windowless walls were in keeping with both the outlandish colors popular during that age and the challenge to authority that time had posed. Or maybe the paint had simply been on sale because no one wanted it. Rows of folding chairs stretched across the floor, all facing the front of the room where a podium and a chart-stand stood beside an American flag. The room already seemed close and stuffy, and Reese wondered if between the hard seats and the inadequate air conditioning the hidden agenda of the design had been to keep meetings short. That was fine by him, as long as it didn't turn them into sweltering pit fights.

He took the cover off his to-go coffee and settled back to think. His meeting with Farlow last night had been less business-like than he'd first imagined it, but overall that wasn't a bad thing. Farlow had been in an expansive mood—or perhaps that was his usual demeanor—but Reese had found him engaging and smart. His intermittent attempts to cajole Betty, the barmaid, into going home with him seemed part of an old ritual they both enjoyed, and it gave Reese the chance to see that Farlow was careful and respectful even in his playfulness. Reese hoped he behaved similarly in a dispute. He had also noticed that Betty brought Farlow a constant stream of drinks, never letting him get to the bottom of one before another appeared. Yet the man seemed as steady and sober after an hour as he had been when he walked in. Either he had one hell of a hollow leg or he was drinking ginger ale.

Farlow had given Reese a good perspective on The Far Out view of things. Like many such groups they ran the gamut from wild-eyed, would-be outlaws who wanted to blow up the dike to solemn and sober citizens who would've liked to avoid conflict altogether. At one point Farlow had suggested that it wouldn't surprise him to find one or two of the gunslinger types "out there messing around" at night, and Reese had had the distinct impression that Farlow intended no threat, but meant to warn him and, perhaps through him, the Westons. When Reese asked him what they might be capable of, Farlow shook his head once.

"They want that dike down," he said. "Some of these old boys have worked all their lives in land clearing, road building, that kind of thing. They're quite at home with bulldozers and dynamite. And they don't trust the government to do squat."

Reese had then given Farlow a summary of the work he was doing. "If we determine that the dike is on sovereignty lands," Reese said, "most likely the State will go forward with an ejectment suit, make Weston take the dike down."

"Again." Farlow said, indicating that the more radical members of his club weren't impressed with the remedies of the law.

Reese nodded. "I don't think you'd see another end-run out of Weston. Things have changed considerably since the early 80s, and he knows everybody's watching him. Right now, I don't see any way that dike isn't on sovereignty lands. It might be worthwhile to at least hold off and see what the State's gonna do."

"It's worth saying," Farlow agreed. "I don't know if it'll make a gnat's worth of difference to some of them. They're just as likely to think I've gone soft."

Reese nodded. He'd seen plenty of that type in his time—guys who just seemed terminally riled and would turn on a trusted ally if he tried to persuade them to be reasonable.

"You seeing Jessie?" Farlow had asked him suddenly.

"No—I, well—I don't know, we just met this week," Reese said.

"Yeah," Farlow twisted his chin once right then back to center, "everybody loves Jessie," he said looking straight at Reese, and Reese had gotten the message. No tomfoolery. She's one of us, and we look out for our own.

"I can see that," Reese had said evenly. He was not about to begrudge the man any attempt to protect Jessie. But he wondered if the warning was simply what it appeared on its face, or if, in the years Chris Farlow had known her, there had been deeper feelings. Perhaps there were still, and Jessie simply couldn't enact such a disloyalty to her family as going with Chris Farlow would appear.

Reese's thoughts were interrupted by the sound of the outer doors being opened. People were coming in. He saw Gus Borman, the State

Lands Director, and he got up to go speak to him. Here we go, he thought.

Borman greeted Reese in the stilted manner Reese had often observed him to have outside Tallahassee. The man was an excellent manager and a good liason to the legislature and the governor's office, adept at garnering resources for vital but obscure programs. But take him out of town and he turned into a nervous nelly, unable to convey the division's intentions or describe its actions in a way that would build trust or confidence. Reese suspected Borman was fearful that the people in these types of gatherings—ranchers, hunters, boaters, outdoors types—would deride him as a pencil pusher with no practical experience in solving the problems of their world.

"Why don't you open the meeting," Borman said, refusing to meet Reese's eyes. "You're more familiar with all the components. Just give a brief summary of what has happened and what we're here to do. I'll be on-hand to answer any legal or administrative questions you feel you can't handle."

"Fine," Reese said. He knew Borman would sit at the back of the room near the door. The man would gladly feed Reese to the sharks if it would allow him to escape unscathed. If things didn't go well, he could blame Reese. If they turned out all right, it would be a feather in his cap. Well, it was probably better than having to sit still while Borman stood up in front of all these people and tried to tell them what was going on in their own town.

Reese decided to stand outside near the door as people came in. He could read their faces better in the daylight, and maybe the sight of him there would create the right impression. As he stepped out he saw Carl Weston and Bud Blake making their way up the walk. He took a deep breath.

"Morning sir, morning Mr. Blake," he said. To his surprise Carl Weston stopped in front of him and offered his right hand.

"Good morning Mr. Kessler. You met Bud?"

Bud nodded and shook Reese's hand warily.

"I understand," Carl Weston said, "that I owe you my thanks for pitching in to save my cow the other day."

"We were glad we could help."

"That was some job getting that old bossy out of that ditch. Jessie said you seemed to know your way around livestock. You a cowman?"

"My granddad. He was the cowman. I used to spend all my time at his place whenever I could sneak away from my home chores. He left me his place—that's where I still live, but the cows were all sold while I was overseas. Between college and getting a career started I never saw the chance to keep any."

Carl Weston nodded and Reese expected him to move on. But he seemed in no hurry to get to the business of the day. "You ever work cattle from horseback?"

"Not really," Reese said. "Granddaddy kept a horse for me while I was growing up. But he was mostly transportation to just go get the cows. Our operation was pretty small potatoes compared to your outfit."

"Well, get Jessie to put you on a Quarter Horse before you wind up your business here. It's an experience you'll never forget."

Reese couldn't believe his ears. "Thank you, sir. I'm sure I'd enjoy that."

Weston nodded and clapped a hand on Reese's sore forearm. Reese did his best not to wince. "See you inside then," Carl Weston said, and he and Bud moved on.

Reese stayed another minute by the door, nodding to the people coming up the walk. He thought he recognized the rigid expression of trouble on a few of the faces, and he was hoping to see Chris Farlow come in. But when he glanced at his watch and saw it was already five minutes after nine, he went in and called the meeting to order. Maybe Farlow was nursing the aftershock of that chorus line of drinks he'd had last night.

"Ok," Reese said, looking out over the thirty-odd faces in the room. "We're here today to put together what we all know about the water levels in Lake Ponder. I'm Reese Kessler with the Bureau of Surveying and Mapping, and it's my job to find out as much as I can about the ordinary high water line of the lake. That's the line that divides the public and private property. As many of you know, our survey crew has been working this week to get some preliminary information on the lake, and that process will continue for another several weeks. What we need from you is the benefit of your long-time familiarity with the lake. Any information you might have about where the water is during the high water season, during floods, during droughts—anything you know about the lake cycles would be very helpful to getting a thorough study and an accurate boundary. We are fortunate to have with us today also Mr. Gus Borman, who is director of the State Lands Division. He'll help us with any legal clarifications we might need as we go along. So let me stop talking so ya'll can start."

A man in the front row wearing a red tee-shirt raised his hand. Reese tapped a forefinger in his direction.

"I'm Roscoe Blain. I have Blain's Fish Camp on the river just above the lake. I don't know why we're here exactly except that it has something to do with finding out what the State's going to do to us." A chorus of chortles rumbled from the group. "I thought the State would come out with a proposal and ask for comments on their line, but you're not telling us anything."

"We're not quite there yet," Reese said. "Nothing's been decided at this point. We're here today to learn what you all know. You live here, you know the lake better than anyone else."

A man wearing horn-rimmed glasses stood up. "I'm Arthur Stern, counsel for the Bar X. "I just want to say I don't think people have had adequate time to prepare for this meeting, particularly in view of the fact that we are not advised as to the position the Trustees are going to take. We're trying to learn to swim in a mudhole, because we don't know what they're doing to us. It's a bad situation from the public standpoint and from a legal standpoint. Apparently you are taking the position in your capacity that the original government surveys of this whole river system are meaningless."

Another voice interrupted and a man with stringy gray hair stood up. "What I want to know, what is the State going to do with the three hundred feet in front of my property if we go to the original surveys. When that land is exposed it is unusable by the fishlife and will be unusable by myself as a developer if I can't get a permit and I have been paying taxes and I have spent money on the property. So I just think the State should have compensation to people who have gone on in good faith and made something useful."

As Reese struggled to sort out the jumble of concerns he saw Chris Farlow come in and settle against the back wall. The sight of Farlow's sardonic grin helped Reese refocus.

"I think we're getting a little ahead of ourselves here. Let me try to put our efforts in a little bit of context. The circumstances that brought about the immediate need to establish the lake boundary are a dispute between the Weston Ranch and The Far Out boating club over approximately four hundred acres of land that is presently impounded by a dike. The dike was breached in the early 1980s and subsequently refilled sometime in the late 80s. As most of you know, this dispute has been going on for some time. The Water Management District issued a permit to pump the water off the property and that triggered a permit challenge by The Far Out. That hearing affirmed the permit and the decision has been appealed. It goes next to the governor and cabinet in Tallahassee to make a decision about the legality of the permit. However, part of the information the Trustees—that is the governor and cabinet—need in order to have a full picture is where the boundary between public and private property is on Lake Ponder. That's the reason we're here, is to provide them any information we can regarding that line. Your deeds and the treatment of the boundary in the original government surveys are not really at issue here."

"But you're saying the line is where?" the horn-rimmed attorney asked. "A change of half a foot in that boundary means hundreds of acres to most of these ranchers."

Another man from the back of the room began speaking, sitting forward on his chair. "I'm concerned over the State's efforts to acquire more and more private lands for the alleged purpose of water storage and other means of water management—lands which are then off the tax rolls. This has done two things, gentlemen. It places a tremendous burden on the taxpayers of the district to purchase the lands concerned. At the same time it removes these lands from the tax rolls and places a continuous increase on the ad valorem tax which landowners then also have to pay. The counties and municipalities are running out of money, and if there is any intention whatsoever that the purpose of these hearings is to establish these lines at some tremendously high level for the benefit of the Trustees, then frankly, right here and now, I am opposed to it."

A tall red-headed man stood up. "This is so typical I can't even believe it. All we hear from daylight to dark is how the State is taking your land. But Carl Weston has impounded four hundred acres of public sovereignty land, which is what we're here to talk about, and all ya'll want to do is bellyache about the State putting the line too high. I want to know what the hell the State's going to do to get Carl's dike off public land. I make my living out on that lake and every encroachment is just cutting into my business the same as it would be yours. So why hasn't the State taken down that dike is what I want to know. Are we gonna have to do it ourselves?"

The man in the red shirt addressed Reese, ignoring the comments of the red-headed man. "One thing you can tell the governor for me is that this so-called solution to the lakes being drawn down is grossly unfair. People who bought waterfront thought they owned to the water and now we're being told we're going to have to pay more to keep the water. That's not right and ya'll know it."

"We're getting so much government we hardly know what to expect from them," Arthur Stern injected. "We can't live with it."

Reese nodded once and signaled that he'd like the floor. "I understand there are a lot of issues still unsettled here. One of the things I can do is give you the information you need to get these issues addressed. But we'll have to do that after this hearing. Right now I'd like to hear from anybody who has boated Lake Ponder over the last ten to twenty years. I need to know where the water used to go on the Weston Ranch before the dike was built."

The redheaded man stood up again. "I can tell you and I can show you. There's one cypress tree left on the upland at the far west end they didn't take out when they put in the dike. It's still got a watermark on it. 'Course they'll go out there tonight and cut it down and burn it, so if I were you I'd get on out there and find it."

There was a chorus of laughter. "You better watch out Red. People get to snooping around down there they're liable to find your handiwork," one man said.

"That there's none of my doin'," Red retorted.

"All right," Reese pushed his voice through the confusion. "A watermark would be very helpful. Anybody else boated back in there when the dike was down?"

"We all were in there a good bit during that time," Chris Farlow said matter of factly. "You could take a pretty big boat through those breaches. I had the "Good'n Gone" in there when it was high water—and she's an old shrimper rig. Got a draft of three feet and more."

Reese nodded and shifted his gaze around the room.

The man with stringy gray hair stood again. "I just want to say that whatever it is you think you're doing out there you have to remember there's a good deal of guess work to these old government surveys—they are subject to question as to accuracy. On the other hand, if we are going to use scientific tests such as you all have today with the fossils and all to determine high water level, you have a problem that is equally speculative. I might say they're still trying to find out where Noah's Ark came to rest."

Another burst of laughter sounded in the room.

Reese grinned. "Thank you. I'll keep an eye out for it. As to the problems of establishing a water line using scientific tests, I agree with you there is plenty of room for error. That's why it's so important to get your testimony about where the water goes. Anybody else?"

In the back corner a short round woman with long, thick black hair stood. Reese had not noticed her before and he now realized she was the only woman in the room.

"I'm Steffee Ninehouse, Mr. Kessler. Everybody knows me. I've lived here all my life. I just want to say I flew over this area a lot from the mid '40s til I sold my outfit in 1977. I ran a charter air business, but I started out doing surveillance for the war office because from the air I could spot submarines lying off the coast. I've seen Lake Ponder in flood and in drought and when everything was regular like. I reckon what Red says about that cypress tree on Carl's place is good help. But there used to be a whole line of 'em right at where the water would get in the rainy season. I'm not talking about a flood now, just regular rain time. You'd find the roots of those trees all along there if you dug down. The evidence is all right there in the ground."

During this testimony Reese glanced in Carl Weston's direction to see how the information was affecting him. Weston looked grim but unprovoked, but beside him, Bud was a different story. His face had reddened and his chest was puffed out. Reese thought he looked like an explosion ready to happen. And, in fact, before Steffee had quite finished what she was saying, he rose to his feet.

"I'm wondering–and perhaps this is a question best addressed to Mr. Borman–what significance any of this can possibly have to my property. Are you telling me the State is going to renege on the deed it issued? Because we have a deed to the land going out into the lake itself. That land has been in my family for fifty-eight years and the State has never laid claim to it til now. Are all of you going to just sit here and let the State tell us our deeds are no good, because your place could be next on the list when you try to make any use of your land or when you decide to sell it."

Reese looked at Gus Borman, waiting for some indication that he would answer. But the man gave no sign. He kept his eyes on the front of the room while carefully avoiding Reese. He seemed not to have even heard the question.

Reese sighed. "We can certainly talk about the issues of deeds that include navigable waters Mr. Blake. I have some specific information that pertains to those questions and I'm sure we can follow up on that. But I'd like to get any further testimony about the water levels first, so people can get on with their day. Is there anybody else who wants to be heard on where the water used to stand?"

Bud Blake was still standing. "Well I can tell you exactly where the water stands because I've lived there all my life and I helped build the dike everybody's so worried about. That dike was built to keep out extremely high water, which is what people are remembering being above that dike. In regular water that dike is on high and dry land and everybody here knows it."

"Thank you Mr. Blake." Reese paused to see if anyone else would speak. In the back a few men stood up and made their way towards the door. "I'd like to thank all of you for taking time to come here today," Reese said over the scraping chairs. "If any of you want information on these other issues, I can provide some contact information." People were filing out, and Reese waited to make sure no one would stay. Then he went to speak to Borman.

"Ok then," Borman said. "I don't know what use any of that was, but at least they can't say they didn't have their chance."

"The cypress tree testimony might come in handy. I'll do a few borings up there and see what turns up." Reese waited for the director's response, further instructions, or feedback. None came. Finally Reese said, "Can I get you anything then–need a ride, a late breakfast, early lunch?"

"No. No thanks. I've got a charter waiting to get me back to town. I better get going."

"Yes sir," Reese said. "I better get back to it myself. Have a good flight."

I guess it takes all kinds, Reese thought, watching Borman make his way to the parking lot. A man in Borman's position walked a peculiar line Reese was glad to have none of. He wondered if Borman knew particular things about this case that made everything Reese was doing irrelevant. Well, that was not his concern. All he could do was give them the best information he could. What they made of it was out of his hands. He reflected with half a grin that it had never much mattered to him before. He felt a thrill run through him remembering Jessie's mouth on his in the parking lot last night. It would be nice if he could manage to keep out of trouble with her stepbrother, but that seemed increasingly doubtful. Bud Blake struck him as a train wreck trying to happen.

Reese wondered if Carl Weston's invitation to ride would hold if Reese tried to take him up on it. Jessie had talked about riding back along the dike to check for cave-ins and make sure cows wouldn't be regularly wandering into danger. He wouldn't mind getting a look at that cypress tree Red had talked about at the far end of the dike. And it would give him a reason to ask her if he could go along. In spite of the morning's stress, Reese felt happy, and he noticed it, noticed the unfamiliarity of it. It might still be possible, he thought, to have some happiness. It just might.

Reese walked the three blocks to his hotel and put in a call to Sam Donnovan.

"Just checking in," Reese said.

"Hey–where are you?" Sam replied.

"In the hotel."

"Where's Borman?"

"Don't know. Last I saw of him he was headed down Main Street with a mob of angry villagers hot on his heels."

"Ah," Sam said. "The venerable salt of the earth."

They laughed.

"No, actually, things went all right. About what you'd expect. The usual confusion, complaining about deeds and science and not enough notice. I got two leads on the water line prior to the dike going in."

"Yeah?"

"Yeah. One guy said there's a cypress tree with watermarks still on it at the far end of the property. And this old Indian lady who used to run a charter air service told me a whole line of cypress used to stand along the ordinary high water line above the dike."

"Hmmmn. You could probably find that, huh?"

"There's a good chance if they left the roots. If they tipped 'em up roots and all we'd have to dig to China to find anything."

"You need extra crew?"

"Let me poke around for a few days and see what turns up before I tell you on that."

"Ok. Ya'll coming in tomorrow?"

"I'll send the boys back tomorrow. I'm going to stay down here and nose around a bit–get some rest instead of burning up the roads."

"And this plan would have nothing to do with Jessie Weston?"

"Well I do have an invitation to see the ranch on horseback."

"Ideal on all fronts," Sam laughed.

"Seriously," Reese said, "I need your advice on a related matter."

"Shoot."

"Who do I want for a divorce lawyer?"

Sam didn't skip a beat. "Joe Hill. Here's his number–you got a pen?"

"Yeah, go ahead." Reese wrote down the number.

"And you don't need me to tell you that the first thing he'll tell you is not to get caught with another skirt until after the settlement is signed. Right?"

"Thanks Sam."

"A'ight. Keep in touch."

"Will do."

Reese sat for a moment thinking about the call to Joe Hill. It suddenly felt so unreal. The thought of just calling up a stranger and saying I want to divorce my wife seemed unaccountably far-fetched. Did he really have the right to do such a disruptive thing? He had always thought he would stick it out with Vivian, and the sudden clarity that he no longer wanted to almost frightened him. It was as if he was just finding out that he didn't know himself at all, as if he might at any moment let himself go and do any fool thing he wanted to. He felt the panic flutter in his chest and he laid back on the bed and shut his eyes. After a moment he realized he was thinking of the way Jessie had looked last night standing in the parking lot–her dark hair framing her lovely face and her sun tanned arms reaching out to him. This was not a foolish fantasy. Jessie was solid, smart, warm. All the longing in his being seemed to come alive, and his body ached to hold her again. He could feel his pulse beating in his fingertips. He reached for the phone and punched in the number for Joe Hill.

Jessie was working at her desk when she heard Bud's car come up the drive. She paused over the ledger she was updating and listened. In a moment she would know from the percussion of their steps how the hearing had gone, know from the rise and fall of their voices if they were angry or exuberant. She liked these sounds that telegraphed so much. Her ex-husband, Foster, had been still and quiet, and she had found herself, over the years they were married, longing for vibrant energy.

She heard the high whine of Bud's voice winding out like an engine. Venting. But that wasn't unusual. He could be ranting over something someone said at the hearing that was really of no consequence. What wasn't usual was that she could hear no answering thunder from her father. It was unlike him to fall silent, regardless of the situation. She waited to hear his boots marking their relentless rhythm across the tile in the foyer, down the wood plank floor of the hall to the thick rugs in his study. Nothing. It was like Bud was raging solo into a void.

Might as well face the music, she thought, pushing back her chair. She wondered what the morning had been like for Reese. Maybe she would get a chance to talk to him later. As she came down the stairs Jessie saw her father sitting in an upholstered chair just inside the living room. This startled her and she hesitated. Given a choice, he would not sit in "dressed" chairs, and he never sat in the living room unless someone had died and he was hosting guests. She could hear Bud clearly now.

". . . and probably never would've seen that watermark if Red Greely would just keep his damn mouth shut. If the State takes it back to that old tree line we've got nothing left. I can't put eighteen holes on thirty acres. Chappy's told me straight out he's got to have at least two hundred acres, and what it would do to the unit number . . . . We might get a hundred tops."

"Nothing has been decided yet," Jessie heard her father say quietly. "But I think it's time to give some attention to a fall-back plan."

"That's exactly what they want us to do is fold. What we should do is get a hold of that lawyer up in Tallahassee. He as much as said the State's taking what's ours."

Carl Weston sighed. "Bud," he said, straightening, "we're going to give it our best shot. But in the interest of prudent business, I want to have a back-up. We ought to go take a look at that property on the Banana River. It's just three miles outside the town limits and the old man has just died. His sons want to sell it. Let's go walk it, see what its potential is. In the mean time, we'll keep the pressure on Tallahassee to see things our way."

"If we divide our resources that way we won't end up doing squat," Bud exploded. "We've–"

"Bud," Carl Weston said, and Jessie heard the low rumble come back into his voice, "the amount of resources I'm willing to devote to lawyers is thin to begin with. I've never gotten anything but bills out of a lawyer. It's better to put your money in the land. That always pays."

For a moment there was silence. Then Bud began to speak. His voice sounded strained as if he could barely breathe. "Well I never thought I'd see you throwing in the towel," he said, "at the first little scuffle."

Jessie stepped off the bottom step where she had been listening and entered the room. For a moment nothing moved, the two men might have been statues. Then her father's posture softened, though he did not look at her. He leaned back in the chair and his eyes stayed on Bud. He seemed to pull something from deep inside himself.

"Maybe you're right son," he said. "But you're thinking about your development. What would be grand and wonderful and everything you envisioned. I know that feeling. It's frustrating to have obstacles to your plans. But there are other things I have to consider along with your development." Bud shot Jessie a dark look, his mouth locked in a tight scowl. Carl Weston went on speaking. "You cool off and think about it. If you want to go look at that property, I'll call 'em."

Bud brushed past Jessie without meeting her eyes and slammed out the front door. They heard his car crank and the gear grind as he popped the clutch and spun out of the drive. Jessie waited for the moment to pass.

"Was it that bad?" she finally asked her father, settling into a chair opposite him.

"He's just finding out he's got some real obstacles with this development," her father answered. "I don't think it ever came home to him before. He's used to these old boys around here cutting him a lot of slack over paperwork and permits. But, it's a new day." Carl Weston raised his eyebrows and almost grinned. "It's good for him to learn this now." He nodded at her, slapped his open palms on his thighs, and rose from the upholstered chair. "Let's see what Juanita's got in the kitchen. I'm starved."

Jessie followed him to the kitchen wondering whether to be happy or alarmed at his manner. He seemed already to have forgotten Bud's outburst, as well as any of his own aggravation about the golf course and development. Juanita had prepared a plate of enchiladas dressed with green sauce, avocados, and tomatoes.

"Eees hot," she warned. She waved Carl Weston away from the stove and carried the plate to the table, her hand swathed in a thick towel. There she stood over him, watching as he sat down and began to eat with gusto. She went to the refrigerator and brought back a bottle of Dos Equis, prying off the lid as she set it before him. He took a long drink and nodded. Satisfied, she returned to her perch at the breakfast counter, where she was sorting grocery receipts. Jessie pulled out the stool beside her and sat down.

"I talked to our Mr. Kessler at the hearing," Carl Weston said between mouthfuls. He glanced up to gauge Jessie's reaction and was not surprised to see her left eyebrow arch and her gaze shift. A second later the corners of her mouth twitched in the unmistakable suppression of a smile. "His granddad ran cattle. He used to slip over there and help out."

"I thought it must be something like that," Jessie responded. "You can just tell."

Carl Weston nodded, mopping green sauce from his mustache. "He's ridden, but it doesn't sound like he ever had a real horse." He let this information settle on her. "I told him you might let him test drive a Quarter Horse." He waited and watched, seeming to busy himself with his disintegrating enchilada.

"That would change his life," Jessie said with a droll grin.

"Oh his life would be changed all right," Carl Weston said, chuckling.

Jessie broke out in a chortle. "I don't know what you could mean by such a remark."

"Well, just see that he doesn't fall off and break something. I'd hate to have him take the ranch in a lawsuit. You'd have to marry him to get it back." He grinned as Jessie got up and started towards him. "He's not already taken is he?" he said, ducking her approach.

"I can see your mind is wandering today," she retorted, darting her hand towards his ribs. "Anybody would think you had nothing better to do than play cupid." She leaned over his shoulder and kissed his cheek. "I, on the other hand, have got horses to work."

"Eees dees tha man who calls with the deep voice? He eees so, ummm, *polite*," Juanita cast a glance at Carl Weston and waggled her eyebrows at Jessie.

Jessie laughed. "Well, if Mr. Right calls you can tell him to be ready to ride tomorrow morning at eight." She went down the back steps toward the barn, unaccountably pleased with the fine spring weather.

April 13, 2001

As luck would have it I was late getting to work. Friday the 13th. The first thing I saw when I got off the elevator was what could only be a staff meeting in the big, glass-front conference room by the director's office. Naturally I had forgotten Bonnie's warning about the early meeting. I slipped in through the door and stood along the wall, surveying the situation. Steve was introducing new employees in the field crew—guys who looked like they'd just as soon get out of this fluorescent, over-air-conditioned, swivel-chaired environment as fast as possible. Bonnie had saved me a chair along the back wall and was waving me over.

"What's going on?" I whispered.

"Nobody knows," she said, her eyes wide.

"What's *he* doing here?" I poked my chin at the deputy director, sitting at the front table. He was accompanied by yet another new assistant—younger and bustier than the last one, who had seemed to leave under duress but without detail.

She shrugged.

"So now I'll turn things over to Ron," Steve was saying, "who wants to address you all this morning with a few remarks."

Ron Lehman straightened his six-foot-two frame and turned to face us. His face was a study of seriousness, and he let his gaze scan across every face in the room before beginning to speak. This looked like his heartfelt mode with maybe a hint of motivational speaker waiting to be unleashed. "I'm here today to allay your fears about job cuts under the Governor's Service First initiative—fears that are being fed by misinformation."

"Oh boy," Bonnie whispered, "I feel better already."

"As most of you know, the Governor was elected on a platform of trimming the fat from state government, making a smaller, more efficient workforce. He wants to see us do more for less. Now you know and I know that's going to ruffle a few feathers. And you know the kind of people who are going to get stuck right there. But I'm here to tell you that you have an opportunity here. In a sense you can look on this as a personal challenge to join the future. Let me just tell you a little story."

Where was Roland Barthes when you needed him? I thought. I had a hunch Ron's little tale would be a classic example of how stories can turn our attention away from the fact that our own interests diverge from those of the elite, ruling class.

Ron began. "My father did essentially the same job in the same company for over thirty years. He was recognized as among the most reliable employees by his supervisors, and one of the most skilled in his craft by his peers. He enjoyed a fair wage and reasonable benefits. He was a good provider."

He paused and scanned our faces to gauge the effect of his remarks. "It is unlikely that we will have careers like our fathers: thirty years in one place. The Governor has envisioned a new and better public service sector for the State of Florida. No longer will we employ individuals with the intent of keeping them for a quarter-century in one place. In the future, we are going to migrate far more readily and confidently between the public and private sectors, and back again, all the while acquiring new skill sets, providing greater value, and commanding performance-based compensation. In the Governor's State, the public service jobs of the future will look much more like the corporate jobs of today. More flexibility to get tasks accomplished, better compensation for those who produce. What I'm here to tell you is that future is already here. The legislature is right now considering a bill that will substantially revamp the State's career service workforce, including our Department of Environmental Protection. This will be an exciting and challenging time for each of us, and I ask you to put aside your doubts and work to bring this unique opportunity to fruition. Your bureau chief will be holding meetings with you to discuss the details of the implementation as they are developed. Now, if you have any questions, I'll answer what I can. But keep in mind we don't have a final version of the bill yet, so some of the factors are still unknown."

We all sat in stunned silence. It was impossible to gauge whether he actually believed the stuff he was saying or just thought we would believe it. What *we* knew about the governor's vision was coming from the people who'd been x'd, as we called it—exited from the system. No paycheck, no benefits, no warning—just fired for no other reason than that the governor had arbitrarily decided we would be more efficient if 25% of all the jobs in Florida's civil service were "privatized"—i.e., contracted out to his "bidness buds." And this nonsense in the face of the fact that Florida's public service was ranked one of the smallest, most efficient, lowest paid professional work forces in the country. It seemed akin to telling a whole and healthy man you were going to hack off 25% of his body because it would make him more efficient. And if this fool standing up here spouting this crap thought that 25% of the public service jobs could be cut without people bleeding . . . I couldn't help it, I stood up.

"Teena Shostekovich, Ron, with surveying and mapping. Good morning. I'm a little puzzled at how the logistics of these cuts are supposed to work. We have 1,300 employees in public service whose jobs have been slated for cuts who live here in Tallahassee. And they are going to go out into the private sector?"

"Yes, and I think they'll be amazed at how much better the compensation is out there. In fact, I'm scared to death that I'm going to lose my best people. But the beauty of this is that they'll be enriched by their tenure in the private sector, and when they come back into public service they will be able to command greater compensation."

"Do you envision these people being employed locally?" I asked in as even a tone as I could manage. "Because I don't know where 1,300 jobs are going to come from in Tallahassee. And what's more, the big cuts are coming in service sectors like janitorial, food services, park services, personnel. Those people aren't going to be enriched by their tenure in the private sector. They're going to be scrambling to get minimum wage jobs at McDonalds." I felt Bonnie's foot bumping the back of my calf.

"But what you don't realize," Ron responded, "is that with those jobs privatized, many of the same employees will still be doing their same jobs—they'll just be working for a private company instead of the State."

"With better compensation?"

"In many cases, yes."

"How is that possible when companies have to make a profit and the State doesn't?"

"Well that's the beauty of the free enterprise system," he said. "People work harder when they make more money. Ok, someone else?"

When no one moved for the count of five, I couldn't help myself. "Excuse me Ron but I also had just one more question about the integrity of the public service sector if it's too closely allied with private enterprise. Historically, an association that blurs the boundaries of civil service responsibility has resulted in massive corruption."

"Well I'm sure we've got plenty of people watching out for that," Ron replied a little coldly. "Ok, I'm sorry but that's all we have time for today. I have to meet with another group. Thank you all."

He shook Steve's hand and hurried out. Everyone else stood up and moved toward the exits like zombies. The gap between the reality of this situation and the spin they were trying to sell us was crazy-making. In the hall a few of my colleagues joked with me. Hey, way to go Shossie. Yeah, Teena, you got a job all lined up to go to? Cause that man gonna fire yore ass. Yeah, but just remember he be doin you a *favor,* cuz you gonna make so much money when you x-it the system you be wondrin how to kerryt'all home. Hey Teena, thanks for stickin' up for us. You can come to my house for dinner when you're out on the streets.

Yeah, yeah. I went to my office and listened to messages. One from our attorney at the AG's office. Let's set up a meeting for next week on Lake Ponder. Get this settlement agreement done. One from Mel. Are you going to make happy hour? We need to catch up. One was from my ex-husband, Mack. Hey darlin. Call me at this number when you get a chance. That was weird. Although we'd parted on friendly terms, he never called. I called Jack at the AG's and set up for the following Monday. I left Mel a message saying yeah, see you there. I scribbled down the number for Mack, trying to decide whether to call him right back or wait til I got home tonight. I calculated that the best time to catch him in his part of the world was about 3 a.m. in mine.

There was a little rap on my door and Richard came in. "Hey, girl. How's it going?"

"Ugh."

"That good huh? You left the camera in the truck last time out," he said, handing it to me. "I downloaded the files to my laptop, so the card's good to go again. I can email you the pictures."

"Oh, the Lake Ponder trip. Thanks, but I guess I won't be needing those."

"Really." He sat down, sprawling his long legs out and slumping comfortably in the chair. "What's going on?"

"If you had to pick something we were vulnerable on in the Lake Ponder case, what would you pick?" I asked.

"You mean what could we lose it on?"

"Yeah."

"Nothing. You've done a great job of showing that none of their arguments hold water. When you really go back and look at the actual record, we did everything right, except maybe played too nice from the git-go. 'Course people holler if we come down on 'em with our big fascist boot, but then you get guys like these who lie and cheat and steal if you don't. Judging from your expression, I haven't given you the right answer yet."

"I need a way to lose this case."

"Seriously?"

"That's what I'm being told."

"Well that's a bunch of shinola. After all this time?"

"Yeah. But I'm not going to be the one saying oh come on let's go for it and then losing all the sovereignty lands down to the low-water line."

"Hmmmnn. That doesn't sound like you."

"Yeah, well, I'm learning to choke in my old age. I'm hoping it'll give my face a rest."

"So you want to identify the places where we're most vulnerable and use those as the basis to give this away?"

"That's what I was asking you, yes. But when you say it out loud like that I just want to barf."

"Ok. Let me give it some thought. Maybe if we could find something from long ago it would make it easier. You know, to say well we sorta kinda didn't know which way to jump during all that screwy legislation that came down in the early '80s, and we might've misled Mr. Wesson."

"Yeah, I'm looking into that angle. I'm also thinking I ought to contact Chris Farlow, just to get his input you know."

Richard grinned. "You mean Chris Farrell, the airboat cowboy?"

"Right. Chris Farrell. I can't help but think he'd be interested to know about any settlement. You know, want to have some input."

"You, girl, are bad to the bone. That case would blow up so fast we wouldn't know what hit us."

"Yeah, well I might need to get old Chris to give me a job driving airboats after that little q & a with Ron this morning."

"You're not wrong about that. Make sure you get his name right if you have to go for a job interview. Farlow's probably the name you gave him in your novel."

"Yeah."

"You better watch out, you're gonna be sitting up there on the witness stand one day citing your characters for authority and calling us all by our made-up names." I nodded, sighing. "So what's my name in the book?" he asked.

"Richard," I said.

"No, that's my real name."

I made a face at him. "I only change the names to protect the innocent," I said. "Nobody thinks you're innocent, so you've got nothing to worry about."

"I like your twisted logic."

"Anyway, my novel got stolen night before last."

"What do you mean? How could it get stolen?"

"Somebody came in my house while I was at Inez's retirement party and took my hard drive out of my computer. Is that weird or what?"

"Took just the drive?"

"Umhmm," I nodded.

"That is weird. Did you call the cops?"

"Yeah, but I don't think they can do much. Even if they catch the guy, he'll probably destroy everything—it's evidence against him."

"You don't have back-ups?"

"He got 'em."

"Man, I hate that. I got robbed one time, and it just made me feel so—violated. I know that sounds girlie but it's the only word that nails it."

"Yeah. He's evidently a creepy type anyway. He called me on my phone when I got home and told me not to call the police or I'd never get my files back. And he left a printout of that window that says this program has performed an illegal function and will be shut down. Only his says 'this *person* has performed an illegal function and will be shut down.'"

"That's not just a break-in. That guy's screwing with you. Got any idea who it is? Who've you been partying with?"

"Dream on hotshot. I've got NO life after hours."

"Do you have a gun?"

"No. I'm not ready to start taking men by force. Yet." We laughed.

"Let's go out to the range tomorrow afternoon and shoot this little 410 shotgun I've got," Richard said. "Then you can borrow it for a while."

"I don't know Richard. I'll probably end up blasting Willow to smithereens."

"No you won't. And if that asshole comes back he'll get a real clear message that the game is over. Really, Teena, you're gonna love this little beast."

"Ok," I said, knowing he wouldn't give up. Richard grew up a military brat, with a father who was hard as nails, and his resilience under fire is legendary. "Come get me when you're ready to go to the range."

"Will do, and if you have any trouble, I don't care if it *is* the middle of the night, you call me, okay?"

"Thanks, Richard. I might have to take you up on that."

"Ok. You going to happy hour?"

"I'll be there."

"Ok. See you."

I spent the afternoon answering correspondence that had been forwarded to our bureau to handle. It was soothing to be able to put out small fires, answer questions motivated purely by curiosity, and send out information that was accurate and would be welcomed by the recipient. At 4:55 Steve came in and closed the door behind him.

"Was that your notice you were giving this morning?"

I let myself wilt in my chair. "Only if it's come to that."

"There wouldn't be anything ignoble about keeping your head down when people are slinging shit, you know."

"I know. I just . . . it feels wrong to let them just spin this out when people are losing their jobs, their homes, benefits. Besides, what Ron was describing this morning is a perfect prescription for taking all the backbone out of environmental policy. It's nothing more than a revolving door between the agency that's supposed to enforce policy and the people who are supposed to abide by it. There's no integrity in it."

"There's sure not going to be if they're able to single out the people like you and can your ass."

"So I'm just supposed to sit there and say nothing?"

"Right. Save it for when it can make a difference. It's just a suggestion."

"I know. But you can only stand so much—"

"A detective came to see me today."

"Oh. Logan Deo?"

"That sounds right. Tall guy with shoulders. Dark hair."

"What did he have to say?"

"He wanted to see employment records for people in the computer section. He knew about your files being copied."

"I told him about that."

Steve nodded. "Are you sure you know what's going on with all this? I got the impression for some reason he was suspicious of you."

"Really?" A firestorm flashed through my neurons. "Actually, I'm not sure about anything. I don't like how little they tell me. But they keep warning me of some kind of danger. I don't know what to think. What made you think he was suspicious of me?"

"At one point he asked me if I knew of a reason why you would be protecting someone you work with. I said I thought it was possible. Then he sat there for a minute just looking around my office. Looking at the pictures of us on the airboat, and on the creek, and everywhere. Then he looked right at me and said is the situation ongoing?

"Steve, I didn't tell him anything."

"I know. That's why he didn't know whether to trust you."

We sat for a minute. Both of us were probably wondering if we had been that obvious to everyone around us, or whether Logan Deo was just that good at his job. I wasn't going to ask how Steve had answered Deo's question.

"I told him I believed you were past it."

We sat there another minute. Then in a strained voice he asked, "Was that right?"

I knew what he was asking. I could see the chasm opening, ready to swallow me up again. If I waffled now I'd have a one-way ticket back to limbo-land. Whether it was right or not, I wanted to believe I'd come too far to go back to those days. Besides, I really wanted to know what Logan was up to. "What did he say?" I asked.

Steve stared at his fingernails. "He said, ok, that was all he needed to know."

So that was it. Logan had sensed I was hiding something from him. Protecting someone. And he had also guessed about my involvement with Steve, either from the way I talked about him, or the pictures in my house and Steve's office, or from Steve—or all of it. I couldn't decide if that accounted for everything weird in his behavior. Was there something else he could have suspected me of?

"What else?" I asked.

"He wanted to know if I'd told anyone else about your files being copied. I told him I'd talked it over with an old buddy in enforcement—that he was going to nose around and see what he could find out. Nothing official."

"He mentioned something to me," I said, "about having seen this before. A pattern. Maybe he's talking about some kind of problems with computer hackers or something. Maybe politically motivated spying. I don't know."

"Yeah, well, *he* may be the one *doing* any politically motivated spying," Steve said with uncharacteristic feeling. "We may both be about to get fired. Don't forget the investigation they launched against me while we were down at Okeechobee—right in the middle of the case. They went through every contract we'd let for the last ten years trying to find something on me. They had me chasing my tail for weeks before I figured out the deal."

"That didn't stop you from making idiots of them in court," I said.

"Just keep it in mind. This whole thing may blow up on us. It's one of the ways they get what they want."

"That would make more sense if we weren't folding."

"Yeah it would. But they don't know what deal we're going to put on the table, so keeping the pressure on doesn't hurt."

We sat for a moment, and I felt like he wanted to say more. "You going to happy hour?" I asked.

"I guess I'll stop by. You going over?"

"Yeah."

"Ok." He got up. "I'll see you there."

I stopped at the bar and got a marguerita, then headed for the patio where our gang usually congregated. Richard waved to me, but he was surrounded by guys from the field crew enacting some wild story, so I just saluted and made my way over to Mel. She was sitting with Ben, one of the lawyers from EARTH JUST IS. We gossiped for a few minutes about the new attorney in their office, trying to decide if she was really an environmentalist or just prepping herself for power roles.

"We get that more all the time," Ben told me. "New hotshot attorneys right out of school—they don't want to work for the environment, they just want to cut their teeth on us so when they interview with the powers they can say they know how to get around environmental laws."

"Send 'em over to us," I said. "They're exactly the type Dud's looking for to carve out Florida's future."

I watched the people drifting out from the bar. Most of our old gang had been around a decade or two, working in governmental offices, grass roots organizations, and other foundations to protect the fragile Florida we loved. It was a good-hearted, politically savvy community, and I always felt proud to be part of it. Some of these people had war stories that would stand your hair on end, and it was a comforting feeling to sit among them, knowing they had survived.

In a minute Ben got up to mingle, and Mel pulled her chair closer to mine. "Ok. Tell all."

"I got an email from creepboy yesterday."

"This bonehead's got some nerve, you know it? What did he say?"

"He's critiquing my novel."

"You're kidding."

"Nope. He gave me an assignment."

"To do what exactly?"

"Make it grim," I said. She scowled. "He thinks I'm a hopeless romantic."

"And how is this a concern of his?"

"I think he fancies himself an editor of the first order. He wants to rescue my talent from my girlish idiocy."

"Did you show it to the hunk?"

"Logan?"

"Logan, huh? Not Detective Deo?"

Inexplicably, I felt my face redden. She grinned.

"Spare me," I groaned. "It's hard to tell what he thinks. Something else seems to be going on besides this break-in. He stopped in to see Steve today and Steve thought he seemed suspicious of me."

"For what? You didn't steal your own hard drive."

"I don't know yet. Something to do with stealing computer data, or political spying maybe. He was interested in my files being copied."

"That doesn't make sense."

"I have another theory," I said.

"And it is?"

"When he was asking me if I had a boyfriend or an ex or anyone who would do something like this, I got a little squirrelly saying there was nobody. I mean, actually, I wasn't even thinking of protecting Steve. It was like it suddenly hit me that it was really over between us—or that there had never really been an us. That there was nobody at all in my life."

"And he thought you were protecting someone and so he got suspicious."

"That's the theory. But it doesn't explain anything. What would he think I was protecting someone from unless some other kind of crime has been committed? I mean there are all kinds of reasons why you wouldn't want to divulge who you're seeing. And then there's this thing he said about the break-in being part of a pattern."

"Of what? Rampant literary criticism? I think he's being nosy about you and pretending it's part of his job investigating the break-in."

"Well that would be thrilling darling, but I think there's more to it. He keeps warning me about someone stalking me."

"Maybe he means him."

She said it without thinking, as part of teasing me, but as soon as she said it I felt the prickle of some survival hormone race through my spine. "How'd it go down with Steve?" she asked.

"What, you mean Logan questioning him?"

"Yeah. Did he come clean?"

"More or less—in his way. He's paranoid that this is actually an investigation of us, to throw us off balance on this case. He said Logan spent a lot of time looking at the pictures of us out in the field. He thinks he put two and two together. He asked Steve if there was any reason why I would be protecting someone, and Steve said he thought that was possible. Then he asked him if it was still going on."

"Really." Mel leaned forward, raised both eyebrows. "What did Steve say?"

"He told Logan he thought I was past it."

"Well that was clever. Is that right?"

"That's the same thing Steve asked me. I'd like to be. But I get the feeling it would be really easy to start up again right now."

"He's worried. He does care about you. He's probably still hung up on you."

"Well you know what? That's the way he wants it. He wants to live with her and be hung up on me." As if to illustrate my point, Steve came through the door from the bar with his girlfriend, Ginger. Mel saw him too, saw me seeing him.

"And what do you want?" she prodded.

"I want my novel back. I want to be able to do my job. I want to be with someone who's there. Mack was never there. Steve was never there. I mean, what is it—"

"Do you like him?"

"Steve?"

"Deo."

"Oh I don't know. I don't know him well enough to know if I *can* like him. And I don't know what's really going on."

"Do you think he's investigating you and Steve, you know, to get you fired?"

"I have trouble believing that's what this is about, but—" I paused, uncertain how to describe my misgivings. "We went to the Blue Moon last night to eat."

"And?"

"I don't know Mel. I think I'm too vulnerable to male attention. Very likely I'm being a total fool. He could've picked my pocket and I would've said, 'oh and here's my credit card too.'"

"Is he coming onto you?"

"I don't know. I pick up signs that he's, you know, interested. But it's like there's a closed door there somewhere. Maybe he's about to get me fired. Or maybe he's married."

"Ask him."

"I just met him. And besides, he's a cop—if he is a cop. It feels funny asking him personal questions."

"Well yeah, but just say there's nothing funny going on, that he *is* coming onto you, that you end up wanting to sleep with him. I mean, if you're going out together it's a fair question—you need to ask."

"I guess. I almost don't want to know. I'm savoring the notion that there's someone on the scene I could get interested in, and I don't want to know yet why it isn't going to happen. I know that's stupid."

Mel patted my hand. "It takes time. Especially meeting under such weird circumstances. Just enjoy getting to know him."

"Yeah. He's already seen me crying and barfing. What's left to know? Anyway, tell me some good news. How's your appeal shaping up?"

"How about I tell you at dinner. If we sit here one more minute you're going to have to talk to them," she said, poking her chin towards Steve and Ginger. "They're working their way over."

"Let's go," I said. We grabbed our bags and split through the garden entrance.

Chapter Six

Watching Reese's jeep come down the drive through the morning light, Jessie was struck by how quickly life could change. On Tuesday she had seen him for the first time, driving in like a man under a spell. She knew that she herself had been sleepwalking for months, simply putting one foot in front of the other to get through the days. Seeing him now with that bright glance and the little half smile as he waved to her, she felt that something was happening right under their noses. Maybe they were both waking up from a past they wanted to move on from. After his call last night, she had lain awake wondering what the day would bring. The logistics of an affair seemed ponderous, with him living in Tallahassee. And she had no idea what kind of family obligations he had. Parents, children, romantic entanglements—any or all seemed likely. In a certain sense she didn't care. She enjoyed his company in a way that seemed apart from everything else. And there was the physical attraction. With other men she had dated since her divorce, she had been lukewarm at best. But with Reese she felt free and open in a way she hadn't felt for a long time—since before she was married. It seemed to her that his slow, easy ways made a space where she could discover her feelings without pressure. For years she had been retreating into herself. But Reese made her feel like racing, flying through the wind at breakneck speed while the green hills blurred around her. She didn't want to be cautious. She didn't want to think about the future. If all she could have with him was a few short weeks, she would make the most of it.

He parked the jeep and joined her in the barn, glancing closely at her face and saying a soft, "hey." They fell into a slow stroll down the aisle, stopping in front of Rocket's stall. Jessie leaned on the stall door. "This is the fella I've been telling you about. This is Rocket."

Reese leaned on the stall door beside her. "Yo buddy," he called softly. The dark ears flicked in their direction, but Rocket kept his nose in his bucket.

"I gave them a handful of feed," Jessie said. "They'll be finished in a minute." They walked on to a stall that contained a big chestnut horse.

"This is Knuckle," she said. "He'll be your ride today."

Reese leaned over the stall gate and watched the big horse thoughtfully.

"You can go in and see him," she said, handing him a lead rope. "Bring him out when he's finished eating, and we'll get saddled."

Reese stepped into the stall and approached the big gelding. He ran a hand along the horse's crest and rested it on his shoulder as the horse turned to snuffle his shirtfront. "Hey Knuckle," he said. "Wanna go for a ride? You'll pretty much have to pack me around. I'm not much of a cowboy."

"You can test drive him in the arena before we head out," Jessie said, watching Reese's face. "If you're not comfortable we'll just ride in there today, let you get used to him. He's a good guy though. He'll take care of you."

They saddled the horses. Fingering the soft reins, Reese felt the odd sense of something familiar from a long time past. He breathed in the smell of the leather, and he felt the years since he was young as a tangible thing, almost like the rein in his hand. The weight of time and things he still wanted seemed to gather a density now that required action, response. His life had been static for too long. He had somehow let the important things slip away. The quiet moments, the good moments, doing something you enjoyed, with someone–really with someone. He watched Jessie lean down to catch Knuckle's girth and then straighten to tighten it. Her motions were economical and sure, like an artist or an athlete. A pang of longing went through him as he thought of all the little routines that should make up a life. Cooking dinner together, saddling horses.

"Ready?" she asked, picking up Rocket's reins, and he nodded and followed her out into the thick, brightening air.

"Okay, walk me through this," he said, mounting the big chestnut and settling into the saddle. "It's been ten years at least."

"He goes forward when you close your calves against him," Jessie said. "Then relax and just let him move. Everything easy. Quiet aids. Touch his mouth a little and get the feel of your brakes."

Reese set the horse off, then halted him. Laying the left rein on Knuckle's neck, he guided the horse to the right and moved off at a walk. He concentrated on the feel of the horse, the steady energy and the rhythm of the walk. After a minute, he closed his legs again and Knuckle picked up a trot. Reese trotted in a big circle, bouncing a little but feeling the motion as consistent. This was going to be fun.

He changed direction, trotted a circle to the right, then brought the horse back to a walk.

"I think we'll get along fine," Reese said, patting the horse's neck. "What do you think?"

"You're a natural," Jessie said, smiling.

"Ok, then. Let's go."

When they had talked the night before, they had decided to try to find the cypress tree Red Greely had described at the hearing. Jessie let them through the gate, and they rode down the driveway towards the road that led up onto the dike. Reese remembered that was the way Jessie had come back the day they'd gotten the cow out of the ditch. It was likely the shortest and easiest route to the other end of the ranch. It was already hot, but the horses strode out eagerly, seeming pleased with the morning and the heavy scent of oranges wafting on the air. When the road rose up sharply to the dike, Knuckle bounded up the steep incline, then settled into a lope. Reese let him go. He could hear Rocket loping along behind, but he seemed to be staying well back. After a minute Reese realized Jessie was being careful not to let the horses goad each other into a race, and he relaxed and rode on. The sun was glinting off the blue waters of the lake, and Reese wondered why he would ever want to be anywhere else. When he felt the big horse begin to slow, he pulled up beside a thicket of Brazilian Pepper Trees. Jessie reined in beside him.

"This is paradise," Reese said.

"Hmmmn." Jessie nodded, scanning the landscape as if seeing it for the first time.

"What do you see?"

Jessie looked quickly at Reese. "You mean besides all these exotic pepper trees overrunning the native flora?" she grinned. "I guess I see it the way it was in the past, the way it could be in the future. I wonder what I should be doing to protect it." She smiled, watching Reese pull gently at Knuckle's mane. "Do you like him?"

"You bet," he said. "He's the horse I always wanted as a kid."

"He's my father's old cutting horse," Jessie said. "But don't let the word 'old' fool you. We had him out working cows this week and he was hunkering down and cuttin' to beat the band."

"I'd like to have seen that."

"You will," Jessie said, grinning. "It's good for him to move out a little today. Keep him from getting stove up."

They walked on lazily now, enjoying the rising sun, the shifting currents on the lake, the slow flight of ibis floating overhead. In the distance, a yellow, twin-engine plane lofted and dipped as if riding the breeze. Reese was conscious of wanting to tell her about his marriage, to get it behind them. But it seemed too strange to just launch into a big revelation about his personal life.

"Chris Farlow seems to be a pretty stand-up guy," Reese said after a few minutes. "Careful, but funny too."

"Yeah," Jessie said. "Chris is a good guy."

"Were ya'll ever an item?" Reese asked. It had just slipped out. He had wanted to ask her about Chris, and for that matter every other man that looked at her when they were out together.

"Oh, a long time ago," Jessie said slowly. "In high school we had something going on. But, of course, nothing ever came of it. We were from different worlds. He couldn't imagine coming over here and picking me up in his beat-up old car. And he wasn't going to ask me to his place. It was really no more than a tarpaper shack, and his dad always three sheets to the wind." She reined Rocket under some willows and dismounted, opening a water bottle and drinking. Reese dismounted and took the bottle she offered.

"So, he never married?"

Jessie laughed. "Oh, he's happily married. In fact you met his wife. Betty, the barmaid that was waiting on us–she's his wife."

Reese laughed. "Okay. I get it. He told me he wanted to meet me at the Granville because there was a waitress there he was trying to get lucky with."

"Yep, that's Chris," Jessie said, smiling.

"So all those drinks she kept bringing him?" Reese looked inquiringly at Jessie.

"Seltzer. He won't touch alcohol."

Reese nodded. "They seem to really like each other."

"I know. It makes you think it *can* happen, doesn't it." She had turned to face him. He knew he should tell her now.

"So what about you, Reese Kessler?" She smiled playfully at him. "I've told you my life story and everybody in this town's life story. You just blow in here knowing all about cows and water lines and waltzing me around the block–"

"I'm the other kind of married," Reese said quietly. He watched her smile fade. "The unhappy variety. Actually, I guess you could say I'm the just barely kind of married anymore." He waited to see her reaction, but she just continued to look at him, listening. "We've been separated over a year now."

"That's tough," she said. She turned and let her gaze lift out across the lake. They were quiet for a minute, as if each one was listening for the right thing to say, for the way forward. "Do you know what you want?" she asked.

"I'm starting to." He could feel the warmth of Jessie's shoulder just inches from his arm. "At first I was just waiting for her to come back so we could get on with our lives. But I'm ready to move on now. What we had got so stuck, I couldn't change it. I can't change it. I don't even want to anymore."

"Does she know what she wants?"

"I can't answer that," Reese said. "If she does, she sure can't talk to me about it."

"Kids?" Jessie asked, still staring out over the water.

"No. I thought we'd have kids, but we never did. I guess that makes it easier to go our separate ways."

Jessie nodded, and Reese turned toward her. She was biting her lower lip. She seemed remote. He waited. He watched her face until she turned to look at him. "I've been looking for a way to tell you that," he said. "I didn't want to presume that it would matter to you one way or another, but, I don't know—in case it might, I wanted to get it said."

She nodded again and the trace of a smile came back into her face. "We're a half hour or so from that cypress," she said, turning toward the horses. "How're your legs holding up?"

"Can't feel a thing," Reese joked.

"Wait til tomorrow," she laughed and swung onto Rocket.

She led the way along the dike now, and Reese watched her shoulders, level and square and softly swinging with her horse's rhythm. He felt relieved to have told her about his situation, but he wasn't at all sure how it left things between them. Her reaction was so contained, and he wasn't used to a woman with self-possession. Of course, it was possible she simply didn't care. But he thought he'd seen the subtle signs of her working to keep her balance. She might be mad. Some people didn't show their anger much, especially when they felt betrayed. On the other hand, maybe Jessie took for granted that his separation from Vivian could be completed without much further ado. But he knew that if Vivian got the idea that he wanted out, she might suddenly decide to block the exit. A week ago, he thought, he would've been glad of it. Now he couldn't imagine going on with the marriage. He supposed the other possibility with Jessie was that she liked him and might want to act on the attraction between them, but that she simply wasn't serious about getting involved. He'd seen women form that kind of liaison with Richard, enjoying each other for the duration of a job, then parting, apparently on friendly terms. Without expectations. It gave him a sinking feeling to consider the idea, and he knew he was incapable of that—at least with Jessie. Maybe with someone else, later on, if he ended up alone. He wondered, if that was the kind of thing she wanted, if he'd walk away, before he got in too deep, or go ahead with it, knowing it would make him miserable and crazy when she was ready to move on.

They passed the gully that had let them down into the ditch to rescue the yellow cow. He marveled that that was only a few days ago, and here he was now, riding along the dike on a horse, with Jessie. They paused for a moment to gaze down at the place where the cow had been stuck.

"Not much sign anything ever happened there," Reese said.

"Not from this distance anyway," Jessie said. She felt a sudden rush of blood to her face recalling his bare arms and shoulders. She wondered if he had already begun to step outside the bounds of his dead-end marriage. Men like him were hard to read. He seemed interested, and the kiss in Nick's parking lot had made her feel there was a lot of heat beneath the cool exterior. But he seemed cautious. She recognized that a restrained, deliberate course might be best with him, but she didn't feel like being cool and coy. She longed for the sort of directness with a man—or at least with Reese—that she had recovered in other aspects of her life since coming back to the ranch. She blushed again as she realized that sexually he made her feel quite reckless. Kissing in the parking lot at Nick's. What was she thinking? They rode on.

In a few minutes he saw her rein her horse in and glance back at him, gesturing at something ahead and off to the right. He brought Knuckle alongside her and Rocket.

"There's something weird up ahead, on the connector arm of the dike," she said. It looks like a big cave-in or something."

"Is that the boundary, where the dike ties back to the upland?"

"Yeah. The old cypress tree is just beyond that point. So that's pretty close to our boundary."

"And that's the Davis Ranch adjoining?"

"Right."

"Let's go see what's up."

They rode toward what looked like a huge cut in the dike. Within minutes it was apparent that it *was* a huge cut in the dike. Freshly turned-up sand formed an even pile on one side of a fifty-foot swath cut through nearly half the depth of the dike. On the waterward side, the lake water lapped against the dike about a foot below the cut. On the landward side, sand had run down from the cut and formed a rough descent to the bottom of the ditch running behind the dike. A single set of tracks dotted the sandy slope. They sat their horses and stared at the ruptured ground.

"Well I guess this solves two mysteries," Reese said.

"How old bossie got down in the ditch without killing herself," Jessie agreed. "Those are definitely cow tracks."

"Yep."

"And?"

"At the hearing yesterday when Red Greely was telling me about the cypress tree, someone said he better watch out or his 'handiwork' would be discovered," Reese explained. "He denied having anything to do with 'that there,' as he called it. I didn't want to ask what *that there* was, but I wondered what they were talking about."

Jessie nodded. "Yeah, I suspect this here is *that there.*"

"Chris warned me about this too. Said some members of the Far Out think the only way this dike'll come down is if they take it down. When I asked him how that would happen, he mentioned they had access to bulldozers. And dynamite. I don't know why I didn't realize he was tipping me off to something actually going on. I thought he was speculating."

Jessie pondered this information. "He probably doesn't know for sure—just hears things. Anyone doing this would know Chris wouldn't want any part of it. They might not even be sure he wouldn't turn them in."

"What are you going to do?" Reese asked her.

She leaned forward and stroked Rocket's neck mechanically. The grim concern on her face made him think of the day they'd hauled old Yeller out of the ditch, and he wondered if she would consider all the options and make a decision before she spoke. He wanted her to talk to him, but he suspected she would not be drawn into confidences she didn't feel sure of. He stepped down from his horse and began a closer examination of the ground.

In a minute she said quietly, "I don't know what to do." She dismounted and, drawing her horse along side Knuckle, dropped his rein and came to stand beside Reese. "I'm afraid this is going to set off a powder keg."

"Are you worried about what your father might do?" Reese asked.

"Actually, I was thinking of Bud," she said. "Even if he doesn't go ballistic over this, he'll want to put some of the hands out here at night to guard the dike. I'm afraid someone will get hurt."

"Maybe it would be a good idea to get the sheriff involved, put some deputies on it, instead of ranch hands," Reese suggested.

"That would be more sensible," Jessie responded, "but I don't know if he'll go for it. I should talk to dad and let him handle Bud. The way Bud's been lately, he's not far from accusing me of doing this."

"I take it the two of you aren't close," Reese said.

"He blames me for—things," she said. "I never mean to get in his way, but the truth is we just see the ranch so differently. If it was up to me, and it didn't affect anyone else, I *would* be out here cutting this damn thing down. I want him to have something that's his, but he's got his heart set on this golf course. And ever since I came back to the ranch I haven't been able to stop knowing—" she shook her head. "This dike shouldn't be here," she said.

Reese nodded. "Well, the State may be about to take a hand in things, and then it won't be up to Bud or you to decide what happens here."

"That would be a relief, at least for my conscience," she said wearily. "I'm not convinced Bud and Dad won't fight it though, and, from what I can see, that could tie things up for a long time." Reese was surprised at the despair in her voice.

"Would that affect your plans?" he asked.

"Bud's development plans take in over three hundred acres. It's some of the best grazing on the ranch."

"Is that with or without the dike?" Reese asked.

"It's less acres without the dikes," Jessie said, "but better grazing—especially in the drought years. The floodplain's wetter than anyplace upland—when it's not cut off from the lake. In dry weather that's sometimes the only grass we have."

"Sounds like you plan to keep ranching."

Jessie nodded. "Probably gravitate more toward the horses," she said. "But I'd like to keep the groves going too."

"You don't like cows?" Reese grinned at her.

"I like cows too much," Jessie said. "I have trouble sending them to market."

Reese laughed. "I was wondering if it was just a coincidence that you don't seem to eat steak."

Jessie sighed. "My family thinks I'm nuts," she smiled ruefully.

Reese chuckled. "When I worked around my granddad's place it bothered me to eat beef. I never did learn to do the butchering. I knew it made him ashamed of me, but I just couldn't do it. Here I'd been taking care of these animals for months, and then I was supposed to *kill* them and *eat* them."

Jessie laughed. "Isn't it funny that you can find your own family so strange in some ways? I wonder why we didn't accept that part of ranching when we loved everything else."

"It's a different sensibility," Reese said, shaking his head. "If you really like the animals you can't imagine harming them. Once I got away from them, I got to where I could eat beef. But in your shoes, I'd be right back to beans."

They led the horses back towards the toe of the perimeter dike, towards the cypress tree in the distance. Jessie followed behind Reese, tracing the clear angle of his shoulders against the languid blue sky. She didn't know what she was thinking, but she was beginning to like it.

She watched him examine the lone cypress tree. He brought out a small camera and photographed the watermarks. Then he measured the distance they were from the ground. They prodded the ground for evidence of the trees Steffee Ninehouse had described.

"I'll need to bring the crew out here next week," he said. "We'll shoot some elevations and do some soil borings. See if we get into any roots."

"How long do you think it will take," she asked.

"Finding the roots?"

"That, and the whole job." She looked away, down the lake to where the river coursed north to St. Augustine and Jacksonville.

"If the roots are here, we'll find them in a day. Altogether, I'm figuring another week to ten days should finish us up." He pronounced the words without inflection. She gazed out at the water west towards the bridge, where the lake narrowed and the river bent north. She seemed absorbed in thoughts that did not include him.

"Have you always lived here?" he asked. "Other than when you were married, I mean."

She turned slightly and he could see her expression soften. "Actually, I was born on this ranch. Mama couldn't get to the hospital because the bridge to town was out. Hurricane Donna had just come through here. Everything was flooded. All the phone lines were still down. It was a mess. Our house keeper, Juanita, delivered me." Jessie turned full toward him now, and he could see that her somber mood had lifted. "Juanita tells the story that Daddy paced a trough in the hall floor that night. At daybreak, he saddled his horse and rode out. He swam that flooded river and went twelve miles over all kinds of obstacles and debris to bring back the doctor. They landed on the front lawn in a helicopter."

"Your father's quite a man," Reese said.

"Of course, Mama and I were sleeping peacefully by the time he got back. But he couldn't know it was going to turn out that way."

"You know, men like him can be stubborn, but you can hardly ever fault them for being indecisive."

Jessie laughed. "No, I don't believe that's ever been one of my complaints."

It was such a good sound to hear her laugh. Reese watched her intently. "You know what I'd like, Jessie?"

She returned his look for a long moment, as if she were mulling over the possibilities.

"I'd like to watch you train your horse. I'd like to see how you get him ready for competition."

He could see no change in her expression, but he sensed a shift: The turning of gears too obscure and complex for him to know the meaning of, the tumbling of pins at the nudge of a key, the unlocking of floodgates. She raked her teeth over her lower lip and gathered Rocket's reins.

"Can we have lunch first? Juanita wants to meet you. I think she has a crush on you."

April 13, p.m.

I should have been tired when I got home, but there was so much to do I couldn't think of sleeping. My mind kept toying with Mel's little joke about Logan stalking me. It seemed almost to make sense of something, but every time I tried to think it through, something about his suspicion of me began nagging my mind, and I could never figure out what it explained. Whatever I sensed between us definitely had the quality of a moving target. I told myself the investigation would be over soon. He would have run through all the possible leads, nothing would turn up, and he would get involved in other cases, fading back into a life completely invisible to me.

I had embarked on this line of thinking as a way of calming my sense of uncertainty, but it didn't give me any relief. There was something unusual about Logan Deo that attracted me, and I would be sorry when I could no longer look forward to his bright glance, the peculiar cadence of his speech, his tall, agile frame stepping through the door into my house. I cautioned myself for the umpteenth time that I didn't know him, that I should be wary of that feeling that something was going on beneath the surface. But even as I said these things to myself I argued back that those hidden stirrings were exactly how you knew you were attracted to someone. I'm just saying it *could* be that, I argued. Why do you always have to be so guarded? Well, because I've made mistakes in the past, I responded, and it hurt. So you're just going to shimmy through the years not taking any risks and not getting hurt and having nada for a life? Stop. Just stop. You don't even know what you're trying to figure out.

Nothing seemed anchored. I have no idea if that condition acts as such a stimulant on people who aren't researchers, but in anyone with my habits of mind, it's like sand in your eye. You just can't forget it. And you keep rubbing it and messing with it until you sort it out or go blind.

I fed Willow and sat down in the den. "Ok," I said when she came to join me, "say the first thing that comes into your mind." She jumped on my lap and settled. "What is it with Logan Deo?" She began to purr. "You're so easy," I told her. "But come on. Something is not quite right. Right? I mean, face it, he talks funny. If he's a local cop, I'll eat your tail." Willow stretched and yawned. I put her on the ottoman and, sliding into my desk chair, booted up my internet search engine. I typed in "Tallahassee Police Department" and hit the search button. The site had personnel listings, but only the supervisors of each division were named. I backed up to the search engine again and typed "Logan Deo." I don't know what I expected. A listing from a college fraternity? Decorated war vets?

In seconds I got back five sites. Two seemed to be computer companies in Yugoslavia—which, as far as I could tell, had recently been wiped off the globe by ethnic wars and so was now usually referred to as the *former* Yugoslavia. Anyway I couldn't read the language. I copied a block of type that seemed to be contained in both sites and plugged it into the translator of my search engine. But the only choices it offered were translations from French, German or Italian. German seemed the closest, so I picked that. But the results were less than great. Only a few phrases translated at all. Nevertheless they were a little out of the ordinary. The original looked like this:

Bežični uređaj za borbu protiv terorista

Mali uređaj, nalik na pejdžer, kome je pre mesto u aktovci nekog japija, nego na opasaču policajca, mogao bi postati važno oružje u borbi protiv terorizma.

Bostonski međunarodni aerodrom Logan, prvi je aerodrom u SAD na kome se testira uređaj BlackBerry, koji će omogućiti daljinski pristup državnim i federalnim kriminalističkim bazama podataka

Uređaj je delo stručnjaka kanadske kompanije Research in Motion (RIM), a u upotrebi je još od 1999. godine. Dosad su ga uglavnom koristili poslovni ljudi za proveru e-pošte i krstarenje Webom dok su van svojih kancelarija.

Uređaj koji se testira na aerodromu Logan deo je paketa u kome se nalazi i softver što omogućava policajcima da šalju šifrirane upite policijskim bazama podataka i da od njih prime odgovor za manje od jednog minuta.

The "translated" version looked almost identical except for the two passages that contained the word "Logan." (So much for free translaters.) Those passages looked like this:

Bostonski me?unarodni aerodrom Logan, prvi ever aerodrom u SAD well kome SE test Irish Republican Army ure?aj BlackBerry, koji?e omogu?iti daljinski pristup dr?avnim i federalnim kriminalisti?kim bazama podataka.

Ure?aj koji SE test Irish Republican Army well aerodromu Logan deo ever paketa u kome SE nalazi i?to omogu?ava policajcima there?alju?ifrirane upite policijskim bazama podataka i there od njih prime odgovor za manje od jednog minuta.

It was a tantalizing peek into a complete mystery. I couldn't decide if it was a letter addressed to terrorists or some type of software designed to keep your computer safe from terrorists, but it seemed a bit ominous that the "translation" kept inserting the phrase "test Irish Republican Army" in the passages containing the word "Logan." But when I checked the original, I realized it was translating "testira" as "test IRA," and I decided the whole thing was just a silly coincidence. It did strike me as weird, though, that I could only get to that page by searching for "Logan Deo." When I went to the website home page and tried to find the "Logan" page, it didn't seem to exist. In addition the "translated" site warned me that "host 200.617.899.340 is not authorized."

The other three sites I found were in English, and they all seemed to refer to some guy who was a faculty member at Brussels School of International Studies in 1996. "Well, well," I told Willow. "That would certainly explain his weird speech if he were a Yugoslavian emigrant to the Deep South via Brussels." Willow didn't seem to find this lead especially promising. "Ok, I admit. TPD probably doesn't have a need just yet for an international relations expert." I gave it up. Somehow, my curiosity about Logan Deo felt too much like an attempt to avoid my life. Just like creepboy said.

Poor Teena (trying to understand hard stuff):
But doctor, why must everything devolve into romance?
Creepboy (sitting behind the analyst's desk in a false mustache):

So you won't notice all the awful shit that's really going on in your life, my dear. Especially the fact that **nothing** is going on in your life, that you are dying of loneliness, that you have a *cat* for a roommate, that you are losing your case.

Poor Teena:

I like my cat.

What I really needed to do was contemplate a response to creepboy. If there should even be a response. I realized that Logan and I hadn't discussed how or if I should acknowledge his little communiqué. Still it couldn't hurt to work on it. I could discuss it with him later.

I decided that I should develop a couple of different reactions, one submissive and meek, one that let fly in his *very* face that he had picked on the wrong girl-child. I was in the mood for the latter, but I tried to sketch out a meek little note.

Dear Ed Itori,

Thank you for your interest in my work. I am trying to think through what you've suggested and understand how to make improvements, but I have a few questions maybe you could help me with. Do you know where I could get a copy of that book you talked about—*Madame Boviney* was it? I don't read French, so I would need a translation. Also, is there a biography on Gustave I should read? You make his life sound very inspirational. Anyway, I don't seem to have a copy of my manuscript to work from. Could you send me something with your comments, you know, done like in yellow highlights or something, so I can see what you mean? I know what you mean about the romantic stuff. It's almost a modern Romeo and Juliet, don't you think? Well, I've taken up enough of your time but like I said I don't have a copy so if you could just send me one from the one you've got I've got lots of great ideas you're going to love.

Ya!
Toddy Shoss

p.s. that's my nom de plum—and I told you I couldn't speak French! "Hahaha"

Well, like I said, I tried. I just didn't have the meek thing going on. I decided to go for the literary smart-ass version.

Eddie—or perhaps I should call you Gussy—

Thanks for reminding me of Flaubert's little dodge. It was good for a laugh. And I appreciate your rather cryptic comment about my writing "drivel." I take it from your juxtaposition of this comment with the GF anecdote that you find my writing old-fashioned, un-*writerly*, if I may so misconstrue a distinction provided by one of my—and, what must be, your—favorite critics. So interesting to contemplate.

Based solely on your objection to my "heroine falling in love with her father's enemy" and "galloping around on horses," I surmise that you have limited your critical attention to subject matter. How quaint. Of course you are quite right that Flaubert's groundbreaking novel contrasted the antithetical themes of romance and realism.

Galloping horses, swooning damsels, deserted pavilions, and all manner of big horrible stuff is everything Emma—that is to say Romance, while Realism fattens its ribs on the here and now, on weak emotions, and material, physical objects. It feeds on boredom, monotony, logic, and tiny little grotesque details.

As I'm sure you know, Emma believes herself to be in one type of novel, while Flaubert has entrapped her in the other, and so *Madame Bovary* provides the most obvious contrast of romance and realism. Again, I congratulate you on your perception of this literary dichotomy. However—and I'm sure you would agree if you'd ever thought about it— Flaubert's real achievement lay not in conceiving this simple thematic contrast but in his invention of the means to embody it artistically. . . .

At this point I was interrupted by my email chime. I quickly glanced to see I had a message from LDeo@aol.com. I decided to press on with my creepboy manifesto while I was in high preachy bitch mode.

. . . His most obvious authorial problem lies in the fact that his character, Emma Bovary, never achieves the perception expected of the reader.

So Flaubert's particular quandary lay in how to convey to a reader what he knows about the situation of the characters that they themselves never understand. Emma, after all, *defines* a character who could not understand *Madame Bovary*—who would read the story, dear me, as *tragedy*.

What was poor Gustave to do? His story is one in which nothing happens. Events aren't emphasized. It's how the events appear to the characters that's important; *i.e.*, the characters' point of view—the internal perception of events, rather than events themselves.

Never fear! He would develop a technique! It would allow him to step into the thoughts of his characters! It would become a mainstay of modern literature!! We would call it *free indirect discourse!!!*

But I'm sure you are too bored with all this twaddle, and—to quote a new correspondent of mine—How *droll* of me to go on so!

And never to have even addressed your kind attempt to provoke me! I shall I WILL I d o P R O M I S E to look to matters écriture. In the mean time, how about returning my files—with your editorial comments if you must—so I will have something to look-to with.

Your thankful subject,
Em On-the-Loose

Oh, and let me let me *pant drool* give the thought for the day: *Romance* is the opiate of the artist. YARYARYAR!! HEEHEE!

I didn't know if creepboy would ever see that, but I felt better. I'd like to see his face, I thought, if he did ever read it. I bet that would cool his jets.

I pulled up Logan's email. Was it too late to call? He had been unavoidably detained on another matter, but he would like to go on with our work. It was 9:45. I hit reply and wrote: Call or come by. I'm up.

Ok. I couldn't help it. I brushed my hair and changed my shirt. I was debating about changing it again when the doorbell sounded.

Wow, that was fast, I thought. He must've been just around the corner. I went to the door trying to remember how to act normal. Not crying or barfing. That would be different.

He looked wonderful walking into my house in a black jacket, pulling in the crisp April air. "Hi," he said in a happy voice. "I brought sustenance in case I could persuade you to imbibe." He handed me a bag with what seemed to be bottles inside. "Actually this is something special a friend just brought me today from New York. You can't get it here. Are you by any chance a brew aficionado?"

"I've been known to investigate the underside of a table or two," I said. All of a sudden I felt great. We went to the kitchen and I pulled out the bottles. Belle-Vue Kriek. "Wow. I've never seen this. What is it?"

"It's a lambic made in Belgium. Black cherry. Full, dry. Best in snifters, if you have them."

I brought out Gramma Shossie's snifter glasses. Somehow the moment seemed portentous.

"I should warn you," he said. "This kicks."

"Ok, I'll just slip into my armor."

"No, don't do that," he said quickly. He poured. It was a striking ruby red. The foam was as creamy and pink as a cloud in a daydream. He lifted his glass to me in a silent toast to enjoyment. I drank. It was delicious. A slight effervescence prickled my tongue and what I thought was going to be a too sweet taste evolved quickly into a clean, dry finish. "Hmmmmmnnnmn. How wonderful." I smiled. He smiled. A spark went through the air.

"Well. I thought we should give some thought to what we might be overlooking. Your lecture on Barthes got me worried about what we might be missing."

"Sorry to be long-winded. Nothing worse than a teacher. They never stop lecturing."

"Not at all. It's completely refreshing to talk with people who care about such things—and know about them." We gravitated to the den. I already felt floaty. I sat down in front of my computer where my draft to creepboy was up on the screen. Logan settled on the ottoman in good position to view the screen.

"I've been drafting responses. I thought maybe something in-your-face, a little preachy and condescending might be a good strategy.

But I want to do one really meek and submissive too. I'm finding that a challenge, but the idea is, you know, to sort of think through the reception each one might get. As a way of thinking at all."

He nodded. "Good. May I?"

I scrolled to the top of the first draft and turned the screen slightly so he could see better, pushed the mouse within his reach. Then I sat watching his face as he read. I might not get to see creepboy read it, I thought, but this was actually more fun. What in the world would Logan Deo think of such letters? From the delight that began to dawn over his face, I surmised he could enjoy the Valley-girl goofiness of the first and the sarcastic contempt of the second. I drank some more of the ruby red Kriek. At one point he laughed outright and said without taking his eyes off the screen, "You are one bad woman." I knew it was foolish to be so pleased, but come on. Anybody who's ever been lonely knows what a pushover you can get to be for a little attention. Besides, it was pretty unusual for anyone to care enough to follow a literary argument. Only my best teacher and one or two of my most talented students would've cared remotely about such matters. I felt a pang of longing go through me as Logan sat back and smiled. "Well that would make a definite impression. You might never see your files again. But he wouldn't make the mistake of thinking you a helpless lass all adrift in the world."

"On the other hand, it might interest him" I said. "I was thinking we might even lure him out. I could offer to meet him once we get into the thick of all these literary arguments."

"Hmmm. So what response would you hope to get from this letter?"

"I'd want to—as you say—sort of set him on his heels. Goad him. The stuff about Flaubert's strategy for writing *Madame Bovary* should evoke some kind of comeback. Even if he has to do a bunch of research. The thing is, though, not just everyone has had the insight into that book that I'm pointing to. I had an unusually gifted professor in narrative theory, who taught in France, and he taught me this book. So creepboy's going to have to go a bit to get up to speed. If he really is someone who lives in literature, though, he should bite. He should want to discuss Flaubert's unmasking techniques."

"What about Barthes? Is that first little bit a push on that button?"

"Yeah, a little one. The distinction of *writerly texts* was Barthes'. So I'm just baiting him a little there to see if he realizes I've recognized his bent."

"Without naming names."

"It's possible he doesn't even know who he's quoting, especially if he's pulling this stuff off the chats or just surfing the web for literary theory.

"Ok. So we might get him focused on the literary arguments and lure him out into the open. But he may respond coarsely, or even violently, if he's already getting out of his element. You should be prepared for that."

"Ok." I paused. "Do you know something about this guy? I mean is this someone you've been trying to catch—has he done something—"

"I know this," Logan said hastily. "We should keep trying to figure out what he wants, who he is. He may be involved in some crazy stuff, and I want to get him. In the mean time, I was wondering if there's anyone you could get to stay with you. I'd like it if you had better security."

"One of my friends at work is going to loan me a gun."

"Do you know how to use a gun?"

"A little. We're going to the range tomorrow."

"And you trust this guy."

"Absolutely."

"Ok." He drank the rest of his Kriek and got up.

I had a sudden panic that he was going. "So what's next?"

"We need sustenance," he grinned, continuing to the kitchen. He brought back two more bottles and poured. "You seem to have an unusual education," he said, settling down in the armchair. "Have you always lived here?"

"I traveled around a bit. I had the wanderlust in my twenties. College came second. I'd move somewhere I wanted to go, and if I stayed long enough I'd enroll in the university."

"What was your favorite place?"

"Bloomington, Indiana. The limestone quarries there are spectacular. Clear, deep water, towering hardwood forests. The campus feels medieval in some mysterious way. Where did you go to school?"

"I was," he paused, "several places—like you. I liked moving around. But I finally finished at South Florida." He spun his fingertip around the top of his glass. I was betting the next thing he said wouldn't be more about him. "Did you ever go abroad?" he asked.

"Not for school. I went over to visit my ex-husband a couple of times—when we were married."

"He always worked overseas?"

"When we first married he was based in Orlando. We actually met working on this case I'm about to lose."

"The hot potato?"

"Yeah. His company had done some engineering designs for the landowner, so I went to his office to grill him on the details."

"And that didn't put him off."

"He's not easily put off."

"Where did you visit him when you went over?"

"The first time he met me in London. That was fun. But things were hard because, you know, I wanted more out of the marriage. I was young."

"It sounds like a hard way to be married."

"It was. But I might do things differently now. Just relax and enjoy what there was. There was a lot good about Mack. But that's just talk. Mack liked his freedom too much to be married. He thought he liked me better than his freedom, but he didn't."

"When did you go back?"

"Actually we were divorced by the next time I went. I went to Greece last year with my mother. She likes to go abroad. She and Mack are great friends. She always sees him when she's in Europe. Anyway, Mack was in Egypt working and he couldn't get away, so he made arrangements for us to come to Cairo for a week. He sent a company plane to pick us up. We had a great time. Rode horses in the desert, right by the Giza Pyramids—although I have to say I was pretty disappointed to find KFC and Pizza Hut, right across the street from the Great Pyramid, adding their glow to the skyline. But, I got to go sailing on the Nile. Ate tons of Baba Ghannong. Mack took us all over the place—I even went on the job with him for a couple of days. He knew I'd be interested in the ecology. He was designing a reservoir system for fish farming in the desert that worked off deep wells. We'd go to this little restaurant at night where all his crew went to eat.

That's when I knew I'd done the right thing to divorce him. We were finally able to just be what we were to each other. It was a relief."

We were silent for a moment. I was trying to decide if Logan's questions were part of his investigation or if they were the kind of normal friendly overtures people make in order to get to know each other. I found myself once again trying to figure out how to ask him more about his life.

"Ok," he said. "I know of no reason why you shouldn't send that last letter. The feisty one. And then let's see what happens."

"Yeah, you think?"

"Let's see if this guy knows his stuff or if he's just full of hot air."

I positioned the mouse pointer over 'send' and pressed the clicker slowly as if it were a trigger unleashing events of unfathomable consequence.

"Now," he said, sprawling back into the armchair and propping his feet on the ottoman, "teach me about free indirect discourse. I believe you characterized it as the most intimate form of discourse a writer could place in the mind of a character. How does it work?"

"You're kidding, right?"

"Not at all, unless you think I can't fathom—"

"No, no." For some reason my heart was thumping wildly. "Just remember you asked for this." I swiveled my chair to face him, took a moment to collect my thoughts. I could feel the beer making me garrulous. On his face was an expression of excited anticipation mixed with playfulness and, well, sincerity. The implications of it were dizzying. "Basically free indirect discourse is all about the author being able to move in and out of a character's point of view. It allows the reader to see the character's emotion and perspective, while making it distinct from the author's perceptions. For example, in *Madame Bovary,* the character Léon, who is a fairly naïve clerk in a small town, is trying to make up his mind to move to Paris. As Flaubert is writing, the scene moves increasingly from Flaubert's point of view into Léon's, from Flaubert's narrative voice into the character's voice, from written language to spoken language. So when Flaubert writes about Léon: What would prevent him going to Paris? He would lead the life of an artist! we know this is Léon's view of the world, not Flaubert's. Flaubert would have some answers to the question of what would prevent Léon going to Paris, and he would have a very different idea of the life Léon would lead there. The exclamation point—He would lead the life of an artist!—" I stroked my finger through the air and jabbed a dot beneath, "registers Léon's excitement, not Flaubert's." I paused. "Had enough?"

Logan shook his head, poured more Kriek. "Show me how he does it."

I pulled a notebook and pen from my desk drawer and moved over to the ottoman so Logan could see the page. "Well, you want to make the discourse sound spoken. At the same time it needs to keep many of the characteristics of written narration. So you blend elements of a direct quote and an indirect quote. In a direct quote the writer would write:

Léon thought, "I will lead the life of an artist!"

In an indirect quote the writer would write:

Léon thought that he would lead the life of an artist.

Free indirect discourse uses the pronoun and verb tense from the indirect quote:

<u>He</u> <u>would lead</u> the life of an artist!

And uses the punctuation of emotion from the direct quote (!)—but not the quotation marks or the speech tag identifying who's speaking. That makes it an interesting blend of something spoken but also something internal, narrated. You can see how it opens the door to the kind of internal monologues that flourish in modernism."

"Why is it called 'free'?"

"I think because of its freedom from the speech tags—the 'he said' kind of denotation. It just doesn't need that because it isn't something you could carry on a dialogue in. It's for moving inside a character."

"You mean I can't talk to you in free indirect discourse? We should try," Logan giggled. "How would it go? I would make captain by Christmas! By jove!"

"Wait," I laughed, "are you the author or the character? Because you have to use the pronoun of the indirect quote. So if you're the author—the narrator—it would be, 'He would make captain by Christmas!'"

"No, no," Logan laughed, grabbing my arm, "it's a dialogue. The direct quote would be, 'I said, "I will make captain by Christmas!"' The indirect quote *in a conversation* would be: You said you would make captain by Christmas. So the free indirect quote would be: You would make captain by Christmas!"

"I think you're inventing a new form. Am I the author when you speak and vice versa?"

"Hmmmmnn. Maybe so. So we now have a shifting narrator—"

"And character. Alternating actually. This is the way it sounds when I argue with myself—"

"Right. So we would be creating each other—which would be fine until we started trying to finish each other's sentences," Logan laughed.

"Then I would say: You would make captain by Christmas! and then you would say—"

"What would prevent me—my—you're joining me—you—? in Paris!" We were getting beside ourselves with silliness.

"We've devolved into simple conditional tense," Logan said.

"Don't you mean conventional sense?" I asked inanely.

"Oh!" Logan shouted breathlessly, "we haven't done we yet. How would you make the indirect quote of we? We wondered what would prevent us joining ____! What? us?"

"No. Each other. In Paris."

"Right, right—"

"For Christmas!!" we both shouted.

We were giddy on lambic and language. I was practically sitting in his lap. We were laughing. Then he drew me into the big armchair beside him and his mouth closed over mine with the deep sweetness of black cherry. I could feel his body conforming to mine, his hands pressing into my back. He held me against him for a moment, my face next to his chest, and I breathed the tantalizing scent of his body. Suddenly he swung his legs off the ottoman and stood up. "I better go before I do something I shouldn't," he said. "I apologize."

I sat up. "No, it's okay. Don't be sorry." I wasn't sure whether he was apologizing for the kiss or for leaving.

He folded his hands into a little church and covered his mouth with the index finger steeple, his dark eyes surveying me as if I were an unexpected cause for alarm. "Ok, I'll call you tomorrow and we'll look at the chat rooms where this guy might've picked you up."

"Logan, tell me what this is about."

He gave me an intensely pained look as if I had asked him to betray himself utterly. "I'll see you tomorrow," he said. "Lock the door." Then he picked up his coat, went down the hall, and out the front door.

I lay there for a while wondering what it would be that finally made me get up. I could feel the black maw of despair close by, licking its chops. Just when I thought things were getting clearer they kept getting more muddled. I called out to Willow, but either she was asleep or she'd gone outside. Grandma Shossie's mantle clock ticked softly, and I found myself longing for my novel, the slow steady time of writing I had found so healing over the past months. I thought about Reese Kessler, how much he wanted his life to straighten out and be something solid—with someone, not just emptiness and problems. Problems would be okay with someone to talk them over with. With with with. The word slumped into nonsense.

I needed to talk to someone. There were times you either called someone or you lost it. I picked up my cell phone and put in a call to Mack. It was 11:45, so I figured I'd wake him up, but he answered like he'd already had his usual gallon of coffee. "Hey darlin', I knew you'd come crawling back someday wantin' me to take you in and forgive all. Make me an offer I can't refuse."

"You old horse's ass, you called me," I said, delighted to hear his crazy gruffness beaming from the other side of the world. "How's the water?"

"Fine if you like it salty. Hard to come by if you like it straight. What're you doing these days?"

"Same old same old. Literally. Can you believe I'm still working on the Lake Ponder case?"

"Good god, you were working on that when I met you. How long ago is that—1991?"

"Somewhere in there. '92 I think. Where are you anyway?"

"Kuwait tonight. I'm supervising four projects though, so I rove."

"That suits you."

"Yeah, well, it gets a little old sometimes. Listen, Teena, are you doing all right? Everything okay?"

"Yeah, for the most part. I've been told to give my case away to those dirtbag clients of yours who diked the marsh. Somebody came in and stole my hard drive out of my computer this week."

"Really. Any leads on that?" It struck me as odd that he didn't seem very surprised.

"Whoever did it is e-mailing me."

"What?"

"Yeah, he seems to have taken all my files as a way to get my attention. But I don't know for what exactly. Lots of smoke and mirrors."

"Well the reason I called you is to give you a heads-up on something. It may be nothing, but I thought you'd better know. This hasn't been reported in the press and I'm not sure how it's being handled, so probably best to keep a lid on it for now."

"Ok," I said, wondering what in Mack's world could possibly pertain to me.

"We had an incident over in Peshawar where somebody contaminated a reservoir with a nasty little bio-hazardous critter—fonseria something, I think. Killed a bunch of livestock—which was only good because it warned the people in the village that something was wrong. Still, two women died later who'd been to the reservoir that morning. A few days later a guy came to see me about what projects BioLogos had in the area. I wasn't sure at first if he wanted to contract us to help with the investigation or if I was being investigated. Maybe some of both."

That, I thought, seemed vaguely familiar.

"Anyway, this guy was asking me all kinds of questions—what kind of systems we design, what kind of security—stuff like that. He wanted to know how I hired people for my field crews, if there was any kind of background check. Anyway, I gave him access to all my files in case he might be able to find something. He was there all day and half the night going through it and we got sort of chummy. Apparently he had looked at my file and saw an old form of who to notify in case of emergency—you know the kind of thing. It had your name on it and the number at DEP. He asked me about you, what kind of work you did at DEP. I was a little in my cups and I rattled on about all the stuff you're involved in. Anyway, later I got nervous about all that talking. I mean, I really didn't know this guy from Adam. And I realized he had set me up to yammer on like that. I think I kinda got slicked. I'm embarrassed to have to say it, but I thought I should let you know."

"Was he with an agency or what?" I had a knot in my stomach the size of a rat.

"I'm remembering CIA or UN, but it might've been some French agency. I overheard him talking to someone in French on his cell and I asked him where he was from. He said he grew up in Paris, his parents were in the diplomatic corps. Canadian maybe or American, I'm not sure. I didn't half pay attention. I didn't really care, you know, hell, I was just trying to help him out. Besides, he probably wouldn't give me a straight story about his personal life."

"He might, if he's who he says he is. I mean, don't those people have friends too?"

"Yeah, you're right. It was probably just the way he got me talking too much that made me nervous. And then when I thought about it, I started remembering talking a lot about you, and you know, it worried me."

"Thanks, Mack. I appreciate you looking out for me."

"Sure darlin', you know I'd be better if I could."

"Mack, do you think he really was CIA or something—you know official, governmental? You don't think he was acting on his own, right?"

"Well I have to admit I hadn't thought of that. I hope to hell he wasn't, 'cause I sure spilled the beans on all these reservoirs I'm building. Maybe I better try to get a hold of someone and ask 'em."

"I think it would be a good idea."

"Good lord, Teena, what was I thinking? And this biohazard thing—frisea or fonsiara, whatever—apparently it has to percolate in a reservoir to get to a toxic condition. It's harmless in rivers unless it gets pooled up somewhere first. I hate to think that I just showed him every reservoir site in the Middle East. Shit. I better get on the phone right now."

"Mack, let me know, okay? And be careful."

"You bet darlin'. *You* be careful. Bye-de-bye."

I was wide-awake now. I needed to think and think good. If Mack's guy was legit, we would know soon enough. But still, someone had poisoned a reservoir in Pakistan with a bio-hazardous agent, and it seemed somehow linked to BioLogos. I realized I should've asked Mack when it happened, when the guy showed up to investigate it. I should have gotten a description.

I thought about Mack's concern regarding me. It seemed far-fetched at first, but, like him, the more I thought about it the more I wondered if there was some connection to my files being stolen. It couldn't hurt to pass the information on. I thought about telling Logan. Emailing him or calling the number on his card. But it felt too much like chasing after him. I could still taste his kiss on my tongue, and a sharp longing went through me. Damn him. I didn't need one more unavailable man playing kiss and run.

I dialed the Tallahassee Police Department and asked for Officer Kirkland. The receptionist put me through to the desk sergeant.

"That'll be a long distance call," he said. "Officer Kirkland's off fishing in Alaska. Do you need an officer or were you just looking for him?"

"I have some information that might pertain to a break-in he worked last week at my home."

"No ma'm, that would be somebody else. Tom's been retired two months."

My heart began pounding in my ears. "What about Detective Deo?"

"Deo? Hmmmn."

I heard him take the phone away from his mouth and call to someone, "Hey Charlie, there someone upstairs named Deo?" I heard a voice reply, but I couldn't quite make out what he was saying. Then the sergeant came back on the line. "I can give you his voice mail ma'm."

"Thank you, I have that number." I hung up. My breath was coming in short, shallow gasps like a cat I once saw dying of heat stroke. I dialed Mel's number, got her machine. "Mel, it's me. There's something—" I'd started to tell her there was something fishy going on with this investigation when it dawned on me my phone might be tapped. I shut my mouth so fast I bit my tongue. "Call me. Um. Yeah, or come over."

Then I picked up my cell phone and punched in the number on Logan Deo's card. His machine identified him as Detective Deo. Leave a voice mail, he said. I hung up and sat there for a moment trying to empty my mind of impressions and longings. Trying to focus only on what scientists like to call "sure knowledge." It didn't add up to much, but there had been some flags along the way I had ignored. I went through the house turning out lights in the order of someone going to bed. Then I came back through the den and stepped out through the French doors into the side yard. The night was cool and pleasant. I gripped my cell phone, feeling my pulse throb against the hard plastic. I made my way around the block, skirting the lighted streets, to the back of the triplex across the street from my house. There were three cars in the parking lot, all unfamiliar. I tried the back entrance door. It opened. To my left there was a staircase. I started up. On the second floor landing I heard voices coming down the hall, and I hurried on to the next turn in the stairs then waited. Two women came onto the landing chatting about a trip they had either taken or were going to take. They went down and out the back door.

I stood there for several minutes trying to decide what I was doing. Did I really want to know whatever it was I might find out on this little escapade? As I debated this question I found myself creeping upwards, listening, then opening the door onto the landing of the top floor apartment. The landing was completely empty. No flower pots, no mat. No sound came from inside. I stuck my ear to the door and hit the redial on my cell phone. Inside I heard the telephone chirp three times, then the answering machine whirred and Logan's voice instructed me to leave a message.

I plunged back down the steps into the lighted street. A man was walking his dog half a block away. A car was backing out of a driveway three doors down. Everything looked perfectly normal, except it wasn't. Logan Deo was spying on me. And he wasn't alone. The question was, who the hell were they and what in god's name did they expect to find out from me? I ran home through my side yard and stepped back through the windows into the den. Who should I call? TPD? Were they really the police?

I wanted to call Steve in the worst way. He would know everything already. We were old comrades-in-arms; he knew so well how to bolster me, help me think things through. If Logan was government, i.e., legit, what did they suspect me of? If he wasn't, who was he and what was he using me for? I wanted to know the answers. I wanted to believe I was safe. But I knew the only one who could really tell me was Logan.

Or maybe that's what he wanted me to think. I curled up in my big chair and pulled my knees up to my chin. Sitting there in the dark I willed all the pieces to fall into place. Clearly Logan was somehow connected with TPD, but not in a regular way. And if Tom Kirkland really was a retired cop, and that really had been Tom Kirkland who came to my house, then some kind of investigation was going on. But it was becoming increasingly clear that I was the one being watched. If I was my political enemy and I wanted to stop me from crucifying him, I would find a way to destroy my credibility. This had to be about work. It had to be tied to Lake Ponder. Someone with clout was after my scalp, and they had the connections to pull in some chits with the local police. The question was then, who had broken into my house? Had creepboy really stolen my hard drive, or was that all part of a ruse to get the so-called police into my house? I buried my face against the tweedy upholstery of the chair and I caught a whiff of Logan's tantalizing scent. A hot flush of embarrassment flooded my face and I felt the prickle of tears in my nose. That kiss was a lie. Just part of the business of getting involved with me, keeping me off balance so I wouldn't put it together. Damn him damn him damn him.

I probably had lain there for half an hour when my email chime sounded. I shifted around enough to see the screen. It was Ed Itori. Just what I needed.

Dearest Em-OTL,
As you so rightly point out, language is never innocent.

[That had to be a direct quote from Barthes—maybe *Writing Degree Zero*. So. He had correctly deciphered my Barthes allusion. What a smart little creepboy!]

So perhaps you would agree that *Madame Bovary* is a hopelessly snooty book. Flaubert takes up the stance of 19th century science—that of a god standing above and outside its subjects. Yet, his writing is also indicative of a terribly conflicted author. His tale, in the end, isn't really about romance but stupidity—that particular brand of stupidity that manifests as a failure to acknowledge the broad sweep of life. As such, one has to admit that the book fails as an indictment of romance. Instead, Flaubert indicts society by creating Realism—the literary form necessary to render the boorish and crass bourgeoisie. But neither he, nor anyone else, could conceive a woman of intelligence in the milieu of this novel. He sacrificed Emma to scarify his own hope for love. Perhaps it made him an artist, but I consider him a coward. Of course he invented techniques that came to characterize modern sensibility. Free indirect discourse, unmasking, double perspective. Am I supposed to be grateful? Why do these things always only expose us as callous fools with small tepid lives not fit for cockroaches?

It's true I did chide you for your heroine galloping around, falling in love. But this is only evidence of my own hopelessly conflicted position. I was in earnest when I told you I wanted more. Not different more. Just more, only more. When I decried your work as a "little romance," I secretly was bemoaning your reticence. I know you are afraid Jessie and Reese will lose themselves in love, will become laughable in the eyes of the world, will overtake all the artistry of your work. But my cautionary tale of Flaubert was meant to warn you not to follow in his steps. The world may think a man wise who forgoes love, but I know him to be the most wretched of creatures. I stole your work because it seemed to me the only way I could ever say these things to anyone. To someone who would hear them. And because I hoped by losing your work you would realize your work. I want you to write the story Flaubert denied Emma.

Your devoted,
Eddie

The letter left me completely bumfoozled. What in the blooming hills was I supposed to make of that? It was smart—very smart. This guy knew Barthes, all right, and a lot of other stuff too. But it was uncanny how he'd recognized the anxiety I'd felt about the romance between Jessie and Reese. The whole tone of the letter seemed so human—a complete turnaround from the scary creepboy. Just like the friend Logan had warned me he might try to be. And yet the message struck me as deeply earnest. In fact, how could you fake such sentiments? A person spent years getting the kind of education that would produce such a letter. Here was a person who loved literature, who cared about the ideas in the world that shape us. And who wasn't afraid to speak of love as a problem for literature, a problem for writing, a problem for me. Maybe he was an academic after all. But how was he connected to all this madness? Was he part of the whole scheme to get me? No. He couldn't be. No one capable of writing that letter could be part of a mean, low plot. Of course, there was always the possibility that I was being duped—just like Emma Bovary—into thinking I knew what book I was in.

I re-read the letter slowly and by the time I finished I had the strangest sense of calm. I went through the darkened house to my room and found Willow already asleep on the bed. I curled up beside her and slept until noon.

Chapter Seven

"So, we weave through these seven poles, just walking, trying to keep his balance on all four feet. Once he can do that, we trot it." Jessie explained the exercise as she guided Rounder through the grid. "Horses are just like people—they have a strong and a weak side. When he turns towards his weak side he tends to fall onto his outside shoulder and it's hard to turn him. When he turns to his strong side, he tends to fall into the turn, and that's when he'll hit a pole and bring it down." Sure enough, as the horse came around to the right, he bumped the pole, and it wobbled precariously.

"I'll be your ground guy," Reese said. "If you knock something over, I'll stand it back up." He watched, fascinated, as Jessie urged the colt with her legs, trying to convey to him the idea of a different posture in his body. He could see the colt trying to understand her as he turned from side to side, working his way through the line of poles. Reese felt he could almost see the neural pathways taking shape in the horse, the learned responses forming, the understanding deepening. It was an amazing way to make a partnership, the two bodies and brains merging into one centaur-like being.

After a few turns through the grid, Jessie asked Reese to close up the distance between each pole. "That'll make it more challenging for him. He's so smart, I have to work to stay one step ahead of him." As Reese moved the poles, she cantered the horse around the arena, letting him stretch out, then bringing him back to a short lope, before letting him go again. When she came back to the poles Reese could see that the colt was much handier going through the grid than he had been earlier in the lesson. Even with the poles closer together, Rounder went through without a mistake, turning easily from left to right all the way through.

Jessie was beaming. "Good, good boy," she told him, leaning down and patting his neck. She stopped him and dismounted. "That's enough for today. He does better with short, intense work sessions when he's first learning something."

"You're really good at this," Reese told her. "Even I could see the difference you made in him in just 20 minutes. His whole balance changed."

Jessie smiled and nodded. She handed Reese her reins and stepped to the colt's side, loosening the saddle girth as a reward for work well done. As they headed to the barn, she smiled up at Reese. "Isn't it funny," she said, "that such simple things can make you so happy?"

Reese nodded, unable to voice his thoughts. He felt an overwhelming sense of completeness helping her with her horse, and he already felt a looming dismay at the loneliness that would descend on him when he went back to his life in Tallahassee.

They unsaddled Rounder and hosed the sweat off of him. Then Reese walked him slowly on the grassy yard beside the barn while Jessie tended to her "crips," as she called them. Two orphaned calves, "Jed" and "Jaybelle"; a blind raccoon, "Rastus"; and a Great Blue Heron with a broken wing, named "Boney Moroney." As Rounder nibbled grass, Reese watched Jessie cleaning pens, filling water dishes, and petting over each of her wards. He loved how un-self-involved she was, and he wanted to bask in her calm aura hour after happy hour. "If I break my leg, can I come live in your sanctuary?" he asked wistfully.

Across the yard Jessie looked up. He wasn't sure if she had heard him or not. He wasn't sure if he had meant her to hear or not. He realized he could no longer tell where the boundary should be between him and her. He suddenly wanted her so badly that he turned away and pulled Rounder back towards the barn. What did she want? What did he have to offer a woman like that?

As he led Rounder into his stall, his cell phone rang. He'd completely forgotten it was still business hours. His crew had left for home the night before, but in Tallahassee, the office was still open. He answered, expecting Sam Donnovan.

"Hey Man. How's it going? You don't know me but I was at the hearing yesterday."

"Ok. How can I help you?" Reese asked.

"No, man, we wanted to invite you. Saturday night's airboat races at the 520 bridge, you know it? The field there by the Lone Cabbage. You know where I'm talkin' about?"

"Sure, yeah. Well thanks. I'll try to make it. What time does it kick off?"

"First race is at 7:30, but we go on, you know, we bop til we drop, you know." The man snuffled a laugh and coughed.

"And what's your name again? I'm Reese, Reese Kessler, and tell me your name?"

"Alvin. Al. One of the founding members of The Far Out. You know?"

"Ok, great. Well thanks Al, thanks for calling and for the invitation. And I'll see you there."

He looked up to see Jessie making her way across the lawn. She motioned to him as she sank into a chair on the little patio beside the wash rack. Amazing. She was beckoning to him. It was like winning the lotto. He went to join her.

"All the crips ok?"

"Happy as clams—whatever that means," she said.

"I just got an invite from someone named Alvin to the airboat races tomorrow night. What kind of scene is that?"

"Up til about ten o'clock it's a family thing. After the wives and kids go home it gets a little wilder."

"I thought Alvin said it was in a field."

"They like the irony of racing their boats on dry land," Jessie said, laughing. "It tickles 'em. There are some stretches of water out there, but those courses are mainly for newcomers."

"I get the picture. Is there any chance I could interest you in partaking of such shenanigans?"

She hesitated, and Reese felt suddenly that he had monopolized her for too long and she was ready to be away from him.

"I'm wondering why you got that invitation," she said. "I don't know who Alvin is, but some of those guys might want a chance to talk to you more one-to-one. If you show up with me that won't happen."

"You're right. Besides, I've monopolized you all week." He grinned at her. "I shouldn't press my luck."

Jessie stood up and came around the back of his chair. "Oh, I think you should," she said. She put her hands on his shoulders and bent down. Her hair fell across his back and her mouth was close to his ear. When she spoke, he could feel her breath on his neck. "I think you should be back here first thing in the morning for a boat ride to Moccasin Island. I'll pack lunch."

Reese's heart was pounding. He tried to concentrate on her words, but the feel of her hands pressed against his arms made it nearly impossible. "I guess that means we're not having steak." He tilted his head back and grinned at her.

She straightened up. Her hands rested lightly on his shoulders. "Peanut butter and sprouts for you, bub, and green algae slime to drink."

Reese scratched his head. "You're a hard woman to deal with."

"I'm not taking you if you're going to whine." She stood up and pulled him to his feet. She hooked her arm through his and walked him to his jeep.

"Can I drive the boat?" he asked, "Or do I need to take out a bigger insurance policy?" He dodged as she punched her fist towards his chest, then took her by the elbow and pulled her to him.

"Don't patronize me Kessler," she said. "I could drive an airboat by the time I was eight."

"What took you so long?" he asked softly, but now he was looking at her dark brown eyes, noticing the ring of green in her irises. She opened his door.

"I can see you're trying to get rid of me," he said. "I guess you've got a hot date tonight, it being Friday." He got in.

"That's right," she said, shutting his door. "The competition is fierce, so don't keep me waiting. Nine o'clock sharp, tomorrow morning." She leaned forward and kissed him hard on the mouth. When he opened his eyes she was walking away.

Bud Blake hung up the phone and turned a gleeful face to his companion. "He'll be there."

"All right," the other man said, giving Bud a thumbs-up gesture. "Good work 'Al'." They both laughed. The man's crooked front tooth hung on his lower lip beside a deep scar that ran almost to his chin. "So, did you want pictures of him doing anything in particular—mingling with the boys, or what?"

Bud thumbed a stack of hundred-dollar bills, peeled one from the top and laid it on the table. "Just blend in and stay alert," he said. "Try to get pictures of him looking real palsy with the boat people." He peeled off another bill and set it on top of the first. "Once the party gets going it shouldn't be too hard. I've arranged for the May twins to be there." Bud arched his eyebrows at the man and placed two more bills on the table. "See if you can't get a feel-good portrait of him with the girls. Make a nice present for his wife."

"Or a good local color photo for the Sunday section," the photographer suggested. "State surveyor appraises local beauties." He waved his hand across the imaginary banner.

"Maybe we'll get lucky and he'll get in a fight. Maybe even get arrested. You never know."

"Ok, I gotcha. I'll see what I can do."

"I appreciate you Fred," Bud said nodding. He laid a final bill on the table.

"Always glad to help out, Bud," the man said. "I'll call you once I get everything sorted, and you can pick out what you want." He stood up and leaned forward. The money was more than halfway across the table from him, and he had to reach out farther than he could do without losing his balance. That Bud Blake was a bastard was not news to him though. He knew Blake was toying with him, but it was nothing personal. Blake screwed with everybody. Fred lurched forward onto one hand and swept up the money with the other, then gave a little salute with the cash, just to keep up the illusion that he had a shred of dignity still intact. It didn't pay to get your nose out of joint. And, on the other hand, it paid pretty well to let Bud have his fun.

When the photographer had gone, Bud sat for a while imagining the prospects he had unleashed. Part of his enjoyment came from the chaos factor. He could never be sure what events would unfold from his little games, but that merely heightened their entertainment value. He had come to the realization early in his life that people who played by the rules could easily be blindsided by a personal attack. They never seemed to wise up.

His anger flared again at the thought of CW inviting that stupid surveyor to ride horses at the ranch. Bud would gladly ship every horse on the place off to slaughter if he could. Goddamn horses. It was always the horses. Jessie and the horses. Lacey and Jessie and the horses. CW and Jessie and the horses. Once his golf course permits were in-hand he would make sure Jessie and her fucking horses relocated to some other part of the county. He was tired of seeing her suck up to CW, and it was beginning to be more than bothersome that she was affecting the old man's judgment. If that old coot had stood up for him, he wouldn't be having to dick around like this. He could get on with building the golf course, and he would finally be in a position of centrality. Then he would call the shots without having to kowtow to Carl Weston or that sniveling bitch, Jessie.

He let his thoughts range for a while to the possibilities. It would be gratifying to fuck with her mind again, but it wouldn't be as easy as it had been before she got married. He had lived at the ranch then, and she had been easy pickin's. Now he would have to arrange things from outside, and that wouldn't be easy. Everyone who worked at the ranch was devoted to CW, so he would have a hard time finding an agent for his mischief. And it was important that the attacks were never tied back to him. Even though CW treated him as a son, Bud knew the old bastard would cut him out of his will in a heartbeat if he knew Bud was messing with his precious Jessie. Besides, he enjoyed the god-like perspective it gave him to manipulate trouble for someone behind the scenes and then sympathize with them and act all friendly to their face. Of course, on a ranch there were other sources of chaos than people. The bull had been great. Bud hadn't really intended for things to go so far, but that was the nature of power. You had to be willing to cut it loose if you were going to use it. Then the trick was to be in position to take advantage of the outcome. Nothing wrong with that. It just meant you were smarter than the rest, tougher, more savvy.

He wondered if CW had a bull anymore. He knew Jessie didn't like the cattle operation, and since she seemed to have CW in her pocket, CW was likely phasing it out. But, it didn't matter. A bull was really overkill. Ha! No pun intended. He hadn't meant the bull thing to end up that way, but, on the upside, after the death of his step-mother, CW had made a concentrated effort to spend more time with him, get him involved in development projects. So that had turned out all right. But the bull thing wasn't really appealing now. He was looking for something more challenging, something appropriate to his more advanced talents. It would probably be easy to slip into the barn, leave a special treat for one of Jessie's horses. Or maybe do something with her stupid petting zoo. But the thought of having to actually get near the animals sent a wave of revulsion through him. With the bull, he'd only had to open a few gates. He knew Jessie rode her pony in those fields and he thought it would be poetic justice for her to get chased by that big monster. Her and her prissy morals—sitting at the dinner table and refusing to eat steak. Let her see how she felt when that fucker was breathing down her neck about to eat *her.*

He knew he would eventually hit on the right thing. He would just have to do as he had advised Fred—blend in and stay alert. Some kind of opportunity would present itself. And that was a lot of the fun of his games—watching the possibilities bob to the surface, being ready to take advantage of them. It made him feel keen and hungry—and horny. He picked up the phone and punched the button for the May twins.

April 14, 2001

I must have been hearing the doorbell for a minute or more before I swam into anything remotely like consciousness. I threw on a robe and staggered to the door. Mel was standing on the porch squinting down her nose at me, her finger poised over the ringer in case my resurrection required further stimulation. Behind her, Richard was making his way up the walk with his big, swinging step.

"Breakfast ready?" he grinned.

"Late night?" Mel grinned.

"Arg," I responded, waving them in. "Cof---fee."

They lounged at the table while I puttered, grinding beans and making toast. I remembered the warning Logan had given me about the Kriek. I was still feeling the effects of being kicked by something, but I wasn't sure it was the brew. Richard was telling us about an article he'd read that tracked U.S.-produced DDT. "We sold it all to Latin America. It's still legal to use it down there, and guess what they do with it. They dump it all over the coffee beans and sell 'em back to us."

"There's a cheery piece of news," Mel said.

I handed them each a piping hot cup of whatever.

"Ok. I'm awake now. And I have stuff to tell you. There's something screwy going on. I think it's tied to my hard drive getting ripped, but I think it's also tied to Lake Ponder."

I saw the flash of concern go over Mel's face. She sat up and put her elbows on the table, leaning toward me.

"What's going on?" Richard's brows wrinkled together and he stuck out his chin in anticipation.

"The police are watching my house. If they are the police. I'm not even very sure about that," I said.

"Are they worried about creepboy?" Mel asked.

"I think they're watching me."

"Why?" they both said in unison.

"I can't think of any reason unless they're trying to get something on me that might discredit me as a witness for the State."

"But what would that be? Why would the police be involved in that?" Mel queried.

"How do you know they're watching you?" Richard asked.

"Ok, the night after the burglary, Logan came over to interview me. He's leaving, right, and as he drives off I notice the curtain moving in the third floor window of the apartment building across the street. Someone was looking out that window. At first I was afraid it was creepboy, because I could tell from his email that he had seen Logan at my house. But the next night I saw Logan looking at that window as we walked out. I had told him I thought someone was watching us the night before. But he looked right at that window." I paused to let that part of the story sink in.

"That could be a coincidence," Richard said. "And it might have just looked like that's where he was looking. It's pretty hard to tell about that kind of thing if you aren't lined up right." Mel and I stared at him. "It was probably a nosy neighbor watching you," he said. "What else?"

"I had a message from Mack yesterday at the office and I called him back last night. Something had happened in Pakistan near a project he's working on. A nasty little bacteria turned up in a reservoir and killed two women."

"Wait a minute," Richard said. "Are you going to tell me this thing with Mack ties in?"

"I'm hoping you might tell me," I said. "Mack said some guy came around investigating the contamination and asked him a lot of questions—who he hires for field crew, what kind of security he has, what his people know about water chemistry. Stuff like that. So he gave the guy access to all his personnel records. My name was on one of Mack's forms as a contact person in the States—with my DEP address. Mack said the guy asked him a lot of questions about me."

"And this guy was what," Richard asked, "CIA?"

"He's not exactly sure," I said.

Richard bugged his eyes out.

"Mack, Mack, Mack," Mel said, shaking her head.

"He's trying to find out right now. Anyway, he showed the guy all the projects he's done—a lot of them are reservoirs. And apparently this bacteria—fonseria, or something like that, has to percolate in still waters in order to get going. But under those conditions it gets plenty toxic."

"So now Mack's not sure if the guy was *the guy* or a real agent for some legit outfit," Mel summed up.

"Right," I said. "Anyway. I called Tallahassee Police last night to tell them there might be some connection. It's remote I think, but Mack was worried about how much the guy wanted to know about me, so I was going to let them know."

"I wouldn't worry too much about that, Teena," Richard said. "I mean, it makes sense that if the guy was asking a lot of questions about you he might break in and steal your hard drive. But it's what, like ten thousand miles away?"

"Well, yeah," Mel said, "but this could be something a little more organized."

Richard lifted one brow. "Maybe we're getting a little paranoid here."

"I know *I* am," I said. "But it gets weirder." They both stared at me, mute. "When I asked at TPD for officer Kirkland they told me he was fishing in Alaska. I mentioned he had worked a break-in at my house this week and they said Tom Kirkland had been retired for two months. I asked for Logan Deo and they didn't know him. They had to ask around and finally they gave me a phone number to leave him a message."

"Who are these guys?" Mel said almost to herself.

"At that point I realized that I knew who was watching me, so I snuck across the street and went up to the third floor apartment."

"Now see, that's what I'm talking about," Richard burst out. "You're not showing good sense, girl. That's when you should've called me and waited. Do you know how dangerous that was?"

"I was pissed off. They're jerking me around, not telling me what's going on. Logan had just been over here acting like he was attracted to me when all the time he's just playing me for a nincompoop. I did try to call Mel but then I realized my phone is probably tapped—"

"All right, all right. But you hear me on this now. No more of this lone ranger stuff," Richard said, pointing his finger at me like a pistol. "Until we get to the bottom of this somebody needs to be around when you go investigating."

I nodded my head.

"And besides," Mel said, "he *is* attracted to you. He can't help it if he also has a job to do."

"Correct me if I'm wrong," Richard said, exasperated, "but you've never even met the guy."

Mel glared at him. "Some things a woman just knows," she said.

"So what happened when you got in the apartment house?" Richard asked.

"There's nothing on the landing like you would expect to see if someone was really living there. No plants, no umbrella stand. So I dialed Logan's number on my cell and I could hear the phone ringing inside, and then the answering machine picked up. It was his voice."

Mel pulled her chair close to mine and put her hand on my shoulder. We all sat there without saying a word.

"What about this creepboy?" Richard finally said.

"I have no idea. Or rather too many ideas that don't add up. He started out seeming really spooky. He was obviously trying to scare me. But I wrote him back this kind of put-down letter, sort of taking him on. Logan saw the letter and he said to send it and see what happened. I was thinking maybe we could get the guy really involved and lure him out. But he sent back this really sweet smart letter that basically made *me* want to meet *him*. Plus he sounded kind of pathetic, like a hunchback or someone hideously burned who could never have love."

"Uh-oh, that's the kiss of death," Richard said. "Women always fall for pathetic guys."

"Oh stop. He just sounded nice, and really smart. And he definitely knows about literature. He's not faking that."

"So, is he connected to this other thing?" Mel asked. "I mean if the police are watching you—or whoever they are—and they could just be trackers working for Wesson or that rabid legislator—anyway, wouldn't it make sense for *them* to break in and steal your hard drive? Why would someone with a real education who just wants to discuss literature be involved with spooks?"

"I'm totally clueless." I picked the crust off a piece of toast. Through the kitchen window I could see a perfectly sunny April day. Crocuses were in full bloom. Everything looked so normal.

"What about this," Richard said. "Suppose they're watching your house but they can't figure out whatever it is they want to know, and then they see somebody break in, and they come over and act like police. And now they have an in with you so they can watch you really close."

"But they must be connected to the police—at least marginally," Mel said. "I mean TPD did know who Logan was even if they didn't know *him*."

"Maybe he's FBI or something like that, and TPD gave him the retired cop to help him with the stake-out," Richard said.

"So why would the FBI be watching Teena?" Mel asked sotto voce.

"Maybe this *is* tied to the thing with Mack," I said. "Maybe they think I'm supplying someone information on Mack's projects."

"That would mean Logan's an agent for somebody and not a thug," Mel said with a little hopeful note in her voice.

"Can you stop playing cupid long enough to make sure this guy isn't going to murder your best friend?" Richard said, trying to sound impatient. "It could also mean he's an international terrorist trying to get information out of Teena."

Mel gave him a withering look.

"Of course, it's a lot more likely that these guys are on the payroll of some dirtbag lawyer trying to get inside info on the Lake Ponder settlement," Richard went on, ignoring Mel. "We still don't know who creepboy is. Do we really think he just happened to be breaking into your house this week? A love stricken student?"

"He doesn't strike me as a student."

"A love stricken prof then."

I gave him a big-sisterly you're-hopeless glower.

"What do you really know about Logan?" Mel was shifting gears now. I could see her lawyerly wheels beginning to turn.

"Nothing," I replied with barely concealed disgust. "He came over last night sort of on the pretext of going on with the investigation. But he brought several bottles of this kick-ass brew and got me pretty ripped. We were joking around about literary techniques and he kissed me. But then he got all flustered like a schoolboy, and he jumped up and left."

"Excuse me but you were joking around about *what?*" Richard asked incredulously.

"Free indirect discourse. We were trying to see if you could carry on a conversation in free indirect discourse. Of course it's ridiculous. It's a form that blends the narrator's and character's thinking. It isn't designed for dialogue."

Richard and Mel sat looking at me as if I'd sprouted asparagus from my forehead. "Teena," Mel finally said, "doesn't that seem a little unusual to you? That a detective would know *any*thing about free indirect discourse, much less be able to joke about it?"

"Well I gave him a little mini-lecture," I said. My head was pounding. "But I have noticed that he's unusually interested in the literary aspects of the case—and he grasps them really fast."

A look passed between Richard and Mel that said are you thinking what I'm thinking?

"What?" I demanded.

"He's writing the emails," Mel said evenly. "They're using the literary stuff to distract you from something else."

I felt the blood drain from my head. My scalp prickled, but when I reached up to scratch it, it felt like a big cotton wad. No matter how impossible it was to know how, I knew instantly that Mel was right. We looked at each other, and she could see it in my expression.

"Does that mean there's no creepboy?" Richard asked. He sounded slightly disappointed.

"We've got to figure out who this guy is," Mel said, ignoring Richard's question. "I mean he could be FBI or he could be some whacko doing god knows what."

"But you guys did call the police when the house got broken into, right?" Richard asked.

Mel hesitated. She looked down the length of the table from one end to the other as if she were guessing its length. "Well, something funny did happen. A sound—a couple of clicks," she said. "I didn't think anything about it because the voice answered 'Tallahassee Police Department'. But what if . . . let's just say they could reroute your calls to a switchboard across the street. They come in and steal your hard drive, maybe hoping to find out something about the case—or who knows what—whatever they think you know that they want to know. Then, when we call the police, Kirkland shows up—but he's working for Logan. Bingo, they're in."

I was getting a very bad feeling in the pit of my stomach. "I'm afraid there's more." They looked at me with blank expressions that I recognized as the first stage of panic. "Let me show you something I found online."

We moved our camp into the den and I pulled up the Yugoslavian software site I'd found searching Logan Deo. I pointed out the bothersome word "terorista" in the opening line, and showed them how you couldn't get to that page from the home page, but only by searching Logan's name with the search engine.

"They're talking about Logan airport," Mel said. "See the word 'Bostonski' here at the beginning of the paragraph. And then 'aerodromu'—that's airport. Maybe the company installed some kind of computer system at Logan."

"It looks like gobbledy-gook to me," Richard said. "But if you leave off the last two or three syllables on those words at the end of that paragraph, you can see they're worried about a federal crime of some kind." He had picked up an empty Kriek bottle I'd left on the coffee table, and he pointed the tip of it at the screen, indicating the phrase "federalnim kriminalističkim."

"Well the good news is I don't think this has anything to do with Logan," Mel said. "They're talking about the airport. The fact that the word 'deo' is included brought this site up. But deo's the Latin word for god, and in Czech it probably has about a hundred meanings, so who knows why it's here, but I don't think it refers to our Logan."

I wasn't really listening to Mel though. I took the bottle out of Richard's hand and held it up. "I am an idiot."

"Don't be too hard on yourself," Richard said. "We all let ourselves go sometimes."

"Last night," I said, ignoring his remark, "this bottle contained a ruby-red lambic bottled in *Brussels.* Logan told me a friend of his had brought it to him, because you can't get it here. I can't believe I haven't put this together before. Let me show you." I pulled up the search I'd breezed over the night before, thinking it irrelevant. It listed the three websites in English that all seemed to refer to the same Logan Deo. The Brussels School of International Studies listed him as a faculty member in 1996. The United Nations listed him as a seminar presenter at the UN International Network on Water, Environment and Health in Ontario in the summer of 1997. He was also listed as a research advisor at the Department of International Relations at the University of Karachi in Pakistan—no date. His faculty profile at the Brussels School showed a doctorate from the Sorbonne, Paris in social sciences and the philosophy of knowledge, and an M. Phil in international relations from Cambridge.

"All right," Richard said. "Now I'm starting to get spooked. This looks like something big you've landed in the middle of."

"What makes you think so?" Mel asked. "Not that I don't have the same feeling—I just want to know what you're seeing there."

"It's got to be tied into the thing with Mack," Richard said. "All the elements match up: International relations, the UN's water-health thing, Pakistan. What are the odds that there are two guys in the world named Logan Deo who come up associated with those particular elements?"

"What do you see Teena?" she asked.

"The Cambridge degree," I said. "It's very slight, but he talks in a strange way. Not like he's translating exactly, but like he's trying to remember which city he's in. I know that doesn't make sense."

"It does if he needs to seem like a native," Mel observed.

"One time he slipped up and said he'd been 'at university,'" I went on. "That's a British expression."

"What about the literary stuff. How does he get that out of international relations?"

"A doctorate in the philosophy of knowledge from the Sorbonne is probably at least as literary as a literary degree in the U.S. Anyway, unlike Americans, the French revere their intellectuals. It would be pretty hard to live in Paris and not know something about the cultural heroes—Barthes, for instance."

"Who?" Richard asked.

"A French culture theorist—Roland Barthes. The creepboy refers to Barthes in his letters."

"Hmmmmn," Richard nodded, "romantic."

"And of course *Madame Bovary,*" I said, ignoring Richard's quip. "That's the book that started all our conversations. With a background like this he could easily know Flaubert like the back of his hand."

"So," Mel said, drawing out the o, "what do we know? Is the guy who's hanging around here pretending to be a cop *this* Logan Deo?" she asked, indicating the profile on the screen.

"Yes," Richard pronounced.

"It would explain a lot," I agreed. "But it opens up a lot of questions."

Mel frowned. "I agree it would explain a lot. But we don't really know anything. There probably aren't two guys with similar experiences named Logan Deo. But that doesn't mean someone with similar interests isn't impersonating him. If this guy is up to no-good, he could be using Deo's identity to appear legit. That said, it probably is really him."

"He does seem to be in earnest about catching somebody doing something horrific, even though he won't ever say what it is," I told them. "Almost like he's on a mission."

"That's easy to fake," Richard said.

We sat staring into our jumbled thoughts for several minutes. I began to wonder how creepboy's emails would seem to me now. I wanted to read them knowing that Logan might have written them. It might explain why they had done such a turnaround. I hoped it would explain anything at all.

"All right," Mel surfaced from her reverie, "we need a plan."

"You need to just pack up and come stay with me and Carmen until this blows over," Richard said. "Let them watch an empty house."

"I think we need to make some contact with authorities we trust," Mel said. "That way if something happens we'll already have people who know what's going on."

"Authorities you trust? And that would be?" Richard asked.

"The Attorney General," she replied. "And I think you should keep Steve up-to-speed," she said, looking at me. "Wasn't he having Gordon look into the computer shenanigans at the office?"

"Yeah. I don't know if that's going anywhere."

"Let's just keep all the lines of communication open," Mel said. "The AG can find out if there's an FBI investigation involving you. He can also find out how TPD's involved."

"*If* they're involved," Richard said.

"All right." Mel stood up and prepared for battle. "Put your things in garbage bags and take them out back to the alley. I don't think they can see back there from across the street, and it might be a good idea if they didn't realize you were splitting. They'll figure it out soon enough."

"What about Willow?"

"We'll have to stuff her in my bag. She's used to staying with me when you're gone, so it would probably be better to let her do that, huh?"

"Yeah, thanks Mel," I said. "I appreciate you guys doing this."

"We should go on to the shooting range from here," Richard said. "That's what we were planning, and that'll give us a chance to see if anyone's following us before we head out to the house."

I nodded. "Would you do me one more favor Richard? Would you call Steve and fill him in?"

He hesitated. I knew it wasn't because he wasn't going to do it. I knew it wasn't because he minded at all. I knew it was because he'd been wondering for a year and a half if there was something going on between me and Steve, and this was one more piece of the puzzle. "Sure," he said.

Mel had moved into the hall and was talking on her cell phone. I heard her apologize to the attorney general's wife for disturbing their day at home. I went to shower and bag my stuff. When I came back Richard flipped open his cell phone and punched three buttons. I listened to him tell Steve the news, wondering what was going through Steve's mind as he listened. While Richard narrated, I downloaded the creepboy files to a disk and stuck them in my bag.

I remembered Logan's response to my dubbing the emailer "creepboy." He had liked it. He'd liked it that, scared as I was by the threat, I'd picked an insulting moniker for my tormentor. I thought about the state I was in when he found me puking on the bathroom floor. Now it made sense that he'd been so alarmed. He'd been surprised and worried at how badly his message had scared me. I wondered if his questions that day had been designed to figure out if I was scared because I was shuttling information to international terrorists and was afraid of being caught, or because someone had broken into my house and then threatened my cat.

"Ok," Richard said, flipping shut his cell. "Steve's going to call Gordon and see if he's run across anything shady. He'll get back to us. I told him you'd be hanging with me and Carmen."

I nodded. Richard was looking at me.

"He said to tell you he's right here if you need him."

I realized my mouth was drawing a tight line across my face. I nodded again. "Thanks Richard."

He nodded slowly. We heard Mel ringing off in the kitchen and we went in to get briefed.

"All righty," she said. "I gave Bill all the details. He's very concerned. He didn't think we could rule out anything at this point, but he's going to call some people right now and get some answers. So we should know more soon. In the meantime he thought it was a good idea for you to stay with Richard. I gave him both your cell numbers, but he'll probably use Richard's. I'm not sure how cell phones work—whether you can track their frequencies or anything, but we know Logan and crew have Teena's number. Probably better to stay off hers unless absolutely necessary."

"Ok, Mel," Richard said. "You get the cat and head on out. We'll hang here for a few before we leave. Let's talk again at five."

We glanced at each other with little nods. There are times when you realize everything in your life is hanging in a precarious constellation that may be about to fly apart. At such times gravity itself seems likely to fail. But if you have real friends, right there with you, holding fast like a great steady planet to a wobbling moon, nothing needs to be said. You each know events have conspired to bring you to this moment, and whatever intersecting and parallel paths your fates once traced have now merged. Whenever I think of this moment I feel a deep sense of privilege to have come to such a brink and found such strong arms around me.

Chapter Eight

Reese had barely reached his hotel room when the phone rang and Carl Weston invited him to the ranch for dinner. "I'm not planning to talk business," he said. "I'd just be glad to have some company and a fresh perspective on the world. Jessie won't be here–she and her girlfriend Beth get up to something on Friday nights, and I'm just calling you on a whim–she doesn't know I'm inviting you." Reese quickly agreed to come and hung up.

Then he began wondering if that was really all there was to the invitation. It was difficult to figure Carl Weston. On one hand Reese knew his reputation as a shrewd businessman. But his sense of Weston so far was of a man who could look at life through a wider lens. Besides, Weston had generously offered him a wonderful day on a great horse with his beautiful daughter as a guide. He really should go and say a proper thanks. He wondered briefly if he was being taken in, and he thought of the ethical guidelines the department sent out every year covering what state employees could and could not accept from "clients." But he felt an odd kinship with Carl Weston sitting at home alone in his big house. He'd spent many a lonesome night in his own rambling house, and he often longed for a friend to talk to, to compare notes about the world and just speculate on what things might matter. He thought he might enjoy getting to know Carl Weston. And if the State was ready to blister his ass over a free dinner, then so be it. Somewhere along the way you had to draw the line on a job and be a person, with human needs and human responses.

Jessie sat at Beth's table and listened to her friend recount her evening with Richard. She felt lucky to have a friend like Beth. What were the odds that someone so cosmopolitan would live in Granville? Beth took the broad view of most things, and had an unfailing faith in biology. She didn't exactly believe that hormones accounted totally for one's behavior, but she aspired to live what she called a "natural" life, by which she meant that you shouldn't let social dictates interfere too seriously in your inclinations. History showed that society had an inordinate interest in controlling women, and Beth suspected it was wholly unhealthy. Her refreshing outlook and saucy sense of humor had helped Jessie enormously in the months following her divorce, when she had suffered the disapproving glances and wagging tongues of Granville's stodgier citizens.

"So," Beth was saying, "enough about that rascal. I want to hear about that simmering redhead who's so smitten with you." She poured wine for the two of them.

Jessie grinned. "We-e-ll, there's not *that* much to tell." Beth waved the fingers of both hands at her, as if coaxing the words from her mouth. Jessie laughed. "He *is* married." Beth slumped forward in defeat. "But they *are* separated."

Beth sat bolt upright. "Oh poor baby," she mocked. "We're *so sorry* to hear it."

Jessie grinned at her friend. "He's a little hard to read though."

"Hmmm. How so?"

"I've laid hands on him—and lips—three times now, and he has yet to really react."

Beth considered this. "I wouldn't worry about it yet. You know how it is when you're still married and wishing you weren't. You've been out of circulation for so long. You're lonely and horny and over-stimulated, and you don't know what the ground rules are anymore."

"That's true," Jessie said. "It's a psychotic time."

"Did you have fun riding with him?"

"I really did. He has this wide-open feel, or he gives me a wide-open feel that I don't remember ever having before." Jessie giggled. "Which is just another way of saying he's making me a wanton woman."

Beth laughed. "I like this guy!"

"But there isn't much time. I mean he'll finish this job and be gone. And I don't want to just let it go. I mean, Beth, he came out to the arena and helped me with Rounder this afternoon. He was out there setting poles for us. And he cooled Rounder out while I cleaned critter cages."

"Wow, that's sexy," Beth said, and they nodded at each other seriously. "So, do you have any plans for the weekend?"

"We're going to Moccasin Island tomorrow for a picnic," Jessie said.

"Far from the madding crowd," Beth said.

Jessie nodded. "I feel like he wants to, you know, get there with me, but . . .".

"Oh trust me girl," Beth said. "He definitely wants to get there with you. He's just having trouble making the crossover from polite company to natural man. I like the Moccasin Island idea."

"Ok." Jessie raised her glass and toasted her friend silently. "Whoever thought it would be so hard to get a guy into bed?" They laughed.

"I took a film class one time as an elective—it focused on Hollywood romances. After watching dozens of 'em, I finally realized I had grown up thinking that the guys I knew were going to act like the heroes in the movies—you know, take charge and get the show on the road. I was totally perplexed trying to figure out why the guys I knew didn't even know how to kiss a woman."

"I've wondered about that too," Jessie said. "I think girls tend to model their ideas of relationships on what they see in movies, but guys—it blows right by them."

"Yep," Beth huffed. "There's a reason guys refer to those movies as 'chick-flicks.' Only women pay any attention to them."

"Well, but then there are the Casanovas who seem to realize that the movies are actually a great "how-to" guide for how to get women into bed. They learn how to be all manly and hot, but for a lot of them it's just an act—'there's no there there,' as Gerty Stein so aptly said."

Beth nodded. They drank. "So, what category is Reese in?"

"Oh he's definitely got the hot manly thing. It's too early to tell about the rest. But I'd be surprised to find out he's shallow."

"Yeah, he's one of those who has been made tender by suffering." Beth grinned. "That kind can be pretty serious. Are you ready for that?"

Jessie shrugged. "I don't know what I am. I'm *seriously* wanting to get his shirt off. And I haven't felt that way since maybe ever. I just hope something happens, you know? I'm going to be *seriously* kicking myself if he goes home without something happening."

"Well then get ye to Moccasin Island and take *your* shirt off," Beth said. "He'll figure out the rest."

Juanita brought plates of beef and chicken, onions and peppers, beans and cheese; fajita shells, lettuce, tomatoes, sour cream, and bottles of salsa, until the table was crowded with food. They sat in the big kitchen, rather than in the formal dining room, and Reese felt this was one more thing he liked about Carl Weston—his ability to be at ease, to share his comforts and avoid the stiffness of formality.

"I understand you met Juanita earlier today," Carl Weston said. Reese nodded as Juanita poured beer.

"We are already friends," Juanita said, patting Reese on the shoulder. "Now, if you two have everything you need, I am going."

"You're not going to join us?" Carl seemed genuinely startled.

"You have your dinner and talk," she said. "I have to watch my program."

"Ah," Carl said. "Ok."

"Thank you, Juanita," Reese said. "This looks incredibly good."

"There is more beer on the ice," she told Carl, and then she was gone.

All through dinner, Carl Weston talked about his grandfather. How he had come to be in this part of the world as a young man, how he came to have land. He quizzed Reese on his own heritage, on his time in the service. When they had eaten their fill, Carl took their plates to the sink and invited Reese into his study.

As Reese settled into an arm chair, Carl Weston poured three fingers of whiskey in two glasses and handed one to Reese. "So, howd'ya like that Quarter Horse?"

"More than I could say," Reese replied. "I appreciate the chance to experience that—and I got to watch Jessie work the young horse—Rounder. That's an art few people understand."

"It's in her blood. Her mama was the best I've ever seen. But Jessie might be every bit as good, if she'll stay at it."

"I can't imagine wanting to do anything else if you've got that in you," Reese said.

Carl was silent, his lips pursed, head nodding slightly. Reese wondered what the man was considering.

"She likes the training," Carl finally said, looking up at Reese. "But she freezes under pressure. In competition. That'll hurt her if she tries to make it her profession. You need those credentials to draw in the clients."

Reese was surprised to find Carl Weston so forthcoming about his daughter.

"She's good enough to hold her own," Carl was saying, "but she chokes when she should punch on through. I've tried to tell her to go for it more, but it seems like the more I push, the more she backs off. I don't know what would help. Her mother would know what to do.

She always knew what to do, even when everyone around her was in a muddle. She knew what to do and she did it, no matter what it cost her."

"That's some big shoes to fill," Reese said.

"You bet it is," Carl said.

"I wouldn't be surprised to see Jessie grow into 'em," Reese said. "Seems like she's got a lot of things she's working out right now."

"Could be, could be," Carl said. He seemed to sink back into his own thoughts again. He held his glass in the air before him, gently swirling the amber liquid.

"You seem to have a pretty good handle on Jessie for not having known her long," Carl said. "Or maybe you already knew each other, I don't really know. Did ya'll meet at school or somewhere?"

"No, just this week." Reese sipped the whiskey. He wondered if Carl Weston was testing him in some way, checking him out. "But she's no coward. I could tell that by the way she worked to get your cow and calf out of that ditch," Reese said. "Careful. Real careful. Worried about the things that could go wrong if she made a mistake–maybe get somebody hurt. But she was determined." He looked up to see Carl Weston looking at him intensely.

"She wasn't quite nine when her mother was killed," Carl said. He hesitated, and Reese had the feeling he was gathering strength for what he had to say. "Lacey was working her competition horse in the front field out there," he waved toward the front of the house, "and Jessie was riding her pony–Joey. She would always sort of tuck in behind Lacey and try to get Joey to do the things Lacey's horse was doing." His face crinkled in a sad smile and he shook his head. "Lacey sent her ahead to practice opening the gate while she finished working her horse. They were going to take a trail ride and cool out the horses." He sighed heavily. "We had a big Brangus bull at that time that we were using to improve our herd. I'd been wanting to get rid of him. He was so damn mean–he'd already killed one of my dogs. He wasn't even careful about the cows–just a mean son of a bitch. He was supposed to be in a field two fences away, but somehow he had gotten into the next field. And when Jessie got the gate open, he came out of nowhere and rammed her pony. Somehow she didn't get pinned when the pony went down, and she tore out running while that bull was mopping the ground with Joey. But she was screaming and crying, and the bull started for her. Juanita heard her in the house and came running with my rifle. She said she could see Jessie wasn't going to make it to safety—the bull was closing on her too fast. And of course Lacey could see it all. She came down the field wide open, spurring her horse and yelling, and she rode up right between that bull and Jessie and hung down off her saddle and grabbed her up. Somehow, she managed to shield Jessie when the bull hit her horse and took him down. Juanita came out and put six bullets in that bull at almost point blank range while he was rampaging over the horse and Lacey and Jessie. I heard the shots from down in the groves. By the time I got there, Lacey was almost gone. Jessie was hysterical and it took a while to see she wasn't badly hurt—she was so roughed up and scared and covered in blood. I sent her with Juanita to wait in the house for the life flight. I held Lacey's hand and I told her Jessie was all right, she was all right, she was safe. And I told her she was the light of my life and I would never get over it if she died on me. And then she was gone."

Reese heard the emotion rise in the older man's voice as he finished his story and he felt his own breath catch. "God, I'm sorry," he uttered thickly.

Carl nodded again and drank his whiskey down. "If you ever have someone like that, don't waste time on things that don't matter," he said gruffly. He held up his thumb and forefinger positioned an inch apart. "Life ain't but about that long," he said. "Do the things that matter, son. Don't wait."

Reese had the uncanny feeling once again that Carl Weston was handing him the keys to the city, or more aptly, the ranch, and all that went with it—most particularly Jessie. He wondered suddenly if the man was dying. He felt shocked and disoriented from the story of Lacey Weston's death, and he began to think what it would have meant to the young Jessie, to grow up with such a horrific and tragic event separating her from her mother. Everything had changed in those few minutes in what had seemed a normal afternoon. It would be no great wonder if that weight settled in on her during moments of stress or danger—the realization that events may conspire to outrun all your expertise and training, all your illusions of control.

Carl Weston straightened in his chair and seemed to make a visible effort to shake off the past. "Working for the State suit you?"

"It has its good points," Reese replied. "But my plans haven't exactly panned out in other ways." Reese paused. He wondered how much he should say to the older man about his situation. He realized Carl Weston was waiting for him to go on. "My wife and I have been separated for over a year now," he said. It sounded odd to call Vivian his wife. It felt odd to be telling Carl Weston things about his life that he was just realizing himself. "I thought for a long time that it would work out, but it's not going to. I'm taking steps to move on."

Carl Weston was nodding again, looking preoccupied. "Lot of opportunity in the world for a man with your skills," he said. "Seems like you could go pretty much anywhere and land on your feet."

"Well that's good to hear. I hadn't really thought that far."

Carl Weston drank the last of his whiskey. "I'd be glad to help you think through some options. There may be a few prospects in this neck of the woods if that's something that would interest you." The older man smiled.

"Thank you, sir," Reese said, standing as Carl Weston got up. "I appreciate you giving me your insights more than I can tell you. And I'll try my best to act on them."

They walked down the long hall and, as they passed the kitchen, Reese called his thanks to Juanita. He was pleased that Juanita came to join them at the door, and to see that Carl's arm went around her shoulders as they stood together bidding him goodnight. The comfort and affection between the two was obvious, and it was a relief to know that the tremendous sadness in Carl Weston's past had not overtaken his great gift for life.

April 14 p.m.

I sat at the counter in Carmen's kitchen chopping vegetables while Carmen shredded cheese. I have frequently wondered how Richard managed to lure this beautiful, well educated, Italian woman to the wilds of north Florida, given his complete irreverence for culture, ethnicity, anything worldly. Maybe after growing up in Rome, the daughter of an embassy attaché, that's exactly what she finds appealing in him.

We were both listening to Richard's end of a phone call with Mel. But apparently, she was doing all the talking because, so far, he'd said almost nothing. My shoulder ached slightly from firing the little 410 shotgun that afternoon, and my right ear seemed to have a wad of cotton stuck in it. Richard looked at me and shook his head slowly, once. I didn't like his expression.

"And Bill feels sure about that? He knows these guys himself? He trusts them?" More air time.

"Yeah. I just think she's safer here. Nobody's going to get through the yard to even get to the house without tripping over Ripper and Duggie, and then they're in for a thrill," he said referring to his two big Dobies.

We waited some more. Richard nodded. "Ok. We'll talk it over and let you know what we're going to do."

"Tell her to come for dinner," Carmen said.

"Carmen says come eat." He signed off and sat down on the bar stool next to mine.

"The AG thinks those guys are watching out for you. He says there is a federal investigation going on, but Mel says either they wouldn't tell him what it's about or he wouldn't tell her. He seems to think you're in no danger from Logan and Kirkland—and that they need to be able to keep an eye on you. He thinks you should go home and act normal."

Carmen looked from Richard to me and back again. "That's asking Teena to take a lot on faith, don't you think?"

"I do," Richard said. "The only thing it has going for it is that Mel trusts him, and he seems to trust his information. He's worried we've taken her out of reach of the people most prepared to deal with the dangers."

Carmen looked at me sympathetically. "What a crazy thing this is," she said. She poured boiling water off a pot of lasagna noodles and began assembling ingredients in a large casserole dish. I watched her layering pasta, sauce, vegetables, and cheese with a growing sense that I was exposing my friends to a danger we could not even fathom.

"What about the possibility that they could tell me what the hell is going on?" I asked Richard.

"Not going to happen. Mel thinks with how tight-lipped Bill was this must be something way over our heads. But she does think it's a good thing that they know the AG is aware of them—whoever 'they' are—and that you're connected to people who will inquire if things get too fishy."

"But Richard, they could disappear like a little puff of smoke," Carmen said, her dark eyes wide. Her fingers puffed the air into nothingness. "They could take Teena in the night and be out of the country before anyone even knew she was missing."

Richard patted Carmen's shoulder. "This isn't the Red Brigades," he said with a patronizing grin. "We don't have political kidnappings in Tallahassee."

"No?" Carmen returned, ignoring his jibe. "Then why are you so worried about your friend?"

We all chewed on that meaty question for a silent moment.

"I have an idea," Carmen said. We looked at her hopefully. "Why don't you invite Logan over here for dinner?"

Richard's face scrunched into a wad of skepticism, but he waited for Carmen to elaborate.

"That would seem a normal thing, wouldn't it?" she said. "You invite him over to meet your friends. He can see where you are but he doesn't have so much control. Maybe if he starts to trust you, he'll tell you more about what's going on."

I could tell Richard was warming to the idea. "You know, if this whole thing is connected to that situation with Mack, Logan and company might have come into it thinking you were involved somehow." He grinned at me. "I haven't actually asked you—you're not hooked up with some towel-headed whackos, right?"

"Richard!" Carmen said sternly. "You will refrain from making your bad ethnic jokes in my presence."

"I thought that was a good one," he ducked and chuckled.

I gave him a withering look and ignored his question. "I think it's likely they thought I was involved in something," I said. "What I don't understand is whether there really is a creepboy and, if there is, do they know he's connected to the Peshawar incident?"

"You mean this creepboy who is writing to you is the guy who poisoned the reservoir in Pakistan?" Carmen asked. A note of alarm sounded in her voice.

"We don't know that," I said. "He might just be some nut I met in a seminar somewhere."

"We can't rule it out either," Richard said. "But I think Logan is the one writing the emails."

"You think Logan is this creepboy?" Carmen asked nervously.

"That's just it," I said. "There are too many unknowns. Logan could be the email writer, the terrorist, *and* the CIA. About the only thing he doesn't seem to be is a TPD detective—which is what he wants me to believe he is."

"Why do you think Logan is creepboy?" Carmen asked Richard.

"Not that he *is* creepboy—that he's pretending to be. He's writing the emails as a way to get in with Teena," Richard explained. "It allows him to manipulate her from both sides."

"So you're saying maybe someone else stole your hard drive but Logan is the one who's writing to you?"

"I don't know what I'm saying. I hadn't actually thought of that."

"Can you tell if he's read your novel?" Carmen asked. "I mean, did he actually steal your computer or is he just pretending in order to get this connection to you?"

"Whoever called me the night the files were stolen had already looked at them enough to know about the novel," I answered.

"And you know that because?" Richard asked.

"Because he talked about the writing issues."

"Ok. And no one you know from work or online had already seen excerpts from the novel?"

That stopped me cold. Of course there had been someone, I just didn't know who. "Actually, there was an incident at the office. Someone 'stepped in' and copied one of my chapters while I was sitting right there looking at the screen."

"You're kidding me," Richard said, looking a little stunned. I could see he was starting to wonder where the boundaries of this mess were. "When did *that* happen?"

"I don't know—a month ago now. I told Steve about it because I was afraid someone was gunning for me."

"What do you mean Teena?" Carmen asked.

"I'm worried about getting fired over Lake Ponder. They wouldn't fire me for anything connected with the case. It would be something like misuse of state resources."

"The powers," she said.

We all nodded. She didn't need any explanation of that. We'd all been living with that for some time now.

"What happened then?" Richard asked.

"I took all my novel files off my computer at work. They were only on my computer at home after that."

"This just keeps getting weirder," Richard said. "So, it may not be Logan sending the emails, it may be someone who was spying on you at work, or—what other possibilities are there?"

"He may be just what he says," Carmen offered, "and he's trying to catch someone who's stalking Teena."

"Well, no. TPD wouldn't be assigned to catch terrorists," Richard said. "Go back to the emails. Is there anything in those that would indicate the sender has actually read your files?"

"Yeah. The first email took up the thematic problem of the novel, and, basically, warned me how deeply entrenched our culture is in that problem. Also, he's apparently a Barthes aficionado and—"

"Roland Barthes?" Carmen's dark eyebrows lifted.

"The one and only."

"How interesting," Carmen exclaimed. "Is Logan French?"

Richard harrumphed. "Could we just focus here? I'm trying to deduce some actual information. Now, what is that thematic trench or whatever you said?" Richard asked, waving his fingers as if to pull it out of me.

"It's an issue of representation I guess. How to write about people's longings without either romanticizing them or making them grotesque—if those are two different things."

"That's gotta be Logan," Richard said. "Some scumbag fanatic isn't going to know that stuff."

"We don't know that Richard," Carmen said earnestly. "Some scumbag fanatics may be very well acquainted with Barthes. In fact, in France, intellectuals are national heroes. My friend in Tours once told me a funny story about Barthes' death which shows that even working people take pride in their intellectuals."

Richard scowled. "You mean as opposed to the typical American grunt."

"Don't be grumpy. My friend who told the story is an American."

"Yeah, one of those treasonous, expatriate bastards, no doubt."

"If you're finished huffing and puffing," I said, "I'd like to hear the story."

Carmen turned to me, and raised her hand to block her view of Richard's antics. "Well you know that Roland Barthes was killed when he stepped out in front of a laundry truck—or maybe it was a milk truck. There seems to have been some evidence that it was suicide. A note, perhaps, or something he'd said. A recent period of severe depression. You know the kind of thing. Anyway, when the truck driver jumped out to see what had happened, he cried, 'Oh my God, I've killed Roland Barthes!'

"Oh how funny," I said, giggling.

"Why is that funny?" Richard demanded. "The famous man was squished in the street."

"Because, Richard," I said slowly, as if explaining to the village idiot, "the truck driver recognized Roland Barthes. Carmen's American friend told it as a joke *because it illustrates* how much the French revere their intellectuals. Of course, it's probably only funny to an American who despairs of America's anti-intellectualism."

"We're not anti-intellectual," Richard insisted. "We just don't want to be bothered with all that crap."

Carmen and I laughed.

"My very own Yahoo," Carmen said. "The point is, Richard, that scumbags may be very well educated people."

"As long as they're not American," Richard mumbled under his breath.

"One of them may be Logan for all we know," I said woefully. "Bill's information only tells us there's an investigation. Nobody's vouching for Logan Deo."

"Does he know you suspect him of being anything other than a Tallahassee Police detective?" Carmen asked.

"I don't think so," I said. "Unless the AG's inquiry tipped him."

"That's not likely," Richard said. "Those FBI guys keep their cards pretty close. I'm betting Bill's contacts are fairly high up—or at least mid-management. They wouldn't bother telling a field operative that his cover was shaky just because the attorney general calls up wanting to know what's going on in his own backyard."

"We're getting nowhere," I said. "Every strand of information dead ends in a muddle."

"Invite him over," Richard said. "Like Carmen says, if all he wants is to protect you then everyone is happy. I'd like to get a look at him anyway."

"I don't know Richard," Carmen said. "Maybe it's not a good idea. They could come with weapons—" she spread her fingers wide and raised her dark, expressive brows—"we don't know what they want."

Richard and I glanced at each other. Even though his inclination was to joke about her concerns, we both knew that Carmen had a lot more experience with these things than we did. She had been visiting her family in Rome several years ago when, a few streets away, a NATO officer was gunned down by terrorists outside his home. Growing up in the Rome of the late seventies, she had become all too familiar with political terror. I noticed that Richard wasn't making jokes now.

"Maybe you should call Mack," he said to me. "See if he's found out anything. Then maybe we'd be able to figure out what's next."

We were all quiet for a moment. I didn't know if they were feeling as suddenly overwhelmed as I was. Probably not. They were together, in their warm, secure home. It felt wonderful to have their help and support. But I was getting increasingly anxious about involving them.

"Ok," I said. "I'll call Mack. Then we'll see where we are."

I took my phone out onto the porch to place the call. Through the screen door I heard Richard's phone ring again, heard him say, "Yeah, she's here. So far everything's fine." Then Mack picked up.

"Mack, it's Teena."

"Hey girl, I just tried to call you. I got a hold of a guy I know at the embassy and asked him to find out who that was that came nosing around here."

"Did he know anything about the Peshawar incident?"

"No he didn't, and that worries me too. Not that he necessarily would, but you'd think there would be some coordination of information."

"Have you heard about it from any other source than the guy who came to investigate?"

"No. Like I said, he told me it was being kept quiet while they tried to find out more about what happened. But that seems odd to me now. Why not warn people? I don't like it Teena."

"Mack, what did the guy look like? When was he there?"

"It was in March. He was here about three days looking through everything. Near as I can figure it was sometime around the 20th."

"What did he look like?"

"Tall, dark, and handsome. You would love him. Like I said he was a nice guy--smart, but easy going. Not stiff like a lot of government types. Hell, I fell for him."

"I think I know the feeling," I said. "When will you hear from the embassy guy?"

"Realistically not before Monday. I tried to light a fire under him, but I'm not sure he exactly shared my concerns. He probably didn't think something important could be going on without him knowing about it."

"That's always the way. Either the guy doesn't get what's important about what you've told him, or he gets miffed because he didn't already know it."

"I think in this case it's some of each. What's going on there?"

"I'm not sure exactly. The police who investigated my break-in seem to be part of a federal stakeout. But they seem to be staking out me."

"Really?" Mack pronounced the word as he always did, the second syllable dropping an octave in pitch. It made it sound as if he were not all that surprised.

"Yeah. They're watching my house and interviewing me daily—ostensibly about my stolen hard-drive—but I wonder about that now."

"Got any idea what they're looking for?"

"Our theory of the hour is that they got my name from you and thought I might somehow be connected with the Peshawar thing since I work on water stuff."

"So they *suspect* you?"

"That's a possibility. But we also haven't ruled out that some part of this is politically motivated."

"You mean the Ponder case?"

"That's the most likely candidate."

"Charlie Wesson isn't like that," Mack said. "Now his step-son, Bobby—he's hard. I wouldn't want to be in his way, especially if I was a woman. But Charlie's a decent guy."

"Charlie Wesson died last year."

"I didn't know that." Mack sighed. "That's a different picture." He sighed again. "So, you can't really rule that out then."

"Mack, I think it's possible that the detective that's working on the case here is the same guy that talked to you."

"Really?"

"There are some possible connections. Does the name Logan Deo ring any bells?"

"That's him all right. I remember that clear as day now that you say it. Logan Deo. What about that? He must be CIA then, or he wouldn't have given the same name."

"That would make sense I suppose." I wasn't sure anything we knew added up to a molehill much less a positive I.D. "Mention that name to your embassy buddy and see if it gets a reaction. I'm still not sure we can know this guy is legit. He told you he was one thing and now he's pretending to be a local detective."

"They're just making sure you aren't involved in whatever this mess is," Mack said. "I bet in a few days they'll pack up and be gone and that's the last you'll hear of it."

It was amazing to me how unreassuring that prospect was. What great choices: Logan the dangerous terrorist, front and center in my life, or Logan the dedicated, sexy CIA agent, gone with the wind. I chatted with Mack another minute. He agreed to call as soon as he heard anything, and we hung up. I sat on the porch and scratched Duggie's head. The idea of Logan moving on left me with the weird feeling that my life was taking place somewhere else, that I was twirling in a dead-end eddy while the real stream of being flowed on without me. I felt a sudden embarrassment thinking of last night. I *had* fallen for the guy—the whole set-up—hook, line, and sinker. They couldn't have found anyone more perfect in the whole of the wide world. Who else could have suckered me with literary theory, all the while discussing Flaubert, of all things. And to think I'd ever believed myself more savvy than Emma Bovary. But Logan would have known how isolating an education can be. He'd guessed from the beginning that my novel would be the way in with me. Feigning ignorance, he'd baited me to see how deep my theoretical bent was, knowing that, in America, theory signed the land of the lonely. And I had hit the bait hard. Now he had me on the hook. What would he do with the biggest ninny in the sea? It had been so wonderful having someone to talk to about books and ideas and art. I felt regret welling up like a tsunami in my chest. To meet someone like that and have his interest turn out to be just a ruse—part of his job.

My phone rang, and I jerked my hand hard against the porch rail. Duggie grumbled and lumbered off the porch. "Yeah," I said into the tiny plastic box.

"Teena? It's Logan."

"Yeah, hi."

"Where are you?"

"I'm having dinner with some friends."

"Oh." He sounded disappointed. "Should I call you later?"

"No, this is fine."

"How'd it go today at the range?"

"Ok. I'm a little deaf, but I think I could hit the broadside of a barn now."

"Did you get a response from Ed?"

"Yeah I did. And he sounded very contrite. I could almost believe the guy has a heart."

"Don't be fooled. He's—"

"Oh I don't think we have to worry about that," I interrupted. "You'll keep me straight I'm sure."

Logan laughed. "I'm sorry to be so overbearing. I know you can see through this guy as well as I can."

"I doubt anyone could do that as well as you," I said. "Anyway, the important thing is I think I could get him to meet me. In his last letter he seemed like a real person—like someone I could talk to."

"Let's see how things develop," Logan said. "I don't want to put you in danger if we can avoid it. We do need to get together though, and see if we can figure out how he's connected to you. Look at your internet sites and talk some more about how your paths might have crossed."

"Hmmmn. It could be something so remote I would never think of it. A stray form somewhere, a talkative friend."

He didn't even pause. "Most likely it is something you aren't aware of. But maybe we can figure it out."

I waited.

"Can we get together later tonight?" His voice sounded hopeful.

"Hmmmmn. I'm going to be tied up til late."

"How about tomorrow?"

"Let me call you when I see how the day's going," I said. I had no idea why I was putting him off. I hadn't planned it, but it seemed, well, normal. Why should I be in a hurry to let this guy toy with me the way he had last night? I could feel myself getting mad and, ordinarily, when I get mad I can't breathe, I can't think, I can't talk, and I repeat myself. But now. Now I felt a steely clarity I'd never felt before. Logan Deo was used to being the smartest kid in his class. Well, so was I.

"Teena," he said gently, "I'm sorry about the way I behaved last night. I want to talk to you about some things, but I can't right now. It's confusing me. I hope you can understand. The last two evenings with you have been very happy for me. I've really liked getting to know you."

"Great," I said. "Maybe after you solve this case or get your divorce or fix whatever the problem is you'll feel like calling me up and telling me all about it. I'll look forward to that."

"Ok. I deserve that," Logan said evenly. He paused. "Let's just try to work together on this case and then see where we are, ok?"

"Couldn't be better," I said just as evenly.

"On that note, there's one thing I forgot to follow up on yesterday. Has Steve heard anything back from Redman about your computer problem at work?"

"Not that I know of. I'll ask him when I see him."

"Will you see him tonight?"

I almost laughed. What was the point of all this cat-and-mouse? Did Logan really need to ask if I was still involved with Steve? "I expect I'll see him Monday at work," I said nonchalantly. "Unless you really need to know. I mean, I could call him."

"Don't bother about it. I've got to talk to him again myself. I'll ask him."

"Fine."

"Right, then. I'll check on you tomorrow. Have a good night." He disconnected before I could reply.

Whatever cool steeliness I'd felt while talking to Logan dissipated rapidly as I sat there with the phone still pressed to my ear. I wanted to go on talking to him. The very vibrations of his voice set something in me humming. Oh get a grip Teena, I said to myself angrily. I flipped my cell phone shut and stood up. Carmen was standing inside the screen door watching me.

"You got man problems Teena?"

"I'm not sure you could call it that Carmen. I've got no-man problems, seems more like it. I guess you could tell I didn't invite him for dinner."

"Richard went to take a shower. He said to warn you that Steve's on his way over here." She watched my face as I came inside and sat down at the counter, leaning my head on my hands. "You got man problems," she said, nodding.

"I don't like feeling so vulnerable Carmen. On every front. I can't seem to protect the land I'm supposed to protect. And I'm afraid of what's going to happen to me professionally if the powers decide to play hardball. I may be about to be arrested by the FBI for being involved in some terrorist ring. I'm not even sure I believe any of that is real—except that Mack's involved. It's just too much of a stretch to think Bobby Wesson could launch an international conspiracy in order to build his damn golf course."

"And then there's Steve," Carmen said, looking at me closely. "What I hear you not saying is there are feelings between the two of you?"

"Were," I said.

"You're sure it's over?"

"It was . . . muddled."

"Because of Ginger or because you work for him?"

"Both I think. He'd be crazy to leave his job. He's built something really important in this State. I mean the Bureau is a work of art. He hand picked each person for the job they would have to do, knowing that this work is controversial, and knowing that what we do would shape all the water policy in Florida."

"You appreciate his vision," Carmen said. "That must be nice for him. So few people even understand what he does."

I nodded. "That's true."

"And you . . . didn't want to leave your job either?"

"I think I would have at one point if I'd felt like we were going to be together. But I was never sure it was really over between him and Ginger. He seemed to think that wasn't the relationship he wanted to be in, but . . . he stayed in it. I love my job, and I'm good at it. I didn't want to leave for nothing."

"And he never makes up his mind. That's very hard on you. It feels like it could change at any time. It keeps you waiting."

I nodded.

"And now this Logan comes into your house," she smiled, "and sits down and talks to you, and listens, and walks through the rooms, and looks at you."

"Exactly."

"He's sexy, yes? He's simpatico?"

"Oh yeah."

"No more waiting. Except—whoops—there's a job in the way! Or is it another woman? A wife maybe?"

"Exactly." I sighed. "Besides, if he *is* FBI or CIA—and I'm not sure I believe that—he's only here for this operation. He'll be gone when it's over."

"Your stars are tangled up," Carmen said seriously. She pulled romaine and tomatoes from the refrigerator and began making the salad.

"Here, I'll chop," I said.

She gave me the cutting board and went to the sink to wash lettuce. "I bet these men's love planets are in your house of work and likewise yours in theirs."

"Oh God, Carmen. I thought it was just Bobby Wesson plotting against me. I never imagined it was the entire cosmos."

She laughed. "Now don't you feel better?"

"Actually I do. If it's just the planets, it isn't so personal."

She gathered my chopped tomatoes to the edge of the cutting board and slid them into the salad bowl. "Ok. Go shower. Dress nice. If he wants to come here and eat his heart out, give him a nice big meal," she said laughing.

I went upstairs and undressed slowly. I felt like a zombie—even though I guess literally it isn't possible to feel like a zombie. I got in the shower and let the water run hard over my shoulders for several minutes. Closing my eyes, I took slow, even breaths, and I found myself thinking about the settlement agreement I was supposed to be writing. It seemed to me I was getting sidetracked there too. Just because it was safer for the Trustees to lose the case didn't mean *someone* couldn't win it. Someone besides Bobby Wesson. There had to be a way to give Bobby Wesson that land that would leave us wide open to a lawsuit. Hell, I didn't care if the State got sued for failing to protect public trust lands. What I cared about was protecting the lands. If I had to look like the fool, so what? I was starting to find it liberating.

I suppose I should have realized that that's the last coherent thought of most stark raving mad lunatics, but I heard Steve's voice downstairs and I got distracted. A flash of nervousness ran through me. What exactly was he doing here anyway? I pulled on jeans, sandals and a tank top, wondering what it was I was feeling. Too much energy. Too much confused energy. I took a deep breath and went downstairs.

"Hey," he said when I came into the kitchen. His eyes searched my face for clues. "You making it okay?"

In spite of everything I felt the old, familiar rush. My insides turned to jelly and hot prickles burned down the back of my nose. I didn't want to cry. I didn't want to collapse in his arms. I clamped my jaw shut hard and nodded. Then I went to the frige and got a bottle of fizzy water.

"I thought we could eat on the porch," Carmen said. "I put everything out on the picnic table." She nodded at me. "Get your drinks and go on out. It looks like a nice sunset. I'm just going to go hurry Richard."

I gave her a doubtful look.

"Go on," she said waving her hands at us. "Richard and I will be out in a minute. But go ahead and eat. He's just making his phone calls. Mel's coming. "

We went outside. Steve stood against the porch rail, gazing at the sunset until I had settled into a deck chair. Then he pulled a chair up beside mine and sat down. "Not a good week, huh?"

"I keep trying to get on top of it. You know, figure out what's going on—"

"Yeah, that's what you do so well," he threw in.

"I'm not doing so good with this."

"Well it's pretty damn weird from what I can tell."

We sat for a minute without talking. That had always been comfortable for us. I could feel myself wanting to relax in that old, familiar way. It made me uptight.

"Roger Jamison got fired yesterday at five o'clock," Steve said calmly.

"Oh you're kidding." Roger was bureau chief of land acquisition, a good man in a no-win situation, trying to deliver on near impossible deadlines while dragging the dead weight of the State's most constipated bean counters.

"Escorted from the building at 5:30. After seven years."

"That'll be the last straw for some of them. They're about as down over there as anyone in the division. Joe Kemp and all the appraisers were just hanging on out of loyalty to Roger."

"Yeah. They'll go out into the private sector now and charge the State double for their work. So much for public service."

"Do you know the details?"

"Looks like straight-up payola. One of Dud's buddies is taking it over Monday morning. They tried like hell to get something on Roger with all those audits the last six months. I'm surprised he didn't blow his brains out. It must have finally dawned on them that they didn't need a *reason* to fire him, and they did need a cushy job for Dud's buddy."

"Those slimy weasels. I guess Dud doesn't know any surveyors or you'd be gone too."

"Give him time. A nephew or a cousin will turn up who once thought he might like to be a surveyor. He'll end up with my job."

"Maybe," I said. "I think it's just possible that nobody on the planet wants your job. Everybody's always mad at the water boundaries guy."

"Only if you're fair. If you're a political whore at least you make one side happy."

I laughed. It was the way we always were together. Spinning deeper and deeper into catastrophic scenarios, indulging ourselves with fantasies of the bleakest outcomes imaginable. We were comrades-in-arms, carrying on like soldiers too long at the front, our cynicism and gallows humor wrapped around us like flak jackets. I looked up to see him smiling his sad smile, and I knew he wasn't there to make a play for me. It made me feel embarrassed, and relieved.

The dogs barked, and Mel pulled into the drive and got out of her Kia, patting Duggie's broad head and fussing over Ripper. "I can smell that lasagna clear out here in the yard," she announced. "I'm starved."

"We're just fine, thank you, and you?" Steve quipped.

"Well I was going to ask," Mel said. "But I could see you had a beer in one hand and a beautiful woman on the other, so it seemed obvious you're doing fine."

Steve tipped his bottle at her with a little touché flair. "Can I get you one?"

"Please and thank you," Mel said. She came up the steps and headed straight for the food. She made a heaping plate and plopped down in a chair. "Willow's fine," she said to me. "How are you?"

"I feel stupid."

"You mean you haven't got this all figured out by now?"

"No. Yes. That's what I mean."

Carmen and Richard came through the screen door behind Steve, returning with drinks. Listening to them exchange greetings and insults with Mel, I felt a twinge of regret that I hadn't invited Logan along. I listened as they settled into the meal and the conversation, and I thought Carmen had probably been right. If he met my friends, hung out with us, surely everything would come clear. Of course, he might just think us insufferably provincial—southern, American, white, middle-class. After all, if he'd grown up in Paris, as he told Mack, he'd likely find us as droll as sticks. But then, maybe not. Everyone needs friends. It could be he was far away from home on a hard assignment. I thought he had sounded lonely on the phone. I remembered his question for Steve about Gordon's behind-the-scenes investigation.

I waited for a lull in the conversation. "Did you hear anything from Gordon yet?" I asked.

Steve had his back to me, and at first I thought he hadn't heard me. He put down the plate he'd been about to refill, turned, and sat down without looking at me. But I could see his face. This was why he had come. He glanced at Richard, threw his hands up and let them settle on the arms of his chair.

"Gordon seems to be missing," he said.

We all sat dumbly staring at him.

"I talked to his daughter. She lives near him down in Wakulla. At first she thought he'd just gone off fishing somewhere and didn't tell her. But she called me this afternoon and said she was getting worried. She said he comes over there Saturday mornings to hang out with the grandson, and he didn't show up this morning. So she went to his house. His car is gone, he's not home. None of his buddies have seen him this week. She notified the sheriff."

"Fuckin' A," Richard said. "This is startin' to get on my nerves. Is this connected with Teena's break-in?"

Steve shrugged. "I told his daughter he was looking into a matter we had talked about. I told her to have the sheriff call me. I haven't heard from him yet."

"Of course he could be off somewhere tying one on," Richard said. "This might not have anything to do with Teena's files."

But we all knew that was not what Gordon Redman was doing. Not big, hard-headed Gordon. Powerful, bull-necked, good-hearted, Gordon. Richard was just trying to dull the shock taking hold of each of us. We sat, looking at nothing, waiting for the world to come into focus again. I was completely blank, like a person who's learned not to think the next thought because she's discovered the one universal truth: however bad it is, it's about to get worse. I could feel a weird sort of quaking deep inside that was threatening to well to the surface. I wondered if I opened my mouth what would happen. I found myself staring into Mel's eyes. She looked as frightened as I felt. But when she opened her mouth she just sounded like Mel.

"Okay. We have to get organized," she said. "If we let this paralyze us, we're not going to like the outcome."

"Let's figure out what we know," Richard said. "Teena, you talked to Mack, didn't you? What did you find out?"

I could hear Richard talking to me, but in some funny way it didn't seem to have anything to do with me. I waited to hear my answer like everyone else was waiting. After a moment when nothing happened, it occurred to me to open my mouth. "We can't figure out what we know," I heard myself say. "No matter what we know, it doesn't tell us anything."

Mel was looking at me with a concerned expression on her face. I could tell she wanted me to say something else. I tried again. "Logan Deo is the same person who talked to Mack. He got my name from Mack. And now he's here."

"But we still don't know anything about him," Mel said. "Is that what you mean? Mack hasn't found out who Logan is working for?"

I nodded.

"You're right," Mel said. "And we also can't be sure from what Bill found out that Logan Deo is part of the FBI operation. Basically, Bill was reassured that there is an investigation, and that your computer files are involved. But they didn't get into the details of whether there's a stakeout or who's working it."

"What about the retired cop," Steve asked. "Can we get somebody at TPD to vouch for him at least? I mean don't they have pictures of those guys hanging on the walls down there?"

"That's a possibility," Richard said. "It's a place to start."

"You know, I don't know all the evidence as much as you do," Carmen said. "But *if* we knew Logan was an investigator trying to solve this case, we would tell him about Gordon. It might—"

"He just asked me that," I said.

"What's that Teena?" Mel asked.

"Logan asked me if Steve had heard from Gordon."

"Why would he do that?" Richard asked slowly. "Why wouldn't he be talking to Gordon himself at this point in his investigation?"

"I didn't give him Gordon's name," Steve said. "Teena, did you?"

"No. I didn't. I'm sure I didn't."

"Well, we're the only two people who knew about Gordon," Steve said. "You're sure he said Gordon's name?"

"Redman. He asked if you'd heard from Redman."

I could feel us sliding together into a vortex of dread.

"Ok," Mel said, struggling to get control of our panic. "It's possible Logan had made his own contact with Gordon through his investigation. If Gordon's been missing for several days, Logan might have noticed. He might be asking if Steve heard from him in order to find out where he is, what's happened to him."

Steve sighed. "Or he knows exactly where he is and what's happened to him."

Mel stood up. "I'm going down to the police station," she said.

Richard stood up. "I'll go with you."

"Carmen I'm sorry to eat and run," Mel said. "The food was wonderful."

"No, no," Carmen said, waving her hands. "This is what matters. Just be careful." She stood up, tipping her face up to Richard.

"Back soon," he said, kissing her forehead.

And they were gone, the taillights of Mel's Kia flashing through the dark woods before disappearing in the twilight.

It seemed there was nothing to do but wait. After Mel and Richard had been gone five minutes, it occurred to me I should have gone with them. I'm losing it, I told myself. Steve and Carmen sat on the porch talking, but I couldn't concentrate on their words. I went in, found the laptop Richard and I use in the field and popped in my disk. The chaotic fonts of creepboy's first message came on the screen.

It seemed plain that it had been designed to scare me, but also to snare me—to set up the connection between Logan and me. My guess was at that point they wanted to find out what I knew and who I was involved with without telling me anything. They probably suspected me of something. But the last email baffled me. If Logan was writing this stuff it almost seemed as if he wanted me to realize it. I mean, could creepboy/Eddie really have written such a letter solely in response to the letter I'd sent him? I wasn't sure he could. On the other hand, Logan and I had talked about Flaubert's techniques, Barthes' theories. I had discussed with him my concern about the lovers in my book taking over. It seemed to me it was our conversations that the last letter responded to—not that bitchy diatribe I'd emailed.

And there was also the complete reversal in the tone of the last email. Instead of the threatening, nasty voice of the first message, there had been the expression of what seemed to be profound misery. "Why do these things always only expose us as callous fools with small tepid lives not fit for cockroaches?" I thought about it for a long time, re-reading the message: "The world may think a man wise who forgoes love, but I know him to be the most wretched of creatures. I stole your work because it seemed to me the only way I could ever say these things to anyone. To someone who would hear them."

It seemed to me that the dangers attached to me from his perspective were at least as daunting as those attached to him from my perspective. If he was starting to believe that I was not part of some terrorist network, if he was beginning to see me as a smart woman with a cat and a thankless job, *if* he was finding himself attracted to me—it would make his job harder. He would be wondering if his loneliness and attraction to me were skewing his judgment about the treacherous person I might be. He would at some point realize that he was as diverted by our literary discussions as he hoped I would be. It struck me that all the normal dangers, faced by anyone reaching out to another person, were in our case ridiculously exaggerated. It was always scary to get to know someone, to let them know you, to trust a little, to rely on them with your heart at stake. But in such a maze of unreality as Logan and I had met in, when life was at risk, when deception might be your only protection—what chance at all did two people have?

I opened an email file and began to type.

Eddeo:

Love is the thing no one has written adequately. Its reality has escaped art. The grotesque is so simple to render. Love is complicated and hidden. Of course you're right. None of the realists even got close. They only point again and again to how absent it is from their creations. Maybe Flaubert protected his love in this way. Maybe we all do this and so that is what realism captures—our inability, or refusal, to come out in the open.

What would it be to write such openness? Can we only know the world by its presence? What of these terrible absences? Perhaps the man who foregoes love knows more of love than we can ever speak of. Think of the romantic rendition of love. Think of the passionate passages I removed from my story. (I'm sure you've discovered my "outtakes" file by now.) Can these passages ever stand up to the plodding daylight? They launch us from ourselves and make of us slobbering voyeurs. Perhaps love is unyieldingly a private thing. To look at people making love, then, might forever cast us as trembling gods looking on Adam and Eve and feeling forsaken. So love defies writing.

I must disappoint you (too). My poor story can only be what it is—lost. Maybe I am relieved that you stole it, so I could stop struggling with it. At least I understand now why it always would have failed. Or maybe instead why it was always only written for you. I have come to see it as an even trade: the unfinished story for the unanswered question.

Who are you really?

Em

I pressed the send button, waited a moment, and checked the sent files to make sure the message had gone. Then I copied the message to my disk, deleted it from the laptop, cleared the trash file, and checked to see that all traces of it were gone from the computer. As I scanned the "sent" items I noticed three messages in the list were to me. I clicked on the first one, not remembering what it was.

It was the camera files Richard had downloaded from our last trip to Lake Ponder. He had sent them to me as attachments to three emails, but I didn't remember receiving them. I could hear Mel's Kia coming down the drive. I re-sent the photo files to myself and went out to see what now.

Chapter Nine

Flying over the water, the warm rush of wind through the narrow space between them. Pelicans floating in morning light. The beach, her laughter. Are there really moccasins here? Nah, that's just an old claimer trick–keeps people away from your little piece of paradise. Give it a name that tells a scary story: Rattle Snake Bluff, Big Gator Cove, Haunted Hollow. Make sure they go somewhere else. So, I will call you Really Mean Woman.

The curve of her cheek, her shoulder, her breast. The long slope of her calf. He would always remember the confusion that overtook him as her shirt opened, dropped to the ground, the sun-dappled ground of Moccasin Island. Where they had gone like animals homing through the sea to the place of merging. Then they were naked and his confusion was gone. Nothing had ever been more clear, more certain. His thoughts evaporated in the trace of her warm hands, her fragrant body, and he felt the deep, ancient fire awake in him, overwhelming the relentless caution of his life. He yielded that caution entirely, gratefully, coming to her again and again through the long afternoon, without hesitation, sensing her, taking her as naturally as breath. Pausing only to reclaim their desire, to savor its building once more to the next fevered coupling that rolled again and again toward release, receding like waves beneath the next swell, until the surge broke in them, leaving them trembling, gasping, their voices ragged. They would lie together, gazing at the swaying pine boughs high above, tracking the shadows across their bodies. And then something would happen. The sun playing across her nipple. Her hand brushing back tangles of her thick, black hair. And he would reach for her, pull her to him again with an urgency he had never known in himself.

April 15

I dreamed of Officer Tom Kirkland standing in a river jumping red with spawning salmon. He was grinning and shouting something over his shoulder, and I came closer and closer to him, trying to hear his words over the crashing water. Finally he turned and held out a huge fish, wiggling and gasping in the air. "We got one," he yelled excitedly. "We got one!" The fish seemed to be trying to speak to me, but I couldn't make out what it was saying over Tom's noise. I could see its wide-open eye, already beginning to cloud, and I woke up.

I lay in the tiny bed in Richard and Carmen's guest room and thought hazily about the events of last night. Richard and Mel had confirmed that Officer Kirkland was indeed a long-time, highly respected, well decorated, and now retired member of the Tallahassee Police Department. They had found a photo and write-up of his recent retirement ceremony hanging on the station-house wall.

"It was definitely him, Teena," Mel told me with clear relief. "That probably means he's working under cover with Deo."

After talking it all over, we had decided to take the attorney general's advice. I would go home this morning after breakfast. Mel would bring Willow home and check on me by early afternoon. Everyone seemed to relax a little.

I got up and wandered out into the living room, searching for the murmuring voices I could hear: two men, on the deck, talking quietly. I realized with a start that Steve hadn't gone home. Richard was still in the clothes he'd worn the night before, and two shotguns were lying under a couple of deck chairs that had been pulled close to the rail.

I pulled back the sliding door and stepped out.

"Better safe than sorry," Richard said in return to my look. "I never did like sleeping when there was any possibility of adventure."

"Yeah, it's like being ten years old all over again," Steve said with his sardonic grin. "Sleepover: get to stay up all night, play tough guy."

"You guys," I said, shaking my head. "You're so great."

Carmen joined us. We made breakfast and ate. I couldn't decide if I was glad to be going home or scared out of my wits. At one point I glanced up and saw Steve staring at me. We looked at each other for a moment and I wondered if he was afraid.

"Get your stuff and I'll take you home, so Richard can go to bed," he said.

I nodded.

I got my bag and we all trooped out to the driveway, where the dogs waited for goodbye pats. I hugged Carmen and tried to thank her, but she shook her head. "You are family," she said, holding up her hand with the index and middle fingers pressed tightly together.

Richard yawned and squinted at me. "C-A-L-L," he spelled out, "at the first sign of trouble." He handed me the 410 shotgun and a case of shells with a sober look. I stuck them on the back seat of Steve's Land Rover without comment and climbed in the front. Steve was fiddling with the cd player.

I caught Richard's eye. "Bye," I said. Steve let out the clutch and we slid away like a leaf in a slipstream.

A heavy silence settled over us as we drove the deserted country road. I tried to shake it off, think clearly, "act normal," as Richard had advised. But I kept wondering why Steve affected me this way—making me tongue-tied and unsure. I tried out the hypothesis that things weren't over between us, but even thinking of us as an "us" didn't feel good anymore.

"Do you feel weird around me?" I finally asked him.

He sighed. Pressed his thumbs against the steering wheel. "Awkward, I guess. Caught between regrets." He glanced sideways at me with a little shrug.

"What do you regret?"

"Starting the whole thing. Messing up our friendship." He glanced at me again. "Then sometimes, I regret not going for it when you wanted to." He turned onto the interstate ramp and accelerated. He sighed again and his hands seemed to relax a little. "I regret ever kissing you," he said vehemently. "I'll never forget what a great kisser you are." He had always made a joke of blaming me for the attraction between us. But now he smiled his sad smile. "Mostly I'm sorry I hurt you."

I couldn't have guessed how much it mattered to me to hear him say that. I knew it, of course. Knew he never meant to steer me down a path of misery and desolation. But over the last six months I'd started to believe that he hadn't known—or hadn't cared—how much I'd wanted to be with him, how much I'd suffered his indecision. We rode the rest of the way to my house in a more amiable silence, not like the old days, but not uncomfortable either. When we pulled into the driveway he turned off the engine.

"If you don't mind, I'll come in for a few minutes," he said. "Just make sure nobody's planned any surprise parties."

I grabbed my bag and the shotgun out of the backseat and unlocked the front door, suddenly wondering if Logan was across the street watching me. Steve checked through the house while I made tea. We sat at the kitchen table.

"Do you have any idea what's going on?" he asked. "I mean, really? Is this just more of the same ole same ole that has somehow gotten completely out of hand?"

I could hear the anger and incredulity snapping under his usual unrippled surface.

"We know Bobby Wesson is plugged in with the governor. It's not the first time they've tried to get one of us fired. I just can't put it together, how it's supposed to work. My hard drive being stolen. This fake investigation with a retired cop and a who-knows-what detective."

"Have you thought about this? Maybe someone knows about us."

"And . . . ?"

"Maybe this whole thing is designed to scare you, get you to call me, we start seeing each other—boom, busted. Too distracted to pay attention to the case. Fired. Lose the case. Wesson wins."

I stared at him, trying to remember something. His head tipped down, his hand turned up, beckoning.

"I'm thinking about it," I said. "There was something right from the beginning. Kirkland wanted to know if there was someone who might want to scare me, to create a situation where I would ask that person to move in with me or stay with me or, you know, otherwise babysit me."

"And you said—?"

"No it was Deo. Because that's when he got the idea that there *was* someone even though I was saying there wasn't. Remember? He was suspicious of us being involved."

"He asked me about it in my office. Right."

"Well what does that tell us? I mean, would he ask you about us being involved if they were trying to catch us being involved?"

"Good point. He saw the photos of us. He got it. Why would he make an issue of it if the idea was to catch us in the act?"

"So, it only made sense to clear that up because he started out suspecting me of something—and I don't think we know what that is, but maybe something to do with this whole thing with Mack. And maybe he thought you were involved. But once he realized I was protecting you from political fallout, not criminal prosecution, he decided I wasn't guilty of whatever it was. Is that right?"

"Could this be any more complicated?"

"Don't ask."

We waited to see if either of us thought of anything else. I was thinking something that I didn't want to think. I was thinking that Logan might have wanted to know—at least in part—if Steve and I were still involved because he had been attracted to me. But I sure wasn't going to hold that thought.

Steve sighed. "There's just one more thing I want to say and I know it's none of my business so I'll shut up then and go away, ok?" He said it without looking at me.

"Ok," I said.

"Don't get involved with this guy because of me. What I mean is, don't make a mistake with this guy because I screwed you over. I mean, I know how it is when you're kicked in the guts and—"

"It's ok, Steve," I said. "I'm not that vulnerable."

He gave me a doubtful look. "I know you're pretty tough," he conceded. "Just, you know—live through this, ok?"

I went to stand behind his chair and put my hands on his shoulders. "I'm all right. Stop guilting yourself."

"Well, I'm going to keep guilting long enough to get up from here and get out the door without trying to kiss you, ok?"

I laughed and stood back, made a wide berth for him through the hall and flung the front door open. We stepped out onto the porch.

"So they're watching you?" Steve asked.

"Yeah, across the street, top floor, far right window."

"Maybe I should just grab you and kiss you one last time."

"I'm sure they already think I spent the night with you."

"Yeah. If somebody's trying to bust our chops over that, I guess we'll hear about it now."

We stood for a moment, shoulder to shoulder, suddenly sobered by all the possible dangers. Then I said ok, mañana. He nodded and went out the screen door without looking back.

It was too quiet in the house and lonesome without Willow. I went through the rooms, pulling back the curtains and opening the windows. I turned on the stereo, put on the Go-Go's, and got out the vacuum cleaner. All morning I'd been wondering what response I'd have from "Eddeo," but now that I was home, I realized I was putting off finding out. The events of the last few days were taking a toll. I felt myself pulling in, like a crab into its shell. I heard myself, in a back corner of my mind, obsessing that this attraction to Logan was muddling my brain. I vacuumed the entire house, cleaned the bathrooms, dusted the furniture, and did my laundry. I turned on the radio and concentrated on Sound Money's retirement strategies while I made myself a sandwich. Then I took my lunch out to the porch and sat down to wait for Mel and Willow. It was starting to rain.

I stared at the window across the street. Why were these people watching me? What was the point of all the secrecy? Why not just come out with it, whatever it was? Put your cards on the table, boyfriends, and let's rock and roll. At the same time, a little part of me was worried that they *weren't* watching me anymore, that no one was over there, that they had packed up and gone home, discovering that I was nobody to watch, nobody to write to or talk to or sit next to on a rainy Sunday afternoon listening to the cars swoosh by in the street.

The radio program had shifted to the news. A U.S. spy plane had collided with a Chinese fighter jet. The pilot maintained there was no reason to apologize to the Chinese. The Jordanian King was warning that the U.S. Middle East policies under the current administration were likely to bring an escalation of hostilities. Saudi Arabia was about to sign a security agreement with Iran. More cattle were being slaughtered in North Kent after being diagnosed with hoof and mouth disease. The Arab-American Institute was calling for the U.S. to halt weapons sales to Israel. A news analyst discussed the botched elections, detailing how thousands of Florida voters had been wrongly prevented from casting their ballots.

Now a former U.S. Senator was being interviewed about activities concerning the Arab Anti-Discrimination Committee. "I started the committee in the 1980's," he was saying, "when FBI agents dressed up like Arab Sheikhs and went to congressmen and senators and said: 'we pay you money if you give us immigration to the USA.'" They had a hidden video camera. Seven congressional members accepted the bribe. And somebody asked the FBI why they chose to dress like Arabs, and they said, "Because we want people to believe that the Arabs are corrupt."

What world were we living in?

At two o'clock Mel drove in, and Willow and I had a happy reunion. Mel fetched glasses and scotch from the kitchen and declared it not too early for a Sunday afternoon.

"What are you doing out here anyway?" she asked.

I drank scotch and considered the question. "Deconstructing the stake-out," I replied.

Mel licked her lips. Her head tilted slightly and her gaze followed mine to the apartment complex across the street. "I've been wondering if there's a way to hack into creepboy's computer," she said without shifting. "Steal your files back."

"Of course creepboy is probably Logan is probably the CIA," I reminded her.

"That might make it ten times easier."

We drank scotch. Willow wound around my ankles, purring and porpoising.

"How would you do it?" I finally asked.

"There's a program—it's actually a kind of virus—you can send in through an email—kind of a trojan horse thing. It grabs any file you tell it to and brings it back to the original sender."

"So you have to know the name of the file?"

"Right."

"And odds are . . .".

"He hasn't renamed your files."

"Although we don't know that they would be on that computer."

She nodded. We drank scotch.

"There's another little feature you can access," Mel said.

I knew she had thought about this a lot. And she was certain she shouldn't be telling me this. Certain that we were going to end up in federal prison for even thinking about this.

"Uh-huh," I said, non-committally.

"It captures all the keystrokes the person makes—anything they type in their email program—and returns them to you."

"A regular little spy, huh?"

She nodded, pursing her lips, her gaze still on the building across the street.

"And how would a person come to be in the possession of such a program?" I asked nonchalantly.

"I suspect it's on your computer right now," she said evenly. "And I just happen to have a utility program on the disk in my bag that will isolate it for us."

"How do you know this stuff?" I asked, trying not to sound as amazed as I felt.

"The mailperson in my office building is a hacker. He likes me. I probed."

We got up slowly and sauntered into the house, taking with us our scotch and Willow. I pulled the curtains in the den, and we fired up my computer and loaded the disk. Within seconds it sounded an alert and identified a "red messenger." Mel scrolled through the code, nodding. A slight smile played along the lines around her eyes. She copied the block and filed it, renaming it "backatcha."

"What's creepboy's address?" she asked.

I pointed her to the last email and she clicked and retrieved and pasted the address into the backatcha code.

"File names," she prompted.

"Novel/Chapter one, on through to Chapter twelve," I said. "Will it pick up anything Novel?"

"We'll try it." She typed.

We both sat staring at the screen wondering exactly how illegal this was.

"What do you think?" she asked. We looked at each other. There really wasn't any choice.

"What's the worst that can happen?"

She chewed her lower lip. "Probably probation. We'd lose our jobs. I'd get disbarred."

I shrugged. "What are we waiting for?"

"We have to attach it to an email that he'll open."

"Hit 'receive mail,'" I said. "There might be a new message from him and he'll be watching for a reply."

We watched the envelopes drop into the inbox.

"There it is," Mel said. "Do you want to open it by yourself?"

"It doesn't matter," I said. "It's all just a game." She looked at me and I could tell she wanted to say something sympathetic, supportive. But, for the first time in the twelve years I'd known her, she had no idea what it would be. I nodded. "Open it."

She clicked, and creepboy/Logan/Eddeo's latest missive came on the screen. I headed for the kitchen and left Mel to read. I put the kettle on and was rather woozily contemplating the assortment of tea when I heard her say, "Wow." Then she called, "You better look at this. I don't know what's going on here."

She gave me her seat in front of the screen and I sat down and read.

Dearest Em,

How clearly you have seen me through. You speak of our inability, or refusal, to come out in the open, and I want to plead that my hidden-ness with regard to you is not of my own making. Yet I know such a plea makes a meaningless rejoinder to your question.

Would that the world were such a place that we could walk out under an open sky and find only those ancient lights that have counseled lovers through the ages. But there is no more dark night of simple stars. The firmament is full of wattage, radio waves, satellites, aircraft, enemies. The misery of the world draws us to account, and I am caught in the mire of my own ineffectiveness. You are a complete surprise to me.

Barthes wrote that the lover's discourse "is today *of an extreme solitude* . . . completely forsaken by the surrounding languages . . . driven into the backwater of the 'unreal'." Because of this "exile," he said, the lover's discourse has no other choice but to become the site of an *affirmation*. I know this is what you are looking for; it is your test of me. And you have already guessed that it is a test I must fail. Have you also hoped—as I have—that it may not always be this way?

Your,
Eddeo

"Oh god," I said, crumpling my knees against my chest and folding into fetal position. "Why does he have to be so . . . so . . . . Mel, he's just so . . . I never imagined I'd . . . meet . . . I don't . . . someone so . . . so . . . DAMN IT ALL TO HELL."

"I take it he's winning," Mel said. Then, in response to my groan, she added, "Are you sure this is just a game?"

I sat up and blinked, drew myself to the full extent of my backbone and took a deep breath. "Let's find out," I said. "What should I write?"

"I have no idea," Mel said. "I've never seen anything like that. It looks like something Lancelot would write to Guinevere. Is he for real?"

"Well, see, that's just it. I don't know what we're playing at here. He has the cover of being creepboy/Ed Itori, who stole my novel in order to make me write better—or some such nonsense. A stalker figure perhaps. Or an interesting nut. Harmless maybe. Maybe even *attractive.* But I start to suspect he's really Logan Deo. And I start to suspect he's *very* attractive. Only maybe he's a manipulative CIA agent just trying to find out if I'm a manipulative criminal of some kind. Or maybe *he's* a terrorist. Or maybe he's lonely in that extremely miserable way that only very smart, very worthy people can be when they're alone, far from home, working on thankless, important jobs. Or maybe he's supposed to sleep with me as part of his mission. Only he can't bring himself to do it because he doesn't like m—" I was spiraling off into the stratosphere when Mel threw up her hands in the universal signal to STOP.

"No. What's happening is that he's really falling for you and he doesn't want to sleep with you as part of his job," Mel said. "You're falling for each other in spite of all this craziness."

I nodded miserably.

"And you're speaking this double talk in your emails to try to figure out what's really going on."

I nodded miserably.

"O-KAY," Mel said brightly. "This could still have a future."

"Mel!" I wailed.

"No, really. This is incredibly romantic. What are you going to say?"

I shook my head, waved my hands in the air. "How about, 'Forsooth fair knight, slay without further adieu the King who forbids our love. Come hither into my arms this very eve."

Mel giggled. "Not punchy enough."

"How about, 'Why don't we call a time out? Come on over and let's get naked."

"Now you're talking."

We laughed. It felt good to laugh.

"Anyway, send something so we can start finding out what's going on—or at least maybe get your novel back."

I considered the options.

"Get me that book," I pointed, "second from the end on the middle shelf—black cover."

Mel picked it out. "Ah, the Barthes man," she proclaimed. "A Lover's Discourse." She delivered the book to me.

I thumbed through the book until I found a likely passage, hit reply and typed:

Dearest El Deo,

Barthes describes it like this:

Language is a skin: I rub my language against the other. It is as if I had words instead of fingers, or fingers at the tip of my words. My language trembles with desire. I enwrap the other in my words, I caress, brush against, talk up this contact, I extend myself to the point of explosion.

I hesitated. I could just send the quote. He would open it and our mission would be accomplished. I could retrieve my files, I could spy on him and find out the thing I most wanted to know that he wasn't going to tell me: who and what he was. But typing Barthes' words, my will began to wilt. Somehow they made me feel how deeply I longed for Logan, for the way he could respond to me in ways no one ever had. He felt this too, I knew he did. He knew and loved the life of the mind and understood intimately its dangerous tie to the sensory world. The truth was, I didn't want to spy on him. I didn't want to win some abstract game. I wanted him in my life. Sensing Mel's curiosity, I told her to go pour the tea. Maybe it was just a game, but I found I couldn't write in the lover's language with an audience. I couldn't pretend that I wasn't sincere.

You've failed no test of mine. The vagaries of desire (so well chronicled by our friend) always impose such confusion, doubt. Affirmation in these times would surely be welcome. But Barthes, of all people, realized that in such a public place as language this could rarely happen. There has always been danger in the world, and very few men who would risk so much to thwart its chaos. I admit I have allowed myself to hope that you are one of these. And so I will go on.

Teena

As I re-read the message, the words seemed to dissolve into meaninglessness. I took the tea Mel handed me and gave her my seat. She got out a sheet of instructions her mailman had given her to insert the spyware.

"I don't know, Mel. Maybe I shouldn't send anything but a blank email. He'll open it and just think it was a mistake."

"Hmm. It might make him suspicious. It should just look normal. Do you want me to read it?" she asked.

"Yeah. Tell me if it's the right thing."

I watched as Mel read the message, and read it again. Her expression changed as the words overtook her, as if she were taking on weight. She went back and read Logan's message.

"It's really pretty Teena," she said finally. "It's like a secret code you guys write in. I mean, I understand it, but in a weird way. Like it's a language I heard in my childhood. I'm sure it makes more sense to you, doesn't it? Do you understand all of what you're saying? Does Logan?"

"That's the way it feels to me. But speaking words with Logan is sort of an adventure. When we talk we're exploring. It's exhilarating, but what we're saying is not a forgone conclusion. Everything we say could be taken several different ways. We keep discovering all these connections that reverberate, all this meaning. I feel like before I met him words were mostly invisible. He makes them . . . build things."

She was pleased with that. I watched her long, fair hands inserting the spy code into my message and felt like a traitor.

"Ready?" she asked.

I nodded. She clicked, and we looked at each other as a current of excitement and dread went through us.

"What will happen now?"

"I think you get back some sort of report as an email. If we're lucky, it'll have the files as attachments. But it may come back all keystrokes run together with no formatting."

"How long does it take?"

"I don't know. Gene didn't tell me how it retrieves. But I would think he'll have to receive the message and open it, at least. I'm not sure what happens next."

"What happens next is that an alarm goes off and his utility program grabs the virus and rats us out. What happens next is that we wake up in the slam."

"Ok, enough with this tea," Mel said, ignoring me. "Where'd the scotch go?"

"In the kitchen," I said. "And let's order food. I want you to help me with a settlement draft."

"Hey. I get paid big money for that."

"Right. So I'll buy the pizza."

We ordered Hawaiian shrimp supreme and I told Mel what I had in mind.

"But that's crazy," she said. "You'd look incompetent."

I nodded. "You said yourself that's what people expect."

"Yeah, but it's one thing to let people think the guys who worked on this case years ago screwed it up. They're long gone."

"Not all of them, Mel. They're living right here in Florida—some of them still working."

"If you do this you'll look like the one that's at fault."

I nodded. "Hopefully, only in the short run."

"But you can't be sure how it would play out Teena."

"Mel, wouldn't you just once like to see the bastards responsible for these messes get their come-uppance? Isn't that really what you went to law school for? Not to broker these deals that let the powers win at the expense of everybody else."

"You're going to do this, aren't you." It was a statement.

I nodded.

She pursed her lips, picked up paper and pen from my desk, and we moved to the kitchen table.

"I never heard any of this. I never told you any of this. Oh, what difference does it make? I'm going to have to flee the country anyway after the FBI busts us for trying to hack their computers."

"We don't know it's the FBI," I protested. "We're just trying to steal my files back from a computer thief."

"I'm sure your mother told you that that smart alecky way of thinking would bring you to no good in this world," she said with a dark look.

But then she set to work. She drew boxes. If this, then that. If A, then go to C. If B, then go to D. The pizza came. We worked on into the if Q then U, X or Y range, figuring out what consequences could result from the various components of a settlement offer. A couple of times we checked my email, hoping for results from our "probe." But there was an ominous nothing in my inbox.

"Maybe we broke it," I said.

"Nothing so insignificant, I'm sure," Mel speculated. "We've probably crashed the entire east coast network."

"I do think the lights are dimmer."

"That, my dear, is scotch and lack of sleep," Mel said, gathering up her things. "As soon as you write the draft, burn these pages."

She kissed the top of my head, called good-bye to Willow, and went out the door. It's a measure of the difference a few days can make that I got up and locked the door as I heard her car crank up and drive away.

April 16

There was still no mail in my inbox Monday morning. I grabbed a coffee and the pages on the kitchen table and went out the door hoping for a good day—a lucky day. It was going to take luck and all the guile I could muster to go through with the plan. I had a 9:30 meeting with Jack Gore at the Attorney General's office to finalize the settlement offer. I was betting Jack would be relying on me to provide the details of the case history. He knew I'd worked on it for the better part of a decade. He probably had dozens of other cases that were crying for his immediate attention. I just had to make sure I set the axe in such a way that if it fell, it fell on me.

At the office, I stuck my head in Steve's door and waved my fistful of pages.

"Settlement offer," I said brightly.

"Wow. Ok. You look, um, buzzed."

"I worked most of the night. I know you want to get rid of this."

"And you're ok with that."

"It's the great tradition of civil servants," I said, with a twisted smile. "You gotta do what you gotta do."

He nodded. Seemed relieved.

"I'm heading over to the AG's office," I said, hoping to get out before he thought too much about my sudden change of heart. "Meeting with Jack Gore to finalize this."

"Ok. Come in for a minute."

My chest tightened. I'd been too obvious.

"When I came in this morning I had a voice mail from Gordon," he said, poking his chin at the phone on his desk.

I let my breath out. "Oh, good."

"He said he'd found something that seemed a little odd. He wanted me to let him know if any of our computer geeks recently quit their job. Wanted the I.D. picture—if I could get it—of anyone who had."

"Sounds like he's onto something. Where did he turn up?"

Steve hesitated. "He hasn't exactly turned up. The Wakulla County sheriff called me this morning. Gordon hasn't checked in with his daughter and there's still no sign at his house. But in his message to me he said he was heading back home, said to FAX info to his house."

I looked at Steve, wondering what he made of it, knowing he wouldn't tell me if he'd decided not to. "When did he leave the message?"

Steve folded his upper lip between his teeth. He sighed. "The message came in Friday night."

"Oh." We looked at each other. I felt completely blank.

"So. I'll get the information out to him and to the sheriff. You better go to your meeting."

"Right," I said. "I'll check with you when I get back—" I waited, wondering if there was something I should be doing instead of going on with this craziness.

Steve nodded and reached for the phone.

I clutched my pages tight against my chest and got the hell out.

I drove downtown past the myriad state office buildings, wondering at all the horrific little dramas playing out behind those cool concrete walls. As I got off the elevator to go to the Special Projects office, I saw furniture piled against the foyer wall. Jack met me in the hall.

"We'll have to work in the coffee room," he said between clenched teeth. "They're moving us out of our offices." He pointed the way to the break room.

"Where to?" I asked as we settled into the little folding chairs and hauled out our files.

"We're being absorbed into the litigation section."

I looked at his face and waited.

"Our office made the mistake of questioning a policy being crafted in the governor's office that would raid the public lands trust fund," he said under his breath. "Overnight our funding was cut, and now I've got seven new cases that a first-year attorney should be handling. Only, guess what? We can't hire anybody because all our positions are frozen or the starting salary is so low nobody will even apply. Every decision we make is now subject to direct review by the governor's office."

"How much do they think we'll swallow?" I asked incredulously.

"How much do you need your job?" Jack said with barely contained rage. "Let's get this over with," he said, indicating the draft in my hand. "This is payola, pure and simple."

He set up his laptop on the folding table and I gave him a disk of my draft. We went through each paragraph quickly. I thought he would make suggestions and we would haggle over the wording as we went along, but he just nodded as I briefly summarized each point. When I suggested an addition or a better way to say something, he typed like a secretary taking dictation. I wondered how many years he had on the job. I knew he had handled countless cases, and headed up at least two appeals, one to the Supreme Court.

"Want me to type for awhile?" I offered. "Or we could get Denise—"

"Denise is gone. They cut our secretary position," Jack said. I felt my jaw drop open. Denise Liddy had been with the AG's office longer than I had been at my job. Everyone depended on her to keep order and meet filing deadlines during the intense pace of litigation.

"Now we share one secretary between eight attorneys," Jack was saying. "There's no way to even file your paperwork in a timely way. I know we're going to miss deadlines." He sounded like he was ready to blow his brains out. "I've got two sons, seven and nine, and a daughter eighteen months. We were hoping Kathy could stay home with her 'til she goes to school. But with no raises, not even a damn cost-of-living increase, health insurance going up all the time—sorry." He broke off and sat staring listlessly at the keyboard.

"This used to be a good place to work," he said finally. "A person could build a solid career. Not a lot of money, but a decent living, doing an important job—time to be with your family. Good colleagues. Now I feel like a slave. If I'm not working, I'm worrying about work, or about losing my job. They're just keeping us scrambling all the time so we won't be able to fight back."

"What bothers me is that more and more the work is this kind of thing," I said, nodding at the keyboard. "Not using the law to protect what it was meant to protect."

Jack looked up. "Let's finish this before we both get sick. I think I'm going to knock off this afternoon and go see my wife and daughter."

We worked another hour, setting out the agreed upon "facts" and outlining the reasoning behind the settlement. I made sure Jack continually inserted the phrase "according to DEP staff" (which would mostly be me) and "the staff historian reports that . . ." (which would only be me). I might be digging my own grave, I thought, but I was determined that the credit for this debacle fall squarely on my head.

I already had the phone picked out. It was in the parking lot of a convenience store between downtown and the Florida State University campus. On the way back to the office, I bought a pre-paid calling card and dialed the number in my shirt pocket.

"River Runs," a husky voice answered.

"Hi," I said thickly, and cleared my throat several times. "I'm trying to reach Chris Farlow."

"I'm Chris Farrell," the voice said. "Will I do?"

"Oh hi, yes, sorry—I knew that. It's hard to explain." I paused, completely embarrassed. "Let me start over."

Chris Farrell laughed. "Hell, I do that all the time—don't worry about it. What can I do for you?"

"I'm calling to tell you, well, to give you some information you might be interested in."

"That sounds mysterious. Do I know you?"

"Not really. I work in Tallahassee. I've seen you a few times at hearings about Lake Ponder—the Wesson property."

"Ok—" His voice sounded the question.

"The State is about to settle with Bobby Wesson and it's being kept very quiet. It won't hit the papers until after it's a done deal."

"No shit."

"So here's the thing—the so-called facts in the settlement don't agree with the record. DEP staff has issued reports in the past that completely contradict what's set out in the agreement."

"Wha—, why would they contradict their own findings?"

"Jobs are on the line. We're being told to settle it. There's no way to do that if you stick to the facts."

"Ok. What do I do about it?"

"Sue us. Have your group sue the Trustees."

"What'll we use for evidence?"

"I'll send you the staff recommendation that was circulated to the Trustees' aids but never released to the public. In fact the governor told the press that DEP staff didn't do an analysis—didn't produce a report. But we did. It was squelched."

"Ok. But there's no way we can move quick enough to stop the settlement."

"You don't have to. Just get ready. I'll send you a copy of the draft. As soon as it's filed you can sue the Trustees for giving away sovereignty land."

"Is there some way I can get in touch with you?"

The blood rushed to my head. Somehow I had failed to consider that question. I tried to think if there was any reason not to have Chris Farl—Farrell calling me. Was I still clinging to some hope that we could all come out of this ok?

"Let me think about the best way to do that," I said. "I'll get back to you in the next few days. Where can I send you these documents?"

Chris gave me an address and hung up still sounding perplexed. I could tell he wasn't sure he believed me, and I suddenly realized it was possible he would do exactly nothing.

But not likely. I drove to the post office and sent the documents, then picked up a sandwich and headed back to the office. When I pulled into the parking lot I saw a sheriff's car and my first reaction was to think they had come to arrest me. Funny thing, guilt. Totally hilarious the way your gut suddenly goes dry. But then I realized it was a Wakulla County sheriff's car.

I hurried into the building and gravitated quickly to Steve's office. Behind the glass door I could see a beefy deputy talking to Steve. As soon as Steve glanced up, he raised a finger and motioned me in.

"This is Dr. Shostekovich. Teena, Deputy Restin."

As I shook his hand, I had the feeling that the world was about to drop out from under us. I looked at Steve and knew it wasn't good.

"You better sit down," Steve said. "It's bad news."

He was giving me the classic preparation. Dropping beats of time between each sentence like warning flags. Sit. Breathe. Brace yourself.

"Gordon," I said, trying to form the unthinkable thought.

Steve nodded once, slightly.

"Mr. Redman was pulled out of the St. Johns River early this morning," Deputy Restin said. His voice was steady, as if reporting the morning traffic conditions to the desk sergeant. "Apparently the car he was driving was westbound approaching the 520 bridge when it exited the highway."

"Oh no." I heard my voice as if from far away.

Deputy Restin paused. He glanced at Steve. "Do either of you know what Mr. Redman was doing in that area?"

Steve sighed wearily. "He was conducting an investigation concerning some tampering with our computers."

"What kind of tampering?"

"That's what we were trying to find out," Steve said. "Dr. Shostekovich had some of her files copied here at the office, and her home was burglarized last week and her computer was stolen."

Deputy Restin's attention swiveled fully to me. "Did you report these incidents?"

I nodded weakly. "I told Mr. Donneroe about the problems I had here in the office. And the Tallahassee Police Department is investigating the break-in." I didn't add that it hardly stopped there.

The deputy stared at me for a moment. I could hear the distant ringing of a phone. Then the deputy took out a notepad and wrote. "Shostekovich?" he asked, glancing up at me from his page.

"Shostekovich." I spelled it for him. For a moment I thought he was going to ask me the proverbial question (what kind of name is that?).

He turned back to Steve. "What information had Mr. Redman given you in his investigation?"

"Nothing, so far. He left a message for me telling me to send the names of any computer tech who had recently left this job."

"And did you do that?"

"I hadn't had the chance to get the information yet," Steve said.

Restin turned back to me. "Who at TPD is in charge of this investigation?"

"Detective Deo."

I could see Restin's eyes narrow slightly and his breathing stopped for a short second. Without pausing I said quickly, "Do you know him?"

"No," Restin said slowly, "I don't. I thought I knew everybody up here, but I haven't heard that name."

"I think he's new," I said. "Officer Kirkland took the call."

The Deputy nodded, opened his mouth to breathe. Then he checked himself again. "I seem to remember Kirkland retired not long ago."

Nobody said anything. Restin looked like a man with too many thoughts. Finally he breathed again and said, "I'm going to need to talk to TPD. Someone will be in touch, probably from their office."

Steve and I nodded and Steve stood up as Deputy Restin left the office.

We watched through Steve's glass door as the deputy made his way down the corridor among the cubicles. I could see heads turning in his wake, people looking back towards Steve's office door. I guess it was because I had just blown the whistle on the Wesson sweetheart deal, had done it behind Steve's back. Maybe sending that spy virus to Logan was eating at me. But I felt like a criminal sitting there, my colleagues glancing at me through the glass door.

"I'm sorry to get you into all this, Steve," I mumbled.

"Yeah, I'm really pissed off about that."

I glanced at him, wondering if I could even look him in the eye.

"Hey, you're the one in the middle of this mess," he said. "I'm the one who's sorry about you—ok?"

I nodded. It didn't seem worth arguing about.

"I feel completely awful about Gordon," I said. "Such a great person. Remember that story he told us down at the lodge at the Christmas party last year?"

Steve nodded. "The one where the elderly woman gets a wrong number and calls his office by mistake—and she was looking for what, a loan, or something wasn't it?"

"Yeah, she was desperate. Her power had been turned off and she was cold. She couldn't pay her heating bill. And Gordon stopped in the middle of whatever thousand things he was handling and called some organization he knew about and got her a city utility grant."

"Over the phone, that day," Steve said. "What luck, getting Gordon's number by mistake."

"Poor Gordon—and his family. I guess his luck ran out Friday night. It must have been right after he called you, huh?" I said. "He probably ate somewhere and was heading back. Fell asleep. Drove off the road. Weird coincidence, huh? Him driving off the 520 bridge right where Wesson's property is. What are the odds of that?"

I glanced at him. Steve was staring at me, alarmed.

"No Teena. It wasn't like that. It wasn't an accident."

"Wha—what do you—" I stopped.

For once Steve didn't sigh. He seemed completely frozen. "Teena, Gordon was shot. That's why he went off the road. He was murdered."

It felt like the back of my head was exploding. "No. That can't be right," I said. "They're winning. We're settling. Why would anyone kill Gordon?"

"I don't know. I think we're in the middle of something much bigger than the Wesson golf course."

We stared at each other. My mind was chanting don't freeze don't freeze don't freeze.

"Do you know how to get a hold of Deo?" Steve asked.

"I have a number but lately he hasn't been picking up. I think they may have abandoned the stake-out."

"Look, get a hold of Mel. Let's meet at your house in an hour. I'll get Richard. We need to call in the AG—Mel's the best one to do that."

"This has to be connected to Wesson," I said. "Gordon died right there by his property."

Steve nodded. "But there's something about your computer files. Maybe Gordon figured it out and that's what we've got to do. I'm going to detour by personnel and get the information Gordon wanted. I'll see you in an hour."

April 16, p.m.

I'm sure there is a way you can be called into your boss's office, questioned by a deputy, and sent home early that doesn't make you look like a criminal being fired. But whatever it is, that wasn't the way it looked to my co-workers. I was too distraught to deal with it. I realized half way down the hall that Bonnie was beside me and, when we got to my office, she stepped in with me and shut the door.

"Something terrible is happening," I said to her.

She waited.

"Gordon Redman has been murdered. It's connected to the Wesson case."

I heard Bonnie's sharp inhalation. "Oh Teena. Oh no. Are you sure?"

"He was investigating some things connected to the case. Someone shot him. I really shouldn't be telling you this. I'm just in shock."

She pulled me over to my chair and sat me down. She backed up and perched on the edge of my work table. "What can I do?"

"I've got to go get Mel and meet Steve at my house. Could you get on my computer and forward all my email since Friday to my home address? I don't think there will be anything in it, but I was expecting something to come to my home address and it hasn't. If there's a large file, make sure it goes through."

"Teena be careful."

"Don't tell anyone about this Bonnie. Don't let anyone know you know about Gordon until it comes out in the papers. And stay clear of me until we get this sorted out."

I could see questions forming in her mind, but she nodded, and I went through the door and down the hall without looking back.

Outside I scanned the parking lot before crossing to my car. I got in and locked the doors. I couldn't shake the feeling of being vulnerable, out in the open. It wasn't lost on me that Gordon had been shot in his car and as I backed out and headed to the street, I glanced around nervously, wondering what to look for. I flipped open my cell phone and speed-dialed "1."

"Teena."

"Mel. Come to my place. I'm headed there now. There's bad news. Gordon's dead."

"I'm leaving now."

As I drove I tried to work out a chronology of everything I knew over the past two days and decide if it was significant that I hadn't heard from Logan yesterday. Mel and I had thought that he had to turn on his computer and fire up his email program for the spyware to do its work. I had gotten back nothing. Where had Logan been? I hadn't seen him since when? Friday night. And later, when I went across the street to check out the third-story window, no one had answered the phone. His car had not been in the parking area behind the apartment house. Still, that didn't give him time to drive all the way to Lake Ponder and kill Gordon.

Kill Gordon. My god. Who else even knew about Gordon?

At home I made coffee. That was all I could think to do. It doesn't seem to matter how much you tell yourself to stay in charge, in the driver's seat, keep thinking, not freeze. When things go so wrong you can find yourself slumped in a kitchen chair just staring at your anxiety. Thankfully, I heard Mel's Kia turn in the driveway, and I went to meet her at the door.

"Steve and Richard are coming. Steve wants you to call in the AG. We have to figure out what's going on."

"Right." Mel sat at the table and flipped open her cell. I took cups from the dishwasher and poured coffee, set out sugar and a carton of half-and-half. So much for my hostess skills. I could tell Mel's call was running into trouble.

". . . yes, I can hold, but could y . . ." she huffed with exasperation, held the phone away from her mouth. "I'm getting a run around here." "Yes, oh Monica—I'm not sure you can help with this. It's something I was working directly with Bill on—the Wesson case." Pause. "I know you know the case well—don't we all by now (small laugh). This had to do with Teena Shostekovitch and Steve Donneroe's investigation." Pause. "I'm not cleared to brief anyone on it. Can you make sure Bill gets the message?" Pause. "Call Mel Costner as soon as possible. That's the message. It's urgent." Pause. Nodding her head side to side. Validations, thank yous. She closed the phone. She looked at me and I thought, I've never seen her scared before.

"So . . . he'll call us?"

She nodded, but it wasn't her decisive nod. It was a jittery shake, her mouth drawn tight. I could hear Richard and Steve coming up the walk. I got up and opened the door, waved them in.

"Mel's been trying to get Bill. So far, not happening." They trooped in and sat. I poured coffee.

"What's the deal Mel?" Richard asked.

"I'm having a big alligator moment," she said.

"A what?"

"You know that book *Beyond the Fourth Generation?* A surveyor named Lamar Johnson wrote it—takes place in the early 20th century. He's out in the Everglades on the first dredge job, digging canals around Lake Okeechobee, and he tells this story about how for entertainment the guys would wrestle alligators. They'd come along side 'em and jump on their backs, truss 'em up and put them in cages on the barge. Then they'd let them all out of the cages at once. The gators would be scrambling to get back in the water, and men running everywhere, and that was a big night for all concerned. But he says one day, as he leaned over this particularly large gator, the gator kind of rolled up and looked at him, and he realized it could just reach up and grab him by the neck and take him under. And after that he couldn't bring himself to enjoy gator wrestling anymore. Of course you're wondering the whole time you're reading this why he hasn't thought of this A LOT SOONER, but, you know how surveyors are."

"And you think we're looking at a particularly large gator now?" Steve asked.

Mel made a swirling motion with both hands, as if to say 'who the hell knows?' "It's not like Bill not to take my call if I say it's urgent," she said.

"So, we're losing whatever political cover we might have had."

"We'll know soon I guess."

We all took a deep breath.

At that moment Steve's cell phone rang and then Mel's. They stood up and walked away from the table, Steve down the hall towards my bedroom and Mel into the den.

"I hope that's Bill," Richard said. "This is getting too hairy for us little people to handle."

I nodded, trying to eavesdrop on both conversations at once.

"In all the crazy years I've spent at this crazy job, I've never seen anything as crazy as this thing," Richard said. "What in the—

"Shuuuuu. I'm trying to hear."

"Oh. Right."

". . . a shock to all of us," Steve was saying. "I appreciate it Reese. Can I call you when we get a plan?" Pause. "I'm thinking I'll be coming down there later today, take a look myself, if we don't get some straight answers soon."

"Who's he talking to?" I whispered to Richard.

"I don't know. Did he say Reese?"

I held up my hand to shush him again.

"Yeah, it is kinda right in your back yard," Steve was saying. Pause. "Exactly. Make things easier if you came along—people down there know you." Pause. "A'ight. Talk to you soon."

I heard his phone close and then he went further down the hall into the bathroom and closed the door. We turned our ears to the den, but Mel's voice was too muffled to make out what was happening. Still, it seemed like her voice was agitated.

"So, who is Reese?"

"Must be Reese Kessler. Used to work for us. I started out working on his crew. He must've heard about Gordon and called Steve. He would've known Gordon from his DEP days. He surveyed Lake Ponder way back when we first sued Charlie Wesson to get his dikes off state lands. Ended up marrying the daughter—Jess, Jane, something like that."

"You must be kidding."

"Not in the least. Love at first sight. Romeo and Juliet stuff. I'm sure you've heard the cow story—how we helped her pull one of her cows out of a ditch the first day we met her. He's got his own survey company down there now."

"What about the dikes?"

Mel came back into the kitchen just as there was a knock on the door. We looked at each other.

"That was fast," Richard said.

She shook her head. "It's not Bill. He's not coming," she said.

I opened the door expecting what? The mail man? My mother? Logan stood there, starring into my face, his own face expressionless.

"Dr. Shostekovitch," he murmured, "you really should check to see who's ringing before you open the door."

"I knew there was something I was forgetting."

"It looks like you're having a powwow. I thought I might be able to shed some light. And finally meet your friends."

"Really."

"May I come in?"

I looked at Mel. She was staring at him rather wide-eyed, as if she'd never seen a dark, handsome spy before. She looked at me and gave a little shrug, 'why the hell not?' I waved Logan in.

I introduced Logan to Mel and Richard, and he was just sitting down at the table when I heard Steve rumbling in the hall, clearing his throat or coughing or something. As he came into the kitchen a dark look went over Logan's face and he stood up abruptly.

"Mr. Donneroe," Logan nodded.

"Mr. Deo." Steve smiled a tight little smile.

Mel was looking from one to the other. "All right laddies and lassies, I guess it's time for show and tell," she said, pulling out a chair at the head of the table and sitting herself down.

I sat down next to Mel and looked around the table. Logan was looking at me as if he was waiting for an answer.

"Where is Chapter 9?" he asked suddenly.

"I haven't written it," I said, suddenly exasperated. "Why did you steal my novel? Why did you lie about who you are?"

"We had information you were potentially involved with a terrorist attack in Pakistan."

"Because my name popped up in Mack's files?"

"And because you know about water, dikes, taking dikes down. You were connected with Mack, you had traveled to Cairo. We needed to get close to you, assess the information we had, determine if you were involved."

"How long have you been spying on me?"

"I first saw your name in Mack's files. I started going through your email and computer files at work."

"How could you do that? Who okayed that?"

Logan shrugged. "The FBI."

"Who at State Lands knew I was being investigated?" I wanted to look at Steve, to see his face, but I would've had to turn my head.

"No one. It was put forward as an internet porn sting. No names. I saw that you were writing about a dike system that was about to be breached. There was concern that you were sharing these files—someone was making copies of them. The way this microbe works is that it has to be in still waters to propagate. That's how it becomes toxic. Then, if it gets released into moving water, a river, it kills everything downstream for hundreds of miles."

"But why would I do that? Why would anyone kill thousands of people? For what?"

Logan looked at me for a moment as if across a deep divide. "That's not a question I try to answer anymore."

"So, what happened? Why did you stop investigating me?"

"I realized you aren't a terrorist. You were working on a novel, not planning to kill everyone from Orlando to Jacksonville."

"It was all fiction."

"Right. No. I mean—not what I said. Not us . . . ."

"So it wasn't you copying her files at work?" Steve asked.

"No."

"Then who?" (Steve.)

"We think someone within the systems maintenance staff was capturing her files but we don't know whether that person was the primary agent."

"Gordon asked me to find out if any of our computer geeks had recently quit," Steve said. "I guess he was on to something. Personnel is checking as we speak."

Logan turned back to me. "The night I broke in, I knew you would be at the retirement party—because of your email to Bonnie and Mel. I took your hard-drive, left the note. We wanted to shake you up, interest you, open a dialogue in a way that might have personal, underground appeal—not as cops. But then we realized something else was going on because when Tom Kirkland dusted for prints there weren't any. Someone had been here—after I left—and wiped everything clean. I couldn't figure that out. We even wondered if you'd wiped it down so the police wouldn't have your prints to compare."

I shook my head and stood up. Steve was saying something else to Logan about Gordon. Asking more questions. Voices grim and faces tense. Mel glanced at me as I left the table, but she stayed put, determined to get every detail.

I went into the den and opened my email to see what Bonnie had sent me. There was nothing that looked important. Another staff meeting to discuss communication. And there were the files I had emailed myself from Richard's house. The photos we'd shot the last time we were at Lake Ponder.

I opened them one at a time and looked at the images: the dikes, the old cypress tree, the little gator that always hung around the big diesel pump, all of us clowning around at the landing outside the Lone Cabbage Bar and Grill. And there it was. The key that made all the pieces fall into place. A face in the crowd at the landing. A man's face, watching me. At first I had trouble placing it, although I knew at once it was a familiar face. And then it came to me: Cairo, Mack's crew in Cairo. Nights in the little restaurant where we all went to eat. Haji the silent one, Mack had called him.

I reeled to the kitchen door. Logan looked up and, seeing my face, stopped talking mid-sentence.

"You better come look at this," I said.

It took less than a minute for Logan to realize all of it. We had done so much talking in those evenings together, and, despite the fact that much of it was designed to have me chasing my tail, he had managed to identify the information that was crucial to him. When I pointed to the picture of Haji at the Lone Cabbage and said I knew him from Mack's crew in Cairo, he got it.

"What is the status of the Wesson dikes?" he asked.

"As far as I know they are intact. The State is about to settle the case and let Wesson build the golf course."

"Is there water in the impounded area?"

I looked at Steve and Richard. "There was when we were there two weeks ago."

"And the pump wasn't operating," Richard said. "Meaning the water was stagnant."

"What would it take to breech the dike—let the impounded water into the lake?" Logan asked.

"A little dynamite in the drain pipe would probably blow a pretty big hole in the dike," Steve said.

"Have you got people down there that know the area?"

"A former employee is one of the land owners. Reese Kessler."

"Can you contact him? I'll notify local law enforcement."

Steve nodded and took his cell phone into the kitchen.

"Get an email address. Let's send him this picture," Logan called after him. "See if he knows this guy."

Logan turned away and opened his cell phone. I heard him working his way up some chain of command in some office somewhere, trying to get authorizations. I wondered what world he really lived in, and, in spite of everything, my heart gave a lonesome lurch.

Steve came back and handed me a little notebook page with chicken scratches on it. "Reese is out of range. I contacted his company. That's the email address. They'll bounce it to him when he checks in. I left urgent messages to call me."

I composed an email to Reese Kessler and attached the picture of Haji. A wave of surrealism washed over me as I hit the send button. It felt like I was becoming a character in my own novel.

"Send that photo to Katey Novalis in personnel," Steve said. "See if she can match it to a security badge photo. Tell her it's what we talked about this morning."

I nodded and typed, attached and sent. Mel and Richard had come into the den. And now we all fell silent, waiting for Logan to finish his calls. I felt like we were hoping a plan would materialize the way you hope the road will emerge when you're driving in a thick fog. Logan was signing off, closing his phone. He glanced at me and then focused on Steve.

"We've got a plane fueling now. We need to get down to Lake Ponder."

No one moved.

"Excuse me," Mel said, clearing her throat, and shouldering her way to a more direct view of Logan. "Would you mind telling us exactly who you are and who you are working for? We've been on the short end of the information stick for awhile now, and I don't really see us going anywhere with you until we get a few things straight."

I saw the slightest hint of a smile cross Logan's face. "Of course." He reached into his jacket and handed her an I.D. card. It identified him as FBI Special Agent Logan Deo, U.N. Task Force Investigations. "I'm investigating a terrorist incident that took place in Pakistan involving a water-borne biological agent that becomes extremely toxic in still waters." He recited the words as if with enough repetition they would sink in. "If it is then released into a more dynamic system—a river for instance—it can fatally poison anyone coming in contact—"

Mel held up her hand, her index finger raised. Logan stopped talking. Mel opened her cell phone and punched buttons, asked for the number of the local FBI field office, waited to be connected. I was looking at Logan's face, wondering if this was a normal day for him, where he lived, if he had a family. "Verifying id of an officer presenting FBI credentials ..." Mel was saying. I realized I was seeing him today for the first time without his undercover persona. Just another working stiff. He looked a little tired. Mel nodded, thanked the person at the other end and snapped her phone closed.

"All righty then," she said, handing Logan his badge. "What's the plan?"

"We've got transport to the landing at the 520 bridge where we'll hook up with a bomb squad. We need to figure out the best way to get them to the area."

"That's going to be airboats," Richard said, looking at Steve. "Do we want to call in field crew . . .?"

"We also need to warn the ranch owners, boaters—anyone who would regularly be in that area," Logan said.

"We can figure this out while we're getting there," Steve said. He looked up at Mel. "Good with you?"

She nodded. "Let's roll."

I rode with Mel to the airport. Steve and Richard took Logan with them. It felt like we should run the red lights, speed all the way, but we didn't. I could see the others in the car half a block ahead. I kept going over and over all the pieces of this mess, worrying that I was missing something, that we couldn't stop this thing before it turned into a disaster greater than anything we'd ever seen. I kept thinking of the St. Johns River, maybe one of the most beautiful rivers in the world, poisoned, and all the people and animals whose lives intertwined with that river. I felt sick. At one point Steve buzzed me on my cell and asked me if I had a number for the Wesson ranch.

"See if you can talk to someone at the ranch," he said. "We need to warn them and let them know we're going to be taking crews onto their dikes later today. I'll probably hear from Reese here soon."

I told him I'd call Bonnie and have her search my files for a contact.

"I heard back from Katey in personnel. This guy did work for us, for almost six months. He had computer science coursework at the University of Massachusetts, came here from Egypt to go to school. The photo matches."

"How long ago did he leave?"

"A month ago."

I waited to see what else.

"If you get a number for Wessons," he said, "call them right away. Try to get someone to understand what's happening. We need to keep the lines of communication going with them, so you stay on that."

I put the call in to Bonnie and in minutes I had the number. A woman answered the phone. I asked for Jessie Wesson.

"She ees training horses," the lady said. "I will give you her cell phone number and you can leave her a message. She turns it off when she is riding."

I told the lady there was an emergency involving the dikes at the ranch, and I asked her to please take a message to Ms. Wesson that there was an urgent message on her cell phone. Then I punched in Jessie's number, wondering what to say, how to convey the danger without seeming outlandish. It was entirely possible she would listen to the message and think the whole thing was a hoax.

"Ms. Wesson," I began, "my name is Teena Shostekovich, with State Lands in Tallahassee, and I have some very important information to give you. Actually it's on the order of an emergency, and it has to do with the dikes on Lake Ponder at your ranch. Please call me at this number immediately when you receive this message." I paused, then added, "Again, this is an emergency. Please contact me immediately."

Then we were at the airport getting on a sleek little jet and soon we were airborne.

I spent the 45-minute flight staring at the back of Logan's head and wondering how this was going to end. Was it even possible for things *realistically* to have a good outcome? If Haji had identified the Wesson ranch as having an impounded area he could use, had he been able to gain access to the dikes? Did he know how to blow up the drain pipe? Where would he get explosives? Could anyone just walk in the dynamite store and buy it? Had he already planted his deadly microbe in the still waters behind the swales? How long did we have before the toxicity was potent enough to trigger its release? And there was another factor affecting Haji's plan. Obviously something had happened that had let him know Gordon was on his trail. In fact, Gordon must have been very close for Haji to decide to kill him. Would that have changed his plan? How were we going to stop him? I wanted to imagine the scenario, the good outcome, but all the pieces were in motion and out of control.

I heard Richard in the seat across the aisle talking on his phone to someone, lining up airboats to meet us at the landing. I had a sinking feeling at the thought of Richard and Steve in an airboat anywhere near those dikes. But they were the ones who knew the dikes, probably better than anyone. They'd walked them and surveyed them and photographed them many times, with the water at different stages. They were the natural choice to take the bomb squad into the area, to show them the vulnerable places where an explosion could take out the dike wall. Then, we could get the hell out of there and leave it to the experts. We could eat chicken boxes at the Lone Cabbage, have a beer, and go home.

I thought about the conversations I'd had with Logan about Madame Bovary, about what kind of story her life was, the dashing romance she thought herself in or the gritty realistic tale Flaubert invented for her. I was wondering what kind of story we were in. I'd spent years focused on the Wesson dikes and how to get them off of the lakebed. They encroached on public lands, and I was appalled at their destruction of the fragile marsh, which plays such an important role in river life. I believed it was important to protect the natural world from rapacious capitalist plundering. So I fought to expose the damage, worked to educate people about the necessity of healthy ecosystems as the basis for all life. The end of my story was to bring to bear all the resources of the law and the hearts and minds of the people to save what mattered.

But now here came Haji with a vision infinitely larger and more powerful. Maybe from his perspective he wasn't so different from me. In his story he was the hero; he was fighting the good fight against a monster that threatened his way of life. But the end of his story was the hideous death of thousands of people. Widespread chaos and fear. Terrible destruction of the natural world that gives us the very possibility of life.

So our story all came down to the end. Whose happy ending would it be? Mine or Haji's? That's what worried me most. Because I'd read enough stories to know the end was here.

We were starting our descent into the Orlando airport. I looked up to see Mel making her way back to me. She had been sitting with Steve and Logan in the front of the plane. She dropped into the seat next to me.

"Ok, we've got a helicopter to take us out to the dikes."

"Cool. Where'd we get a helicopter?"

"Forest Service—they use 'em to fight fires. Logan wants to see the dikes from the air first—see if anything seems amiss before people go in. Chris Farrell is meeting us at the landing with airboats, so we'll touch down there. Reese will be there too. He'll go with Logan in the helicopter to show him the way. If everything looks clear from the air, Steve and Richard will take the bomb squad on in and show them the layout. Then they're out of it."

"Where are we going to be?" I asked.

"We'll hang at the landing and coordinate communications," Mel said. "Did you hear back from Jessie?"

I shook my head.

"Try her again when we get on the ground."

"You doing ok?" I asked her.

She smiled. "I feel like I'm in one of those naked dreams. I don't even have my purse with me. When you called I just grabbed my wallet and headed to your house. I don't know what I was thinking."

"You were thinking this day wouldn't turn into a massive biological attack on a major Florida river and you'd be back in your office in a couple of hours."

"Right. Silly me."

She grabbed my arm and squeezed it. "He's interesting," she said, nodding towards Logan.

I sighed. "That's a heartbreak for another day."

We touched down and exited the spiffy little jet in record time. We were in a part of the airport I'd never seen before and there was a large helicopter already running on a pad barely 60 yards away. A man in camo fatigues ran out to meet us, and, after a short conversation with Logan, waved us toward the big whirlybird. I saw Logan turn and look at me. It was impossible to guess anything from his expression.

He waited for me to come alongside him and he leaned toward me and shouted over the whick-whick-whick of the copter. "Can you come sit with us on the way to the landing? I want to diagram the dikes and finalize our plan."

I nodded. His hand came against the small of my back and he propelled me into the aircraft. I tried hard not to think about his touch. But it's always a bad sign when you're trying hard not to think of something. It generally means that whatever you don't want to be thinking of is exactly what you *are* thinking of and that you can't quit. Spare me, spare me, spare me, I prayed to the god of fools.

As the copter lifted, we huddled around a notebook. Steve had sketched the general area in quick strokes on the page. Richard pointed to the place where the big drainage pipe came through the dike, and Steve wrote "pump" in a little box, drew two lines through the dike and labeled it "drain pipe." They put a big "X" over it, indicating it as a likely target of destruction. Then I pointed to the area at the far end of the dike, where it tied back to the shore. There had been a breech there years before when Wesson was first busted by the State and made to restore the marsh behind the dikes. It was the place where Jessie and Reese had found the cut in the dike the first day they rode out together in my novel. Maybe Haji had copied that chapter thinking that it was pertinent information about where a breech could easily be cut without detection. Steve marked it with another big "X."

By the time we got to the landing, we had added other notes: the Wesson ranch house, groves, and stables; the road along the dike where Haji might gain access. Logan pointed to a spot on the map and looked up at me. "Is this where the cow was?"

I nodded and got up, turning away to avoid the quizzical looks from Richard and Steve.

"I think my cow story ended up in the novel," I heard Richard say.

At the landing, I tried Jessie's cell phone again. When she didn't answer I left her a more detailed message. "Ms. Wesson we think it's likely that some type of poison has been introduced into the impounded waters in your dike system. An Egyptian national named Haji is connected with this action. He may well be in the vicinity and is very dangerous. We think he may be planning to open the dike and release the poison into the river. It's possible he will try to detonate an explosive device on the dikes. Please get everyone out of the vicinity until we have given the all-clear. And please call me at this number when you get this message."

Chris Farrell and another man were there with the airboats. He came forward and shook Richard's hand, then Steve's, and introduced the other man as Pat. It was hard to believe I had talked to him on the phone just this morning. The bomb squad arrived along with several officers from the Orange County sheriff's department, and Logan began briefing them while the rest of us took turns using the facilities. I came back from the bathroom in time to see a man who could only be Reese Kessler looking at the image of Haji on Steve's phone. As I watched, the color drained from his face and I heard him say, oh no, he works for us. Frantically, he flipped open his phone and punched in numbers. Waited, tried another number. I listened to him leave Jessie a message warning her about the man calling himself Hanif, telling her the water in the impoundments was poisoned, that there might be an explosion on the dikes. Wait for me at home, he said. Call me when you get this message.

When he closed the phone he said, "I've got to get home. That man has been helping with the horses. My wife is there." Logan was waving the sheriff over. After a short powwow, Reese got into his truck, followed by the sheriff and a deputy, and they drove rapidly away, their tires spewing gravel as they pulled onto the highway. My mind was chanting keep us safe, keep us safe.

When I looked up I saw Logan and Steve discussing something in an intense whisper, then Steve looked at me, waved me over. "We need you to go with Logan. You know the layout as well as anyone and we don't have Reese now."

I nodded.

"I wouldn't send you but Richard and I have to drive the bomb squad in on the airboats. I can't let Farrell and his guy go in in case something happens. We're only contracting the airboats, you understand?"

I nodded.

"You'll be safe in the helicopter—they're going to keep enough distance that if anything happens—"

"Steve," I said, "I get it. It's fine. I'm glad to have something to do. Let's go."

Mel pointed her finger at us. "Come back in one piece. That's an order."

I saluted, and then Logan motioned me into the helicopter and we lifted off again.

Jessie mounted her dark bay stallion and reined him towards the gate. "Let's take a nice easy trail ride today, son. I'm not ready to get back to work." She still felt exhausted from the past weekend, when she and Rocket had competed at the District 3 Reined Cow Horse Championships. She knew it wasn't so much the travel and training that made her tired, it was her same old Achilles heel that brought her so low. Once again, she thought, I held you back. "You're such a great horse," she told Rocket, "and I can't seem to get out of your way." She had worked so hard to get her edge, even had several sessions with a sports psychologist to help her handle the stress. But nothing had changed. When it came time to pull out all the stops, she back-pedaled, feeling as if freezing water was filling her arms and legs. Shaking her head in disgust at the memory, she turned onto the road and headed up to the dikes.

She wondered how much longer the dikes would be there. It was her firm intention and ardent hope that they would be gone very soon. Bud had wasted so much time and money fighting with the State over these dikes, and then, when her father died and left her the entire ranch, Bud had challenged the will, tying things up for the last eighteen months. Never mind that her father had left Bud a six-hundred acre property on the Banana River that was ideal for a golf course and condo development. Bud had hung on like a bulldog, determined to "get what he'd earned." But Jessie thought the only thing he'd earned was a swift kick in the pants. They had become completely estranged since her marriage to Reese, and lately, Jessie had heard disturbing rumors about her step-brother that made her even more inclined to steer clear of him. She felt confident though, that her father's will would hold up in the probate court. He had made it crystal clear. The ranch went to Jessie.

Still, she would miss being able to ride this road once the dikes were gone. It was one of her favorite places to go on a horse. The footing was great and the views spectacular, and, she would always associate it with her first days with Reese. As she rode along, miserable with disappointment in herself, she noticed that even now, five years after her marriage to Reese, the thought of him lifted her spirits like a balloon rising into the clear blue sky. He was warm and solid, yet he had that wide open quality that made life with him an adventure. She felt so lucky that they had met, had been able to negotiate the difficulties facing their relationship. When she was down, only Reese could sympathize with her in a way that picked her up, put her back on her feet.

Suddenly she felt Rocket stiffen. His head came up and his ears pricked. There was something ahead on the dike. White, stirring in the breeze. As they came closer, Jessie could see it was the carcass of a white heron. Its wing was catching in the wind off the lake as if in a last attempt to fly. They drew alongside and she studied the bird for a moment, thought about dismounting to examine it. But she didn't want to dwell on it. Creatures lived and died. It was the natural order of things. She felt a sharp pang of longing for her father, and reining Rocket around the carcass, she rode on.

They hadn't gone fifty yards before she saw another bird, this time an ibis, then another, dead on the road. She urged Rocket forward, and as they came closer, she saw that the side of the dike, as far as she could see, was dotted with carcasses. A shudder of fear went through her. She reached for her cell phone and switched it on.

As the signal bars came up, her message light began to blink, and she speed-dialed her voice messages and put the phone to her ear. By the time she had heard Teena's two messages and Reese's one, she felt that the earth's axis had lurched onto a crazy angle like a top spinning out of control. Hanif, the believer. She had asked him one day when they were cooling out horses, washing down tack, what his name meant. He had shrugged as if it were no great matter. The believer, who follows the one true prophet, who destroys the infidel.

Reese had said to meet him at home. But in that moment Jessie realized what Reese couldn't know. What the police couldn't know. What no one could know, except her. There was no more time. No time to meet. No time to share information and strategize. Hanif's plan was in motion. This morning two things had happened out of the ordinary. The first was that Carlos had called her to ask if she knew where the new spool of electric fence wire had gone. He was ready to replace the old wire, but the new roll was missing from the equipment shed. The second was that Hanif had not shown up for work.

For a moment she hesitated, wondering what to do. And then she realized she was thinking about the far toe of the dike, a place where it was unlikely anyone would notice someone setting an explosive, running wire. In fact, there was a partial cut in the dike there, a cut made years before by someone with a bulldozer. She and Reese had discovered it during their first ride together, and it had never been completely refilled. It was a perfect place to blow out the dike. Jessie looked at the dead birds along the slope. Then she pulled down her visor and sent Rocket into a fast lope.

As the helicopter lifted off, Logan waved me to the front. "Sit up here by the pilot," he said. "Show him where we need to go."

I saw the rough diagram Steve had sketched spread out on the instrument panel. I pointed to the square marked "landing" and then to the toe of the dike where Steve had marked my "X." The pilot gestured through the windshield to the southeast and I nodded.

"Let's stay out over the lake," Logan called to him, and he gave a thumbs-up.

I saw Logan open a long slender case and take out a rifle. Only then did it occur to me that I'd been wondering about that case since I saw him lift it out of his car at my house and stow it in Steve's trunk. It had somehow made it onto the jet and into the helicopter. Now he lifted out a large scope and began attaching it to the gun.

"I thought we were just here to take a look," I yelled over the whirling blade.

"I can see an ant with this scope," he yelled back.

He reached into a canvas bag and handed me a pair of binoculars. He motioned for me to start watching out the window. As I was adjusting the glasses, I caught glimpses of him putting on a vest, and then he slid out of his seat and made his way to the cargo area behind the seats. He shrugged his way into a harness that attached to the ceiling, and pulled open the cargo door. The roar of air and sound rushed through the cabin, and I felt the prickly black of dizziness sweep over me.

We were approaching the western end of the ranch. I could see the dike system, its familiar signature etched in my mind from years of seeing it in aerial photos. And then I saw something else. "There—" I shouted. It was just a flash, a reflection, like sun on a windshield, just south of the old cypress tree on the far western end of the dike. I peered through my glasses trying to get oriented as the pilot maneuvered for a better view.

"There's something shining, right . . . there." I pointed and saw Logan nod then sight through the scope on the rifle.

Suddenly we saw a figure break from the edge of the dike and run toward the glint. The helicopter was closing in. Something was in his hands. Then he disappeared under the trec line.

"He's hooking up," Logan yelled. "We need to get lower."

"He says go in lower," I yelled to the pilot. The helicopter swept down and came past the tree line.

"It's a car," I shouted. "With the hood up." The copter swept past and began to circle back.

"Can you see explosives Teena?" Logan yelled. "Cylinders, anything?"

I scanned backwards from where the man disappeared, out onto the dike. "Go down," I yelled. "What's that?"

"Garbage can." Logan yelled.

"Is that it?" I yelled.

"No . . . ." He was scanning the dike frantically through the scope. "But *that* is."

As the copter swept over the dike and turned out over the lake, I saw it in my glasses. A pipe end, sticking out of the dike, and wire running up the bank. The copter swung around and started a pass back along the shore. I fought down a wave of nausea and scanned the tree line.

"There," I yelled. "He's under the trees by the car.

"If he gets to that battery, it's gonna blow," the pilot shouted. "We've gotta get back."

"Take me in," Logan yelled. "Take me right in on him."

I felt the hesitation in the pilot's mind, a split-second that seemed to hang in the air between us, and then the helicopter surged towards the trees again, lining up to bring Logan directly over the car. We could see the man reaching under the hood, wire spooling from his hands.

And then he swung around and lifted his hand toward us and we heard the shot.

There was a spray of glass, then the helicopter staggered and began to nose toward the ground. I saw the pilot slump forward, saw his hand drop from the controls. I yelled to Logan, he's hit, and I reached across the console, grabbed the stick and pulled. The copter lurched violently and banked left, and I saw Logan crash against the wall, then scramble up against the harness. I eased up on the stick, and the copter seemed to level out, but began to swing slowly back around toward the trees. In a moment the front of the copter would be directly in front of Haji and he would have another clear shot at us.

And then to my right I saw her coming. Her dark hair was streaming behind her, her red visor a blur across the green land, and there was no hesitation now, only her sitting centaur-like, at one with the dark horse galloping wide open towards the man with the gun. The man was looking at me, aiming his gun at me, and he didn't hear her until the second before the horse hit him and knocked him to kingdom come.

Then the copter looped slowly toward the dike, hung one arm of its landing gear on the edge, hop-scotched down the bank, and tumbled into the waters of Lake Ponder.

"Can you get his belt off?" I heard Logan yelling. The water was coming in fast and my right leg was submerged up to my hip. I decided I was lying on my side and I tried to straighten up. The pilot was hanging against his seat belt, all his weight slumped toward me. I groped for the buckle. Then somehow Logan was beside me. He reached forward and pulled a lever, turned a key. The copter engine groaned and cut out. I could hear the blades slowing down.

"I'm going to try to lift him so you can undo the buckle," Logan shouted.

My hand felt like a jaw that had spent an afternoon in the dentist's chair, shot full of Novocain. I pushed and prodded while Logan wrestled the weight of the pilot's body.

"Teena, get your belt off and get out," Logan yelled. "Come through this door and get out." He waved toward the cargo door behind him.

I found my seat buckle by following the belt down and felt an irrational surge of hope as I felt it release under my prodding fingers. But the water was gushing in, pushing me against the right side door. I tried to crawl past Logan, made it to the rear seats, but the water was too strong.

"I can't get out," I yelled.

Logan was digging under the jacket of the pilot. I saw him reach into his own vest, saw the gleam of a knife blade, and in seconds the pilot dropped onto the console between the seats.

"Help me pull him out," he yelled.

I had a firm grip on the rear seat back, and I tried to get hold of the pilot's right arm. Logan was trying to lift him and pull him back. The water was swirling into the cockpit in a foaming torrent.

"Ok, wait a minute," Logan said. He grabbed my arm and held it against his chest. "Save your strength. Wait."

I thought he must be mad.

He gave my arm a shake. "Once the cockpit fills up we can swim out. We'll be able to get him out. We're not in deep water. We'll be able to swim out in a minute."

I stopped struggling and looked at him. It was amazing how quiet it was now that the copter blade had stopped.

"That's a good idea," I said. I almost giggled at how normal it seemed to be discussing our plans this way. "But if he's still breathing he'll drown."

Logan nodded. "I'll cover his mouth with my hand—try to keep him from taking in too much water."

I pointed to Steve's diagram clipped onto the console. "The clips," I said. I made a clipping motion onto my nose and pointed to the pilot. Logan nodded. The water was slowing down now. It was getting higher. I could see blood from the pilot's jacket billowing into the swirling water. We got as ready as we could. We clipped the pilot's nose shut and held his head out of the water until the last second.

Then Logan looked at me and I felt my heart stutter.

"You do know how to swim, right?" he asked, a little smile playing in his eyes. Then he ducked under the water and began maneuvering the pilot past the seats towards the cargo door.

I took one arm and started swimming. It was disorienting trying to swim under the overhang of the cargo door and maneuver the pilot between us. But once outside the copter, we got quickly to the surface, and laid the pilot against the dike. As I leaned over him to check for breathing, I heard the high-pitched whine of approaching airboats, and I glanced up to see the sun setting over the lake in one of those spectacular displays that make you happy just to be alive.

April 16, into the night

We sat around a wooden table in a military-style building somewhere near Cocoa. But it could have been the moon for all I knew. Someone had given Logan and me dry clothes, which seemed to be some kind of mechanics' jumpsuits. I thought we looked funny, but no one seemed to notice. I heard the sheriff talking, and some guys in uniform were in the mix. Logan explained several times about the Pakistan incident. Two guys in suits showed up. It seemed to me everyone was moving through a mist and talking with cotton in their mouths.

Steve wanted to know about Gordon. I knew he felt responsible for getting Gordon involved in the first place. Big, gruff Gordon, who should have been fishing, playing with his grandkids. I tried to concentrate on what Logan was saying. Something about Officer Kirkland and Gordon being fishing buddies. So, Gordon had been working with them, doing the same investigation Steve had asked him to do: Find out who was copying my files and why. He had found Haji, who worked a few months at DEP, while honing in on his target. Then, with enough information to make his plan work, Haji had gotten on at the Wesson ranch.

The suit guys wanted to know about Mack, about how Haji had followed a trail to me. I tried my best to explain. The divorce, the trip to Egypt with my mother, the little restaurant where Haji the silent one met me, heard all about me from Mack the gregarious.

At that point, Logan sat down beside me and took over explaining. That fall, he said, Haji entered the U.S., as so many bright young people do, to go to school, to follow a dream of a better life. Only Haji, it seems, had been bitten by the bug of martyrdom, infected by the message of *jihad.* After a year of computer science classes, he applied for a job at the Florida Department of Environmental Protection as a computer tech. He had been stalking me and my rivers since our days in Cairo.

But his problem was, that even though he wanted to believe I wouldn't remember his face, would never really have noticed him at all, he couldn't be too careful. He must have crept around the halls during those weeks he was at DEP, dreading to turn a corner and run into me. He must have felt so lucky when the new capability came online for the techs to commandeer our computers from their own. Everything was going his way. It was the will of Allah.

Until the day of the picture. At the Lone Cabbage, on the deck, clowning around. Haji must have realized the camera had captured him looking at me. And, in the end, he couldn't be sure I wouldn't know him. So, he had come to my house to steal the pictures. Except my hard drive was already gone, because Logan had just been there to take it.

At that point, Logan told the suits, they suspected me of being involved, and it was only after extensive interviews concerning my work and the stolen files, that they determined I was not a threat.

When I heard Logan make this statement, I realized what had happened between us. I had been a job. Maybe not a job, pure and simple, but a job. He had needed to determine what kind of person I was and whether I was an enemy, and he had done that in an efficient and wildly creative fashion. Now he would go home. Wherever that was.

I was holding my head in my hands, my elbows resting on the table, and wondering if I was grateful to him for not taking me to bed as part of his investigation, when I heard him say my name.

I looked up and turned around to find him standing with Reese Kessler. I had the oddest sensation that fiction had jumped its tracks.

"Can you smell it?" Logan asked me.

My head reeled. "What?" I looked from Logan to Reese. "Mr. Kessler, I'm Teena," I said, getting out of my chair.

He smiled. "I know. I've been hearing about you." He reached out to take my hand.

And then I smelled it. The scent Haji left behind in my house.

"It's the oranges," I said.

"Yes," Reese said. "This time of year we pulp what's left of the crop for our local rescue organization. The oil gets in your clothes. It has a very powerful scent, but you get used to it. You forget you smell so strong."

We talked a little more. He invited me to the ranch to meet Jessie. He told me it was her hope to take down the dikes. "Not right now, of course," he added quickly.

I asked him if she was all right. If her horse was all right.

"Nothing some R&R won't take care of," he said.

"That was a very brave thing she did."

He nodded, his eyes shining.

Then Logan was taking my arm, leading me away. "This one needs some R&R now too," he said. I waved good-bye to Reese.

Outside, Logan put me in an SUV. I was surprised to see Mel at the wheel. They looked at each other. "Is this over?" she asked.

"I think so," he said. "You know the way to the hotel?"

"Yep," she nodded. She turned the ignition. She waited. Logan caught my elbow and turned me toward him. He bent forward and kissed me, quickly, pressing something into my hand, and then he was gone.

I opened my hand and held out the object. The light from the street lamp angled in. It was a thumb drive.

It took me two days to get home. I just didn't feel like hurrying. I sent Mel back to Tallahassee with Steve and Richard after we ate breakfast on Tuesday morning. I told Steve I would be in towards the end of the week. Then I drove to the St. Johns River Water Management District Offices. I checked in at the desk, saying I was here to do some research in their files. The receptionist showed me on a big wall map where I was going and sent me off in the right direction. But a little further down the hall was a list of offices and their directors. I scanned the list, wondering if Eddie Barfield was still in enforcement. Probably retired by now. I looked at each director's name for the initials JC, remembering the staffer who had made the only record of the secret meeting with Wesson's attorney Andy Ratzlaff, in which the executive director had verbally okayed the dike "reconstruction." But there were no directors with the initials JC. Probably JC didn't last long—what with making notes of secret meetings and all. Not the kind of staffer you want hanging around when you're trying to get business done.

What was I doing? Wandering the halls hoping to find ghosts of people who had helped me over the years? My case was over. I should have been elated that Jessie Wesson wanted to take down the dikes, that we had just prevented the largest environmental catastrophe ever imagined. Instead, here I was, hoping to be able to thank two people who didn't know I existed, who had probably long forgotten about the dikes on Lake Ponder.

I wandered into the break room and bought a cup of coffee. I was about to take it outside into the garden area, when I noticed an old man moving slowly through the café line. I waited until he came up beside me. "Excuse me sir," I said, "do you work here?"

He looked slightly startled. "Yes ma'am, for twenty-three years. Can I help you with something?" He motioned to a table against the wall. "Would you like to sit down?"

"Thank you," I said. We settled ourselves at the table, he introduced himself as Marvin Webber, and I told him a little about my quest. He remembered Eddie Barfield.

"He's been retired for some time now," Marvin said. "I believe he took early retirement. Didn't like the way the wind was blowing." He chuckled. "I thought about going out about the same time, but I just never could say 'uncle.' Just ornery that way, I guess."

I asked about JC, but he couldn't come up with a name that fit. "You got me on that one," he said. "We could go over to Records and ask Alice Fitz. She's been here almost as long as I have, and she's got a better memory."

"No. I don't really know why I'm here," I said. "I just thought I would say 'thank you' if I could find either Eddie or JC. They've kind of been my heroes for the last several years."

"Well, I think that's fine, very fine" Marvin said. "As you know, most of the work we do in these places is largely unappreciated. A lot of folks would just as soon we not bother them with all our taxation and regulations and oversight."

"Yes, that's true," I said. "Why do you think that is, that some people don't seem to understand how important it is—to try to protect the water and the land?"

"Beats me," Marvin said. "Some people take care of things and some people don't. Then, there's those who think individuals can take care of the environment just fine, that you don't need government mucking around in it. But individuals can't work in tandem, and an ecosystem is a bigger thing than most individuals can grasp. So, I'm a believer in having government oversight."

I finished my coffee. "Well, let me at least thank you for your work through twenty-three years. I'm sure you've made a valuable contribution."

"It's hard to feel so anymore. There was a time when I thought we were going to make amazing advances—make Florida really beautiful again, the way it was when I was a boy. But we sold it instead."

"Yes. That's the way it feels, isn't it?"

He nodded.

"What do you remember from when you were a boy?"

"Crystal clear water you could swim in. Catch fish, eat 'em without it killing you. And you could go up in a plane and the sky was clear. Not like today—there's always a brown layer of dirt in the air, hanging over everything. Beaches. Miles of beaches with no high-rises. No crowds. It was a magical place at one time. Now people think the magic is at Disney World." He snorted. "We sold all the things that really matter, and now they're gone."

We sat for a moment. Then I stood up and thanked him again and said good-bye. Walking out, I felt about as miserable as I could ever remember being.

I called Mel and asked her to stop in and feed Willow. She sounded concerned about me and I told her I was planning to sleep a lot and do a little sightseeing. She asked me if I'd heard from Logan and I told her no, I didn't expect to. She let it drop. She knows me so well.

On Wednesday I drove to the Wesson ranch. I had called Jessie the night before and made an appointment to see her, but I wasn't sure what I had in mind. I didn't exactly want to interview her, but I couldn't bring myself to ask her if I could just hang out with her. I had a feeling I wasn't making much sense to people. Thankfully she didn't seem perturbed or puzzled, just told me to meet her at the stable. She would be working horses.

I guess I should have been prepared for the sense of unreality that came over me when I stepped out of my rental car into Jessie Wesson's world. I had created this world so completely in my mind, in my novel. Now I felt like a person returning to a beloved childhood home after many years away. Some things were exactly as I'd thought, and many things were different.

The beauty and solid presence of the horses astounded me, even though I had imagined them in detail. I was mesmerized by their motion, their clean, sharp smell. I watched Jessie finish a training session with a quiet lope around the arena. Then she dropped the reins on the horse's neck and proclaimed him the best horse in the world. As they came toward the gate, she caught sight of me and waved.

"You must be Teena! Hi, glad you could come," she called. She motioned me to join her in the barn. "Come on in, we can talk in here."

I watched, fascinated, as she stripped off her saddle and bridle, haltered the horse, and hosed him down, adjusting the water temperature and checking it carefully before aiming it at the horse. "They don't like cold water on their warm muscles," she explained.

"He's just beautiful," I said.

"Thank you. He's a wonderful horse," she said. She finished spraying him and slushed the excess water away with a squeegee. Then she called a young woman who was cleaning stalls to come and walk the horse until he was cool and she guided me to a small veranda adjoining the office area.

"We can sit out here," she said. "I love this little place. I feed the birds here so I can watch them."

I glanced around, but the petting zoo of rescued critters was nowhere in evidence. "Thank you for taking time to see me. I know you're busy, and with everything that's happened, I imagine you don't need strangers turning up to bother you."

"Well, that's true," she said, meeting my gaze. I was surprised at her directness, at her striking face, her soft-spoken manner. "But I don't think I've talked to a single person over the last 24 hours who hasn't told me how much I owe you for your incredible bravery on Monday, not to mention the tenacity you've shown for years to protect the environment here."

A confusion of sensations rushed through me. "But you saved us all Jessie," I said. "You and your beautiful horse. If that dike had blown . . . the damage . . . I can't even imagine," I stammered. "If I live to be a hundred, I will never forget the sight of you and your horse on that day."

"I think together, all of us, did something good," she said. "I still don't understand why that man was trying to kill so many people, but it was very clear to me he needed to be stopped."

"You saved my life," I said, choking a little on the enormity of the statement and the pressure in my throat. "He was aiming at me. The helicopter was swinging toward him. There was nothing I could do."

She put her hand gently over mine, and I saw tears on her lovely face. "My mother taught me what to do when things really matter," she said, "and I've never forgotten it. For a long time it seemed like too big a burden to carry around, but now I know I just didn't need it until that moment. And when I did, it was like I'd been practicing for it all my life. It was like she was right there with me, riding with me like we used to. I lost her, you know, years ago in an accident. But she made quite a mark on all of us here before she went."

We sat together for a moment in silence. "What will happen to your marsh now?" I asked her.

"It's so odd how things happen," she said. "I have wanted to take down those dikes for years, but my brother was against it. As you know." She huffed and shook her head in exasperation. "We are increasingly at odds since my father died and left me the ranch. He is contesting the will."

I shook my head sympathetically.

"But now that there is this toxic substance in the impounded waters, I'm not sure what will happen. The biologists at the Water Management District and the CDC are out there now, trying to figure out what to do. It's so sad. So many creatures died. Even the poor frogs." She took in a deep, ragged breath. "Still, it could have been so much worse. There have been times when I've taken my horses swimming in that impoundment," she said. "Can you imagine? What was that man thinking of?"

We looked at each other. "I think that's something that is going to haunt me," I said. "Maybe for the rest of my life. I don't know much about what he was thinking, or whether he had suffered some terrible injustice that he felt had to be avenged, or what. But he went to great lengths to find an American target. It frightens me to think why that would be."

"I know what you mean," Jessie said. "I've realized for years that we're involved in a lot of what happens over in that part of the world, things I have no idea of, and probably a lot of it isn't good. It makes me feel that we're sitting on a ticking time-bomb."

"I realized recently that I don't even know the basic geography of the Middle East," I said. "I have a feeling that's too much ignorance about something that's playing a big part in my world."

"Yes, me too. I usually just go along, focused on my little problems on my little patch of dirt."

"I know. Even though in my job I focus on problems all over the state, all of a sudden that feels terribly provincial." I sighed. "This is such a beautiful place."

"Someday you should come back and see the dikes on horseback—when it's not so dangerous. And maybe we can still get the dikes taken down one day. Wouldn't that be fun?"

I smiled. I would definitely like to help with that, I told her. We agreed to stay in touch, and I got back in my rental car and headed north to Tallahassee.

It took awhile to get settled. I checked in with Mel and my mother, had a long hug-up with Willow, and threw out a few cartons of unidentifiable aliens that had invaded the refrigerator. I took a long shower and put on my favorite pajamas. Then I sat down at my computer and looked at the contents of the thumb drive Logan has given me. It was my files, all the chapters from my novel. And that was all.

Inevitably, it seemed, I ended up sitting on the porch starring at the building across the street. It had almost happened, this thing between Logan and me. And he still seemed so nearby, like he might materialize at any moment with his warm, strong arms and broad, quick mind.

It was a humid night, and a light breeze had begun to stir the fresh new leaves in the oak trees. Off to the west I saw lightning flash over the top of a towering thunderhead. I felt in my bones that changes were coming, changes none of us could imagine. And I longed for a way to be connected to Logan in this world that suddenly seemed so dangerous and so unknown.

I felt entirely inadequate to understand what had happened with Haji. In spite of my education and my political savvy at some level, I had only the vaguest idea why someone would hate Americans so much. Logan had dodged my question about why someone would do such a thing as Haji had attempted, but it was clear he had thought a lot about it. Logan had had an education in many ways similar to my own. Not exactly a preparation for life as a special investigator for the UN. Somewhere along the way he had set aside his plans for an academic life and opted for something more hands-on. I wished I'd had the chance to learn his story, to know how it was he'd become involved in tracking down Haji.

I went inside and sat at my computer. I wasn't sure I could face opening my email and finding nothing from my creepboy. But really there's never an alternative, is there?

As my email loaded, a window popped up on the screen, showing file after file downloading. Did I want to save them to disk or open them, it asked politely. I saw immediately the titles: Chapter 1, chapter 2.... It was the Backatcha spy program Mel had used, returning my files. I chose "save to disk" and selected a location, dumbfounded at our success. Holding my breath, I clicked on a file, half expecting to get a message saying the file was corrupt and could not be opened. When the familiar pages filled my screen, I found myself laughing ridiculously. I had never really believed it would work.

And there was more. Several of the emails between "Creepboy" and me—the early ones. They were attached to what evidently were Logan's reports to his superiors. In the reports he had clearly been on the defensive, arguing that this tactic of engaging his target (me) intellectually would yield the most effective information. The first reply told him to get on with it. The next ordered him (paradoxically) to engage the target romantically—there was no more time for "dicking around."

And that was it. Either he had not filed further reports, hadn't shared our last exchanges with his bosses, or Mel's little spy program hadn't ferreted them out and returned them to me.

I thought about the night he kissed me, then left so suddenly.

Maybe life has always been so full of ambiguity, illusion, veiled purpose. But it seems to me that more and more we live in a world of exploding contexts. I think I am in one world, and find it is only one small bubble in the wave of an ocean. And you can never know what shore you might wash up on.

Logan might have liked me. He might be married, or in love with someone else. He simply might object to bedding a woman as part of a job. Or maybe all of those. Whatever the situation had really been, I would likely never know. But now I could feel something in myself come back.

About the Author

Sara Warner is a third-generation Floridian and environmentalist. At various times in her life she has taught literature at Florida State University, bred and trained champion horses, and worked as a musician. She has a Ph.D. in History, Theory, and Culture from Emory University. She makes her home in the wilds of the Florida panhandle with her husband P. V. LeForge, several horses, dogs, cats, and assorted wildlife friends. She is the author of *Down to the Waterline: Nature, Boundaries, and the Law in Florida*. *Still Waters* is her first novel.

Photo by Jeff Stockwell.

Made in the USA
Charleston, SC
07 September 2012